March 2015

THROUGH
STAINED GLASS

To: Linda Troutman,
God has blessed you
with a special son
Aaron
Thank you for sharing
His love with
all you meet.
Blessings
Marlene Walters

THROUGH
STAINED GLASS

MARLENE LOUISE WALTERS

TATE PUBLISHING
AND ENTERPRISES, LLC

Published by Tate Publishing & Enterprises, LLC
127 E. Trade Center Terrace | Mustang, Oklahoma 73064 USA
1.888.361.9473 | www.tatepublishing.com

Tate Publishing is committed to excellence in the publishing industry. The company reflects the philosophy established by the founders, based on Psalm 68:11,
"The Lord gave the word and great was the company of those who published it."

Book design copyright © 2014 by Tate Publishing, LLC. All rights reserved.
Cover design by Gian Philipp Rufin
Interior design by Jomar Ouano

Published in the United States of America

ISBN: 978-1-63418-092-4
Religion / General
14.10.03

In honor and love of my dearest two friends: my husband Tom and my mom

Tom and Marlene at Mom's 105th birthday

CONTENTS

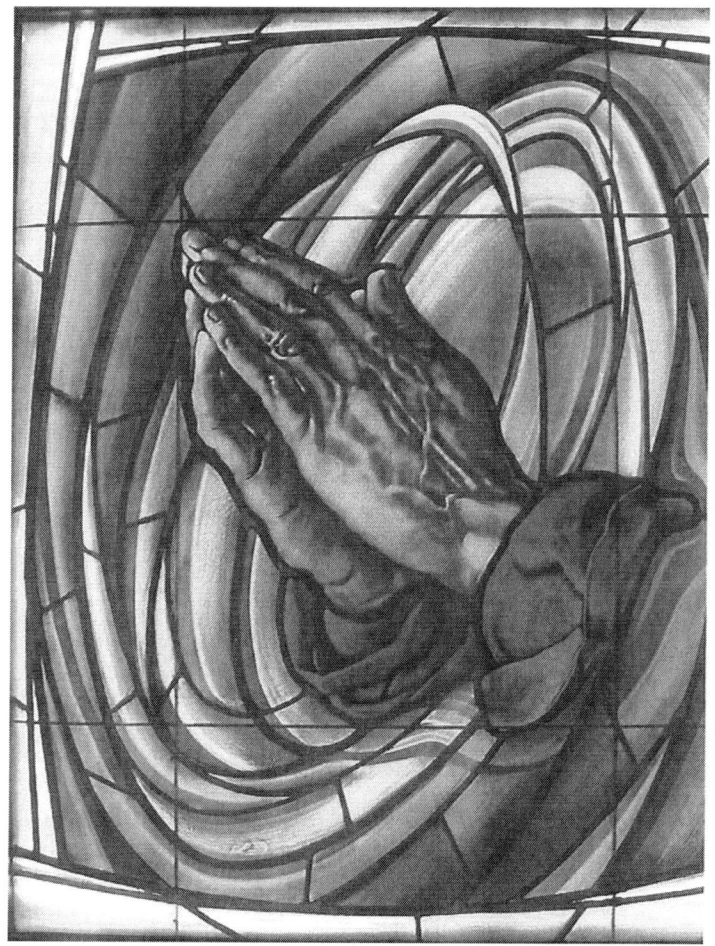

Stained Glass Praying Hands

INTRODUCTION

The last forty-five years of my life have been quite a journey from housewife/mother and volunteer, to responding to an ethical dilemma I encountered in 1969, in Wilmington, Delaware.

And now, after these years in the ordained ministry, I'm reflecting, not only on medical ethical problems, but where my response led me. I hope this will enable the readers to look back on their lives and see where God nudged them, as I believe our Lord touched me.

After graduation from Palmer Theological Seminary, in Philadelphia, Pennsylvania, I spent eight years as a hospital chaplain for Wilmington General Hospital, three years as associate minister for Grace United Methodist Church, and twelve years as senior minister of Mt. Lebanon United Methodist Church, in Wilmington, Delaware. When we retired and moved to Florida, I preached for ten years at our chapel in Florida.

One of my responses to serve the Lord was to start support groups for those in need in the hospital and churches I have served in. This became a full-time challenge to witness the tragedies that we humans must endure, as I facilitated a variety of support groups. These support groups included suicide prevention, one for teenagers (Youth Suicide Prevention Program, YSPP), and another for adults (Adult Suicide Prevention, ASP); grief recovery for loss of child (Grief Recovery Loss of Child, GRLC), Families of Suicide to Enable Recovery (FOSTER); You're Not Alone, for widows and widowers, HOPING (Helping Other People In Normal Grieving), and Supporting KIDDS (Kids Involved in Death, Divorce, and Separation).

Throughout my ministry, I've attempted to reach people who were suffering from life's rough edges. This book, *Through Stained Glass*, attempts to capture those direct observations of life, comingled with my religious training. To that end, I've tried to address these situations in each chapter, allowing the reader to choose which dilemma you might encounter.

Faith, Anger, Courage, Peace of Mind; Life changes, Living with the Gray, Good and Evil, Gratitude, Forgiveness, Overcoming Discouragement, Love, Death, Birth, Patriotism, Starting Over, God's Will, Not Ours, Choosing Faith, Blessed Are You, God and Suffering, are samplings of this effort. What would God want us to do? Where is God when I'm suffering? What is my response to difficult situations?

As I responded to the medical ethical issues that I encountered in 1969, I taught medical ethics to interns at the Wilmington Medical Center for ten years; Eastern College in St. David's Pennsylvania, for six years; Washington College in Chestertown, Maryland, for five years; and the Nursing School of Wilmington for five years. Teaching and continuing education enabled me to follow medical ethical issues such as abortion, infanticide, euthanasia, and physician-assisted suicide through the years. Some of these observations are addressed.

My hope is this book may guide and shepherd your journey through the trials and tribulations of your life.

Many thanks to our daughter, Debbie, and my husband, Tom, for editing as they did for my other book, *Virtual Grace*, and our son-in-law, William Hawthorne Sharp (WHS), for his insightful poetry scattered throughout the book.

The Holy Bible Scripture passages are cited from the New King James Version.

In the Beginning

The chapel committee person came buzzing around the golf cart path of the fifteenth hole, as I was riding in my golf cart down the street where we live.

"Pull over, Marlene. Pull over!"

As I skittered over to the side of the road, he blared, "You're 100 percent retired! You're 100 percent retired" he echoed.

Well, I am eighty-one years old. I've been preaching in our community for about ten years, and there are two ordained new residents in our neighborhood, who can lead our chapel worship services.

However, I'm disappointed to be 100 percent retired, especially now, because our chapel just dedicated the stained-glass window, and Tom and I were a part of this special project.

We've had a very small area in Colony Hall, until Norm Neill arrived and transformed our chapel into a pastoral church reflected by an incredibly inspirational stained-glass window that brings humbleness and awesomeness to your inner self.

Norm Neill was one of the finest leaders and faith-centered persons I've ever met. He arrived in our community several years ago, set the new chapel in motion, and the Lord took him home eighteen months later. My husband, Tom, and I have been grieving ever since.

I've been in this ordained ministry for over forty years now. What is next? How did I get into this ministry anyway?

It was 1969 and I was a volunteer with the Junior League, Easter Seal, and Mancus organizations in Wilmington Delaware where my husband and our three children, Debbie, Becky and Carrie, lived.

My main position as a volunteer was to teach swimming to the handicapped children and adults in those programs. It was amazing to see those who had handicaps actually walking in the water, moving their limbs with great joy. "Mrs. Walters, watch me! I can really move my legs." Even our own children became involved, helping those who couldn't always help themselves.

Then I was approached by a Junior League friend, whose husband was a politician. He asked me if I'd bring some of the handicapped children down to the capital of Delaware, Dover. "We really need you all to help us at an upcoming important hearing. Will you come please?"

We had been working hard on getting handicapped ramps put in the many state-owned office buildings, so I was delighted to hear that hearing was finally in the process.

"Yes, of course," I replied. "When do you want us?"

"Next Thursday," came the response. "Be sure and get permission slips from their parents."

With permission slips from the parents in hand, we traveled to Dover, about an hour's drive from Wilmington.

When I emptied the handicapped van and entered the colonial capital building, the kids were joyfully singing, "We're going to get our ramps. Yippee!"

Then it was time for my politician friend to start the hearing, and he nodded for me to wheel my kids around the Senate hall.

"Ladies and Gentlemen of Delaware, we must pass this House bill that will allow women to abort their child if they're known to have a handicap."

Period.

End of quote.

Shock!

"Does anyone object?" intoned an unfamiliar voice sitting on the chamber floor.

No one answered, and my throat was caught in glue. How could I speak? I had never spoken in public before. What would I say to these people who obviously never swam with, sat with, talked with, or cared for a handicapped person?

So I gathered the handicapped kids and went directly to the van, without uttering a word.

On the way home, one of the kids spoke enthusiastically, "Mrs. Walters, are we gonna get ramps now? Did we do good?"

I leaned my chin on my left shoulder so they wouldn't see tears flowing from my eyes as I drove back to Wilmington, Delaware. And then I said something that led me on a forty-year journey with myself, God, and whoever would listen. "Oh, God, forgive me that I said nothing. What can I do? I will follow your lead, but please, please lead me."

As I was praying "What can I do, Lord?" the very next day there was an advertisement in the Wilmington News Journal: "Come Visit Eastern Baptist Theological Seminary." And another advertisement: "Lancaster Theological Seminary Is Waiting for You."

These ads seemed to jump out of the newspaper in front of my eyes. I knew I had to do something, but what?

I got in my Mustang the next day, and drove to Lancaster, Pennsylvania, frequently getting lost.

The following day, I visited EBTS in the suburbs of Philadelphia, also getting lost.

Both seminaries wanted me to enroll as their first female master of divinity student.

At EBTS, now known as Palmer Theological Seminary, I met Dr. Norman Maring, the Christian history professor, who encouraged me to sign up for a class. However, my husband, Tom, and I didn't have extra money for my schooling, as we were saving for our children's education. And when I approached Tom, he said absolutely no. He asked, "Why do you want to go? What's the point? How will that change the abortion issue?" And, he was right. What was I doing and why?

Then, two days later, another advertisement in the *Wilmington News Journal* flew out of the paper into my eyes, literally. This ad? "Come hear Dr. Joseph Fletcher, writer, author, lecturer, on 'Euthanasia. The good death.' Where: Wilmington Medical Center (WMC). All are invited."

So I packed up my Mustang and attended this meeting.

This meeting changed my life as much as the House Bill to allow abortions for women "who would be emotionally and mentally disturbed if they had a handicapped embryo."

At the lecture, Dr. Fletcher, world-renowned author on medical ethics, preached the importance of dying a "good death." "Too much money is spent on the last months of life when the person is dying anyway, why keep them alive?" he boldly claimed.

And his presentation was eloquent, even convincing the likes of me to temporarily agree with him.

Somehow I found my voice and with great gusto. "Why don't we allow everyone over the age of seventy-two to have a choice of living or dying? Perhaps give them a 'hemlock pill' in case they want to die. Of course, it would be their choice," I sarcastically implored. And then, I snidely added, remembering Delaware's original abortion bill, "Of course, it would be with the approval of two doctors, one a psychiatrist and the other a medical doctor."

I was disappointedly surprised when so many people turned, looked at me, then applauded. Was it possible that people would choose a hemlock pill if they were ill?

After the meeting at WMC with Dr. Fletcher, I walked up to speak with him as I was trying to understand a man of his intellect, promoting such an anti-life position.

It was then I met the chaplain of the medical center. He was so pleased I spoke about giving people "hemlock" pills, because, as a chaplain, he had seen everything wrong with the medical system. "They continued hooking people up on machines and giving them chemo when their veins collapsed and stints became infected," he boastfully proclaimed.

He misjudged me, thinking I actually approved the "good death hemlock pill" option.

Then he talked about needing someone to help him visit patients at the Wilmington General Hospital (WGH), better known as the Alpha/Omega Hospital. This hospital was a place where most babies are born, and most people die. There was a large oncology unit at the General Division. During 1960 to 1980, most cancer patients died in the hospital.

I knew I had no choice. I volunteered, and blurted out, "I've been to Eastern Baptist Theological Seminary two days ago, and might be attending classes there."

The chaplain immediately replied, "No kidding! I am a graduate of EBTS and if you volunteer at the General Hospital, our chaplain's office can't pay you to visit patients and families, but we could pay for your seminary classes and books."

Are you kidding me!

I rushed home and told my husband, "I've got my books and classes paid for."

Tom uttered, "At what price?" He was referring to the time I wouldn't be home to fix everyone's breakfast, dinner, and be the mom I had been since our first daughter, Debbie, was born in 1956, second daughter, Becky, born in 1959, and third daughter, Carrie, born in 1964.

The following day, I drove up to EBTS and signed up for one class, "The History of Christianity," given by Dr. Norman Maring.

It was early September and I was volunteering at the General Division three days a week, two days at seminary, and I didn't have a clue how I was going to study after all these years, or speak to dying and sick patients.

And I had no idea how to approach my United Methodist Church to endorse me as a candidate for ordination. There were no other women applying for their master of divinity degree at Eastern Baptist Seminary, in our Peninsula, Delaware, conference back in 1972.

And my female friends thought I'd totally lost my marbles. "Women aren't in the ministry." Didn't you read about St. Paul and how women aren't allowed in the church, except in total silence. And that's from the Holy Bible!" they collectively stated. "Why would you, a woman, want to be a clergy? Jesus only called men."

Jesus, Our Feminist

I really needed to find out more about my Lord and Savior, Jesus. After all, I wouldn't want to be ordained if it's true that Jesus didn't want women to preach His word. How did Jesus treat women? What does the Holy Bible say?

My research became twofold.

First, who was Jesus?

Jesus lived in Palestine more than two thousand years ago, and we Christians acknowledge him as our Lord and Savior. And I do believe He is my Lord and Savior.

Second, how did my Savior treat women?

As I began my research, I wondered if Jesus said or did anything which would indicate that he advocated treating women as intrinsically inferior to men. What I found was that Jesus said and did things which indicated He thought of women as equals to men, and that in the process He willingly violated pertinent social mores.

Let me explain.

There were very important factors in existence in Jesus's time of history which are quite significant.

How were women treated? What was the status of women in Palestine?

During the time of Jesus, women were treated as inferiors. According to most Rabbinic customs of Jesus's time, women were not allowed to study the Scriptures, the Torah.

In the virtually religious area of prayer, women, along with children and slaves, were not allowed to recite the Schema, nor prayers at any meals. In fact, the Talmud states: "Let a curse come upon the man whose wife or children says grace for him."

In the great worship temple at Jerusalem, women were limited to the outer portion, the women's court, which was five steps below the court for men and three steps below the court for children. Besides the ostracizing women suffered in the areas of prayer and worship, there were other restrictions in the private and public forums of that society.

It was thought positively disreputable to speak to women in public. The Proverbs of the fathers contained the injunction: "Speak not with a woman in public." It was written in public documents, "Who speaks much with a woman draws down misfortune on himself, neglects the word of the law and finally earns hell."

It sure wasn't easy being born a woman in those days. In addition, save the rarest instance, women were not allowed to bear witness in a court of law.

Some thinkers in that era, Philio, a contemporary of Jesus, for example, wrote that, "Women ought not leave their households, girls ought not cross the threshold that separated the male and female apartments of the household."

In general, the attitude toward women was epitomized in the institution and customs surrounding marriage. For the most part, the function of women was thought rather exclusively in terms of childbearing and rearing. Women were almost always under the tutelage of a man, either the father or husband, or, if a widow, the dead husband's brother. Polygamy, in the sense of having several wives, but not in the sense of having several husbands, was legal at the time of Jesus. Divorce of a wife was very easily obtained by the husband. He merely had to give her a writ of divorce. "Honey, I'm home, but I don't want you around anymore, here's your writ of divorce."

Women in Palestine, on the other hand, were not allowed to divorce their husbands.

Rabbinic sayings, and remember Jesus was a Jew and a Rabbi, provide an insight into the attitude toward women. One of these sayings was: "It is well for those whose children who are male, but ill for those whose children are female. Even the most virtuous of women have four qualities. They are greedy at their food, eager to gossip, lazy, and jealous."

The condition of women in Palestine was indeed bleak.

With this in mind, I began to look at the good book, the Holy Bible, especially when our Lord walked the earth.

What are the Gospels?

The first four books of the New Testament—Matthew, Mark, Luke and John—are eyewitness reports of the events in the life of Jesus of Nazareth.

They are four different faith statements reflecting four primitive Christian communities who believed that Jesus was the Messiah, and Savior of the World.

They were composed from a variety of sources, written and oral, over a period of time. Consequently, they are many layered.

What's important to remember is the fact that no negative attitudes by Jesus toward women are portrayed in the Gospels. When you set side by side the treatment of women of the times, it's totally amazing to see how Jesus treated women.

When I began my journey, the word *feminist* was just beginning to emerge. Being a feminist really means a person who is in favor, and promotes the equality, of women with men. A person who advocates and practices treating women primarily as persons.

Now, let's look at how Jesus touches the untouchables: women.

One of the first things noticed in the Gospels about Jesus's attitude toward women is that He actually taught them the meaning of the Scripture and religious truths in general.

When you remember that in Judaism, it was considered improper and even "obscene" to teach women the Scriptures, this action of Jesus was an extraordinary and deliberate decision to break with a custom invidious to women. A number of women, married and unmarried, were regular followers of Jesus. "Jesus made his way through towns and villages preaching and proclaiming the good news of the Kingdom of God. With Him went the twelve as well as certain women who provided for them out of their own resources" (Luke 8:1-3).

Jesus's first appearance after his resurrection to any of his followers was to two women—Mary Magdalene and the other Mary from whom Jesus cast out seven demons. And these women were commissioned by Jesus to bear witness of his resurrection to the eleven disciples. This is recorded in three of the Gospels: John 20:11, Matthew 28:9, and Mark 16:9.

And, in typical Palestinian style, the eleven disciples refused to believe the women. Remember, according to Judaic law, women were not allowed to bear legal witness. As one learned in the law, Jesus obviously was aware of this stricture.

Jesus first appearing to and commissioning women to be a witness to the most important event of Jesus's career, His Resurrection, couldn't have been anything but deliberate.

Other intimate connections of women with the resurrection of the dead are also written in the Gospels.

The first account is that of the raising of a woman, Jairus's daughter, recorded in three Gospels: Matthew 9:18, Mark 5:33, and Luke 8:41.

The second resurrection Jesus performed was that of the only son of the widow of Nain. "And when the Lord saw her, He had compassion on her and said, 'Be well,' and He touched the casket and said, 'Arise,' and Jesus delivered him to his mother, and all were amazed" (Luke 7:11).

The third resurrection Jesus performed was of Lazarus, at the request of Lazarus's sisters, Mary and Martha, from the Gospel (John 11:1-29). From the first, it was Martha and Mary who had sent for Jesus, but when He finally came, Lazarus was dead four days. Martha met Jesus and pleaded for Lazarus's resurrection. "Lord if you had been here, my brother would not have died and even now I know that whatever you ask from God, God will give you" (John 11:21). And then He raised Lazarus from the dead and immediately following, Jesus declared himself to be the Resurrection.

To Martha, Jesus said, "I am the resurrection and the life. He who believes in Me, though he may die, he shall live. And whoever lives and believes in Me shall never die. Do you believe this?" And Martha said to Jesus, "Yes Lord I believe that You are the Christ, the Son of God, who is to come into the world." (John 11:24, 25).

Jesus once again revealed the central event, the central message in the Gospels—the resurrection. Jesus said these words to a woman.

In other places in the Gospel where women were treated by others not as persons but sexual objects, it was expected Jesus would do the same.

Their expectations were disappointing.

One such occasion occurred when Jesus was invited to dinner at the house of a skeptical Pharisee.

> And, behold, a woman in the city who was a sinner, when she knew that Jesus sat at the table in the Pharisee's house, brought an alabaster flask of fragrant oil, and stood at His feet behind Him weeping; and she began to wash His feet with her tears, and wiped them with the hair of her head; and she kissed His feet and anointed them with the fragrant oil. (Lk 7:36-38)

Here's a woman of ill repute, washing Jesus's feet with her tears, wiping them with her hair, and anointing them. The Pharisee saw her only as an evil creature. The Pharisee said, "If this man, Jesus were a prophet, He would know who this woman is, who is touching him, for she is a sinner" (Luke 7:39).

But Jesus deliberately rejected this approach of the woman as a sinner. Jesus rebuked the Pharisee and Jesus spoke of her love and her being forgiven and her faith, and then Jesus addressed her. Remember, it was not proper to speak to a woman in public, especially an improper woman.

And Jesus spoke to her as a human being, "Then He said to the woman, 'Your faith has saved you. Go in peace'" (Luke 7:50).

A similar situation occurred when the Scribes and Pharisees used a woman reduced entirely as a sex object to set a legal trap for Jesus.

> But Jesus went to the Mount of Olives. But early in the morning He came again into the temple, and all the people came to Him; and He sat down and taught them. Then the scribes and Pharisees brought to Him a woman caught in adultery. And when they had sat her in the midst, they said to Him, "Teacher, this woman was caught in adultery, in the very act. Now Moses, in the law, commanded us that such should be stoned. But what do You say?" (Jn 8:1-5)

It is difficult to imagine a more callous use of a human person than the "adulterous" woman being placed by the enemies of Jesus.

First, she was surprised in the intimate act of sexual intercourse, and then dragged before the Scribes and Pharisees, before an even larger crowd that Jesus was instructing, "making her stand in full view of everybody." The Scribes and Pharisees told Jesus that she had been caught in the very act of committing adultery.

And they reminded Jesus that Moses had commanded that such a woman be stoned to death. From the Old Testament, "If the woman is found in the act of adultery, they shall bring out the damsel to the door of her father's house and stone her with stones that she die" (Deuteronomy 22:21).

So, the Pharisees asked Jesus, "What do you have to say?" (John 8:5).

The trap was partly that if Jesus said yes to the stoning, he would be violating the Roman law, which restricted capital punishment, and, if Jesus said no, He would appear to contravene Mosaic Law.

Jesus eluded their snares by refusing to become entangled in legalisms and abstractions.

Rather, He dealt with both the accusers and the accused directly as spiritual ethical human persons. Jesus spoke directly to the accusers in the context of their own personal ethical conduct.

Jesus said, "He who is without sin among you, let him throw a stone at her first" (John 8:7).

To the accused woman, He likewise spoke directly with compassion, but without approving her conduct: "'Woman where are those accusers of yours? Has no one condemned you?' She said, 'No, not one Lord.' And, Jesus said, 'Neither do I condemn you. Go and do not sin again'" (John 8:10, 11).

Now, remember the law concerning divorce at the time Jesus walked in Jerusalem? A man would write a writ of divorce for any reason and the wife had to leave the home. What does Jesus say about divorce? The Pharisees tempted Jesus, saying, "Is it lawful for a man to divorce his wife for just any reason?" (Matthew 19:3).

And Jesus answered, "Have you not read that He who made them at the beginning, made them male and female, and said, For this reason a man shall leave his father and mother and be joined to his wife, and the two shall become one flesh?" (Matthew 19:4, 5).

And the Pharisees asked, "Why then did Moses command to give a certificate of divorce and to put her away?" And, Jesus said to them, "Moses, because of the hardness of your hearts, permitted you to divorce your wives, but from the beginning it was not so."

"And I say to you, whoever divorces his wife, except for sexual immorality, and marries another, commits adultery; and whoever marries her who is divorced commits adultery" (Matthew 19:8, 9).

Again, when I recalled the Palestinian restriction on women studying the Scriptures or studying with Rabbis, it is difficult to imagine how Jesus could possibly been clearer, that women were called to the spiritual life, just as men were.

In many ways, Jesus strove to communicate the notion of equality. And I was finding the Gospel lessons of Jesus were as I thought and was taught from my early years. Jesus, God the Father, and the Holy Spirit accept all people regardless their gender, their handicap, their being.

All are unconditionally loved.

I'm certainly not going to get into a debate with each person who wonders why, me, a woman, would become an ordained minister serving people communion, leading a church, and, preaching the Good Word. But after my research on Jesus, I felt as though I would qualify in Jesus's kingdom because of his loving treatment of women when He walked this earth.

What's Next?

As to the abortion issue, about 99.5 percent of my female friends agreed that women have a right to their own body, and should be allowed an abortion, if they so chose.

I don't know what possessed me. Why did I believe in the sanctity of life?

Why did I believe that taking the life of a human being was wrong? And, was "it," the embryo, even human?

After all, the Women's lib groups were claiming "it" was a zygote or embryo, therefore not a person. I'm not sure of the whys. But I do know what has happened since I started "believing," and it feels right.

Convincing my husband of nineteen years that I had to go to seminary and I had to work with the oncology patients wasn't going to work with my old-fashioned but loving husband, Tom.

His first response, after I found out the WMC's chaplain and the medical center was going to pick up my seminary tab in exchange for hours of volunteer work, was, "What? I didn't marry a minister. You have us to take care of," referring to our three daughters and himself.

But I promised I'll only take one course at seminary, and probably won't do much more. I'll flunk out, or phase out, or poop out. But, in my heart and soul, I knew I had met my destiny.

The first time I saw the packed nursery at the Wilmington Hospital, I felt an overwhelming wave and spirit that whispered to me, "You'll never change the minds of any person but you have to try to protect the sanctity of life."

I didn't know what that meant then, but I had to continue my journey and I felt I would never walk alone.

My newfound agape angel was with me always.

And, as time moved on, my beloved husband became my most ardent supporter.

This was now 1973, and the abortion on demand was approved by the Supreme Court of the United States of America. The worst Supreme Court approval since the Dred Scott Case that stated Negroes were not deemed as human beings, just as the Abortion Bill, *Roe vs. Wade*, stated that embryos weren't human. What's more, the United States Supreme Court didn't know when life began.

In my search for "Who am I?" and "What does God want me to be and do?" I started the Delaware Right to Life Society, along with Dee Becker and Jean Piziak in 1973, but the Roman Catholic members didn't feel very comfortable with me, a Protestant, who believed in the use of contraceptives. I believe in some kind of birth control. My concern is not to kill the baby once it is formed at conception.

The month before I attended seminary, I made appointments with, and talked to, forty-one ministers, rabbis, and priests about their opinion concerning their views on abortion and euthanasia. All Protestant and two rabbis agreed women had the final right to choose if they wanted an abortion. Of course, they all added, "We would hope they'd choose to keep the baby or put it up for adoption."

Only the priests were against abortion on demand. Several said, "That's the teaching of the church."

So, why do I believe the way I do? I'm not Roman Catholic, although many times during the abortion debate I've thought of becoming one. But, as a woman, I could not be a priest. I'm unsure of where I am going, but I know, with all my being, that I was being called to do something. I didn't want to carry placards at abortion clinics. I've never been much to demonstrate in that fashion.

However, I did climb into a Dr. Martin Luther King Jr. bus from Wilmington, Delaware, to Washington, DC, on August 28, 1963, to protest the wrongness of the treatment of the black people in our country.

It was at the Lincoln Memorial in Washington, DC, that Dr. Martin Luther King Jr. delivered his classic "I Have a Dream" speech. It was another unbelievable and touching event in my life. I've always been a firm believer in justice and equality for every living thing—black, white, yellow, red, and handicapped.

We are all God's children and loved equally by our Creator.

My future as a United Methodist minister was not yet established, so I considered going into psychology and opening a practice. Every time my thoughts went in that direction, I would be led back to ministry. I already enrolled in seminary, and had a volunteer acting-chaplain badge, and some of the Methodist male clergy were angry. I hadn't gone through the bells and whistles necessary to become a deacon and elder yet.

Crying, but not in front of the clergymen, became a side job for me. I couldn't figure out why no one wanted me to talk about God and Jesus and the Holy Spirit, when many of the same accusers seldom visited their own parishioners.

To this day, I've felt a lot of judgment against women in the ministry. However, I did find a friend in Rev. Paul Thomas, an associate minister at Aldersgate United Methodist Church. We had been members of Aldersgate since we arrived in Wilmington in 1958. He was instrumental in procuring approval of my becoming a deacon in the United Methodist ministry. This endorsement meant I was a person attending a Methodist-approved seminary, a person in good standing with the Methodist Church, and one "called by God."

Most of the patients and their families at the hospital were pleased with what I was doing, which was visiting, caring, praying, and showing up as often as I could.

By the time the second semester of EBT Seminary began, I realized studying was very difficult. Running back and forth from seminary to home to hospital day and night, and keeping track of my fast-growing daughters became quite a chore. I had a talk with the family and told them I would probably continue my newly found life of run, run, run. Our daughters were great. Each of them decided to help by taking turns preparing breakfast and dinners. Debbie was, and is, an outstanding chef, and she loved participating in that way. Becky, was busy with her vigorous athletic life, but nevertheless was supportive, and Carrie joyfully pitched in wherever she could.

I also studied with Carrie a lot, because her study habits were much better than mine.

Seminary was quite a ride. I was the only woman registered for the master of divinity degree at that time. I started at EBTS in 1972 and graduated in 1978 with ninety-six credit hours for my Master of Divinity degree. I graduated magna cum laude, and was forty-eight years old.

After two full years of working on my doctorate, as well as being a part-time chaplain, I earned my doctor of divinity degree. My doctorate dissertation is entitled "Sanctity vs. Quality of Life."

I was still volunteering at the Wilmington General Hospital many hours, day and night, and the hospital lived up to their original promise. All my seminary fees, including books, were paid for in full.

At the WGH, where I was a chaplain from 1973 to 1980, there wasn't an area for meditation or Sunday services. I was pleased when the junior board of the hospital said they would purchase a stained-glass window if I could find a spare room. After a lot of haggling with the general hospital's administration, they finally gave us a room. It was small, but a real place for ecumenical religious services and meditation. The beautiful stained-glass window was designed by my husband, Tom, and crafted by Willet Studios, who built stained-glass windows in Philadelphia, Pennsylvania.

Many years later, I contacted Willet Studios for another stained glass window here in Florida, and they recommended C. Paul Pickel, a stained-glass window company in Vero Beach, Florida. Paul Pickel and his design team completed the stained-glass window in the chapel of our Florida community.

The Wilmington General Hospital stained-glass window depicted praying hands, and symbolisms of many religious groups. Unfortunately, the lovely stained-glass window was destroyed when the hospital was leveled in the mid-1980s. The stained glass chapel had been special for many patients and their families, through many years.

Even our youngest daughter, Carrie, came with me Sunday after Sunday wheeling patients down to the little chapel.

We were fortunate if we could fit fifteen wheelchairs in the chapel area, and many of the patients became exhausted after fifteen minutes, so my preparation for the Sunday chapel service was minimal, to say the least.

However, more and more patients and families asked for pastoral care and I had to find someone to help administratively.

Then along came Mildred Bromwell. Her beloved husband, Roy, was a patient in our General Division hospital off and on for a year and we became good friends. After he died, Mildred volunteered to assist.

She was the perfect secretary as she typed, made appointments, and in general was a dear friend. She even typed and retyped my original doctoral thesis in 1979. Our entire family treasured her friendship until her death many years later.

Mildred was my surrogate mom, as my own mother lived in Ohio, and, although Mom and I talked on the phone almost every day, at that time we only saw one another about fifteen days a year. Mom knew I was beginning a new "adventure," as she called it, and gave me my second teddy bear to watch over me when she was in Ohio. The first teddy bear I still have, even after all these years. Mom and Dad gave it to me when I was born.

My mom was one of the greatest women I've ever known, and Mildred comes in as a close second. It was through friendships such as theirs I continued my faith process.

We are a small family with absolutely not one relative within a five hundred-mile drive. So, we frequently would call good friends "aunt" or "uncle" even though they weren't direct aunts or uncles. Mildred Bromwell was "Aunt Mildred." "Aunt Virginia" and "Uncle Lawson" Hall, our Grubb Road neighbors, were another. And "Aunt Erminine" and "Uncle Dave" Hall rounded out our surrogate family members. I thank God they were part of our lives.

My "teddy bear journey," as I named it, began to take all kinds of twists and turns.

I entered the ministry because of the abortion issue, but now I'm involved with death and dying. In fact, my husband designed a bumper sticker in black letters against a bright yellow background.

I was proud to drive my old Mustang around with that sign on my back left bumper. It said, "Abortion-Euthanasia then who...you?"

Death and Dying

My first encounter with a dying patient was with the WMC's chaplain as he was guiding me around to visit hospital patients. The patient was elderly, comatose, and hooked up to some strange-looking machines.

The chaplain, right in front of the patient, said, "Marlene, this is the kind of person Dr. Joseph Fletcher was talking about. She should be dead if not for all these contraptions hanging off her already dead body."

Another chill went through me. Why did I feel such compassion for this poor soul who probably would be better off dead and living with Jesus? I didn't understand my deep anger at the chaplain for saying what was obvious to everyone but me: "She would be better off dead."

My job was undefined, so I could walk around, see patients, talk with families, nursing staff, and everyone in the hospital. I didn't know where to start, so I just went from room to room. In the 1970s, patients usually died in the hospital, especially if you had a "tumor" or a "lump." No one called it the C word—Cancer. However, most every patient I visited knew they had the Big C, and asked me if their family members knew that they knew.

I didn't know. But soon I found out.

Family members would ask me, the acting chaplain, "Do they know I know that I have 'it'? How can I talk with them?"

There was one important lesson I learned when I was a "chaplain-in-training" at a hospital in Philadelphia. Their "teaching" chaplain department was training a few of us wannabes. As we entered one room, the teaching chaplain advised, "This patient is in a coma and she hasn't woken up from her last alcoholic binge."

After the chaplain spoke, the so-called comatose patient sat up in bed and loudly proclaimed, "I was not a drunk!" and zoomed back into her comatose position. I thought perhaps the chaplain had the wrong room. But the chaplain fainted and we all ran for the nurse. Apparently the comatose patient had been in that state for six weeks. To my knowledge, I don't know when or if she died, as the teaching chaplain never answered questions about what happened to her.

One thing I did learn: Hearing is the last thing to go, so never, but never, speak out loud in front of the patient about anything you don't want them to know or hear, even if they're comatose.

When it comes to talking about the big "C," even the staff, doctors, and nurses, didn't want to talk about it, but they whispered among themselves about each patient.

Only the housekeeping staff would tell me that "so and so" needs you to drop by, they're crying in their pillow.

Little by little, I arranged to have family meetings in one of the corridors. And, little by little, each family member would tell their story about their loved one. As I began knowing the people, their stories, their anxiety, their anger, their hopes, and their fears, I began to understand the depths of our being. We are complicated, even when our lives are going smoothly. We hurt, we wail, we cry, and we need each other.

I was fortunate at that time to encounter Dr. Elizabeth Kubler Ross, who'd just written a book on death and dying. She became an instant bestselling author and traveled around the world identifying the stages of death and dying. I became personally involved because our hospital invited her for several lectures and I was asked to accompany Elizabeth. She lived with us for a few days. It was during that time I listened to and talked with many cancer patients, with Elizabeth guiding me along the way. And when Elizabeth's mom died in Switzerland while she was visiting our home in America, that bonded our relationship as we frequently corresponded through the years. I learned quickly the different stages of dying, which will continue to be valid throughout our lives.

Just as the person dying goes through stages of dying, the immediate family will experience the same emotional reaction. When anger, resentment, and guilt can be worked through, the family will go through a phase of grief, just as the dying person does. Denial, isolation, bargaining, and anger usually accompany these stages, but the most difficult stage is acceptance. If members of a family can share these emotions together, they will gradually face the reality of impending separation and come to an acceptance of it together. The most heartbreaking time for the family is the final phase when their loved ones are slowly detaching themselves from their worlds, including their family.

Probably the most difficult time for everyone concerned is the moment the patient no longer feels pain, when the mind slips off into a dreamless state, the need for food becomes minimal, and the awareness of the environment all but disappears into darkness.

This is a rough time for the relatives as they are not sure whether to stay or leave. "How long before death takes place?" they frequently ask.

This is the time when families need help the most. It is the time for therapy of silence with the patient. It is hard to die, and it will always be so, even when we have learned to accept death as an integral part of life, because dying means giving up life on this earth. But if we can learn to view death from a different perspective, to reintroduce it into our lives so that it comes not as a dreaded stranger but as an expected companion to our life, then we can also learn to live our lives with meaning and with full appreciation of our finiteness of the limits on our time here.

Then how do we learn to live with the word *death*?

When Socrates was told that the time had come for him to prepare for his death, he asked reasonably, "Knoweth not that I have been preparing for it all my life?" He knew that death was not something he could get ready for in one last moment of fear or high resolve. The only way to get ready for death, as a part of life, is to get ready for it, throughout your life.

Jesus walked toward His own death with such courage that the closest of His friends couldn't believe that he was about to die. Such courage does not come from steeled nerves or whistling in the dark, it comes from living so constantly in the company of the eternal God that one really feels the grave itself is but a covered bridge which leads from light to light, through a brief darkness.

As we stand in the presence of death, there is no Scripture more thought-provoking that the one from the Epistle of Romans.

> Who shall separate us from the love of Christ? Shall tribulation, or distress, or persecution, or famine, or nakedness, or peril or sword? As it is written: "for Your sake we are killed all day long; We are accounted as sheep for the slaughter." Yet in all these things we are more than conquerors through Him who loved us. For I am persuaded that neither death nor life, nor angels, nor principalities nor powers, nor things present nor things to come, nor height nor depth nor any other created thing, shall be able to separate us from the love of God which is in Christ Jesus our Lord." (Rom. 8:35-39)

God's love stands at the heart of death. Paul says it in his letter to the Corinthians church: "Death is swallowed up in victory" (1 Corinthians 15:54).

The secret of faithful living in every stage of life was beautifully expressed by St. Francis of Assisi. One of his ardent followers came to him as he was hoeing his garden and said, "Sir, what would you do if you were suddenly to learn that you would die at sunset this very day?" And with a benign smile that reflected the deep serenity of his soul, St. Francis replied, "I would go on hoeing in my garden."

So we must live through every phase of our life in faith and security of knowing God's with us, through every stage.

The prayer of St. Francis of Assisi says it well.

Lord, make me an instrument of thy peace.
Where there is hatred: let me sow love.
Where there is injury: pardon.
Where there is doubt: faith.
Where there is despair: hope.
Where there is sadness: joy.
Where there is darkness: light.
O, divine Master, grant that I may not so much seek to be consoled: as to console.
Not so much to be understood: as to understand.
Not so much to be loved: as to love.
For it is in giving that we receive.
It is in pardoning that we are pardoned.
It is in dying that we are born to eternal life.

Stained glass window

BETTING AND SUPPORTING

My first funeral was a young man, forty-six, my dad's age when he died. I'd become quite close to their family, his wife and three children, as they reminded me of my family. They asked me to wear a clergy robe for his funeral, and I had no idea where to get one my size. Cokesbury was the United Methodist Store for books, clothing, and all kinds of clerical needs.

When I entered the Cokesbury store, I felt strange when I asked for a woman's clergy robe. The salesman told me they didn't have women's robes, but he had a small-sized man's robe that had just been returned, so the price was reduced.

When I put the robe on, another chill went through me, and amazingly it fit perfectly.

"I'll take it," I exclaimed proudly.

"That'll be $128.50," he said with authority.

"Okay", I said, as I reached in my purse and brought out our checkbook. No Visa/Mastercard in those days.

As I was writing the check, I realized I didn't have enough money in the bank to cover the cost of my new robe. But I wrote the check anyway, the first time I'd ever done anything like that without conferring with my beloved husband. As I drove back to Wilmington, I wondered how I was going to admit this lack of judgment to my husband, who is financially disciplined.

"Hi, honey," I sheepishly murmured, ready to step up and tell the truth about the check.

Arriving home, Tom said, "Hey, don't forget we're going to my Rotary party at the Brandywine Race Track. It starts at 5:30 buffet then the races follow."

Oh dear, now when am I going to tell him about the overdraft? We'll need to do something soon, else the check will bounce! Tom had already asked our eldest daughter, sixteen-year-old Debbie, to babysit her sisters. Our middle daughter, Becky, was thirteen, and our youngest, Carrie, was eight.

I stuffed my newly purchased robe in the hall closet, out of sight, and then we went to the harness race track, the first and last time I've ever attended.

I didn't know how to choose horses then or now, but my Tom asked if I wanted to bet the "daily double."

"What's that?"

"It's when you choose two horses, one in the first race and one in the second race."

"I'll bet on number 5 and number 3," I responded, not registering why I chose those numbers.

"Why those horses? What are their names?" he inquired.

"I don't know."

So Tom dutifully put two dollars on number 5 and number 3. Obviously they won, or I wouldn't be telling this story, but the irony is that the win of the daily double was $128.50, the exact price of my new clergy robe.

Tom, who's seldom impressed, asked me why I chose numbers 5 and 3.

"I have something to tell you, honey. Today I bought a robe and it cost $128.50, And, I remembered on the back of the robe's collar there are the numbers 5 and 3. I put the robe in the hall closet," I sheepishly responded.

To prove myself, I asked Tom to call our daughter, Debbie, and ask her to look in the closet, open the zippered robe, and look on the back collar.

"Yes, Dad. There are numbers 5 and 3. Why? What's going on?" she queried.

"Nothing, just your mother."

None of the Rotarians knew I was going to seminary, or anything about the robe, but they knew I won the daily double and all asked me, "Who are you going to bet on for the next races?"

I didn't bet a penny after that, and haven't bet on horses since. But you can bet I put that $128.50 in the bank the next morning to cover the check.

Not only that, but I could never tell anyone about how I got that money, else the whole Methodist church would've forbidden me to enter the ministry at that time, I'm sure. United Methodists were totally against all gambling and made antigambling their prime policy for many years. Interestingly, the United Methodist polity agreed on a woman's "choice of terminating her pregnancy, aborting her child," but don't dare bet on anything.

Supporting

At our Wilmington General Hospital area, there's a special place for downstate cancer patients called "Robin Hall." People with cancer and their families traveled from lower Delaware to receive their radiation and chemotherapy treatments. Each room at Robin Hall had double beds and a small bathroom. It really was an old-fashioned home converted, originally to house patients who had tuberculosis, and when that disease was finally conquered, cancer patients and their families used it. A very large parlor became a meeting place for all the patients and their families. Dozens of them came each week, and they knew no one.

I started a Bible study, but most of them just wanted to talk about their lives, and the frightening radiation, chemo, and emotional problems that were bombarding their whole being. Support groups became my focus, because it was their focus. They wanted and needed to talk with people who were going through the same emotions that they were experiencing.

When I first thought about support groups, there was already a support group helping cancer patients cope openly with their feelings and assisting them in relating better to the mourning of their loved ones. It is called Make Today Count.

The motto for the program is, "Don't worry about the future, just get the most out of each minute of each day." A book by the same name is the story of Orville Kelly, a Burlington, Iowa, newsman who lost his world in June 1973 when he discovered he had cancer and only six months to live. But, for some reason, his radiation and chemotherapy began to work, and even though he was nauseous, his hair fell out, and he was riddled by pain, he regained his world in 1975 when he started "Make Today Count."

This is an organization that brought new hope to people every day. I was asked to start a chapter where I worked at the medical center and it was well received by many patients and their families. Their teaching is not unfamiliar, but vital to remember. Today is all we have. This moment is all there is. This is it. This is life right now. Work on living one day at a time, sometimes failing, but discovering a new joy of living. First of all, we have to die to yesterday. Each day is a new day to begin again. Today is all we have (Frank Crone, "Just for Today," 1921).

Just for Today

There are two days of the week on which and about that one should never worry. Two carefree days kept sacredly from fear and apprehension. One of these days is yesterday. Yesterday with all its frets and cares and with all its pains and aches, all its faults and blunders, has passed forever beyond the reach of our recall. All that is, holding onto our life, the wrongs, regrets and sorrow, is in other hands than ours.

Except for the beautiful memories, sweet and tender, that lingers like perfume of roses in the heart of the day that is gone: we have nothing to do with yesterday.

The other day that we should not need to worry about is tomorrow. Tomorrow, with all its possibilities, adversities, its perils, its large promises, and poor performance, is as far beyond the reach of our mastery as its dead sister, yesterday. Its sun will rise in roseate splendor or behind a mask of weeping clouds, but it will rise. Until then, the same love and patience that held yesterday and will hold tomorrow, is not in our possession.

There is left for us but one day of the week, Today. Any man can fight the battles of today. Any woman can carry the burdens of just one day. It is only when, to the trials and cares of today we will fully add the burdens of these two awful eternities, yesterday and tomorrow, that we break down. It isn't the experience of today that drives a person mad. It is the remorse for something that happened yesterday. The fear of what tomorrow may bring.

I will try to live through this day only, not to tackle my whole life problem at once. I can do things for twelve hours that would appall me if I had to keep them up for a lifetime.

Just for today, I will be happy. This assumes that what Abraham Lincoln said is true. "Most folks are about as happy as they make up their minds to be."

Happiness is from within, it is not just a matter of externals.

Just for today, I will try to adjust myself to what is, and not try to adjust everything to my own desires. I will take my family, my business, and my luck as they come and fit myself to them.

Just for today, I will take care of my body. I will exercise it, care for it, nourish it, not abuse it or neglect it, so that it will be as good as possible.

Just for today, I will try to strengthen my mind. I will learn something useful. I will not be a mental loafer. I will read something that will require effort, thought, and concentration.

Just for today, I will exercise my soul in three ways. I will do somebody a good turn, and not get found out. I will do at least two things I don't want to do, just for exercise.

Just for today, I will be agreeable. I will look as well as I can, dress as becomingly as possible, talk low, act courteously, be liberal with praise, criticize not at all, nor find fault with anything and try not to regulate nor improve anyone.

Just for today, I will have some kind of a program. It will eliminate two pests, hurry and indecision. Just for today, I will have a quiet half hour all by myself and relax. In this half hour, I will think of God, so as to get a little more perspective to my life.

Just for today, I will be unafraid, especially I will not be afraid to be happy, to enjoy what is beautiful, to love and to believe that those I love, love me.

My Roman Catholic priest friend, Father Bill Ketch, and I were in a number of clergy meetings together and we talked frequently about the abortion issue. Soon we realized our deep concerns for the widow and widowers, who felt so alone in this couple world of ours. Of course, my mom becoming a widow at the tender young age of forty-four made me realize how lonely life can be for a widow.

When I started this support group, I called it "You're Not Alone," concentrating on widows and widowers. I asked Father Ketch to help me cofacilitate the group every Friday from 1:00 to 3:00 p.m., at the American Red Cross building in Wilmington. We were there every Friday for over ten years.

The support groups certainly helped me understand pain, loneliness, and suffering as I vicariously lived my life through their journeys.

After eight years as chaplain at the hospital, in 1980, I was appointed associate minister at the Grace United Methodist Church, in downtown Wilmington.

Grace United Methodist Church

Grace Church was a stunning edifice positioned in a historic area that was once a popular meeting place. The congregation was accepting of their first female minister, because many attended the support groups I facilitated at the hospital.

It wasn't long into my new ministry at Grace that I started more support groups. The support group for grief recovery (GRG, Grief Recovery Group), was attended by anyone who was in the process of recovering from the loss of a loved one. There was also a support group for grieving the loss of a child (LCG, Loss of Child Group). You're Not Alone was also continued for widow and widowers.

After three years at Grace United Methodist Church, I was appointed minister of Mt. Lebanon United Methodist Church, and brought my support groups to that location.

A church "in the dogwoods," as the locals called her, Mt. Lebanon, founded in 1812, built in 1834, was ready to close her doors. Fewer than twenty people were in attendance, but our bishop wanted someone to minister until the sesquicentennial anniversary, to be celebrated the following year, 1984.

Mt. Lebanon United Methodist Church, painted by Carolyn Blish

The support groups started at Grace were now located at my new appointment, Mt. Lebanon. And those support groups led to new ones.

Many people who attended the Grief Recovery Group were recovering from their loved ones who committed suicide. They asked if I would start a group just for families whose loved ones had committed suicide, because their feelings of a suicidal situation were much different from grieving from a "normal death," that other attendees of the GRG were feeling. I named it Families of Suicide to Enable Recovery (FOSTER).

I was surprised at many people came to this group bringing their entire family and supporting friends. Their biggest issues were blame, shame, guilt, and anger. They always blamed themselves. "Why didn't I see this coming?" "I should've done something…anything." And then the blame was on someone else, most often another family member. Frequently, spouses ended up needing grief counseling, because everyone grieves so differently.

And, the shame of a family member committing suicide remains with the entire household. "Why did they do that to me?" It was quite normal for loved ones to take it personally. They felt it was a direct assault against them. Many felt that suicide was a "sin," and were concerned about how their loved ones would be judged by God and society. And when the family members could finally work through their feelings of despair, anger was next. Anger at the one who committed suicide, anger at society, anger at everyone. All of these feelings are felt by all families whose loved one has committed suicide.

The families of our FOSTER group asked me why I didn't start a group for people who were suicidal. "You've got the cart before the horse," they would exclaim. And that was true. They were attending a support group whose loved one already committed suicide.

"What should I call the group?" I asked.

To the person, they said, "Call it like it is, 'Suicide Prevention.'"

So, I put a small ad in the *News Journal*:

> If you feel depressed or suicidal and want to talk about your feelings, come to Mt. Lebanon United Methodist Church Thursday at 7 p.m.

When that Thursday arrived, I was ready with a small pot of coffee and tea, and some of the church women provided cookies.

In the church fellowship hall, over fifty people arrived!

"Oh God, what will I do now? How in the world can I help all these people who must feel suicidal? Please lead me, Lord," was my constant prayer.

We all sat in a large circle in the Fellowship Hall. There were all ages, the youngest sixteen, the eldest fifty-eight.

I was the lone facilitator. I tried to get another facilitator. None of my clergy friends wanted to help. Their reason? Potentially big lawsuit issues. None of my psychologist friends wanted to help either, they wanted to be reimbursed.

We never charged a penny to any person or their families in our support groups.

I had overcommitted myself. I had no choice. I started this, and had to continue even though I didn't know how. Immediately I realized I had the wrong idea. I thought everyone would talk about their feelings, and they did, but in a much different way than I anticipated.

The elders of the group were chastising the younger set when they told them, "You don't know problems until you're older! You haven't seen anything yet!" That was in response to the younger kids mentioning they were suicidal because they were jilted by a boyfriend or girlfriend.

It was at the end of that first disastrous meeting I decided to split the groups into two groups—younger and older. The younger had only teens, and the older group with a different set of problems. Two different nights to facilitate another two support groups.

Many of our attendees at our group meetings became church members. They felt hope and nonjudgment from other parishioners. It actually helped that our church had only a few members in attendance. They didn't dare be too judgmental of people who were different, else we'd have to close the church.

Our suicide prevention support groups grew precipitously.

Since my time was becoming more and more limited, I thought a buddy system might work, similar to having a buddy swimming with you. I taught swimming b.m. (before ministry), and we always swam with a buddy, for safety purposes.

"Wouldn't it be helpful to have a buddy system for those who feel suicidal?" I asked the support group. And they promised one another that if they felt suicidal, they would call, and meet each other no matter what time of day or night.

I prayed it would work. And it did. Not one of our group members tried to commit suicide over all those years. Many continued feeling depressed, but found other ways to reach out, besides reaching in. That doesn't mean it was all rosy. It wasn't. Often I found myself meeting them in different places, trying to listen to their problems and calling my psychologist friends to advise me.

I certainly was learning too much about suicide. But what I was learning I passed on to others.

Speaking to many different organizations became a biweekly occurrence. Several of the young members of our Suicide Prevention Support Group joined me in my presentations.

No matter how much I would talk about the prevention of suicide, the people who had actually felt suicidal and found the support group helpful could describe their situations accurately. Speaking in public about their feelings helped heal their wounds, as nothing else could. We were invited to speak on television, radio, even in Hamburg, Germany, where we gave a major talk at the AASP (American Association of Suicide Prevention) Conference.

I was always so proud of their courage and openness to discuss their fears, depression, and suicidal thoughts. It's through sharing and caring that healing begins.

My most memorable moment of speaking was in an auditorium at William Penn High School, to a large group of seventh, eighth, and ninth graders. The subject the school wanted me to speak on was "Signs of suicide and how you can help each other."

As I was being introduced, the school secretary put a note on the podium, addressed to "Chaplain Walters."

Here is what it said: "Your daughter is having a baby."

Our oldest daughter, Debbie, was in the process of having a baby and my secretary knew where to reach me. The school secretary delivered that special note, which I still treasure.

My first comment, to those middle-school kids, was, "This is why you live for another day. There's always a tomorrow that will bring you much joy."

After the presentation, I immediately drove down to Herndon, Virginia, where I saw our grandson, Benjamin Joseph, being delivered.

Our beloved Ben is now twenty-nine years old, married, and serving in the United States Marine Corps.

Stained Glass Two Keys

WHERE IS GOD
WHEN THERE'S SUFFERING?

There are many lessons to be learned in life. Experiences that are unforgettable.

I reflect back on my time spent at the Wilmington General Hospital. Our hospital delivered most babies in our area. And it was a public hospital, so abortions could be performed. We had a paging system in those days, and when I heard "Chaplain Walters, call OB or ER," I knew a family was suffering some kind of loss. Usually it was a still born.

I was amazed at how many babies were not born alive.

The first family who called upon the pastoral care office to help them wanted me to conduct a funeral service and baptize their stillborn.

There were no guidelines to follow in writing a memorial service for a person who hadn't lived yet. Nor was there anything mentioning baptizing one.

However, I learned what not to do for families who had a stillborn.

The first couple I met who had a stillborn were very angry that I hadn't asked for their stillborn's name. I hadn't thought about naming a stillborn, hence I didn't ask.

But what a mistake. And I should've known better.

We had three children, all of whom were in my tummy for nine months and we'd come up with a lot of names in the process.

A baby dying at birth is a tremendous loss, and most people who haven't dealt with this kind of loss don't understand the grieving that is inherent in the loss of a child at birth or shortly after birth.

Another page, and I assumed it was a stillborn. But it was not. Alive, but dead.

One of our obstetricians who believed in abortion, had aborted a baby that was born alive. In our state of Delaware, there was no time period that babies could be aborted, so the doctor had not committed a crime. Many of our obstetric nurses were of the Roman Catholic faith, so two of them saw the baby in the waste area trying to breathe. They immediately tried to resuscitate the aborted baby, and they wanted me to witness the event.

Administration had already been notified and they were trying to cover the act of the doctor and intervening on the nurses' attempt to resuscitate.

And, the "mother" of the aborted fetus was furious that the nurses were resuscitating her "baby." She was threatening to sue the hospital because she wanted her baby aborted, and that meant a dead baby.

This raises so many other questions.

When does life begin?

Is it at birth?

Is it when we can resuscitate it?

Is it at conception?

When will we begin to value a human life?

Abortion leads to so many other ethical issues.

Infanticide is one. Allowing a baby to die because it has a disease, handicap, or deformity.

Another ethical issue is fathers not being involved in the decision of abortion.

Doctors not being held accountable to any ethical standard.

Euthanasia, hastening the death of a dying person.

The list goes on and on.

But nowhere is it more alarming than in the decision of doctor-assisted suicide. A society could eliminate themselves from an entire group of handicapped, diseased, and worthless people.

Were they considered to be unworthy of life?

When is a person a person, with rights of personhood?

This is the toxic atmosphere of which the entire abortion issue has brought into our culture. A belief that life is not precious, and quality of life is more important than sanctity of life.

I can actually buy into it, after seeing people struggle as they live with severe pain; a lifetime of being unable to move, talk, or communicate; and end of life diseases that are cruel to our bodies, minds, and souls.

Why would my savior allow this to happen? On the other hand, why did my Father allow His Son to suffer on the cross?

And I kept wondering, as I visited patients, families, and watching in the emergency waiting rooms the vast number of injuries, grief, and suffering, where is God when there's so much suffering?

We've all wondered about this question, and ask it many times throughout our lives.

Indeed, where is God when there's so much suffering?

In fact, if you stop for a moment and tune in your awareness to the sum total of human suffering going on in this very instant, physical suffering such as that caused by auto accidents, with mangled cars and smashed bodies, or mental suffering caused by the demons of the mind scourging the minds of many with unearthly fears, or emotional suffering caused by betrayed or strained relationships, if you think about all the suffering, you can almost be totally undone.

War, famine, political tyranny, natural disasters, all add to this horrible total.

And the mind cries out. "Where is God?"

Is He able to prevent suffering, but not willing?

Then how is He good?

Is he willing to prevent suffering but not able? Then how is He God?

Is He both willing and able to prevent suffering?

Then, whence cometh suffering?

One explanation the ancients came up with was that suffering was linked with wrongdoing. This was the message of Job's friends:

> Does God subvert judgment? "If your sons have sinned against Him, He has cast them away for their transgression." (Jb 8:3)

If iniquity were in your hand and you put it far away and would not let wickedness dwell in your tents. (Jb 11:14)

Surely such are the dwellings of the wicked, and this is the place of him who does not know God. (Jb 18:21)

But Job insisted they were wrong and answered the Lord: "I know that You can do everything and that no purpose of Yours can be withheld from you" (Jb 42: 2). "God is mighty, but despises no one. He is mighty in strength of understanding" (Jb 36:5, 6).

Job knew he was not perfect, but he insisted that there was no correlation between anything he could have done and what had happened to him and his family.

Is God really punishing us for wrongdoings?

Hear the words from the Gospel of John: "Jesus and the disciples met a man who was born blind, and they asked the Master, 'Who hath sinned, this man or his parents, that he was born blind?'" (Jn 9:1).

Jesus's answer was direct and emphatic: "Neither hath sinned. The man was born blind so that God's works might be manifest through him" (Jn 9:3).

So, our Lord will not let us say, when we see a person greatly suffering, the person or their family had sinned and they were being punished for their problem.

Life isn't like that.

So, this old solution, "God is punishing you," is too limited to be applied across the board. Here is a little child two years old found to have leukemia. How could that child deserve such a thing? How could a still born deserve not to experience life?

As I pondered these unanswered questions, and became involved with families who were asking me for answers, I remembered reading C. S. Lewis's book, *The Problem of Pain*, and his four categories of human suffering.

- First is the law of gravity
- Second is our human ignorance

- Third is our interdependence
- Fourth are our wrong choices

The first is suffering caused by the operation of natural law. Aunt Nelle slips on the pavement and breaks her hip. Whom shall we blame?

The Law of Gravity, I suppose. And being a lovely and charming person doesn't mean that Aunt Nelle will step one inch from the pavement and just levitate until friends help regain her balance.

Tropical Storm Faye, which swept through our area and raised the water level six inches deep into our home, who or what caused it?

Tropical storms are freaks of our planetary wind system and the sun is surely one of the culprits.

But it doesn't help to shake your fist at the sun.

So whom do you blame when your house collapses and your family is injured?

Insurance contracts sometimes call these natural disasters "acts of God."

I dislike that term, because I do not believe that God intends these events at all. They are just part of the way things are in Mother Earth.

So, there is a lot of human suffering that simply shows up our vulnerability before the forces of natural law.

Another kind of suffering is caused by human ignorance.

Job had a wretched affliction. "And now my soul is poured out because of my plight; the days of affliction take hold of me. My bones are pierced in me at night, and my gnawing pains take no rest" (Jb 30:16, 17).

But we had no knowledge of antibiotics or skin medication. So, Job just sat there and became more and more miserable.

Our ignorance of medicine prevented him from ending his ordeal.

Or, try to imagine, if you can, what surgery must have been like before the discovery of anesthetics. Our anesthesiologists are being especially hard hit by our current malpractice madness, but think of going to surgery without anesthesia. Formerly, when a doctor had to amputate a limb, he would get his patients as drunk as possible.

It is recorded that one British surgeon could remove a leg in under two minutes.

Suffering was surely related to ignorance. We didn't have the anesthesia available as we do today.

If you're my age, you'd remember the ravages of infantile paralysis before Jonas Salk and the research pioneers.

I had a dear friend, Marjorie Willock, who had polio from the age of nineteen, and lived in an iron lung for twenty years, until she died. She suffered greatly but kept her faith, even though her body was twisted and torn beyond belief.

There's a lot more to human life than a twisted body.

What is the value of life, if it's only measured by the obvious handicaps?

God didn't intend people to get polio. And when the vaccine appeared, I can picture a holiday in heaven with all the angels let off duty to celebrate.

New knowledge eradicated one more item of human suffering.

That's why it's so important now to continue our reverence for life and not pull the plugs on those suffering.

It's through suffering that knowledge is built.

Another kind of suffering is rooted in our interdependence. I think of a woman I met in the hospital. She is a beautiful lady with a lovely voice that projected a deep faith experience that came through each song.

But, now you seldom hear her sing.

Why?

Her childhood years had been scarred by tension arising from an alcoholic father.

Think of all the suffering people in Africa, the Middle East, the shrouded tent people in our own country. We are all related to one another in a tragedy of history.

None of us are immune.

Catholics, Protestants, Muslims, atheists, Jews, all have suffered from killings, bombings, and starvation throughout history.

St Paul said it well: "We know that the whole creation has been groaning in suffering together" (Rom. 8:22).

There is a corporate suffering which arises from our linkages with one another.

That's why carelessness with one's own lifestyle and health can be so cruel and selfish.

I was a chaplain in the emergency room many times and wished I'd never seen the results of motorcyclists riding without a helmet. They wanted to "feel the wind blowing their hair," which was an all-too-familiar comment by their families when they saw their motorcyclist loved ones dying from trauma to the head and brain.

No person is an island. We sometimes make wrong choices and they always touch others, even if we're a recluse.

And we can all supply our own illustrations of wrong choices. You can't live to be ninety going ninety, too much alcohol, smoking, drugging.

Nowhere does God promise to bail us out of our own folly.

Now that we know four groups of suffering: Natural causes, human ignorance, interdependence, and our own wrong choices, even so, can you think of a world where these causes of suffering would not operate?

Can you think of a world where a person would never fall and break a limb, where the law of gravity would simply be turned off by God whenever someone was likely to be hurt by it?

Can you think of a world where humans would know everything, including the future or a world where people would not be interrelated? Where the suffering of one person would not pull in others?

Can you think of a world where we would have no freedom to make wrong choices? Where God would simply veto all our mistakes? I cannot conceive of such a world.

Life as we know it involves risk, danger, and the possibility of joy and sorrow. Living on planet earth leaves us vulnerable, but vulnerability is part of what it means to be human.

Now, let's look at the Christian in such a world.

Has God written a special contract with Christians? Sometimes we talk and pray as if this were so. How many times I've heard. "Why did God do this to me? I've done everything I could to help others." "Why me?" But what do we find? Christians are hit by drunk drivers. Christian homes are robbed and burned. Christians are murdered. If this were not so, God would have to suspend the whole natural order, just for Christians.

Then Christians would not be full participants in the world. Not only that, but we would extort people to become Christians for the wrong reasons. But what a gigantic membership we would have, if we could promise immunity from suffering!

But what a bunch of phonies we would be!

Some of us talk as if we brought a note with us signed by God when we were baptized. "Dear world, please excuse Sophia/Bradley from all that is unpleasant." But the truth surely is that we are human before we are Christian and we are human after we are Christians. And, as human beings, we have a solidarity with every other human being in the whole world, and, in fact, with the fate of the world itself.

Then, we imploringly ask, "Almighty God, what wilt Thou give us?"

The Scriptures give us some answers. "In everything God works for good with those who love Him" (Romans 8:28).

Whatever our situation is, however bad it may be, God is there with us, working with us, suffering with us, moving the situation toward our good.

So, the "contract" is *not* to be excused from suffering, but to have God as a companion through suffering. Our Old Testament says it well. "When you go through the waters, I will be with you" (Isaiah 43:3).

But you have to go through the waters.

Psalm 23 gives us a similar answer: "Yea, though I walk through the valley of the shadow of death, I will fear no evil, for Thou art with me" (Psalm 23:4).

You never walk alone.

Finally, a word about God Himself.

When I began thinking about suffering and my struggles to identify where God is in suffering, I felt as though suffering put a cloud over the goodness of God.

Can we find anything to make faith and suffering compatible? Our world is incomplete, as a growing developing organism, still unfinished. If the world is still undergoing the process of change, then God is in those processes.

The Hebrews said God is the living God. "My soul thirsts for God, for the living God."(Psalm 42:2).

Paul said, "Likewise the spirit helps us in our weakness" (Romans 8:24).

So, God is at work in every area of our lives. God is at work providing care and love for the terminally ill. Not "I'll get you out of this misery by pulling your plug," but "I'll be with you through your suffering."

God is at work in the laboratories in every affliction and disease, as research pioneers unveil the mysteries of illnesses.

God is at work as people reach out to weaker brethren.

God is at work in the movements for freedom and justice.

God is working with us on the whole agenda of human suffering.

He is unchanging morally, but He advances creatively in the process of the world changing.

God is our companion, even our fellow sufferer: witness the cross.

So, how do we cope with a crisis of suffering when it hits us?

We can learn to draw strength from recognizing the forms of God's presence with us in our situation.

That presence may come into my hospital room with the nurse on the ward. It may come in my awareness of the vast network of research going on to conquer illness. Even the presence of God in nature can be reassuring. Dietrich Bonhoeffer in his Nazi prison cell drew strength from watching springtime return to the German countryside. God is with me. I can learn to cultivate his friendship, because in the end, He is all I have.

One thing more. Even if my action is limited; even if I can't move, see, or hear, I can find out where God is working to relieve human suffering and I can join Him there. If I do this, I will not only transcend my own suffering by attaching my life to a larger meaning, but I may also serve as a beacon light on a high hill to give hope and strength to others who are suffering.

I quote the memorable words of Albert Schweitzer from his classic book, *The Quest of the Historical Jesus*, written in 1906, long before he went to Africa to live out these words: "God speaks to us the same two words, follow me, and sets us to the task which He has to fulfill in our time. God commands. And to those who obey Him, whether they be wise or simple, God will reveal Himself in the toils, the conflicts, and sufferings which they shall pass through in His fellowship; and as an ineffable mystery, they shall learn in their own experiences, who God is."

"Many nations shall be joined to the Lord in that day and they shall become My people. And I will dwell in your midst, then you will know the Lord of Hosts has sent me to you" (Zechariah 2:11).

As a chaplain at WMC, I conducted many memorial services. There was one lady who lived downstate where there were few, if any, oncology units. She was a caring and thoughtful person and I would visit her as often as possible. When she died, her family gave me this touching parable to read at her Celebration of Life service.

The origin of the writing is unknown, but it might have been Rev. Robert Lovell or Richard Hunter. Nevertheless, it sums up "Where Is God When There's Suffering?"

I've read it many times, as a sermon, an emphasis in a lecture, and to myself, reminding me of what God really promises.

Behold the preacher mounted the pulpit, and one hundred faces looked up. And, they were as the sons and daughters of earth, three billion faces, captured in one hundred.

And the preacher placed a throat disc on the tongue, so that the voice became both sweet and oily. And, smiling the smile of those who see but do not understand, said, "Let us give thanks." And, one hundred voices murmured, "Amen." But there was no joy in that Amen.

"Let us give thanks," said the preacher, "for the wholeness of our bodies, for legs that walk and run, for ears that hear the song of the bird, for eyes that see beauty in flower, fruit, earth and sky, and for arms that envelop, and hands that hold."

And sadly, without a word, there arose the blind and deaf people, crippled and paralyzed, and those who had lost a limb and, behold, twenty people made their way out of that church.

But the preacher continued and said, "Let us give thanks for our health, for lungs breathing in soft air and for enjoyment of food and drink."

And there arose and departed those with TB, those with cancer, and those in great pain, and, behold, twenty more left the congregation.

But still the preacher continued the rhapsody and said, "Let us give thanks for earthy benefits, the comforts of this world, the rivers of wealth that this fruitful world has bestowed upon us."

And there departed of the poor who had seen their children die of malnutrition and their parents of cold. Twenty more.

But the preacher, eyes raised in riveted contemplation of comfortable thought, saw none of this and said, "Let us give thanks for home and hearth."

And there departed out of the congregation, the dispossessed, the refugees, the old people from the welfare homes; in all, ten more.

And the preacher persisted and said, "Let us give thanks for our friends."

And then from the congregation there arose forgotten people from lonely corners of our cities, the painfully shy who eat nightly in cheap restaurants alone, and all who by their fellows are considered odd or of wrong race or background, and quietly there slipped away ten more.

But the preacher, drawing from comfort and unction, said, "Let us give thanks for our beauty, surely no supernatural beauty, for we are humble people, but that which makes us graceful, gracious, and good to be with."

And Sally, who knew her cancer left her weak and ugly, and George, whose eyes were crossed, and Ann, whose hair had disappeared due to chemo treatments, and Jack, who had a colostomy, and ten more arose and departed that place.

Yet still the preacher spoke, "Let us give thanks for our wonderful minds, through which we understand art and science and for those who are productive."

And those who could no longer intellectually probe, due to sickness and ill health, and those who were no longer productive, all arose, ten of them, and walked to the door.

And then, the preacher look out upon the congregation.

And there was no one there.

And there was no more sweetness or oiliness in the preacher's voice. And the pastor cried out, and the voice cracked, "O Lord, my Lord, where have they gone?"

And, behold, a voice spoke from heaven, a still small voice and it said, "Because you have exalted what I have not promised, and since the heart of people knows easily the taste of bitterness, they have departed thy congregation.

"When have I promised thee wholeness of body, health or earthly comfort?

"When have I promised thee unbroken bonds with family or friends?

"When have I promised thee continued possession of beauty, intelligence or virtue?

"When have I told thee that in this world people will always know justice and peace?

"When have I promised thee no suffering, no pain, no insidious diseases?"

And the preacher cried out, "Oh Lord, then what wilt Thou give us?"

And the voice replied, "Myself."

And the preacher ran to the doorway of the church, and there, sitting in the shadows of its great pillars and lofty spires, mute and with eyes of three billion.

And the preacher took out the box of throat discs and hurled them into outer darkness, and the preacher cried with a cracked, but human, cry, "O my friends, I have deceived you. We may have health, we may have friends, we may have justice, but all we are sure of is that God gives to us Himself and we continue the circle of love by giving it to someone else."

And a blind man wept, and a friendless woman grasped her neighbor's hand, and a cancer patient found agape love with his roommate, and the poor knew their struggles were worthwhile.

Behold, the preacher mounted the pulpit and one hundred faces looked up.

And the preacher said, "Let us give thanks that God Himself is with us and His love passes to us and we give it to each other, world without end."

And, one hundred voices cried out, "Amen!"

Stained Glass Descending Dove

God's Will, Not Ours

Praying

As I walked the hospital halls into the rooms of those suffering, I couldn't understand why God didn't answer all the prayers.

Why pray, if prayer isn't answered?

As I was struggling with this question, I met a minister's wife who was a stage four cancer patient. All of the members of her congregation prayed continually for her, day and night.

I wasn't going to interfere with another clergy's family, but his wife called for me one day. When I entered her room, she asked if she could be alone with me.

The other people left and I sat beside her bed. "Chaplain," she said. "I hear you're having family meetings where the patient and family can talk together."

"Yes," I replied. "Will your family come? They're on Wednesdays at seven in the evening."

"I'm not sure. You know they expect me to get well. They pray over me every day and night of all of our lives."

"Do you think it's not working?" I murmured with my head down.

"Oh, you understand, don't you? I may not get well. I think my body is dying." And she began to weep, then sob, and I sat on her bed and held her.

She'd realized her death was imminent and her precious Lord and prayers of her adoring hopeful congregation could not stop the dying progress.

We began to talk about God. I'd been around people with cancer long enough to know, once it's on the move, it's a real chase to stop it.

"What are you feeling now?" I asked, hunting for the right words.

"I'm going to let my husband and church family down."

"You're feeling guilty," I replied, knowing that's how I would feel.

"Yes, and none of them will listen to me when I tell them I think I'm dying. They all say, 'Don't say that. You'll get well, you just have to have faith.'" And, she quietly murmured, "I think I'm letting God down too. I just don't have enough faith."

"Faith is a difficult word," I said, again reflecting my own questioning.

This lovely lady was a deep believer in God, family, and church, and demonstrated it with her faith, hope, prayer, and love. But she was also in touch with her own reality. That death was around the corner.

"Can you help me talk to them?" she inquired. "Please tell them how I feel. My doctor is playing their game too."

"I'll try to talk with them when they're here together. Will you introduce me to them and say a few words about how you feel?" I asked.

"Yes."

A few hours later, the entire prayer group from her church came in to pray, along with her minister husband.

I entered with caution, and she immediately introduced me as the hospital chaplain. And they all wanted me to have a prayer. I said one. It was similar to this: "Lord, please be with this family guiding them to accept that Thy will be done, not just our will. Amen."

They didn't like that prayer, but I've learned that everything is in the Lord's hands and His will, will be done. They never spoke to me again, and this lovely lady died two days later.

God's will be done.

There are times that prayers do alter the disease process, but we never know why.

One time, a group of prayerful souls were in a room of a dying friend, and invited me to come in and pray with them. I did, and the room lit up with all of us feeling a tremendous presence.

There was no question the room was full of the Holy Spirit, and the dying friend began a full healing process from stage four cancer.

She lived for quite a while experiencing good health and a spirit of thankfulness.

We never know when the Lord might intervene, but I have witnessed prayer changing events in our lives.

No matter what your belief, I would say pray and pray and pray. And what does our Scripture say about praying?

> So Jesus answered them and said: "Have faith in God. For assuredly, I say to you whoever says to this mountain, Be removed and be cast into the sea', and does not doubt in his heart, but believes that those things he says will come to pass, he will have whatever he says. Therefore I say to you, whatever things you ask when you pray, believe that you receive them, and you will have them. And whenever you stand praying, if you have anything against anyone, forgive him, that your Father in heaven may also forgive you your trespasses. But if you do not forgive, neither will your Father in heaven forgive your trespasses." (Mk 11:22-26)

With these words, we can learn how to respond to the bumps on our roads as we drive through life. When confronted by these life transformations, good or bad, slow or sudden, big or little, the believer's response is prayer.

Michael Ramsey, the former Archbishop of Canterbury, writes this definition of prayer. "To pray is simply to choose for the while to be with God, no more, no less."

Now, that sounds simple enough, doesn't it? But in a world of tight schedules and over-entertainment, how simple is it really? I think prayer calls for a conscious isolation of the heart. It might occur in the middle of a crowded room, or even in the midst of a heated meeting, or while lost in the eyes of a loved one, but it always involved a willingness to disengage from the trivialities of the moment and "surrender to the presence of God."

Of course, God never departs from us. It is we who step away from God.

So, prayer is a deliberate visit with Almighty God.

Bishop Ramsey goes on to explain that it is the attitude with which we come to God that determines the nature of our praying.

To be with God wondering: that is a prayer of adoration.

To be with God gratefully: that is a prayer of thanksgiving.

To be with God ashamed: that is a prayer of contrition.

To be with God while concerned about others: that is a prayer of intercession.

And to be with God open and adaptable: that is a prayer of submission.

So, prayer, real, authentic, life-changing prayer, is not a matter of what we say, it is a matter of what we feel. It is not a matter of well-crafted phrases, or even heartfelt laments. Prayer is a matter of willingly entering the presence of God, no matter who is watching or what they might think. So the person praying must believe in the power of God. Then those who seek power in prayer must first find peace in forgiveness.

And we need to seek a support system. Human beings are not built for isolation.

We need other people, and this is never more true than after we have experienced a major life change.

Unfortunately, the more painful the problems might have been for us, the deeper is our need for a support system. That's why the support groups are successful. They met the needs of people in pain and grief.

The late Joseph Campbell, brilliant scholar, mythologist, and student of human behavior, often made note of the manner in which most of us are quick to blame ourselves for life's disasters. We like to believe that what we do, or fail to do, is often destiny's final straw.

God's going to get us. When children fail to excel, parents think they failed to educate. When parents separate, children often think they made the break-up occur. When houses burn, or cars crash, or finances fold, victims often find fault with themselves.

A lot of this, says Campbell, is due to our religious backgrounds, where we are taught to concentrate on our errors or our sins. For some reason, religion has managed to communicate the silly notion that the value of the person is directly paralleled by how "good" he or she behaves.

The purpose of forming a support group is to give ourselves permission to proclaim:

> Bless me God, for I am still good.
> Bless me God, for I can grieve and grow in the process.
> Bless me God so the God in me recognizes the God in you.

Sometimes we just don't know what will happen to us, but with faithful hearts and open minds, we trust more in God's tomorrow than in our own today.

Stained Glass Window

MUSIC

Besides volunteering at the hospital, we seminary students had to choose field education projects as part of our credit hours toward graduation.

I chose going to our state hospital three times a month for three years.

And what an experience it became.

Those in charge placed me in the elderly mentally and physically handicapped building. After visiting numerous times and finding no one that could or would speak in sentences, I found some magazines and hoped to find some who would read them. On one occasion, a lady picked up a *Life* magazine, and began to read. Or so I thought. I immediately sat beside her and she exclaimed, "Did you know President Roosevelt just died?"

The *Life* magazine was actually current, 1973. But in her mind, President Roosevelt had just died. Since I knew when FDR died, April 1945, and this was 1973, I acknowledged that I remembered him well.

"What do you remember?," I asked.

And she promptly remembered that her husband was killed in WWII, and her son was somewhere, she couldn't remember where, but she did remember some songs. She asked me if I knew the song "If I Had You." How about "When the Moon Comes Over the Mountain?" And she continued to hum these songs, all of them. She also remembered the words of those songs.

As we sat there, other women, whose heads hung motionless in their laps, began to hum along. I couldn't believe it. One by one, these women, who were judged "retarded" and unable to contribute to anything, began to sing, lifting their heads in joy.

When I left the state hospital building for the elderly mentally handicapped, I went home, dug out my old ukulele, and began to practice. Tom and I played the ukulele together for years. However, the only people who heard us were our kids, and they would occasionally sing-a-long, but not for long.

I couldn't wait to return to my newfound "music" friends at the state hospital. To this day, I can still see their faces light up when I began to strum my uke to the old favorites. I still have all my ukulele books, even though Tom and I haven't played those songs for many years now. But what a difference music made in the lives of those women deemed "severely mentally and physically handicapped." They remembered every song and the words were as clearly sung as if they were performing on stage.

One woman understood what it meant to be handicapped, yet wanted people to realize they have a need to try and do everything they can for themselves. She gave me this poem to remember her plight and her blessing:

Blessed Are You

Blessed are you who take time to listen to spastic speech, and sing songs with us.

For you help us to know that if we persevere we can be understood.

Blessed are You who walk with us in public places and ignore the stares of strangers;

for in your companionship we find havens of relaxation.

Blessed are you who never bid us hurry up

and more blessed are you who do not snatch our tasks from our hands

to do them for us; for often we need time rather than help.

Blessed are you who stand beside us as we enter new and untried ventures; for our failures will be outweighed by the time when we surprise ourselves and you.

> Blessed are you, when by all these things you assure us that the
> thing that makes us individuals is not in our peculiar muscles,
> not in our wounded nervous systems; but in God given self
> which no infirmity can confine.
>
> —Author unknown

What a gift music is to all of us.

I've heard that music is called the "Democracy of the Planet." And I believe it is the one commonality that touches the souls of good and evil alike.

Today, the same feeling of oneness in wonder prevails whenever we are listening to the music of composers. Music brings a time of deep satisfaction, the soul moving at one moment, stirred at the next, and at last, assured of an enduring love which embraces all the dimensions of human existence.

The Psalmist says it very simply, "I will praise You, O Lord, with my whole heart; I will tell of all Your marvelous works: I will be glad and rejoice in You; I will sing praise to Your name, O Most High" (Psalm 9:1, 2).

And it happens to be true that there are more ways to accomplish that task than praying and preaching. Music is certainly another way to "praise the Lord."

We live in a world where many voices are struggling to be heard. Politicians call this *havoc*. Sociologists call it *pluralism* and, in the artistic world, it is labeled *textural variety*. Still, the fact remains that music is the one medium that has the capacity to bring us all together.

Music is the common language of every person and breaks all barriers of culture, religion, and race. Music embraces the themes of a spirit that pervaded the church throughout her life.

Since the late 1700s, music and congregational singing received great stimulation from John and Charles Wesley, the founder of Methodism in America. His first hymn book, published in 1787 in Charlestown, South Carolina, soon became popular. It was called the *Collection of Psalms and Hymns*. It's the first book of Hymn…ody.

The religious movements both in England and America made great use of singing hymns. It is said that in many early revivals and camp meetings, the people became completely unrestrained and they would create a whole new body of song.

A book entitled *Ragtime Jazz* is a history of composers and music. It has this account of a camp meeting: "The hollow square of the encampment was filled with people listening to the mid-day sermon and its accompanying exhortations. The excitement was intense. Men and women of all races sang and prayed together."

The first time I heard a Dixieland jazz group play at a church was Sunday, November 2, 1992, at my church Mt. Lebanon United Methodist in Wilmington. I received a call from a dear friend who said he was bringing High Sierra Jazz Band from California to Delaware for his forty-first anniversary that Saturday, November 1, and he wondered if I'd like this jazz group to play at my church the next day. Well, of course I wanted them, and even though I presented this opportunity to my church board who were not in favor of the jazz musicians being in a church sanctuary, I forged ahead.

I called the High Sierra Jazz Band leader asking him which songs would be sung, and most of them were familiar, except I'd not heard his version of "This Little Light of Mine." And he actually sung it on the phone all the way from California.

The day High Sierra played at our little church in the dogwoods, my parishioners were sitting, glaring, with arms folded. Until the leader of the band called the children of the church forward and he sang to them, "This Little Light of Mine."

This hymn was originally a black spiritual hymn, adapted to the Gospel of Matthew.

> You are the light of the world. A city that is set on a hill cannot
> be hidden. Nor do they light a lamp and put it under a basket,
> but on a lampstand, and it gives light to all who are in the house.
> Let your light so shine before men, that they may see your good
> works and glorify your Father in heaven. (Mt 5:14, 15)

"This Little Light of Mine," theme is on the importance of allowing God to give us His light in the face of our struggles. It was written by Harry Dixon Loes in the early 1900s, and became one of the top civil rights anthems in the 1960s.

I can assure you, during the rest of the worship service, people were clapping, standing, singing in-beat, just like the old Gospel camp meetings of yesteryear.

It was a fantastic hour we shared together with people of the church and the entire community, standing in the aisles, praising the Lord.

And when I preached at our little chapel in our community here in Florida, I would invite many different bands to join us. The Salty Dogs, The Golden Eagles, The Zebra Band, Hal Gibson's Colony Singers, and many soloists, including a lovely soprano soloist, Betty Craven, a member of the choir at Mt. Lebanon United Methodist Church, and dear friend throughout my ministry.

Tom and I have literally followed these different jazz groups and their festivals since we've retired. We love music, especially Dixieland traditional jazz.

God appears to us when we join in singing the good news of His love to people, regardless of their difficult situations. That is the good news of the lyrics of many hymns. We are at our best when we shed little shafts of light on others.

Do you remember Victor Frank? He was a prisoner during World War II, and tells of one night when he could not go further in his struggle to survive the death camp at Auschwitz. Everything was gray. The earth was gray, the clothes of the men were gray. He laid down to wish death for himself, but then something happened. He looked out the window of his prison camp to a house in the distance that had one single candle. "That light saved my life," Victor would say many years later. "That candle became my hope and the visual image of God who will finally penetrate every dark corner and lift us all to eternal light. That light pierced the dark with hope, warmth and peace. "That light became my soul,"

Music, the democracy of the planet. The one medium that brings people from all races and all walks of life together. The light of our souls.

Finally, knowing the electric nature of this music, we understand why its sparks leaped from the Holy Bible, with the people from the Old Testament.

> And it came to pass when the priests came out of the Most Holy Place (for all the priests who were present had sanctified themselves, without keeping to their divisions), and the Levites who were the singers, all those of Asaph and Heman and Jeduthun, with their sons and their brethren, stood at the east end of the altar, clothed in white linen, having cymbals, stringed instruments and harps, and with them one hundred and twenty priests sounding with trumpets-indeed it came to pass, when the trumpeters and singers were as one, to make one sound to be heard in praising and thanking the Lord, and when they lifted up their voice with the trumpets and cymbals and instruments of music, and praised the Lord, saying, "For He is good For His mercy endures forever," that the house, the house of the Lord was filled with a cloud, so that the priests could not continue ministering because of the cloud; for the glory of the Lord filled the house of God." (2 Chr 5:11-14)

Thanks be to God for the music in our Houses of Worship throughout the world.

Cleft and Staff

CHOOSING FAITH

Take a trip with me.

We're walking along a beach and all of a sudden a bottle washes up on the shore directly in front of us. We pop the cork and out comes the proverbial genie. "Today is your lucky day," the genie says. "I am prepared to grant you the gift of your choice to present to your loved ones. You pick it and you got it."

What would you choose?

Would it be wisdom? When God offered Solomon his choice of attributes, the king chose wisdom because he believed it would give him access to all else. Would wisdom assure your loved ones of all they ever needed?

What about power? With power one can virtually build a world of his or her own.

How about choosing wealth? And then there's beauty. If you're beautiful, you can get anyone you want. Wealth would be wonderful too. With enough money a person can buy enough wisdom and power to sit in the lap of luxury for as long as they live.

Health? Can't have anything without health. And what about love?. We all know it's the secret to happiness. Love would be a great choice.

Wisdom, power, health, wealth, love. The choices are mind boggling.

There was one that towers over all the others.

If I had but one gift to give my children and grandchildren and great grandchildren, I would give them the gift of faith.

Why?

Because without it, the smartest, most luxurious, loved, health-centered life rings impotent and hallow. With it, no challenge is insurmountable and no joy beyond reach. God is always with us. Our creator will never leave us.

As we read from the Old Testament: "The lord loves you; the Lord has brought you out with a mighty hand, therefore, know that the Lord your God is a faithful God" (Deuteronomy 7:8, 9).

Faith.

What is it and where does it originate? And, when we feel it fading, how do we restore its strength?

Looking at the Epistle of Romans, we get some direction.

> But the righteousness of faith speaks in this way, "Do not say in your heart, 'Who will ascend into heaven?' (that is, to bring Christ down from above) or, 'Who will descent into the abyss?'" (that is, to bring Christ up from the dead) But what does it say? "The word is near you, even in your mouth and in your heart" (that is, the word of faith which we preach) that if you confess with your mouth the Lord Jesus and believe in your heart that God has raised you from the dead, you will be saved. For the heart one believes to righteousness, and with the mouth confession is made to salvation." (Rom 10:6-10)

Here is Paul setting forth the distinguishing characteristics of Christian faith. His problem is that he is confronted with a bunch of rigid, law-abiding, over-disciplined people who are convinced that behavior is the bedrock of the divine human relationship. Thoroughly familiar with the laws of the temple, they are certain that keeping the law, observing the rules, and walking the straight and narrow paths will lead to peace with God.

The Apostle Paul has another idea. For openers, he applauds their zeal, their willingness to work hard to look for God. Then he says it clearly and succinctly in Romans 10:8: "Believe with your heart." What we do isn't nearly as important as what we believe in our heart. The only thing essential to peace with God are to: "Believe with your heart and confess with your mouth that Jesus Christ is Lord."(Romans 10:8, 9).

Faith does not originate with action, and it is not proved by performance. Faith starts with the heart.

I think one of the major obstacles between the average person and a living faith is a matter of unfair expectations. Expectations of ourselves. Having heard the claims of zealous, rigid believers, we define our faith by their behavior, thinking we must act the same way if we are truly linked to the master. That's a mistake. In fact, I have developed a clear sense of suspicion of people who are absolutely confident of all they profess. If you don't have some doubt, I'm not sure about the depth of your faith.

Frederick Buckner writes this in his book, *Wishful Thinking*:

> Faith is better understood as a verb than as a noun, as a process than as a possession. It is on again, off again. Rather than once and for all, faith is not being sure where you're going, but going anyway. It is a journey without maps. Doubt isn't the opposite of faith, it is an element of faith.

Isn't that refreshing? Of course we doubt. We're finite human beings who simply can't see and understand everything, so we doubt. We're uncertain, and we wonder. And we should. It's perfectly normal.

"Lord I believe, help thou my unbelief" (Mark 9:24).

So the first challenge of opening the heart is to be open to ourselves, accepting our doubts as part of the ongoing process of establishing a relationship with God.

Next, look for the presence of God at the same time.

There was a story about the Abbott of a distinguished monastery who approached an Indian guru with a difficult problem. The monastery was dying. For some reason, the flow of new aspirants had virtually dried up. With a heavy heart, he described to the guru the empty hallways, neglected gardens, and dusty dorms. The whole community was desperately in need of more caring people. At last he blurted out, "Why would God do this to us? Have we committed grievous sins?"

"Yes," said the guru.

"And, what sin might that be?" the head of the monastery asked.

"You have committed the sin of ignorance, because one of your number is the Messiah in disguise and you are ignorant of this."

Having said this, the guru closed his eyes and returned to his meditation.

The Abbott rushed back to the monastery, assembled the monks, and described what the guru said. "There is a Messiah in disguise amongst us," he exclaimed excitedly.

The first response was a nervous chuckle. Then the monks began to look at each other.

Could it be Brother Eric? Or Brother John? Or Thomas?

Who was it? Whoever it was, if it was the Master in disguise, it was highly unlikely they would recognize him. So they took to treating each other with a whole new level of respect and kindness. Where once it was drab and depressing, people not treating each other pleasantly, now it was alive with joy and caring for each other.

And soon, dozens of aspirants were seeking admission to the order and once again the church echoed with the holy and inspiring chant of monks who were aglow with the spirit of love.

What a message there is in that story, for those who would be open to the presence of God.

If we are serious about establishing our faith, it starts with an awareness of the presence of the Master in the people around us. Seeing God in everyone.

It continues as we shift our efforts from earning God's love to simply accepting it.

This was the main problem Paul had with the zealots in Rome. They thought their salvation hinged on their behavior. They wanted to make themselves more important than God, shackling the Creator's will to love, with their power to perform.

Sound familiar?

How many of us worry ourselves sick over personal problems, while the healing balm of the grace of God is but a request away?

I read an article about Dr. Eben Alexander, a noted neurosurgeon who, after a near-fatal car accident, was in a coma, with his brain cortex completely severed, experienced things he never thought possible—a journey to the afterlife.

In one section, Dr. Alexander was describing a beautiful world in light, color, and love that "blew through me like a warm wave." And, writes Dr. Alexander, he received a message from that next world: "You are loved and cherished, dearly, forever. You have nothing to fear. And, there's nothing you can do wrong."

Isn't that amazing? It's God's story to every one of us. And I thank God for Dr. Alexander's book, *Proof of Heaven*.

I was also reading about some orthodox religions that make people sit in sin boxes, or do some kind of man-made penance to right their so-called wrongs. Their zeal is admirable, but for those who believe in the saving grace of God, it seems misplaced. When we decide that our performance is the password to peace, we're a short step removed from worshipping ourselves.

The Apostle Paul wanted everybody to understand that salvation, and eternal peace in the presence of God, is a gift: "For whoever calls upon the name of the Lord shall be saved"(Romans 10: 13). It cannot be bought. It cannot be bartered. And it cannot be earned. It can only be accepted.

Two thousand years after grace became real in the person of Jesus Christ, why do some people still believe in works and earning our way to eternity? Many people were taught and hold to be true that they must be "doing something" to have God favor them.

We choke on the concept of grace because it makes us debtors. Some people feel they must earn God's love.

Wrong.

The call to faith is not a call to performance. It is a call to believe in our hearts and confess with our mouths that Jesus Christ is Lord. And that's it.

Faith is not so much a matter of what we do, as it is a matter of who Jesus is and accepting his grace and love.

So, faith originates in the heart, not the head, and it takes strength from an effort to accept as opposed to an effort to earn. The most important way to feed your faith is to claim your faith. That's why Paul puts the emphasis on confession. Confession is not confessing sins. Paul is not talking about hanging out ones dirty laundry, he's talking about confessing our beliefs, by openly acknowledging what we believe, even when others may not agree with you.

Stand up for and proclaim your beliefs. Something happens when we stand up and say what we believe. Suddenly there is not room to slip and slide anymore, as your convictions are reinforced by your confessions.

I think of my architect husband telling me that to get buildings to actually stand, you need posts and braces in order to make the construction stable. Talking about our faith works the same way. The more we stand up for what we believe, the more stable those beliefs become.

Our United Methodist founder, John Wesley, said, "Preach until you believe, and if you don't believe, preach until you do."

It's true in every area of allegiance.

Author David Redding captures the image of this faith. In his book entitled *Amazed by Grace*, he tells of Colonel Dick Lockhart, who was an officer on Admiral Richard Byrd's last expedition to Antarctica. Colonel Lockhart was a seaman, tough and independent, not a believer in God. Nonetheless, he couldn't help but feel a twinge of excitement and adventure as they sailed into those frigid unsheltered waters.

Suddenly Lockhart explains in his book: "A wall of ice twelve hundred feet high loomed beside us as far as the eye could see. Everyone on board came on deck speechless and spellbound."

The chaplain started softly singing "Amazing Grace" and the crew joined in, kneeling one by one. The crusty old seaman continues, "I remained standing until the third verse, then I too kneeled down and met Christ.

The third verse of Amazing Grace says. "Through many dangers, toils and snares, I have already come; 'tis grace has brought me safe thus far, and grace will lead me home."

Grace, is the foundation of our profound faith.

Feeding Five Thousand

But, you might ask, what do we do about facts? Faith doesn't seem to be doing much in the face of facts. Our prayers often seem to be unanswered. We even wonder if they are even heard. God appears to be either unmindful of our situation, or is as inadequate to its demands as we are. It seems that the whole burden rests upon our shoulders and ours alone.

And, so, we worry a lot.

So did the disciples. They worried a lot and they did this even while Jesus was in their midst. To understand this, let's look at the Gospel of John (also found in Matthew 14:13-23).

> After these things Jesus went over the Sea of Galilee, which is the Sea of Tiberius. Then a great multitude followed Him, because they saw His signs which He performed on those who were diseased. And, Jesus went up on a mountain, and there He sat with His disciples. Now the Passover, a feast of the Jews, was near. Then Jesus lifted up His eyes, and seeing a great multitude coming toward Him, He said to Philip," Where shall we buy bread, that these may eat?" But this he said to test him for He Himself knew what He would do. Philip answered Him, "Two hundred denarii's worth of bread is not sufficient for them, that every one of them may have a little." One of the disciples, Andrew, Simon Peter's brother, said to Him, "There is a lad here who has five barley loaves and two small fish, but what are they among so many?" Then Jesus said, "Make the people sit down." Now there was much grass in the place. So the men sat down, in number about five thousand. And Jesus took the loaves and when He had given thanks He distributed them to the disciples, and the disciples to those sitting down; and likewise of the fish, as much as they wanted. (Jn 6:1-11)

The disciples, along with Jesus, had gone by boat to a pleasant lakeside spot and were hoping to have a little time in private to be with Him.

I've been fortunate enough to visit the Sea of Galilee, and it's a beautiful place, ideal for rest and renewal.

But the disciples' hopes were doomed to disappointment. The crowd kept following Him. Their boat had barely touched the shore when they were confronted by a great multitude, five thousand in number, who wanted to be close to the Master, to hear his every word, and to receive his touch.

The hours were hectic and demanding, even beyond the ordinary. At last the shadows lengthened and dusk began to settle in. Still the multitude did not leave. Having been all day without food, they were hungry. In such a lonely spot, there was no bread and no place to go to buy it. No bakery in those days. Besides, there was no money, even if bread was available. To make matters worse, Jesus seemed to be totally unaware of the seriousness of the situation. From morning to dusk, He had been occupied with the needs of the people. They were hungry to hear His words. They were thirsty for His healing calm.

"Then Jesus lifted up His eyes, and seeing a great multitude coming toward Him, He said to Philip, 'Where shall we buy bread, that these may eat?'"(John 6:5).

Now, we need to remember that Philip was an eyes-on pragmatist. Remember when he heard Jesus declare, "I am the way, the truth and the life, No one comes to the Father except through Me" (John 14:6), it was Philip who observed, "Lord, show us the Father, and it is sufficient for us" (John 14:8). Philip didn't need any smoke or mirrors, just facts.

So when Jesus asked Philip how they were going to feed those people, Philip answered, "Two hundred denarii's worth of bread is not sufficient for them, that every one of them may be a little"(John 6:7).

On the face of it, he was absolutely right. He assessed the situation and dubbed it disastrous.

Ah, but there was another disciple watching all of this, who thought at a different level. Andrew, the open-minded one, the phenomenal searcher, who grew up in the shadow of his glitzy brother Peter. Andrew was searching as he said, "There is a lad here who has five barley loaves and two small fish, but what are they among so many?" (John 6:9).

In that instant, what appeared paltry became plentiful in the hands of a loving Lord.

Human calculations can never contain the power of God.

If we sincerely seek to draw nearer to Jesus, to imaginatively experience the vibrancy of God in the midst of our lives, then we should learn to give ourselves over to the experience.

I shudder to think of the losses I have incurred by overcontrolling my own pilgrimage. By erecting walls of will and interpretation around what I will or will not allow myself to do.

Someone once asked the great mythologist, Joseph Campbell, about the biblical phrase, "He who has ears to hear, let him hear." (Matthew 11:15).Campbell responded that the key to authentic hearing is in "yielding yourself to the moment."

"Yielding yourself to the moment" means letting go.

The problem is a matter of thought constricting what we know, over denying ourselves the privilege of learning something new.

Philip couldn't see how to feed the people, and closed off any new possibilities. Andrew, on the other hand, made room for the magic of the Master.

Creative spirituality demands that kind of openness and flexibility when we drop our own calculations, and allow the power of God to embrace our lives.

The Gospel of Matthew records the disciples telling Jesus to send the multitudes away. "When it was evening, His disciples came to Jesus saying, This is a deserted place, and the hour is already late. Send the multitudes away, that they may go into the villages and buy themselves food" (Matthew 14:15).

They decide there was nothing Jesus could do, so they must take matters into their own hands.

What can they do? They decide to escape. It was a solution, not a good one to be sure, but it was one solution. It certainly is not different from our own approach to tough situations.

Sometimes, like the disciples, we want to escape responsibility by passing the buck: "Send the multitude away," the disciples ordered (Matthew 14:15). Get them out of here. They are a burden to us.

Whatever needs to be done for these hungry men and women and children will have to be done by somebody else.

How familiar does that sound? Pass the buck. Let someone else take care of the needs of the multitude. Many of us are inclined to do the same thing. We do not want to take on the responsibility ourselves. Often we are guilty. Guilty of avoiding. Guilty of procrastination. Sure, we can pass the buck or we can escape from life's demands by running.

We've lived through some tough times. Often we want to neglect our responsibilities. To say, "I've tried and tried. I want someone else to fix it. I've already done my part."

We are not alone in this feeling. Many people run from their problems. So many times running seems to be the only answer. I don't mean a respite time, a breathing room to reduce stress. I'm talking about running away from our situation just because it is hard.

Running away is futile. The trouble from which we are running from is often within, and sooner or later we realize we cannot escape from our self. It is not a viable solution.

The disciples were not indifferent to the needs of the multitude. They were not selfish. They were, in fact, genuinely concerned. Why, then, did they seek to send these hungry folks away to shift for themselves?

There is but one answer. They felt there was nothing else to do. There was no other way out. They were plain, practical people, not fanatical dreamers.

But what are the facts? When the disciples found themselves face to face with the hungry crowd, they took account of their resources. Then, with a decision that has a striking resemblance to good sense, they brought the following report to Jesus: "And they said to Jesus, 'We have here only five loaves and two fish'" (Matthew 14:17).

And, like a good committee facing a desperate situation, a motion is made and passed unanimously.

The disciples said, "There is only one course open to us: We have to send the multitude away" (Matthew 14:15). They had overstated the problem. They were not aware of the resources. " We have but five loaves and two fish," they said (Matthew 14:17).

But the question we should put to them and to some of the responses we are making in our own present day is simply this: Does that sum up all of our resources? Do we have no wealth at all except those five loaves and two little dried fish? Are there no other options?

This brings us face to face with the impotence we feel as Christians today.

Do we feel as though we are lacking in resourcefulness?

Intellectually sane, yet often we are spiritually drained. We have room for physical exercise, reading, playing, but praying? Looking for other positive options to our problems?

No. We are so taken by facts, we have undermined our faith. Facts are so important to us that we leave God out, as we imprison Him in His own universe out there somewhere.

The disciples failed to realize they did not have to face this trying situation alone.

Jesus was there. And the disciples discovered with amazement that Jesus had a plan. This emergency did not take our Lord by surprise. He remained calm in the situation. He had seen the problem and had made plans for meeting it. Therefore, the whole responsibility was not on the disciples' shoulders.

> Jesus said, "Bring them here to Me." Then He commanded the multitudes to sit down on the grass. And He took the fives loaves and the two fish, and looking up to heaven, He blessed and broke and gave the loaves to the disciples; and the disciples gave to the multitudes. So they all ate and were filled, and they took up twelve baskets full of the fragments that remained. Now those who had eaten were about five thousand men, besides the women and children. (Mt 14:18-20)

We, too, need to know God has a plan for us and for his world. He never forgets or forsakes us. Not only are we to know God has a plan for us, but also we need to believe God has a plan to every human being. God is the architect and we are the builders. Our Lord makes the plan, we are to execute His plan.

The disciples came to understand the simplicity of Jesus's method. The needs of the multitude were met. "All ate and were filled, and they took up twelve baskets full of the fragments that remained."

It was brought about by Jesus, his disciples, and the people working together.

When faced with choosing a solution, we need to ask ourselves: "Is our present approach based more on facts than faith?"

What about us in today's world? Do we have a problem with no obvious solution?

List your options, and let others share in your solutions. Because Jesus says, "Don't send the people away." Let them share in the solution. Don't take the burden of responsibility on your shoulders alone. In the making of this world, God is dependent upon us, the people. Our Lord walks to his missions on human feet. God ministers through human hands. Our Creator speaks his message through human lips.

If anything is to be done toward building a better life, a stronger, more social order, we must begin to acknowledge our resources and do the job God expects us to do.

The disciples forgot Jesus was in their midst.

We forget God is in our midst too.

Even now, we are prone to take this whole task of building our life upon ourselves. When we do this, we get discouraged. It is too much for us. So we say, as the disciples did, "Send the people away." Send our problems away. But, through our very failures, God keeps impressing upon us this truth: "Apart from me, you can do nothing. With me, all things are possible"(Matthew 19:26). Jesus does this in Holy love, patiently waiting for us to understand, waiting for us to respond, waiting for us to work together to support each other, to use our many God-given resources, and to choose faith.

Even as the disciples couldn't imagine how the Master could feed five thousand people with five loaves and two fishes, because it was beyond their experience, I also am concerned about the limitations we place on the spirit of God through our own myopic experiences.

Through stained glass will reflect the love of God to every person, regardless their handicap, their ethnicity, their gender, their religion.

After all, if our Lord can feed five thousand people with five loaves and two fishes, who knows what our Savior can do with a searching heart?

The Fig Tree

Joseph Shriven was in love. I mean, real love. This guy couldn't take a breath without thinking about his beloved Sarah. She was his first thought in the morning and his last at night. For Joe, perfect peace was a whole day with Sarah and no agenda. He was totally devoted to this woman.

So, it was not surprising when they were engaged to be married. The entire village of Dublin, Ireland, celebrated their joy. Then, just a few days before the wedding date, Sarah was swimming with some friends, dove into a nearby lake, cracked her head on a submerged stone, and drowned.

Shriven was devastated. Nothing had meaning for him. Slipping further and further into depression, he wouldn't eat, talk, or attend church. At last, weak with despair, he walked out into a grassy meadow to a gnarled old hickory tree, under which he and Sarah had spent many a bliss-filled afternoon, and fell on his knees.

"Help me, dear God," he prayed, "to overcome my sorrow and have faith in you and honor Sarah by restoring myself."

With that, he fell asleep. When he awoke, he scribbled his thoughts on a piece of paper and stuffed it into his pocket. A while later, his mother discovered that wad of paper and sent its contents to a publisher.

And billions of us sing the beloved hymn that Joseph Scriven wrote: "What a Friend We Have in Jesus."

> What a Friend we have in Jesus
> All our sins and grief's to bear,
> What a privilege to carry
> Everything to God in prayer.
> Are we weak and heavy laden,
> Cumbered with a load of care?
> Precious Savior still our refuge
> Take it to the Lord in Prayer."

Few words have ever summed up the divine-human relationship, the essence of the Christian faith, better than these.

Faith is not a matter of good behavior. It's a matter of a phenomenal friend who never forsakes us, no matter what happens to us.

In the Epistle of Hebrews, we find St. Paul telling the believers, "Now faith is the substance of things hoped for, the evidence of things not seen" (Hebrews 11:1).

If there's a better definition of faith, I don't know what is.

"The substance of things hoped for, the conviction of things not seen."

With these words, Paul makes it clear to us that faith is first and foremost a matter of inner renewal. It's an inner conviction that you can do something. But first you have to try, and then you proceed.

There's a good illustration of this in the Gospel of Matthew:

> Now in the morning, as He returned to the city, He was hungry. And seeing a fig tree by the road, He came to it and found nothing on it but leaves, and said to it, "Let no fruit grow on you ever again." And immediately the fig tree withered away. Now when the disciples saw it, they marveled, saying, "How did the fig tree wither away so soon?" (Mt 21:17-22)

Jesus has already cleaned the money changers out of the temple and is walking with the disciples when he spots a fig tree in the distance.

He is hungry, so he walks up to the tree to get a fig. But, lo and behold, the tree is barren.

Jesus speaks to the tree, "Let no fruit grow on you ever again," and before the disciples' eyes, the tree withered away. And they asked, "How did the fig tree wither away so soon?"(Matthew 21:20). But Jesus wasn't angry with the tree. He was making a point with his friends.

Jesus answers:

> Assuredly, I say to you, if you have faith and do not doubt, you will not only do what was done to the fig tree, but also if you say to this mountain, "Be removed and be cast into the sea," it will

be done. And all things, whatever you ask in prayer, believing you will receive. (Mt 21:22)

Faith flourishes when convictions are firm. Faith fades when confidence withers.

What is the key to that confidence? It is heavily dependent on a healthy understanding of yourself and your relationship with God. Faith is much more a matter of what God does for us, than what we do for God.

Think about a man named Noah. This man was a respected citizen. His neighbors probably saw him as a regular nine-to-five breadwinner who never caused any trouble. Probably could've coached a little league team.

The story is recorded in Genesis chapters 6 and 7.

God asked Noah to make him an ark, the length three hundred cubits, its width fifty cubits, and its height thirty cubits (Genesis 6:15). Certainly more than long enough to make a mess of the yard and catch the attention of the zoning commission.

Noah would certainly look a fool. What would people think of him? But he did it anyway. Sensing what God wanted, he had no choice but to do it.

That's trust and faith.

Theologian Lloyd Ogilvie says that Jesus Christ is the instigator of audacity. If we really pay attention to the Master, we'll find ourselves doing a lot of things against the grain.

As our faith builds, we find ourselves moving from an emphasis on the assurance of eternal life to the audacity of the abundant life on earth.

God wants us to reach for the brass ring. To go for the gold. To be all that we can be.

What did Jesus say? "I have come that they may have life, and that they may have it more abundantly" (John 10:10).

Taking risks means taking risks in total dependence upon God. It means praying to God to help restore ourselves, even in the midst of our losses. It means building an ark when the skies are clear. Standing up and speaking what you believe even as you risk the loss of friends in the process.

"A man's heart plans his way, But the Lord directs his steps" (Proverbs 16:9).

When the Lord decides, the Lord provides.

Once we've committed ourselves in Jesus's name, we open all our sensors to receive God's answers. We start looking for God's response, and we believe God will provide. This kind of attitude isn't nearly as radical as we might think. If we look closely, we'll discover it was behind every major act of faith in Scripture.

It happened on the Sea of Galilee when Peter stepped out of the boat (Mark 6:48).

It happened in the plains of Haran when Abraham packed up the family and set off to find a promised land (Genesis 12:4-9). It happened on the shores of the Red Sea when Moses led his people to freedom (Exodus 13:17-4:29).

In every instance, the format is the same. God's people seek God's will. And when we find it and we act upon it, every time God meets our every need.

When the Lord decides, the Lord provides.

We have to be ready for those answers to come from unexpected places.

When God first decided I should go into the ministry, I didn't have the money to go to seminary. Our education money was in our bank account for our three young daughters. Trusting the call, I followed where I thought God wanted me to go, and ended up at a workshop on euthanasia and doctor now known as physician-assisted suicide.

Faith.

It starts with a sense of confidence. The kind of confidence that makes an older woman, wife, and mother try something new. Going to seminary and having faith enough she could study after being away from books, other than Dr. Spock and Good Housekeeping magazines.

Faith in God means to continue hoping and knowing full well that "when the Lord decides, the Lord provides."

Shadrach, Meshach, and Abed-Nego

One of my favorite television personalities was Andy Rooney. A while back, Andy wrote a list it "it's hard to do."

> It's hard to…tear something along the dotted line when the instructions read "Tear along dotted lines."
>
> It's hard to…let down a Venetian blind the first time without pulling the cord this way or that.
>
> It's hard to…cut the fingernails of your right hand with your left hand, if you're right handed or visa versa.
>
> It's hard to take something out of your eye without your glasses on which you had to take off.
>
> It's hard to…get at what is in your pants pocket when you have your seat belt fastened.

And, I would add, it's hard to choose faith, in an age of cynicism. Faith is difficult to grasp.

St. Paul found it hard to convince people about his Lord, Jesus.

Paul is saying, "I perceive that in all things you are very religious, for as I was passing through and considering the objects of your worship, I even found an altar with this inscription: To the Unknown God. Therefore, the One whom you worship without knowing Him I proclaim to you"(Acts 17:22, 23).

The people of Athens simply didn't believe in anything. It was a place not unlike your hometown. A place where cynicism ran rampant. Athens was a center for research and education. A bastion of well-earned success and ongoing development. St. Paul tells us a lot when he says, "His spirit was provoked within him when he saw that the city was given over to idols"(Acts 17:16).

The people didn't believe in anything but themselves.

Remember the sixties? The cover of the April 8, 1966, edition of *Time* magazine asked the question, "Is God Dead?" It stands as a faith-filled response to the human preoccupation with only reason and rhetoric, not with faith.

Now, some fifty-five years later, I can still see the theory has moved into a new direction.

God is not dead.

However, the cynics' game is alive and well. Their constant theme? Consider all. Commit to little. Do anything, if it makes you happy. However, it is a game plan for despair.

How do we choose faith over this game plan that chooses nothing but "making you happy?"

Did you ever experiment with two tin cans, drill holes in them, run a string between the two, and attempt to talk to each other from sixty feet apart?

Sometimes, it even worked. But never if the string was not taut. The only chance of hearing any vibrations from the other end hinged on stretching that string as tightly as possible.

In fact, faith cannot exist in isolation. By definition, it demands to be held in tension along with despair.

St. Paul said it best in his letter to the Hebrews:

> Now faith is the substance of things hoped for, the evidence of things not seen. For by it the elders obtained a good testimony. By faith we understand that the worlds were framed by the word of God, so that the things which are seen were not made of things which are visible. (Heb 11:1, 2)

So, the first step in choosing faith is confidence in God against the world. Confronted every day with opportunities to live by the standards of the world, the faithful believer makes a habit of choosing God.

One of the great faith epics of the Old Testament involves three characters by the name of Shadrach, Meshach, and Abed-Nego (Daniel 3:14-29). Confronted by King Nebuchadnezzar, these three were forced to choose between God and the world (Daniel 3:15). Before thousands of watchers, the king ordered Shadrach, Meshach, and Abed-Nego to denounce their God and kneel before the king, God of the humanistic world.

Said the king, "But if you do not worship, you shall be cast immediately into the midst of a burning fiery furnace. And who is the god who will deliver you from my hands?" (Daniel 3:15).

For most of us, this would have been a no-brainer. We know about fire. We've seen what it can do. We've felt its fury. On the other hand, as nice as all the theory might be, very few of us claim to know, to see, or to feel God. So, based on our experience, we would probably avoid the fire and deal with God later. Perhaps with a quick prayer, "Now, God, I know you understand why I didn't jump into that furnace. I know about fire. Certainly you understand why I won't do that."

The difference is a matter of faith.

Shadrach, Meschach, and Abed-Nego had a ton of faith. Refusing to kneel, they were tossed in the furnace, only to emerge unharmed (Daniel 3:24, 25). Would we do what they did? Would we trust God against the world?

Our experience forbids us that pleasure.

But wait.

If experience is our benchmark, then fortune is our God. So our belief becomes, "As long as our life is good, we can believe in God. So, I'll trust God, as long as all is well in our lives."

But what happens if life turns sour?

We know the taste of despair. It's as close as a doctor's diagnosis or an emergency call in the night.

Where do we turn for help?

Perhaps we see a clue by looking at our individual communities. Wherever there's death, sickness, a need for help, the community in which we live should be ready to support one another in the midst of our hurting.

No, the loved one wasn't coming back.

Yes, life had gone sour fast. But people helping people mean the world to each of us. Remember Jesus said, "This is my commandment that you love one another as I have loved you. Greater love has no one than this, than to lay down one's life for his friends" (John 15:11, 12).

Life may have gone sour, but in it still are caring people. For the believer, a distant message sounds softly to the ear, "I will not leave you orphans. I will come to you" (John 14:18).

As the Scripture from the Gospel of John says, "A little while longer and the world will see Me no more, but you will see Me. Because I live you will also" (John 14:19).

> But the Helper, the Holy Spirit, whom the Father will send in My name, He will teach you all things, and bring to your remembrance all things that I said to you. Peace I leave with you, My peace I give to you; not as the world gives do I give to you. Let not your heart be troubled, neither let it be afraid. (John 14:26, 27)

Jesus's promise to us? We will not be left alone.

And, that brings us to the second step in choosing faith.

First, we hold God against the world. Choose God against the false idols.

Second, we hold the spirit against the senses. Follow your heart.

Paul's biggest problem with the Athenians was their soul-sapping intelligence. Their heads smothered their hearts denying them the luxury of taking a step in faith. Sometimes, the only barrier between "what is and what can be" is a willingness to open the door and take a leap of faith. Those who would choose faith must make it a point to consider the impossible, to check out all options, to give the spirit a chance to overcome the rational sense, and take them where they've never been before.

Lastly, make a lifestyle of choosing the future against the present by knowing God is with you.

I think it's interesting that those cerebral intelligent Athenians in St. Paul's day made it a point to keep some "kind" of God at hand. The Bible tells us they had an altar complete with the inscription, "To an Unknown God" (Acts 17:23).

As cocky as they were about their intelligence, they wanted to make sure not to insult God, just in case.

At the same time, they wanted no commitments. Therefore by claiming God was unknowable, they freed themselves for total externalism. Concentrating on the moment, eat, drink, and be merry, for who cares about what comes tomorrow?

Those who believe in God don't tarry in expressing that belief of "eat, drink, and be merry for tomorrow we die." That is the world of alcohol, crack, and cocaine.

Those of us who believe in God know that there is a God who cares and wants us to embrace His love.

There's a story about Ernest Freemont Tittle, the famed pastor who shepherded in the plush northern suburb of Chicago. Dr. Tittle tells a story of a moneyed tycoon who lost control of his Mercedes and plunged into Lake Michigan. When he awakened, he was in the next world. Surrounded by servants dressed in white, he beckoned one of them.

"Could I get something to eat?"

"Yes, sir, what would you like?"

"How about a filet, baked potato with butter and sour cream, no need to sweat the cholesterol any more, right? Tossed salad on the side and an order of pecan pie, to wrap it up."

"No problem," said the servant, and within seconds, the feast was there. A while later, our friend called for a selection of books. Again his wishes were instantly met. Next, a sports car. The Porsche was there before he finished his sentence.

And so it went for several weeks. Then, surrounded with all the things he could imagine, the tycoon began to slip into depression.

He called a sterile-attired aide to his side. "Look, it's really nice to have all these things, but what I would really enjoy would be some companionship. I mean, you guys are okay but you never engage in conversation, and you have to admit, you are a bit like robots. I need some friends, someone who cares about me. Can you manage that?"

"Sorry, sir, we cannot."

"What do you mean you cannot? You can do everything else. Why can't you get me some people who can care for me?"

"Because, sir, there are no such people here."

"That's ridiculous. I'd rather be in hell."

To which the servant smugly replied, "Where do you think you are, sir?"

It's one thing to be surrounded with material blessings, it's entirely something else to be recognized as a unique, unrepeatable miracle of God, cared for by God.

I started this by saying some things are hard to do. Having faith can be hard, or with practice it could be easy. If we work at a faith formula, by choosing God against the world of worldly "things," and making a lifestyle of choosing the future, knowing that God is with us, cares for us, and loves us.

Choose faith!

Come Follow Me

Now that's Faith, with a capital F.

It's challenging to become familiar with the many Scripture versions, practices, and commands, especially to see how they apply to this time and place in history.

Take the Old Testament Book of Numbers, chapter 15, verse 27: "And if a person sins unintentionally, then he shall bring a female goat in its first year as a sin offering."

Of course we don't offer up goats to God when we sin anymore, but it is scriptural. And if we believe in the literal translation of the Bible, then we should be still offering goats to our Creator when we sin. But some parts of the Bible were written for that period in history.

Another Scripture command is:

> Let your women keep silent in the churches, for they are not permitted to speak; but they are to be submissive, as the law also says, And, if they want to learn something, let them ask their own husbands at home; for it is shameful for women to speak in church. (1 Cor 14:34)

Of course women speak in church now. I see women speaking to each other every Sunday. But, in Apostle Paul's day, women were not even allowed to enter a synagogue. They had to sit behind their children outside the synagogue, and, of course, Paul was a rabbi and knew the Rabbinical Laws. So, actually, St. Paul was a man ahead of his time because he allowed women to actually enter the church.

Nehemiah says:

> In those days I also saw Jews who had married women of Ashdod, Ammon, and Moab. So I contended with them and cursed them, struck some of them and pulled out their hair and made them swear by God, saying, "You shall not give your daughters as wives to their sons, nor take their daughters for your sons or yourselves." (Neh 13:23, 24)

Those of us whose families moved from other countries to the United States of America are foreigners and have all intermarried another foreigner. My families are from England and Germany.

So, this is another scriptural passage we're not following in today's world.

There are many verses of Scripture that are not germane to our living today.

If you look for something in the Holy Bible, you will find what you want to find, especially if you have not investigated the history or taken Scripture out of context, nor studied Greek, Hebrew, or Aramaic, the language which the Old and New Testaments were written in.

The Holy Bible has been translated into 518 languages, while 2,798 languages have at least some portion in the Bible. We all take our own expectations to the Bible when we read it.

I like the story of the Christian education teacher who held children sermons on Sundays.

She decided one Sunday morning that she would give the children a little puzzle to solve. So, she gathered the kids all around and started to give them clues to see if they could guess what the answer to the puzzle was going to be.

She asked, "What lives in the forest?"

No one answered, no one raised a hand.

She said, "It likes to eat nuts."

Again, the kids looked at each other and no one made a move.

The teacher then said, "All right, kids, here's a good clue. It runs up and down trees." Again, silence. In exasperation, she said. "All right, this has to give you the answer. It's gray and has a bushy tail."

Finally, one little lad in the front row raised his hand. He said, in a strained voice, "Well, it sounds like a squirrel, but I think I'm supposed to say 'Jesus.'"

Our expectations sometimes get in our way.

Sometimes the Bible has many different versions of the same situation. Most of the time every version of the Bible differs in its interpretations of the words.

Take the "Come Follow Me" phrase that Jesus used that are recorded in all four Gospel readings. "And when Jesus had called the people to Him, with His disciples also, He said to them, 'Whoever desires to come after Me, let him deny himself, and take up his cross, and follow Me'" (Mark 8:34).

Recorded also: "Then as Jesus passed on from there, He saw a man named Matthew sitting at the tax office. And He said to him, 'Follow Me.' And he arose and followed Him" (Matthew 9:9).

And: "And whoever does not bear his cross and come after Me cannot be My disciple" (Matthew 9:9).

Finally, from the Book of John: "If anyone serves Me, let him follow Me; and where I am, there My servant will be also. If anyone serves Me, him, My Father will honor" (John 12:26).

Jesus said, "Come Follow Me."

What does "Come follow me" mean? Where are we going if we decide to follow Jesus?

We are all called to be ministers, to be disciples of Jesus. How can we be disciples and follow Jesus today?

I'm going to suggest four ways.

First, as we move toward a unity in Christ and wish to be followers, we need to remember that, given a trend or movement in history, given a time or a call, beginnings are relatively easy. It's the continuing on that's hard. Not giving up, not turning back.

When we're disciples of Jesus, it does not mean God will put a protective shield around us. Not one of Jesus's disciples claimed to be a child of special privilege.

Nor does the Christian automatically expect to be given the inside track in the race of life. The point is not: "Lord, may I bypass problems," but rather, "May my pain be usable and fruitful?" The point is not, "May I avoid heartaches," but rather, "May I have the courage to face my heartaches and achieve a Christian victory over them?" The point is not, "May I skip all suffering," but rather, "Lord, may the sense of my weakness add strength to my faith."

The second way we're called to be disciples in following Jesus is to have faith. Sometimes our faith is misplaced. We would rather trust what we can see than what we cannot see.

Hundreds of definitions of faith have been painfully written and shaped, but St. Paul's definition still stands the test of time. From the Epistle of Hebrews: "Now faith is the substance of things hoped for, the evidence of things not seen" (Hebrews 11:1).

Too often we tend to think of faith as being somehow linked uniquely to the Judeo-Christian tradition. And it is true that faith did bring the early Christians storming up out of the catacombs. They not only moved mountains, they also changed the face of the civilized world. But just as it was faith that brought those first-century Christians out of the catacombs of Rome, let's not forget that it was also faith that brought the twentieth-century Nazis out of the cellars of Munich.

And that literally changed the character of the modern world for you and me.

Faith, you see, can work both ways. It's no respecter of persons.

It's like a tree. It shades the evil as well as the good. The crucial question is this: In what soil are you rooting your faith?

You are free to take your pick.

If you can have faith in your ability to lift yourselves to the level of the highest fulfillment by your own bootstraps alone, then humanism is your God.

If you have the abounding faith in Judas's thirty pieces of silver, then money is your God.

If you have faith in someone else paying for you, then government is your God.

Or your faith could be a hope of unconditional love and salvation for all people, then Jesus is your God.

What is your choice?

A third way we are called in following Jesus as His disciples is to be there for others. And that is the challenge of any church and community of believers. Jesus didn't just spend an hour a week with his disciples. He traveled with them, he lived with them, saw their moods, shared in their fatigue, when he worked with the crowds hour after hour. The disciples shared in the elation, as people were healed, the hungry fed, and the evil spirits of their society were rebuked. They prayed, got angry, wept, and they laughed together. That's what churches and communities should be. A place to share every mood, feeling, ups, and downs.

Lastly, to be disciples of Jesus and follow Him, we can be givers of what the meaning of life really is meant to be.

Do you feel your life is unfair, loaded down with worries and concerns? If so, look again and realize that Jesus calls you to do something beyond yourself.

Be aware that every choice is a new beginning. Recognize the presence of Jesus charting your course. And pray, not for victory but understanding. Not for power, but perspective. Not for your solutions, but for God's answers.

The year is 1932, a year before I was born. And like so many great hymns of faith, the song was inspired by a horrific tragedy in the life of its composer.

Thomas Andrew Dorsey was born in rural Georgia in 1899. By the age of twelve, Dorsey left school to become a pianist. He played at house parties throughout Atlanta's black districts. In his early twenties, Dorsey settled in Chicago and played and sang secular songs. In 1925, Dorsey married Nettie Harper, and a year later, he experienced a nervous breakdown and was unable to work for two years.

To survive, his wife took a job in a laundry to support them. At the urging of his sister-in-law, Dorsey attended a church service where he experienced a spiritual healing. That event prompted Dorsey to commit himself more fully to God and Christian music. Then, in August 1932, Dorsey was scheduled to be the featured soloist in a large revival meeting in St. Louis. His wife, Nettie, was living in Chicago pregnant with their first child. That night after Dorsey finished playing, a Western Union messenger came up to the stage and gave Dorsey an urgent telegram. The telegram said: "Your wife just died."

Racing home, he learned that his baby boy died too, and he withdrew completely from all friends and his music. Dorsey told everyone: "I felt that God had done me an injustice. I didn't want to serve him anymore or write Gospel songs." Then, in the midst of his despair, a friend visited Dorsey and begged him to sit with his piano. It was then Dorsey said he felt "at peace, and felt myself playing something I'd never heard before." And Thomas Dorsey wrote this beloved hymn entitled "Precious Lord, Take My Hand."

> Precious Lord, take my hand, Lead me on, help me stand.
> I am tired, I am weak, I am worn; Thro' the storm, thro' the night,
> Lead me on to the light. Take my hand, precious Lord, lead
> me home.
> When my way grows drear, Precious Lord, linger near; When
> my life is almost gone; Hear my cry, hear my call, Hold my hand
> lest I fall,
> Take my hand, precious Lord, lead me home.

And Jesus said, "Come Follow Me."

We answer, "Yes, Lord, no matter what happens, even when we're weary and downtrodden, there will be peace in the valley for me. And, when Thou asks, 'Come Follow Me,' we will answer, 'Yes, Lord, I will follow You.'"

I heard a cute fictional story about a man who dies and goes to heaven. Of course, St. Peter meets him at the pearly gates.

St. Peter says, "Here's how it works. You need one hundred points to make it into heaven. You tell me all the good things you've done, and I give you a certain number of points for each item, depending on how good it was. When you reach one hundred points, you get in."

"Okay," the man says. "I was married to the same woman for fifty years and never cheated on her, even in my heart."

"That's wonderful," says St. Peter, "That's worth three points."

"Three points, it that all?" he says, and quickly adds, "Well, I attended church all of my life and supported its ministry with my tithing and service."

"Terrific," says St. Peter. "That's certainly worth a point."

"One point? Golly, how about this. I started a canned good project and delivered it to those who were hungry."

"Fantastic, that's good for two more points," St. Peter proclaimed.

"Two points!" the man cries. "At this rate the only way I get into heaven is by the Grace of God!"

"Well," St Peter replied, "come on in!"

There's an interesting book entitled *Making It* by Norman Podhoretz. In the preface, the author writes:

> Let me introduce myself. I am a man who at the precocious age of thirty-five, experienced an astonishing revelation, it is better to be a success than a failure. Money, I now saw, was important. It was better to be rich than poor. Power, I now saw, was desirable; it was better to give orders than to take them. Fame, I now saw, was unqualifiedly delicious. It was better to be recognized than anonymous.

Podhoretz said that it took him until he was thirty-five years of age to make these amazing discoveries because he was caught, as many of us are, in the contradiction between the American Gospel of success on one hand, and the Christian Gospel of service on the other. The author, Podhoretz, resolved the contradiction by coming out four square for success, unashamed, unapologetic, ungainly success. The book offers a new beatitude to the American scene: "Blessed are the aggressive for they shall reach the top."

That author might have been pleased with the Zebedee boys, James and John. They weren't backward in their ambitions either. They came to Jesus and said, "Teacher, we want You to do for us whatever we ask." And He said to them, "What do you want Me to do for you?" They said to Him, "Grant us that we may sit, one on Your right hand and the other on Your left, in Your glory" (Mark 10:35-37).

No guile, no deal, just straightforward power play for the top jobs in Jesus's new administration.

What kind of power do we want? With whom? Over whom?

James and John knew the kind of power they wanted. That was power in Jesus's administration which they thought would take political, even military force. However, Jesus's administration was not going to be political or controlling, which was much different from what the disciples expected.

When Jesus told James and John and the others, "But to sit on My right hand and on My left is not Mine to give, but it is for those for whom it is prepared"(Mark 10:40).

And when the ten heard it, they began to be greatly displeased with James and John. But Jesus called them to Himself and said to them:

> You know that those who are considered rulers over the Gentiles lord it over them, and their great ones exercise authority over them. Yet it shall not be among you; but whoever desires to become great among you shall be your servant. And, whoever of you desires to be first shall be slave of all. For even the Son of Man did not come to be served, but to serve and to give His life a ransom for many. (Mk 10:41-44)

Jesus knew how difficult it is to withstand the seductions of power.

It is amazing what power does to a person. We all know the poison of power. Lord John Acton said, "All power corrupts and absolute power absolutely corrupts."

What kind of power does Jesus have? He has the power in the form of servant. Jesus taught us to be a servant to others by including them, rather than controlling or having power over them.

One of my seminary professors once said to always include others, no matter what their problem is, for every person you meet is carrying a secret burden, and sometimes its weight makes them cry out unreasonably.

The Gospel does not have a single syllable to say about what others should do...to you. It's concerned only with what you and I should be doing for others, and doing it with unflagging compassion. This is why one of the indelible marks of a practicing Christian is that he or she unfailingly returns good for evil, and not evil for evil, or revenge for revenge. It does, indeed, take two to injure one another. Your foe cannot long feed her or his malicious behavior, if you give it nothing on which to be nourished.

This is why a poem written by Edwin Markham eminently deserves a place in the heart of us all.

Hear these four short but poignant lines:

> He drew a circle that shut me out.
> Heretic, rebel, a thing to flout.
> But love and I had a wit to win.
> We drew a circle that took him in.

If Jesus laid extra stress on anything, it was to be a servant to people.

Jesus isn't seeking power, He's seeking to draw a circle to draw us in. This doesn't mean there are not ethics. Jesus embraced plenty of them, but he made it clear these ethics and principles existed for the sake of protecting the oppressed people.

If persons were the number one priority of Jesus, what was His ministry?

In His first sermon, which He appropriately preached at His home synagogue in Nazareth, He took a text from the Old Testament Book of Isaiah, where the author describes the Messiah, not in triumphal terms, but in terms of lowly service.

"The Spirit of the Lord God is upon Me, because the Lord has anointed Me to preach good tidings to the poor; He has sent Me to heal the brokenhearted, to proclaim liberty to the captives, and the opening of the prison to those who are bound" (Isaiah 61:1).

Then Jesus closed the book, and gave it back to the attendant and sat down. And the eyes of all who were in the synagogue were fixed on Him. And He began to say to them, "Today this Scripture is fulfilled in your hearing" (Luke 4:20, 21).

He was saying, in effect, "I am the Messiah, but not the kind of Messiah you have been expecting." Jesus's ministry is not political, or powerful, but supremely human. It is to serve the poor, the hungry, the blind, the oppressed. But this did not please the pious people of Nazareth. In fact, they got angry and ran Jesus out of town. They were not impressed by a servant image of the Messiah.

Jesus was a servant. He had everything to give and He gave it freely. On the hillsides He patiently taught the common people lessons about God and the good life in word pictures they could understand. In the city streets, He found the despised and the downcast and gave them back their dignity as human beings in the sight of God. People brought their sick to Him and He healed them holistically in body, mind, and spirit.

He healed and anointed with oil many who were sick (Mark 6:13).

He healed the blind and the lame (Matthew 21:14).

He healed a leper crying, "Unclean" (Luke 7:22).

He healed a woman who had sinned (Luke 8:48).

Whoever needed Jesus was not denied Him.

At times, He felt the awful weariness of one who spends himself in service to others, but he went on spending Himself until it took Him to the last full measure of devotion on the Cross.

Jesus committed that servant ministry to His disciples. He made it crystal clear that just as He had come to serve, so they must be willing to serve, if they wanted to follow Him.

As the Epistle of Philippians says, "Let each of you look out not only for his own interests, but also for the interests of others. Let this mind be in you which was also in Christ Jesus" (Philippians 2:4).

Follow Him: be a servant to others.

Faith and Football

Do faith and football have anything in common? For me they do.

Hear the words from the Epistle of Hebrews about the community of faithful people.

> Now faith is the substance of things hoped for, the evidence of things not seen. For by it the elders obtained a good testimony. By faith we understand that the worlds were framed by the word of God, so that the things which are seen were not made of things which are visible. By faith, Abel offered to God a more excellent sacrifice than Cain, through which he obtained witness that he was righteous, God testifying of his gifts; and through it he being dead still speaks. By faith, Enoch was translated so that he did not see death, and was not found because God had translated him, his translation he had this testimony, that he pleased God. But without faith, it is impossible to please Him, for he who comes to God must believe that He is, and that He is a rewarded of those who diligently seek Him. (Heb 11:1-6)

These beautiful Scripture passages from Hebrews are about the community of faith.

No matter your age, place of birth, or where you now live, you've developed some community of friends. You've lived though a number of disasters, and happiness over the years.

We know religion is like that too. The biblical communities have been battered and torn in both AD and BC. It has been churned by towering waves of philosophy, blown like a spindrift by the fierce winds of change, buried in the abyssal depths a hundred times by its enemies.

And yet, here it is. Different, yet the same. God's task is never done.

As I look back over my eighty-one years, I have many memories rushing through the corridors of my mind. Happy ones, sad ones, times of prayer, struggles to raise our kids, meet our budgets, weddings, funerals, and we come to the present.

Keeping the faith throughout these years has been especially vital. The Hebrews passage from chapter 11 are about the heroes of faith, but it's the words that follow I find especially provocative.

> Therefore we also, since we are surrounded by so great a cloud of witnesses, let us lay aside every weight, and the sin which so easily ensnares us, and let us run with endurance the race that is set before us, looking unto Jesus, the author and finisher of our faith, who for the joy that was set before Him endured the cross, despising the shame and has sat down at the right hand of the throne of God. (Heb 12:1, 2)

After reading these verses, I find several points that might guide us on our journey, as we follow Jesus in today's time and place.

I'm going to use the language of football because football is our favorite sport to watch.

The year was 1950, my freshman year of college. I met a cute fellow at the Tri-Delta sorority and Sigma Alpha Epsilon fraternity pledge party. He came up to me while I was playing the piano, and we talked, especially about Ohio State football. In fact, my first date with Tom was supposed to be November 21, 1950, the day now known as the "snow bowl:" Ohio State University against Michigan.

Actually, our "first" date was Tom, my mom and dad, but without me. Tom drove many miles through over a foot of snow to my home. Unfortunately, I couldn't get there, nor could I call from my sorority house, as the telephone lines were down. However, my mom and dad were so impressed by "your young man traveling through thick snow just to see you," they wanted to see Tom again and again.

Two years later, on March 14, 1953, they were as delighted about our marriage as I was, and, sixty-one years later, still am.

Then and Now

The first verse from Hebrews says, "Since we are surrounded by so great a cloud of witnesses" (Hebrews 12:1). Remember, the heroes of faith from two thousand years of Christian history, and nearly two thousand years more of Hebrew history, have had their turn on the field.

So now, they are the alumni, cheering us on, in our time and place. They are the witnesses to what the life of faith in God meant to them, in their time. In that sense, they are in the stands.

So our first witness, in football language, says, "Listen to the fans."

If I could draw animated films I would have Martin Luther, John Calvin, John Wesley, St. Francis of Assisi, and many of my friends who are now living with Jesus. All of them would be leading a cheering section in heaven's reserved seats, yelling in unison, "Go, my friend! The race isn't over."

The people of faith in Hebrews chapter 11 did what needed to be done. Aware that God was in their midst, they experienced God's love and truth in their own history and their faith in God wrote a biblical record that still endures.

So our first shout from the witnesses of faith is: listen to the fans, those friends who walked before us paving the path and encouraging us to continue our faith in God.

The second shout from those witnesses of faith is to discard the weights. "We must throw off every encumbrance, every sin, every weight to which we cling" (Hebrews 12:1).

Football players have all kinds of weights. Their ponderous equipment is necessary for their protection. Christianity is not a pillow to rest on, but a race to run, a race which requires training, discipline, strenuous exertion, the commitment of an athlete.

Are we committed? What can prevent me from running this race of life as well? If we were to list our weights, what would they be?

Perhaps we worry too much about everything. Remember the old adage, "Of all the trouble, great or small, the greatest are those that do not happen at all."

And remember the Gospel spoken by Jesus in Matthew: "Therefore I say to you, do not worry about your life, what you will eat or what you will drink; nor about your body, what you will put on. Is not life more than food and the body more than clothing?" (Matthew 6:25).

Also from the Gospel of Matthew: "Sufficient for the day is its own trouble" (Matthew 6:34).

We need to discard our weights. Get rid of the heavy problems that are on our minds. Throughout the years, I've always found that talking with others about my innermost problems can help to discard the weights that pull me down.

Witness any surviving people of tragedies or those who have been through difficult dramatic experiences. They need to get their feelings out. As my mom always said, "Talk about what's troubling you and you'll get rid of it." That may be a good reason why she lived to be 105 and a half!

Here's another point that Scripture is telling us from Hebrews: "Run with endurance the race that is set before us" (Hebrews 12:1b). Don't take this race of faith too grimly. After all, a race is a sport and sport is supposed to be fun.

Tom and I always watched the Super Bowl game together. Some years ago, our daughter, Carrie, met her future husband, Bill Sharp, at a Super Bowl game we watched at the house of our dear friends, Ann and Bill Sharp. This coming year, 2015, Carrie and Bill will be married twenty-five years, and their other "mom and dad," Ann and Bill, just celebrated their fiftieth wedding anniversary.

In recent years, Tom and I flew to Ohio to be with my mom on Super Bowl Sunday, as her February 6 birthday frequently coincided with Super Bowl weekend. We always enjoyed watching football together. I think it's a good place to release your frustrations and energy. That's why I'm a good fan, I yell a lot.

Did you hear about the devil and the Lord, and football? One day the devil challenged the Lord to a football game. Smiling, the Lord proclaimed, "You don't have a chance. I have all the greatest football players up here."

"Yes," snickered the devil, "but I have all the umpires!"

Sports are enjoyable. The race of the Christian faith is fun too, or it can be. Perhaps a better word is exhilarating, for it can be serious at the same time.

Running the race of faith should be caring for others, as a friend demonstrated. His name is Jim and he's a doctor in Delaware. He heard about an Indian doctor in North India who couldn't afford to purchase medical journals to keep up his skill. So the Delaware doctor sent him some discs with medical lectures. So pleased was the Indian doctor that now every month a group of Delaware doctors sends big parcels to India for distribution in a hospital. The medical DVDs represent hope and excitement for colleagues in a common calling; in a land long on sick people and short on money.

The fourth shout from these witnesses of faith in our Book of Hebrews: "For consider Him who endured such hostility from sinners against Himself, lest you become weary and discouraged in your souls" (Hebrews 12:3).

Keep your eyes fixed on Jesus.

The faith heroes of Hebrews chapter 11 were good, but every one of them was flawed. Every one let God down, in some way or another.

Noah got drunk (Genesis 9:21). Abraham lied (Genesis 20:1-2). Jacob stole his brothers' birth right (Genesis 27:36). Moses killed a man in anger (Exodus 2:12). David committed adultery and murder (2 Samuel 11).

So with the Christian saints. Paul agreed to the stoning of Stephen (Acts 6:8). Peter denied his Lord three times (Luke 22:54-57; Mark 14:69-70; Matthew 26:73-75). Calvin consented the burning of Servenus. John Wesley had severe marital problems.

And, every minister you've ever had, including this one, has sinned at some time or another.

No one of us can be a model.

Christ only is the model. But until faith is turned into service, until the last weight of selfishness drops away and we stand in the Presence of God, we cannot be adequate models.

Only sign posts, like John the Baptist.

Jesus is the only pioneer of faith and perfector of faith.

May we too be witnesses of faith as we listen to the fans, those who have walked before us, paving the way by encouraging us to continue our faith in God.

Discard our weights—the weights of hostility, anger, anxiety—the weights that separate us from God.

Run with resolution. Enjoy your Christian life, spread the joy to others.

And always keep your eyes on Jesus.

And what of ourselves?

"Looking unto Jesus, the author and finisher of our faith, who for the joy that was set before Him endured the cross, despising the shame, and has sat down at the right hand of the throne of God" (Hebrews 12:2).

Jesus, who, for the sake of the joy that was set before Him, is sitting at the right hand of the throne of God.

Stained Glass Anchor

ANGER

More and more I was learning about how people felt when they were beset with cancer.

A seventeen-year-old boy was diagnosed with Hodgkin's, a rare form of cancer that eats away quickly in a young person. As a chaplain, I was asked by the nursing staff to visit the young lad who didn't want to see anyone: his family, his friends, his football team, nor his caring girlfriend. He had totally isolated himself from everyone.

So, here comes the chaplain. Obviously he didn't want to see me, and I didn't know what to do. There are no books at seminary or elsewhere that help direct your conversation.

Well, I thought, *he doesn't want to see me, so I'll just tell him I'll be back later.*

No response. He was glad I was leaving. However, as I'm starting to leave his room, outside the door I could see two nurses peering in, with hope in their eyes, hands clenched as though in prayer.

I turned around and faced the quiet silhouette lying in bed.

"Okay", I said with total defeat in my voice. Of course, the young boy lay still without voice. So I pulled up a chair and sat with him. Quietly, without motion, just as he was sitting, I began to stare at the ceiling and counted all the little dots in each square. A thousand one, a thousand two.

I looked at my watch.

Good grief, I had only lasted eighteen minutes in total quiet.

Now I'm getting mad. First I was mad at the nurses, who asked me to come visit this stubborn sick lad, then I was mad at my seminary, because there were no books to guide me on how to handle this situation. And then I was mad at God, because He got me here somehow. And, of course, I finally got mad at the person I should've gotten mad at in the first place.

Myself.

I'm in a difficult situation and I don't know what to do.

So I get out of my chair and begin to prance around the lad's hospital room, telling him all the people I'm mad at and why.

Immediately, for the first time in many weeks, he spoke.

And he was mad. Mad at the doctors, mad at the nurses, mad at the dieticians, the unit clerks, his parents, and, most of all, his girlfriend, "Cause I told her to leave, and she did."

Finally he spoke, and began to talk expressing his frustrations, his disappointments, his fears, his depression, and all the rest of his emotions came tumbling out.

Once again I was finding out how vital it is we talk and listen to one another.

When this young lad became angry, he came out of his feelings of isolation and shared his feelings of anger.

Sometimes anger is good. It helps us get a handle on our feelings.

One of the most difficult of our human behaviors that people always feel, which our suicide prevention support groups continually mention, is anger.

Webster's Dictionary tells us that anger is "a form of emotional excitement induced by intense displeasure." In other words, it is a form of response to personal discomfort, confusion, and disappointments.

The funny thing about anger is that you can throw it and lose it and still not get rid of it.

Granted, some people handle it better than others, but the truth is, nobody avoids it.

Not even God.

Anger in the Holy Bible

The biblical record is amply sprinkled with references to divine anger.

In the book of Isaiah, God is saying, "I will trod the people in my anger and trample them with my wrath (Isaiah 63:3). And the Book Job observes. "Therefore I say, He destroys the blameless and the wicked." (Job 9:22). And, who can forget the New Testament scenes with Jesus driving the money changers from the Temple (Matthew 21:12)?

Yes, anger is a universal phenomenon with the potential to hurt and destroy life.

And even if we manage to control it, anger still has the capacity to virtually eat the innards out of every one of us. If we keep it inside, we are in danger of a heart attack, stroke, and suicide, whereas pent-up anger will reveal itself later as we strike back when we don't deal with it in one way or another. And we usually strike back at the wrong person. On the other hand, if we let it out, when we immediately feel it, we can wreck our marriages, alienate our friends, and forfeit all gainful employment.

In short, anger is the most difficult of all our emotions

So, how can the Bible help us with our anger?

St. Paul writes, in his letter to the church at Ephesus: "Be angry, and do not sin, do not let the sun go down on your wrath" (Ephesians 4:26).

Interesting, isn't it?

The old apostle doesn't suggest that we avoid anger. He knows better. What he suggests is that we learn how to harness it.

So lets' look at some of the basic causes for emotional explosions in Dr. Willard Gaylins book, *The Rage Within*. The first is the feeling of disapproval. It seems that all of us have a root need for the safety offered by authentic love. We crave acceptance despite ourselves. We long to be loved without limits. So whenever we are told we are "not okay," particularly by someone who is important to us, we tend to respond with anger.

It's the old phenomenon of rejection breeding rejection. Perhaps this is most readily observed on the elementary school playground when a youngster having a bad day decides to stick out his tongue at a classmate.

It is almost like a mirror. You can bet there will be a response in kind.

Another impulse for anger, when we feel the sting of disapproval, we are enraged by betrayal. It is one thing to be judged unacceptable by someone who does not know us. But when that judgment comes from someone who we thought loved and supported us, it is almost unbearable.

This is why most crimes of passion involve people who live together. Whether spouses, parents, children, or roommates, there is an invisible bond that has a tendency to shatter even before it cracks. Betrayal involves the fear of rejection compounded by the humiliation of defeat. Not only are we surprised to be spurned, but most often we feel personally hurt in the process.

Perhaps the best biblical illustration of such anger occurred in the Garden of Gethsemane, when the soldiers came to seize the Master:

> And while He was still speaking, behold a multitude, and he who was called Judas, one of the twelve, went before them and drew near to Jesus to kiss Him, But Jesus said to him, "Judas, are you betraying the Son of Man with a kiss?" When those around Him saw what was going to happen, they said to Him, "Lord, shall we strike with the sword?" And one of them struck the servant of the high priest and cut off his right ear (Luke 22: 47-50).

Jesus the Christ knew what was coming, but this was not the case with the apostle Peter. Watching Judas give the betraying kiss, the hot-blooded disciple Peter seized a sword and lopped off the ear of one of the arresting officers.

I would suggest that the soldier was really not the object of Peter's rage. He may have suffered the consequences, but it was Judas who generated the feeling of anger.

Judas. Judas, the one who shared their table. Judas, the one who had been with them when they trekked the dusty hills of Nazareth. Here was one who had shared their prayers only hours before in the Upper Room. Having been trusted, Judas broke that trust and Peter's passion just couldn't handle it.

Betrayal begets anger.

And that leads me to the another source of anger.

No one wants to feel deprived, picked on, or accused of being morally corrupt, and they get angry. Interestingly, fact has little to do with feeling. One can be basking in the lap of opulence and still feel deprived; and one can live in abject poverty and not feel deprived.

The question is not what we have, or do not have, but what we think we have in comparison to what we think others have.

Anyone who has more than one child knows how this works. When the kids count the loot after Christmas, there needs to be some sense of equity and fairness or the kids will be angry. All of us like to believe we are equally valued and any evidence to the contrary leads to a seething feeling inside that almost always culminates into a explosion.

And that's another impetus for anger. This one doesn't have the hair triggering effect so frequently associated with feelings of: disapproval, betrayal, hardship, and feeling used or exploited.

To be treated like a fool may be the most dehumanizing of all human experiences, and it usually leads to indignation.

Finally, we lose our cool when we are annoyed.

I know how I feel when one of my new technical gadgets doesn't obey "my command." Frustration is almost always anchored in feelings of inadequacy. Sometimes I feel so frustrated that I can't get my computer to complete all my commands. It wasn't the fact that the computer won't work that gets to me, it's my awareness that I just can't figure it all out. That's when I felt anger. I worked with my computer getting more and more frustrated and finally gave up on learning how to cut and paste until a later date. But in the meantime, I thought about heaving it into Langford Bay.

It's a ridiculous gesture of my frustration, but a perfect example of what happened when my emotional circuit got overloaded and I couldn't figure out the problem.

For the most part, every outburst of indignation can be linked to one or more of these situations: feelings of disapproval, betrayal, deprivation, exploitation, or frustration.

Even the Holy Bible reports many incidents of anger. It hurts to have a gift rejected. Cain tilled the soil. Abel cared for the sheep. Cain brought fruit and vegetables to praise the Lord. Abel brought a lamb.

According to the scriptural record in Genesis, Abel's gift was celebrated, but not Cain. And a few days later, it came about that the brothers were in the field together and Cain rose up and killed his brother And God called out to Cain, "Where is your brother Abel?" To which Cain uttered the famous reply, "How should I know? Am I my brother's keeper?" (Genesis 4:9).

It hurts to have a donkey make a fool of you.

Balak, the major of Moab, invited Balaam, the Hebrew prophet, to visit his city and save it from the Israelites. Hence, Balaam saddled his donkey and headed for Moab. But God didn't want him there, so He sent an angel to block his way. When the donkey saw the angel, it went berserk and charged off the road into a cornfield. While his servant roared in laughter, Balaam was embarrassed to tears and smacked the donkey upside the head.

At this point, the donkey began to speak, "What did I ever do to you to deserve such abuse?" Angered, Balaam said to the donkey, "Because you have abused me. I wish there were a sword in my hand, for now I would kill you" (Numbers 22:29).

And, from the Gospel of Matthew, we hear more anger.

> Now when they had departed, behold, an angel of the Lord appeared to Joseph in a dream, saying, "Arise, take the young Child and His mother, flee to Egypt, and stay there until I bring you word; for Herod will seek the young Child to destroy Him. When he arose, he took the young Child and His mother by night and departed for Egypt, and was there until the death of

Herod, that it might be fulfilled which was spoke by the Lord through the prophet, saying, "Out of Egypt I called My Son." Then Herod, when he saw that he was deceived by the wise men was exceedingly angry; and he sent forth and put to death all the male children who were in Bethlehem and in all its districts, from two years old and under, according to the time which he had determined from the wise men (Matthew 2:13-16).

From the moment he saw them, Herod didn't trust them. Three overdressed travelers from a distant land claiming to have followed a star in search of the King of the Jews. Surely this was some kind of scam. But Herod was no fool. He asked them when the star had first appeared, then he prevailed upon them to find the child and report back to him.

He would nip this nonsense in the bud. But the Magi, having found the Babe Jesus, returned, but not to Herod's door; and when the powerful Governor of Galilee learned they had fled Judah, his stomach knotted. "A fool he could not bear to be." Thus, in an icy rage, he issued the decree: "All male children two years and less, must die" (Matthew 2:16).

Another biblical record of severe anger was from the rabbi, Saul. It's recorded in the Book of Acts:

Now Saul was consenting to Stephen's death. At that time a great persecution arose against the church which was at Jerusalem; and they were all scattered throughout the regions of Judea and Samaria, except the apostles. And devout men carried Stephen to his burial, and made great lamentation over him. As for Saul, he made havoc of the church, entering every house, and dragging off men and women, committing them to prison. He was angry and he began stoning those who had witnessed Jesus' miracles. (Acts 8:1-8)

This is the Saul before he meets our Lord on the road to Damascus. You see, the Bible is saturated with incidents of anger.

If it's not Cain slaying Abel, it's Balaam beating his donkey; and if it's not Herod murdering children, it's Saul killing the Christians, before he met Jesus on the road to Damascus.

Anger. It's everywhere, including the Holy Bible. But that's what makes the Bible not only spiritually holy, but a record of all the struggles of humanity, highlighting anger and destruction.

What is the ingredient that marks the difference between anger and destruction? What is it that pushes us from utterance to ignorance, from feeling tension to acting tensely, from snarling to gnarling? Most of our anger centers in unmet needs.

So, what is it that turns sister against sister, man against beast, governor against the governed? What is the common ingredient that transforms a feeling of frustration into a deed of destruction?

In every one of the biblical illustrations that I mentioned at the beginning of this chapter, we can see the devastating role of pride. Cain was most angry because Abel was the one most blessed. Cain felt put down. Balaam was embarrassed because he couldn't control his donkey and appeared the fool in front of his friends. Herod, in an icy rage, killed because his pride was hurt. Rabbi Saul was angry that people loved Jesus, and killed for his personal prideful beliefs.

And here is an important point concerning anger. With the exception of instances of brain damage, or drug-induced euphoria, when a person is aggressive, there is a point where that behavior is chosen. Preceding every act of aggression, there is a point of cognizance, a split second when the "Yes, I will, no, I can't" decision is made.

Cain chose to kill Abel.

Balaam chose to abuse his donkey.

Herod chose to massacre the children.

Saul chose to stone Stephen.

The difference between propitious aggression and lethal aggression is the influence of pride. Personal affronts are much more difficult to hold and measure than generic injustices. So, the link between anger and destruction is an overbearing "sense of self" robbing us of balanced judgment. The real root to our destructive anger is our preoccupation with ourselves.

When we're too proud to admit we can't start a computer, or ask for directions, or say we are wrong or say we are sorry, we inflict damage and generate great harm. And we do this not only to others, but ourselves as well.

The challenge is clear. If anger and pride substantiate the lethal link, how do we keep them apart? We have to learn to remember, no matter how painful the moment, that the big picture is more important.

Consequences

Consider the consequences.

One jailbird writes this line, "Five short minutes done cost me twenty long years in jail."

We must work to be aware of the consequences.

Look at the big picture. Who are we hurting? Not what do I want, but who am I hurting?

Anger activated by pride is a destructive force. In a few seconds, it can destroy the efforts of a lifetime and, without fail, it leaves an ugly aftertaste that forever taints the image of its author. That was the problem with Herod, Balaam, Cain, and Saul. All of these people were centered on themselves. They were negative, bitter, and angry because their pride was stepped on.

We've all known people like that. Having tasted the gall of life, they seem intent on staining the lives of others with the same misery. By choice, they let their pride dictate their lives.

Whenever I get angry, I ask myself, "Is my pride stimulating my anger because I've been hurt by someone?" And, "Can I forgive with pride in my way?"

We all ask, from time to time, "Why is this happening to me?"

Certainly my pride was hurt, when the chapel committee person pulled my golf cart over, telling me, without my input, I'm going to be "100 percent retired."

Even when we feel most helpless, we still have choices. What can happen through us is more important than what has happened to us.

Consider Helen Keller, Franklin Delano Roosevelt, Ray Charles, just to name a few. All of them tremendously handicapped. They could be easily and understandably filled with anger. But every one of them focused on their God-given gifts, not their tragedies. And our world is the benefactor.

How can we keep anger and pride safely distanced from each other? No matter how painful the moment, the consequences of the large picture are much more important.

Choose carefully and don't let your pride direct your anger and choice.

Then we must learn to trust in the grace and love of our Lord, as the Author of our lives. You might believe there is nothing more important than you being in control, until you have a heart attack. You might think the most important thing in your life are children or spouse, until you come face to face with their noncaring attitude about you.

You might think the most important thing in your life is your home, until you come face to face with a hurricane or fire or flood. You might think you have friends who like you, until they betray you. You might function as one who has the political clout to achieve anything you want, until your son/daughter ends up as a drug addict or dead, or in a mental hospital.

Our lives are simply too fragile and too fickle to center anywhere other than in the Grace of God and Trust in our Lord.

The Epistle from the Book James helps us with anger.

> Let every man be quick to hear, slow to speak, slow to anger, for the anger of man does not work the righteousness of God. Therefore put away all filthiness and rank growth of wickedness and receive with meekness the implanted word, which is able to save your souls. (James 1:19)

Remember, the book of James does not assume that anger could be avoided. But he does suggest it needs to be controlled. "For it does not work the righteousness of God." Even so, anger has a lot more to do with how we look at things, than it does with what we feel. What we need to do is reassess how we look at things. We need to have a positive attitude about ourselves. How often do we look in the mirror and see nothing positive? All we'd need then is a snide comment and we'd begin to become angry.

Several authors have stated that people with low self-esteem are destined to be angry forever, if for no other reason than to belittle others. However, if we perceive that we are unconditionally loved, we've got a real chance to master our cynicism and reduce our capacity for anger.

We may still hiss a little from time to time. And, well, we should. But we will rarely bite.

What is that key to self acceptance? It is a sense of honesty about the fact that life constantly changes and not a one of us has it together all the time. If we are to conquer our anger, we have to start by being happy with ourselves. I think this is what James has in mind when he suggested: "Therefore, put away all filthiness and rank growth of wickedness and receive with meekness the implanted word, which is able to save your souls" (James 1:21). What in the world does it mean to "receive the word implanted" if it does not mean to recognize that we are unconditionally loved by God? When the word was implanted in a tumble-down stable in Bethlehem, God was saying loud and clear, "I love you more than you can mess up."

We are all blessed with unconditional love and need to accept that blessing.

If we have to be perfect before we can know ourselves blessed, we will never ask for the transfiguring power of God's love. We need to know that it's okay to cry out, "Help me, Lord." So, if we want to master our anger, we start by accepting ourselves as unconditionally loved. No matter what.

Then, having changed our concept of ourselves, we must work on changing our concept of others.

We are not foreordained judges. God did not grant us the gift of life so that we might study the performance of our peers with an eye toward keeping them on the straight and narrow.

My thoughts are of my high school band performance days. I had practiced over and over again on my French horn for the finals held in the state capital. We were playing against tough competition to be the High School Band of the Year for the entire state.

I had several notes that were solos. My band director pointed his baton at me during the concert, and I blew those notes. All of them. All wrong notes.

Later, the band director and my peers didn't waste any time turning their wrath on me. "Marlene, why oh why did you blow those foul notes?"

Oh, I practiced and practiced until I was blue. My mom and dad almost went berserk listening to those notes day after day. Many were very angry at me for a long time. I hung my head for many moons, and have remembered the incident now as if it happened yesterday. It was an eon before I could forgive myself.

And, so it is we must learn to forgive others too. "Let everyone be quick to hear. Slow to speak, and slow to anger. For our anger does not achieve the righteousness of God" (James 1:19).

If we blow up in exasperation, we'll probably reduce the pressure and change the situation, at least for the moment. Of course, we can always blow up and make a fool out of ourselves. On the other hand, if we manage to contain our indignation, the immediate situation will probably remain the same even when we buy the time to manage it better at a more opportune moment.

So the question remains: shouting or thinking? And which is the best thing to do?

Shouting. Letting it all go obviously brings the immediate release of tension. Rather than seething inside, we just dump the whole mess and get it out of our system.

How many times I've heard someone say, "He'll never have an ulcer. He doesn't keep anything long enough for it to do any damage." Now, a second reason to opt for yelling is the simple truth that it almost always results in immediate change.

If we really can't stand a person or a situation, we can usually alter it in the instant with a few well-chosen words uttered at a loud sound level. It's a common fact of human behavior that when people scream, others listen. How often you watch the picket lines for some issue and people are screaming their views. And something might change in the process. Also, there are a few more commanding ways to announce our priorities than by coming apart at the seams.

We can rest assured that when we shout, everybody around us will know about our concern. They might not agree with it, but they will have no doubt it exists.

Our Lord let people know his ire in the Gospel of Luke: "Then Jesus went into the temple and began to drive out those who bought and sold it, saying to them, 'It is written, My house is a house of prayer, but you have made it a 'den of thieves'" (Luke 19:45, 46).

When we look at the most memorable explosion accredited to our Lord, we find all three of these achievements taking place. When Jesus charged into the temple, dumped the tables of the money changers, and drove them into the street at the sting of a cat of nine tails, He relieved His anger, changed the situation, and let the whole city know this was important to Him. Then, when we are filled with anger, if these are our goals, being angry isn't so bad. But the sad truth is that research indicates those three reasons of shouting—relief, instant change, and announced concern—are rarely the motivators behind human anger. Rather, the most dominant factor contributing to our emotional explosions is our own unmet needs. And we turn our wrath on those who love us the most and unfortunately these are usually the people we love and need the most.

Remember the song, "You only hurt the one you love, the one you shouldn't hurt at all?"

This is where our short fuses take a terrible toll.

True, a frontal assault just might result in a momentary change, but the downside of delivering such a scene is worth nothing. There are consequences in exploding. When we assume the right to explode, we also assume the right to virtually take over the space of those around us. It's really a form of thievery. Often, after a robbery, we hear the victim explain how terrible it is to "feel violated."

It's an insult. By assuming that our feelings are more important than others involved and by pushing their feelings aside, we too deliver a similar insult. We announce: "My thoughts, my values, and my opinions have more meaning than yours. I'm going to smother you with venom and volume until you accede to my wishes." Undoubtedly, this is why we usually reserve our "yelling" for friends, family, and followers. Basically, we tend to blow up only at people with whom we feel safe. It inflicts pain on people we really don't want to hurt. There's another downside effect of losing one's cool as we explode. It clouds communication with everyone who sees it.

Yes, it lets people know we care, but I'm not talking about expressing a feeling of anger. We all feel angry from time to time and need to let people know.

But when your anger is shrouded with unmanaged fury, it is nearly impossible to understand. It's one thing to purposely announce, "This is making me angry," it's another to "explode."

The writer of Proverbs hits the mark: "In the multitude of words sin is not lacking, but he who restrains his lips is wise" (Proverbs 10:19).

So, how do we manage this " restraining of our lips?" I always suggest a person writes a personal journal. Write out how you "wish" you could respond. Then, make it a point to learn your own anger signs. The best thing to do is ask one of those people you need and love to tell you what that is. I asked my husband a while back what my anger signs were and he said I start to talk too fast and pace. And that's the point of learning our symptoms. When we know them, we have a much better chance of "bridling our tongue," as my mom used to say. Then, we need to make it a point, whenever the symptoms pop up, to immediately ask ourselves the question, "What do I want here?" Short-term satisfaction or long-term understanding? Most often, that's the difference between shouting and thinking.

The root challenge for all of us remains the same. It's been that way for thousands of years, according to the Bible. And that is to delay action in order to reduce damage.

Mark Twain said it. "When angry, walk away and count four. When really angry, walk away, count four. Then ten, then one hundred."

Proverbs said it too. "They who restrain their words have knowledge and understanding" (Proverbs 10: 23, 24).

Even so, how do we manage painful feelings?

Believe it or not, it's okay to be angry. It's okay to be depressed. It's okay to feel sick to your stomach. What's not okay is to pretend such passions are not present when all the time they are boiling inside. One of the best ways to handle such feelings is to see them as barometers from past experiences.

The truth is, most passions are hinged to previous events. Paralyzed by painful feelings, a good first step is to consciously complete this sentence: "The last time I felt like this was…" And, the follow-up sentence is: "And this is what I did to feel a little better."

You'll be amazed at the perspective this brings.

By the way, there are two common developments which you should not avoid. If you feel like crying, do it. God didn't give us tear ducts solely for the purpose of washing our eyeballs.

Secondly, don't hesitate to blame God for your situation. It is all right to be angry with God. God can handle it. Remember, we usually get mad at the ones we love the most. Good relationships mean some anger. Almost every biblical situation involves some anger with God.

Jonah's first prayer to God was one of anger. " It displeased Jonah exceedingly and he became angry, so he prayed to the Lord. Therefore now, O Lord, please take my life from me, for it is better for me to die than to live!" (Jonah 4:1-4).

It's a fair prayer.

If God answered the death of Jesus with His Resurrection, what makes us think our anger will stop His affection?

Then, how do we manage our painful feelings? Primarily by accepting them for what they are. And express them without injuring others or yourself. Try to control your feelings. This doesn't mean we bury them. It just means we defuse their dominance.

And don't forget to laugh. Of course there are some crises that are too painful to laugh about. At least for a while. Even as tears liberate healing endorphins into our systems, so does laughter. In fact, even more so.

When I worked with cancer patients at the hospital and home, we would encourage watching funny movies or comedy routines.

Norman Cousins, who was dying of cancer, wrote a book entitled, *Anatomy of an Illness*. He writes this poignant line: "Life is a crisis. Many times to be able to laugh at yourself and your predicament can help the process of healing."

Crises are not pebbles, but they can often be put in perspective by a good laugh.

And, finally, a way of controlling painful feelings is to "put it in a drawer."

Leslie Weatherhead writes this one in his book, *The Will of God*. It was a time when he was dealing with the horrors of German bombing raids in World War II in London. He regularly encountered problems without answers. Emotional mazes from which there appeared no exit. After months of sleepless nights, he virtually labeled the second drawer on the right side of his desk with a slip of paper saying: "Awaiting Further Light." Dr. Weatherhead wasn't denying the existence of the problem, he was just taking control of it.

We can do the same thing with our feelings, once we have identified and expressed them. We, too, can take control of our feelings, sometimes by writing them down and placing them in a drawer.

Meantime, God is with you as you await further light.

Stained Glass Spiritus

COURAGE

I mentioned my dear childhood friend Marjorie Winlock, who was crippled by infantile paralysis when she was nineteen years old. And from that day until the day she died twenty years later, Marge didn't know what it meant to experience a single day without total inability to breathe on her own. The longest she could come out of the iron lung was thirty minutes a day, and then on a chest respirator.

Can you imagine what that would be like? Can you even think of living like that? It's because of Marjorie that I began to think about suffering and God. Trying to link up the understanding of why we still should be thankful, as Marge was thankful. Throughout her illness, she always believed God was with her, helping and guiding her. One time I was visiting and I told her of a problem I was having. Marge said, through her laborious breathing, "You know, Marlene, give thanks for your problems because it's teaching you something. When you realize God is there with you, then you will be able to hand your problem over to God. God will see you through." Marge was gently telling me that God will be with me when I give thanks and trust in Gods' presence.

What if we feel we have nothing for which to be thankful?

Martin Rinkhard was the son of a poor coppersmith and worked his way through college in Heidelberg, Germany, three hundred years ago. At the age of thirty-one, he was offered the position of Archdeacon in his native town. A year later, in 1618, the cruel thirty years war broke out in Europe. Then the plague, and the plague was followed by a terrible famine. Martin was the only remaining minister in the besieged town.

Having made a hospital of his own home, there was a point where, on one single day, he conducted forty-eight funeral services.

But, like my friend Marge Willock, Martin still breathed an unbounded spirit of faith in God by giving thanks.

Martin is best known as the composer of the words of one of the greatest of German hymns, "Now Thank We All Our God."

> Now thank we all our God. With heart and hands and voices
> Who wondrous things hath done. In which his world rejoices.
> Now Thank We All our God. whose wondrous things hath done.

Wondrous things? What's so wondrous about a war?

Of course, Martin and Marge knew that God was not the perpetrator of war or polio. They knew that wars are the results of uncontrolled passions and desires in the hearts of people. And, certainly, the plague wasn't sent by God, any more than God sent polio to Marge.

Marge Willock and Martin Rinehart praised God for wondrous things, for common spiritual graces that they saw through their suffering and heartaches in their lives. How often I have found people who have tremendous physical problems giving thanks.

A dear friend of mine was told by the doctor her surgery was unsuccessful, the cancer had spread. When I went to visit, her hand outstretched to mine, the news is shared, and then her words, "I have so much to be thankful for." And then she began counting her blessings.

This does not mean she didn't feel loss, anger, frustrations, and sadness. Yes, she still felt those, but still, much thanksgiving.

This is not saintly stuff.

This is not pollyannaish.

I have found that people who are buffeted by adversity often give the most evidence of deep thanksgiving. Not for their adversity, but because their hardships help put their priorities in proper perspective. The truly thankful feeling seems to come best when we interrupt our daily round of duties and reflect and pray.

In Scotland, there is a little hamlet on the top of the hill called "Rest and Be Thankful." The name suggests a profound truth. Rest and be thankful, you have to rest in order to be thankful.

And then, there's courageous courage. My health was excellent until several years ago, after my first retirement from the active ministry. I was a chaplain for eight years, associate minister at Grace United Methodist Church for three years, and I was the only minister of Mt. Lebanon United Methodist Church for twelve years, and preached here at our Florida retirement community for ten years. Tom and I decided to move to Florida for our twilight years and we love it here.

However, with my many illnesses, I've discovered a new meaning of the word *courage*. Being a frequent patient at Mayo Clinic in Jacksonville, Florida, I've observed people from all walks of life and with all varieties of diseases. And I've witnessed one human commonality.

Courage.

Courage to face the upcoming journey you know is ahead of you.

One of the cutest get-well cards I received had a picture of Charlie Brown talking to his dog Snoopy, and it said, "Wouldn't it be nice if life was like a DVD, and you could fast-forward through the crummy times."

It takes courage to get through our difficult situations. You know, there is a thin line between courage and craziness.

What is courage?

Over the years we have watched quite a masquerade in the name of courage. How much courage does it take to: Ride a barrel over Niagara Falls? Walk a tight rope between two tall buildings? Make a necktie out of a team of slithering rattlesnakes?

Are risk and valor synonyms for courage? Or have we misconnected brash recklessness, arrogant indifference, and macho bravado with courage, at the expense of the deeper values of creativity, integrity, conviction, love, honesty, and humility?

Scripture always helps me. The Gospel of Matthew gives me a special insight into what I consider to be the true foundation of courage.

> And when He had sent the multitudes away, He went up on a mountain by Himself to pray. And when evening had come, He was alone there. But the boat was now in the middle of the sea, tossed by the waves, for the wind was contrary. Now in the

fourth watch of the night Jesus went to them, walking on the sea. And when the disciples saw Him walking on the sea, they were troubled, saying, "It is a ghost!" And they cried out for fear. But immediately Jesus spoke to them, saying, "Be of good cheer! It is I; do not be afraid." And Peter answered Him and said, "Lord if it is You, command me to come to you on the water." So He said, "Come." And when Peter had come down out of the boat, he walked on the water to go to Jesus. But when he saw that the wind was boisterous, he was afraid; and beginning to sink he cried out, saying, "Lord, save me!" And immediately Jesus stretched out his hand and caught him, and said to him, "O you of little faith, why did you doubt?" (Matthew 14:23-31)

This Scripture passage takes place early in the morning. Several of Jesus's disciples have spent the night battling a storm on the Sea of Galilee. Such storms were particularly vicious due to the combined influence of the shallow water and a natural wind tunnel created by the hills around the lake. In a matter of minutes, *Genesarat*, as the locals call it, can go from a placid glass-surfaced pond to a raging cauldron complete with eight- to ten-foot waves.

That morning, the exhausted disciples were draped all over the boat having survived a lashing by the winds, when they looked up and see the Master walking toward them, directly across the water.

Their first thought: "This is a ghost" and they cry out in fear. "It is a ghost, it is a ghost!" (Matthew 14:26). The disciple Peter, always the showboat, suspects it is Jesus and he shouts to him, "Master, if it is you, call to me and I will come to you." The Master replied: "It is I. Come" (Matthew 14:29).

To what must have been his total chagrin, Peter's bet was covered. So he walked on the water to go to Jesus. Then, after only a few steps, he started thinking about what was going on, and he lost it. But even as he began to sink, Jesus reached out and took his hand, shaking his head in gentle disappointment. "Oh, you of little faith, why did you doubt?" (Matthew 14:31).

It's a classic piece of Christian literature. I believe it contains the solitary key to courage. But let me make a few observations about what courage is not.

It certainly isn't foolhardy. You see, I am convinced that in a world defined by Madison Avenue and directed by Hollywood, we often fall dreadfully short of providing accurate images of courage because we acknowledge the wrong heroes. For example, take this whole concept of negligence. What kind of message do we give to our youngsters when we endorse thoughtless, impulsive, high-risk "hot doggers?"

I did some really temerarious things as a youth. I'll never forget the time I jumped on a bread truck running board, just on a double dare from some young, reckless friends. I was lucky. I only had bruises and a bloody nose. Was I courageous? No. Foolhardiness is a poor substitute for courage.

Also, courage is not an indifference to others.

Truth is, people who really have inner power, as well as outer, don't need to feel superior to show off. They don't have to. At peace with who and what they are, their courage is most often displayed, not through a sense of superiority, but through caring about others.

Real courage has a lot more to do with compassion and service than privilege and command.

And courage is not cocky.

It's not nice to treat any human being as an expendable commodity. It's not right to use power, whether it be physical, financial, or political, just to erase the rights of others.

When it comes to courage, the macho mindset is, without exception, an indication of its absence. When I look at these courage imposters, there's a common thread. Whether the style be a foolhardy, apathetical, or cocky mindset, everyone of these substitutes self centeredness for genuine strength of our soul.

What is recklessness but a scream of "Hey, look at me"? What is indifference but the assumption that I am more important than you? And what is cocky macho but self-centeredness.

Courage, true courage, comes when we surrender the self to a greater cause and trust it all to the care of our Creator. As we look back at our Scripture passage, it shows us the best and the worst of human nature, all in a single glimpse. Peter is the primary player. To me, that seems totally appropriate. Do you know why? Because from time to time, old disciple Peter displayed every one of the phony courage characteristics.

When Peter lopped off the centurion's ear in the Garden of Gethsemane, that was foolhardy. When he rebuked the crowd for pressing too close to the Master, it was indifference. When he swore he would never deny the lord, and then denied Jesus three times the night before Jesus was crucified, that was cocky.

Peter was human, just like you and me.

So, Jesus approaches the disciples early in the morning after a night of horrendous storms. The others think it is a ghost, but Peter let his mouth run. "Lord if it is you, call me and I'll come out there too" (Matthew 14:28).

Right. He didn't think there was a frog's chance in a bowl of hot sauce. Jesus calls him and, here comes the courage point. Peter stepped out of the boat.

Wow!

Can you imagine solely on the basis of the Master's invitation that anyone of us could or would step over the side of the boat and start to walk on top of very deep water? Sometimes we display our courage when we flex our faith. When we step forward with nothing to support us, but the promise of the love of God.

But what happens next?

Peter gets out there and starts thinking about himself. He is doing fine as long as he keeps his focus on the Master. But as soon as he realizes what he is doing, and how it must look to the others, and what people are going to say when they hear about this, and all the other things that go through our minds when we get a rush of self-centeredness, we, like Peter, start to sink.

What is the solitary key to courage? It is nothing more than a coalition with the Creator. When we really need a dose of courage there is only one place to get it. Like it came to Peter, it will come to us if we keep our consciousness focused, not on "What's in it for me," but, "What is in it for you, God."

I like Hank Williams singing and writing lyrics. I especially like his song "I Saw the Light."

> No more darkness, no more night, now I'm so happy, no sorrow
> in sight, praise the Lord, I saw the light.

It lifts us beyond ourselves to a place of dependency on the Master. Truth is, we are always in that position, but it often takes a crisis of immense proportions to remind us how frail and inadequate we are on our own.

"Courage is fear that has said its prayers," said either Karl Barth or Dorothy Bernard.

Real courage is innate in every human being, even more so in those who have developed a trusting relationship with God.

What is courage? Mr. Webster's Dictionary tells us courage is "the mental and moral strength to venture, to persevere and withstand danger, fear or difficulty." But I think it's more than that.

I believe courage is also the appropriate word for the tenacity it takes to hold a course or cling to a dream even when the masses turn the other way.

What are the characteristics of that illusive word, *courage?*

Again, our Scriptures help us in the search. In the Epistle, we find Paul explaining to the believers at the city of Corinth the need to hang in there when the going gets tough.

> We are afflicted in every way, but not crushed; perplexed, but not
> driven to despair; persecuted but not forsaken; struck down, but
> not destroyed; always carrying in the body the death of Jesus so
> that the life of Jesus may also be made visible in our bodies. For
> while we live, we are always being given up to death for Jesus'
> sake, so that the life of Jesus may be made visible in our mortal
> flesh. (2 Cor 4:8-10)

Simply translated, Paul is saying we are here to love, as Christ loved, because we are love-in-Christ, we can endure adversity without despair. Our goal is to grow through it all. And there we have the telltale symptoms of Christian courage. It all begins with mastering the ability to express love. At the heart of our faith is the deep-seated conviction from the Gospel of John: "God so loved the world that He gave His only begotten Son that whosoever believes in Him would not perish, but have everlasting life" (John 3:16).

This spiritual wagon train with God taking the risk, with God jumping in the water, with God figuratively and literally saying to all humanity through the person of Jesus Christ, "I love you."

Courage is finishing the task and accepting the risk of rejection. Loving is a high-risk business, and yet it is at the very heart of the Christians' experience.

I'll never forget the sympathy card I received when my forty-six-year old Dad suddenly died over sixty years ago, just ten days after Tom and I were married. It was a simple phrase on the card, written some ages ago by Elizabeth Barrette Browning's poem, and it said, "'Tis better to have loved and lost, than never to have loved at all."

I didn't believe that phrase at the time, because death is so final that I wished I hadn't loved Dad so much. Grieving is so much more unbearable the more you love. But that's part of the paradoxes of life. It's hard to love and lose, but think of the memories and lessons learned when you have loved.

I believe a mark of Christians' courage is the capacity to love and never count the cost.

Then, you must rise above adversity.

A word about perspective. You see, along with St. Paul, I believe that the manner in which we deal with difficulties is largely determined by the perspective from which we confront it.

The apostle rattled off all those inspirational phrases:

Perplexed…but not driven to despair.
Persecuted…but not forsaken.
Struck down…but not destroyed.

Just what is it that makes it so possible for Christians to endure all these problems, yet never be conquered by them?

It is perspective. The way we see life's challenges is largely defined by the background against which we perceive them.

We have visited many United Methodist churches in Florida, and in one I saw the largest cross I've ever seen. In the hallway of the church was a picture that shows that cross before it was perched atop the building. A giant crane is holding it upright and a woman is standing beside it. The minister explained, "We took that picture so people would know how big the cross really is. We knew once we got it up on the church, people would have no way of truly judging its size."

And he was right. Seeing how that cross dwarfed that woman, I sensed it was a whole lot larger than it looked up against the blue Florida sky. Background has an amazing impact on perspective.

In the same sense, Christian courage takes on a whole new meaning when we realize how believers view challenges, not only against the cross, but against the empty tomb.

If your life is centered in material gain, keeping up with others can paralyze your life. If your life revolves around what other people think, you're going to spend a lot of time sweating over exterior trappings and public perceptions.

If you are confident that God knows your name and has reserved a place of peace for you, then none of that stuff can break your spirit.

Yes, you may be afflicted, but never crushed.

Yes, you may be perplexed, but never driven to despair.

And you may be struck down, but never be destroyed. It is all a matter of how you choose to perceive the problem.

I think of the traveler who was nearing a great city and asked a man seated by the wayside, "What are the people like in this city?"

The man replied, "How were the people where you came from?"

The traveler responded, "They were untrustworthy, detestable in all aspects."

"Ah", said the sage. "You will find them the same in the city ahead.

No matter where we go, there will always be people who are a "terrible lot," but more importantly, there will always be people who are a "caring lot."

When we really need a dose of courage, there's one place to get it. Like the Apostle Paul, it will come to us if we keep our consciousness focused, not on: "What's in it for me," but "What is in it for you, God?"

The old hymn "What a Friend We have in Jesus" says it well.

> Have we trials and temptations? Is there trouble anywhere? We should never be discouraged, take it to the Lord in prayer.

Real courage turns our eyes upon Jesus. It lifts us beyond ourselves to a place of dependency on the Master. The truth is, we are always in that position, but it often takes a crisis of immense proportions to look at our inner soul, to remind us how frail and inadequate we are on our own.

Can things go wrong? Sure.

Is there a chance we'll be hurt or disappointed? Absolutely.

Can disaster strike? Are we prone to auto accidents? Life-threatening diseases? Hurricanes? Fire? You name it, it can strike, without question.

Still, no matter what comes our way, we put it in our Awaiting Further Light drawer, knowing our personal relationship with a God who loves us without condition, and one day will grant everyone of us His presence.

I'd like to tell you about a diploma and a man. He was my mentor and teacher at my seminary in Philadelphia. He was a tall, articulate man who always had an air of dignity and intelligence about him that was complimented by a wealth of warmth and caring. The man was every bit as impressive as his office. That's why the document on the wall of his office was so significant. It is a second-grade report card. Upon close examination, one notices that it is an evaluation of this man, my mentor.

It is not good. In fact, it is atrocious. He failed math, reading, and writing. On the conduct and manners side, the disaster reaches tragic proportions. He spent a lot of time in two places—the hall and the office of the principal. And finally, scrawled across the bottom half of the report card in large block letters are the words "Not Promoted."

As I stood in his office looking at the sad diploma, my seminary professor said, "You know, I think that silly report card has contributed as much to my ministry as any degree I have ever received. I've kept it on my wall ever since I entered the ministry. People come in all broken up, ashamed, disappointed, crying, and then they see that report card and they start to grin. Usually they look at me, half smirking, half questioning, and all I have to say is, 'Yep, it is the truth.'"

It's amazing how fast people start to heal when they sense it's really a possibility to overcome their problems.

We are afflicted in every way, but not crushed.

Perplexed, but not forsaken.

Struck down, but never destroyed.

Real courage involves risking love, rising above adversity, and knowing we have a friend in Jesus who is with us always and in all ways.

The Wizard and Company

As a youngster, and even now as an oldster, I love the movie *The Wizard of Oz* by Frank L. Baum.

It's a fictional story about a great cyclone blowing a child named Dorothy and a dog named Toto from her farm home in Kansas to the Land of Oz. Oz is a strange and beautiful land, but Dorothy, above all, wants to get home to Uncle Henry and Auntie Em. She is told that the only one who can help her return is the Great Wizard of Oz himself. And so, Dorothy sets off down the yellow brick road toward the Emerald City to find him. On her way, she is joined by three remarkable creatures, each of whom has his own favor to ask of the Wizard.

The first is a scarecrow who wants a brain more than anything else.

The second is a tin woodman, who yearns for a heart.

The third is a cowardly lion, who is searching for some courage.

I won't attempt to describe all the hair-raising adventures they have along the way, except to say that they come through them in an unexpected way. Whenever some kind of physical danger confronts them, it is always the cowardly lion who somehow manages to help fight their way out of the problem. Whenever the obstacle is more mental in nature, it is always the scarecrow who figures out a way to get around it. As for the tin woodman, who is journeying in search of a heart, very often he tends to be more of a hindrance than a help. He is so given to being moved by the plight of others that everyone keeps having to rally around him with an oilcan to make sure that his tears of compassion do not rust him. The climax of their tale comes when, upon reaching the Emerald City at last, they make the shattering discovery that the great wizard is not really great at all.

In fact, he's not really even a wizard. He is a helpless little man who tells everyone that he is a humbug and he cannot grant the requests of this little band that has journeyed to him from so far away. But is this really true?

Is he really a humbug, a fake? Is he actually unable to give them what they want?

Here we have to listen closely, for at this point, the fairy tale becomes something more than a fairy tale and the journey down the yellow brick road becomes a journey of more than just a cowardly lion, a tin woodman, and a scarecrow.

For what this helpless little man, who is not a wizard, points out is that each of the pilgrims already have what they have traveled such a distance to find.

Such things are always and everywhere available to each person. But we discover that we've got them only when we put them to use.

Wisdom, courage, and compassion.

These were not gifts awaiting them on a silver platter at the end of the journey. They were the gifts these three strange pilgrims acquired as they journeyed. As they met each day's crisis faithfully. This seems so obvious that we would think that one would have to be a scarecrow not to see it, but that simply isn't so. We want very much what these three wanted. We want to be fully people, to become authentic persons, or "children of God" (John 1:12).

We want this for the same reason that Dorothy's friends wanted this.

Take my heart. It is so much less than my heart should be. Small, weak, shut off behind a wall of tin. And my brain? It's a thing stuffed full of the straw of other people's ideas. And courage? There are times when I don't even have the courage to face myself. I am not the person I would like to be, but someday I will become that woman. When things straighten out. When all the pressures on me let up a little.

Like Dorothy's friends, we expect that what we want will simply happen to us one day by some sort of wizardry. One day, I will have a heart big and strong enough to care about and feel for all the people I sense I ought to be caring about. One day, I will have the wisdom to see clearly what is important in life and begin to establish some intelligent priorities and make some sound decisions. One day, I will have the courage to face the things that scare me now. Even enough courage to face myself.

One day.

Of course, the hard truth is that the day we are thinking about probably will never come if we are expecting it to simply happen to us automatically. True humanity does not come to us all at once, by some kind of wizardry. True humanity is something that is born and grows in us as we meet the challenges day by day. With the tiny amount of courage and compassion and wisdom we happen to have at the moment.

Frederick Buechner, minister and author of *The Wizard of Oz*, to whom I am indebted for some of these ideas, writes this: "A brain. A real brain, is his who knows that he is as much a fool as a scarecrow. Yet manages somehow to do all that a scarecrow can. A heart is his who is willing to let it be broken. And courage is his who, with his scalp cold with fear, yet acts courageously."

What is your heart set on?

St. Paul had his heart set on going to a province of Asia. There he saw his great opportunity. But instead he landed in Troas. He was greatly disappointed. However, it was in this city he saw a vision of a man from Macedonia saying, "Come over and help us." Paul obeyed, and it was this vision and his courage that changed the world (Acts 16:1-10).

George Washington had his heart set on becoming a sailor in the King's Navy. His trunks were packed and his ticket purchased to sail for England, but at the last moment his plans were changed. His disappointment was almost unbearable, but out of this disappointment came a great leader and our first president.

What is your heart set on? Perhaps you lack courage? I'm always humbled by the story about Ludwig Van Beethoven, a poor boy made poorer by a drunkard, improvident father. However, Ludwig was a musical genius. Barely had Ludwig reached maturity, when the greatest tragedy that can befall a musician struck him. He became deaf. The first signs appeared when he was only twenty-nine years old. When his great Ninth Symphony was played for the first time, he was seated upon the stage. He had to be turned around to face the audience to see the applause. But in the isolation and utter detachment which his affliction brought him, Beethoven continued to write music, which he could hear in his mind.

Amazing courage.

Every confirmation class I facilitated in my church ministry would include a visit to the Jewish Community Center to hear the stories of the Holocaust in Germany. These stories weren't about Emerald City. They were stories about raw courage of the Jews and Gentiles who tried to save the Jewish people, oftentimes at the expense of their lives. Many of the survivors of the Holocaust recalled their experiences of hiding in the forest, going to labor camps, and witnessing the atrocities inflicted on the Jewish people.

What does this mean for our everyday living?

There's hardly a week that goes by when we are not touched by some impulse to do a brave thing, given at least a glimpse of a truth to ponder, perhaps to speak, or some nudge of compassion that might be expressed. The kind of human being I am going to be in some future week or month or year depends on the kind of human being I am willing to be, despite every obstacle right here, right now. We need to listen to those nudges, those feelings of trying to change. Listen to the Holy Spirit as we're sent some impulse to do a brave courageous thing, some glimpse of truth that makes our heart feel compassion, some nudge of wisdom that makes us speak up.

The tragic thing is the way we consistently give these tiny inspirations little value or attention. We push them to the back of our minds while we get through what has to be done today. These impulses, nudges, and glimpses seem so insignificant compared to the ambitions, fear, and pleasures that clamor for our attention, our time, our energy.

"After all," we say to ourselves, "with my problems I can't possibly be the one to do or say that. Perhaps someday I really will be brave and wise and truly compassionate and ready to follow such nudges, such impulses, such glimpses, but not now."

What if, what if, that fleeting insight or thought is not just one of those "passing" things? What if it is the very movement of God's Holy Spirit somehow trying to work its way into our hearts? Then those little nudges of wisdom, those impulses, those glimpses of truth, become significant. They are the points where the living God confronts us, trying, as He always has, to embody His love in our daily lives. God doesn't want us sometime in the future in Emerald City. God wants to meet and use and fill us right now.

Yet this isn't Oz. It's earth. And we have no wizard to bring us to our senses, remind us of these nudges, these impulses, these glimpses. We have no wizard who is a humbug.

What we have is a God who became human. A God who will be with us from birth, and through our entire life, even beyond death.

Sometimes people try to turn God's Son, Jesus, into some sort of wizard, a "being" from a different order than us. But the truth is that Jesus is God incarnate and the Holy Spirit is with us always, granting us the power to become what we were meant to be, what we already are. The simple fact of Christ's humanity both judges and gives me a great and shining hope. It judges me because in its light I must recognize a real fact about myself. The reason I am only half a woman, a scarecrow, a tin woodman, a cowardly lion, all in one, lies not in God's failure, but mine. It lies in all the times God sought to bring Jesus the Christ to birth in my life, and somehow I failed to see Him in my life. But I am redeemed because in God's light, I see door after door opening into a new life.

My hope rests not in some impossible transformation far off in the Emerald City, it rests in the small changes I can begin to make right now to help God bring to life a whole new spirit in each one of us.

"But to all who received Him, who believed in His name, He gave power to become Children of God" (John 1:12). I believe that each of us participates in the story of Jesus, and that all of us stand at different points in our lives. No matter where we are or how we feel, what happened in Him, and through Him, can happen to us.

One Step at a Time

Courage builds one step at a time.

Take the Khutu Pyramid. It stands about six miles southwest of Cairo and it is recognized by many as one of the seven wonders of the world. It's height is 455 feet, 2,500,000 cubic meters. It took twenty years to build, involving installing 800 tons of stone every day. Similarly, since it consists of an estimated 2.3 million blocks, completing the building in twenty years would involve moving an average of more than twelve of the blocks into place each hour, day and night.

Nearly five hundred feet tall, covering thirteen acres, it has been calculated that St. Peter's, the Cathedrals of Florence and Milan, Westminster Abbey, and St. Paul's Cathedral could all be grouped inside this single edifice. It is mind boggling that, while constructing the pyramid, the rate of delivery was one stone weighting 2.5 tons every minute. And what makes it even more phenomenal is the fact that it was built more than two thousand years before the birth of Jesus the Christ.

It wasn't done with bulldozers and cranes.

It wasn't done with wheelbarrows and cement.

In fact, it wasn't even done with ropes and pulleys.

It was done over a period of thirty years by thousands of human beings. Many of them lost their lives shoving those huge blocks of stone up a steadily increasing embankment until the final rock was perched at the peak.

Keep that image in mind, as we continue looking at that valorous word: *courage*.

All great things are built one step, one stone, one brick at a time, and often over a considerable period of time. Courage is no exception.

It would be nice if, when the need arises, all of us could simply sign up to take a crash course on developing the mental or moral strength to venture, persevere, and withstand danger, fear, or difficulty. But it doesn't work that way. Courage forced is most often courage compromised. Real courage, the kind that enables us to stand firm in the face of persecution, or confront injustice, or leap boldly into the future, is born over a long period of time.

Few biblical writers understood this any better than St. Paul. The man who was transformed from persecutor to prophet on the Damascus Road, only to end up in a dank Roman prison cell because of his beliefs, offers us some brilliant insights into the building blocks of courage in the third chapter of his Letter to the Church at Philippi:

> Not that I have already attained this or have already reached the goal, but I press onto make it my own, because Christ Jesus has made me his own. Beloved, I do not consider that I have made it my own; but this one thing I do, forgetting what lies behind and straining forward to what lies ahead, I press on toward the goal for the prize of the Heavenly call of God in Christ Jesus. Let those of us then, who are mature, be of the same mind; and if you think differently about anything, this too God will reveal to you. Only, let us hold fast to what we have attained (Philippians 3:12-15).

When I read those words, I get the feeling that Paul wasn't too happy about people who were rigidly positioned. Clearly, he puts a priority on moving forward when he says, "Forgetting what lies behind and straining forward to what lies ahead, I press on toward the goal." The idea is to constantly seek improvement.

I believe if we are to develop a reservoir of courage, it means more than simply being familiar with a cornucopia of theories. It is not enough to know all about Christianity, Buddhism, Judaism, and all the religions. It is not enough to have read the great philosophers and theologians, Tillich, Brunner and Barth. And it is not enough to have sat at the feet of Weatherhead, Kosher, Bonhoeffer, or Graham. Somewhere along the way, we have to take all this information into ourselves and let it influence the way we live.

Some years ago at seminary, I heard Dr. Ernie Campbell, the one-time senior minister of Riverside Church in New York. Campbell was then perceived to be one of the finest preachers in the world. During a casual discussion sitting on the seminary steps leading into the chapel, someone asked him, "How do you come up with fresh sermon material week after week?"

At that, he reached in his coat pocket and produced a small black notebook. "I keep my eyes open all the time for 'life lessons,' and when I see them, I write them down in here. Of course I do a lot of reading, but almost all of my messages are initiated by incidents from this book."

That's what I've been doing since my early hospital chaplain days. I've been "journaling." I believe God is constantly communicating with all of us. The problem is we are too busy or too indifferent, or too into ourselves, to realize what is going on and write it down. During my facilitating our adolescent and adult suicide prevention groups, I asked every participant to write a journal. Not only could they witness new events happening to them, but more often than not, they realized they had grown and matured and became more confident in themselves. But we can't stop there.

God is constantly trying to communicate with us, but we must open our minds and hearts and souls and listen. The bottom line remains: what we care about, we hang on to.

Another step in building courage is soul centering. It is unfortunate that our lives are so cluttered with crises and calamities that we so easily forget how spiritual we naturally are.

St. Paul knew it. He said, "I press on toward the goal for the prize of the heavenly call of God in Christ Jesus."

Real courage isn't a matter of muscle or nerve or daring.

Real courage is a matter of the soul. As St. Augustine observed, "Thou hast made us for Thyself and our hearts are restless until they find their rest in Thee." If I am not at peace right here, in my heart, there is no way I will be able to muster the courage to endure trials or initiate action or challenge injustice. The soul must be at peace in order for the mind and the body to fully function.

I believe that was the intent behind the admonition to "honor the Sabbath day and make it Holy" (Exodus 20:8). We need to take a day to refresh our souls.

Courage finds root in the fertile soil of a soul, attuned to God. We use courage to accept opportunities to stretch and grow. We use courage to express love, affection, friendliness, and vulnerability. We use courage to rise above adversity and grief. We use courage to be honest with ourselves in confronting weakness and illusions. We use courage to quiet fears, doubts, and worries. And we use courage to persevere and honor our deepest values, convictions, and principles. All of these process centers are in our soul.

When I feel myself spiritually indifferent, I always remember a line that was given to me by one of my seminary professors. He challenged us to always be aware that "Jesus is the answer to all our questions." To be centered in our soul, we must all remember "Jesus is the answer to all our questions." When I think I am doing the right thing, I ask myself, "What's in it for the Master?" When I am faced with difficult choices and I wrestle my way to an ultimate answer, I ask myself again, "What's in it for the Master?"

And that brings me to the final building step.

Remember, first we build courage by listening for the Lord's messages throughout our life.

Then we build courage by centering in our soul.

Finally, we build courage by pressing on toward our calling in Christ.

Believers accept no position as final. Every station of life, every incident, every experience, good or bad, is just a step along the way. We are always moving toward the Master. Pressing on toward Jesus's calling often entails "letting go" of things that keep us from being complete.

The old saying is: "Let go, let God."

A major contribution to personal courage is mastering the ability to release problems and people over which we have no control and that can only control us if we insist on clinging to them. The tragedy for most of us is that someone or something controls us.

How often I have personally let that happen. If someone doesn't like you and you've done nothing wrong, you must learn to "leave them to heaven," as the old movie title tells us.

I started this book with an incident that was very hurtful and painful, but I've learned to "leave the situation to God in Heaven" and He will lead me.

St. Paul said, "Brethren, I do not count myself to have apprehended; but one thing I do, forgetting those things which are behind and reaching forward to those things which are ahead, I press toward the goal for the prize of the upward call of God in Christ Jesus" (Philippians 3:13, 14).

The final building step in our foundation for courage is *trust*. When we trust in a God of unconditional love, we learn to endure all trials with a sense of triumph and hope.

We all remember Terry Waite, the renowned man who was taken hostage in the Middle East. For over seven years, he endured pain, humiliation, indignity, torture, and dehumanization at the hands of his captors. Even now, when he looks back at those years, he is amazed at his survival.

What kept him alive? Was it training? No. What about anger, revenge, or hate? No.

Terry said even those things dimmed as the years passed.

What kept him alive was faith. The conviction that there was more to come. In his testimonial dinner several years ago, Terry said these words:

> Faith was really the key to my survival all those years. Faith in my God, faith you were praying for me, faith in my little Chapel, faith it would continue to be open, because attendance was down when I left. Faith that I would some day return. I even thought of the many times our Minister asked for money and how often

I scoffed at why I should tithe my hard earnings, and, oh, when I was held hostage, I would wish I could be right here in Church to give from the bottom of my heart. I learned never to take my Chapel for granted.

Our lives are a continuing journey; and we must all learn to grow at every bend as we make our way. Sometimes we'll be stumbling, but always moving forward toward the finest that is within us, by building one stone at a time, as they built the Khufu Pyramid.

As Miguel de Cervantes said: "They who loose their wealth, looses much. They who loose their friends, looses more; but, they who loose their courage, looses all."

The most courageous of all are those who live through their suffering, accepting it, knowing that God is with them, granting them courage, through His abiding love.

Stained Glass Two Keys

LIVING IN THE REALM OF GRAY

Often I've been asked, "What do you think about the gays?"

As I'm from a generation of people who thought gay was happy and gay, I wasn't sure what they meant, until I met Paulette. Paulette was a brilliant caring nurse who was willing to help anyone and she could've been an excellent doctor. I knew Paulette through the oncology unit and called upon her many times.

One day she asked to make an appointment with me. "Of course," I responded as we met in my office.

"I'm having trouble with my soul mate," she exclaimed.

"Tell me what's happening?" I asked.

"We're angry at each other all the time."

And the conversation continued until at last I said, "What is he doing to help the situation?"

"He?" queried Paulette." My soul mate is a *she.*"

Oh, I see, and I didn't.

After trying to guide Paulette as I would a heterosexual couple, I realized the lesbian couple was just like a male-female couple. Same problems, same caring, same love, same jealousies, same, same, same.

So, I asked myself, *What's wrong with me? You've known Paulette as a wonderfully caring nurse. Why would you even think of judging her as a lesbian? She's a person, not a sex object.*

Thus ends my story.

From that time on, I've learned not to judge someone by their sexual orientation.

However, my straight-arrowed husband made a poignant observation. "If God wanted the homosexual people to partner together, we'd only have one generation of people on earth."

End of his story.

The truth of the matter is, we all live in a realm of gray. Life isn't black or white, but a variety of gray.

It's a long way from the mountaintop to the valley, and somewhere in between, what was once black and white has become authentic gray. Nearly four thousand years have passed since Moses climbed Mount Sinai to receive the Ten Commandments and, in the interim, what was etched in stone is now scratched in sand (Exodus 20:1-17).

The people of God were told to place no other God before Yahweh, but they never heard of trust funds, or "who's who" in the world. The people of God were instructed not to take the name of the Lord in vain, but they didn't know about it, not even a silent prayer in schools. The people of God were told to keep one day of the week holy from end to end, but they had no idea what it is like when the service of worship runs fifteen minutes too long, or their daughter had a soccer game, or their son had a swim meet on Sundays.

The people of God were told not to murder but nobody told them what to do about abortion or the death penalty. And stealing? Not surprisingly it was dubbed improper, unless, of course, one nation conquers another, or there are riots in the streets, then it's only to take whatever you want. So, really, it should be no surprise that what was so clear at the foot of Mount Sinai is so fuzzy on the south side of Chicago or the communities in Florida.

If we know anything, we know how experience changes perspectives. And perspective establishes perception, and perception is the essence of integrity. It's a nebulous world of gray out there. The land between absolutes where circumstances and consequences shape the course of our action. It is that space between right and wrong, black and white, good and evil, where, like it or not, most of us live.

Good and evil, and, in between, gray.

From the Gospel of Mark, we see Jesus setting out on a journey, when a bold young man literally ran up to catch up with Him. "Good teacher," he pleaded. "What must I do to inherit eternal life?" (Mark 10:17, 18).

So Jesus said to him, "Why do you call me good? No one is good but One, that is, God." I've never heard words offer a better perspective on the march of history than those: No one is Good but One, that is God.

It is the weakness of the historical process that tends to categorize its subjects into columns of villains and heroes, bad and good. Still, time has a way of tempering all this, blending the good with the bad, resulting in an authentic gray that is undoubtedly more accurate than extreme. Isn't it amazing how people believe everything they read in the press? If anyone does one thing wrong, they are doomed forever by their peers, the judges. There are many people who come to mind: The late Penn State coach, Joe Patterno. After the Sandusky incident, the opinion was that Joe was a bad guy. But then, very few people saw Joe walking the halls of hospitals or helping assist other players. And what about the legacy of Richard Nixon? He might be the most controversial American. But that same person built a bridge to China and executed an excellent foreign policy for our country.

Good or bad?

It is the misfortune of public people that their persona is forever open to judgment. When they make an error, it's criticism and instant judgment. And all along the truth lingers in the center.

Neither good nor bad, all are just like you and me: Gray.

Although most of us would like to be good, the simple truth remains, none of us are.

After Jesus told his questioner in Mark that: "No one is good except God alone" (Mark 10:18), then Jesus prompted him in the next verse, "You know the Ten Commandments, Do not murder, do not commit adultery, do not steal." And the young man interrupted, "Jesus, teacher, I have kept all these things from my youth up" (Mark 10:19).

This young man really knew his Bible teaching. Nevertheless, when he assured the Lord he had kept the Commandments, the Master, filled with understanding and compassion for one who worked so hard to be good, said, "One thing you lack, go and sell all your possessions, take up your cross and follow me" (Mark 10:21).

Isn't that the way it always is? Just when we think we have it all together, someone highlights a nearly impossible goal. This business of following Christ is more complicated than strict behavior. It's not just a matter of what we do not. Murder, steal, commit adultery, it's equally a matter of what we do. Faith is never a matter of what we cannot do, it's always a matter of what we can do. Yes, that young man, responding to Jesus, had covered one end of the virtuous spectrum, he had observed the Commandments. Nothing more was needed. He was oblivious to the call of service. Goodness, faith, virtue are all connected with the doing.

One philosopher put it this way: "Wisdom is knowing what to do next; virtue is doing it."

Undoubtedly, it was this awareness that caused St. Paul to confess to the Romans.

> But now, it is no longer I who do it, but sin that dwells in me. I know that nothing good dwells in me. For the good that I will to do, I do not do; but the evil I will not to do, that I practice. Now if I do what I will not to do, it is no longer I who do it, but sin that dwells in me. I find then a law, that evil is present with me, the one who wills to do good., that is in my flesh for the wishing is present in me; but the doing of good is not, for the good that I wish, I do not do; but I practice the very evil that I do not wish. For I delight in the law of God according to the inward man. But I see another law in my members, warring against the law of my mind and bringing me into captivity to the law of sin which is in my members. O wretched man that I am! Who will deliver me from this body of death? I thank God-through Jesus Christ our Lord! So then, with the mind I myself serve the law of God, but with the flesh the law of sin. (Rom 7:17-25)

Good? No one is good but God alone.
In between stands the realm of gray.

One of my seminary professors said, "When all is said and done, when I'm standing face to face with my Maker, I'll be asked only two questions: First, 'What did you do with what I gave you?' Second, 'For whom did you do it?'"

Martin Buyer, the noted Jewish philosopher, built a whole system of thought around the idea that all of us will one day be measured by our ability to maintain the "I-Thou" relationship, not only with God, but with our fellow human beings.

Ultimately, our lives will not be measured by awards received, fortunes amassed, or achievements recorded. Rather, we will be judged by the manner in which we have related to God through other human beings.

In the Gospel of Matthew, Jesus once again encounters those lawyers, Sadducees and the Pharisees, and our Lord eradicated his political opposition by telling the followers of Herod to "render unto Caesar that which is Caesar's and to God the things that are God's" (Matthew 22:21b). Later, Jesus is confronted by the best trial lawyers the Pharisees can find. After smirking at the adoration with which the crowds are admiring the Master, the lawyer asked a double-edged question, "Teacher, what is the greatest commandment in the Law?" (Matthew 22:36).

It's a wonderful trap.

If Jesus singles out a commandment, He will be accused of compromising all the others. One the other hand, if He does not, he will be chastised for the lack of knowledge.

> Jesus said to him, "You shall love the Lord your God with all your heart, with all your soul, and with all your mind. This is the first and great commandment. And the second is like it: You shall love your neighbor as yourself. On these two commandments hand all the Law and the Prophets." (Mt 22:37-40)

In other words, our highest calling is to love God, and prove it by the way we relate to each other.

Ella Wheeler Wilcox penned the lines that help our choice:

Two Kinds of People

There are two kinds of people on earth today,
Just two kinds of people, no more I say.
Not the good or the bad, for 'tis well understood
That the good are half bad, and the bad are half good.
No, the two kinds of people on earth, I mean,
Are the people who lift, and the people who lean."

Which are we? The lifters or learners?

Do we seek to take as much as we can, leaning on everyone and everything around us, expecting the world to support our weight and bend to keep us happy? Or are we among those rare characters who have learned living is giving, who accept each day as a fresh opportunity to help others, as much as our physical bodies allow us to do.

The Old Testament prophet Micah makes the challenge clearer when he says, "God has told you what is good. To do justice; to love kindness and to walk humbly with God" (Micah 6:8).

Sometimes, in order to do that, we have to overcome terrible events in our past, we have to rise above bad memories, or blot out the pain of a bankruptcy or divorce or death or not-so-nice family members. Still, the promise of God is to help us do exactly that.

There are many true stories of what God does with our lives.

It was a snowy December evening and Adie didn't want to be where he was. Sure, his sister had asked him to stick around for her sixteenth birthday party. But the rest of the kids were all teenagers, and Adie was only twelve. He really didn't fit in. So he stood staring blankly out the living room window. One of the boys who had been away at school spotted him.

"Hey Adie", he shouted. "I learned the manual of arms last semester. I really learned how to arm a gun and disarm, and how to twirl it. Would you like to see how to do it? Do you have a gun or rifle?"

Adie knew there was an old .22 rifle in the hall closet, so he fetched it for his friend. Sure enough, the guy knew the manual of arms. In fact, he taught several parts of it to Adie. And, so it was while he was twirling that old rifle that Adie accidentally pulled the trigger. The gun was loaded and fifteen-year-old Ruth Merwin never knew what hit her.

She fell to the library floor, dead. Adie dropped the rifle, stared unbelieving at the dead friend of his sister. Although the death was appropriately rendered an accident, it would haunt Adie for the rest of his life. Self doubt and feelings of unworthiness would plague him.

Feelings that would plague him, but not destroy him.

Adie would go on to graduate from Northwestern University and practice law in Illinois. He would serve his country in the field of foreign economics, become an Assistant Secretary of State and assume the highest office of one of the largest states in the union.

Then, in 1952, he would receive an honor far beyond imagination, yet, not so far removed from that snowy December evening forty years earlier, for upon his nomination for the Office of President of the United States, Adali Stevenson would respond: "I am honored to accept this nomination. I've tried to grow and not allow my most difficult hard circumstances to control my life."

Living with the gray, is learning to overcome the valleys even as we conquer the mountains of problems.

Good?

"No one is good, but One, that is God" (Mark 10:18).

Fortunate
We grasp for something
yet not knowing why
we stumble at times
and wish we could cry
the depths of our pains
are sometimes not met
as life passes by
we too soon forget
the gift of a child

the gift of each breath
the knowledge of God
who conquers all death
so while we await
the fullness of time
and hope for a day
when evil turns kind
help us to find peace
in this world of sin
show us the way to
let Christ enter in.

(WHS)

Living with Criticism

For ten years I taught medical ethics for the interns in Dr. Janet Kramer's program at the Delaware division of the WMC. It was a challenging weekly event, with many differing opinions. I always started out each time together with the remarks: "It's okay to have differing views. When we debate our opinions, one point I want to make clear, we're not attacking the other person, but their theorem. Everyone has a right to their theory, each person will present their supposition, and we'll debate together."

I used the same approach when I taught medical ethics at Eastern College in St. David's Pennsylvania for six years. And teaching at Washington College, Chestertown, Maryland, as an adjunct professor for five years.

However, we need to be prepared to accept criticism. Most of us find criticism an intolerable and stressful experience. No one can go through life without being criticized. Parents stand up to criticism from their children. And children have to live most of their lives under criticism from their parents. Wives and husbands hear criticism from each other. Business people, politicians, preachers, all come in for their share. The public is restless. We have grown used to change through confrontation.

What responses can we make to being criticized?

We must realize criticism comes regardless so we must learn to expect it. Whenever the self-centeredness and self-interest that are so much a part of human nature appear in ourselves and others, criticism will come our way.

Jesus was criticized, and by responsible religious intelligent people. In fact, he was seldom spared criticism. But He learned to live with it.

When Sir John Simon served as Britain's Chancellor, there hung on his wall this motto: "To escape criticism, say nothing, do nothing, be nothing." Anyone given a leadership role to fill, be it a coach, referee, commission chair, nurse, teacher, minister, any position, simply must come to term with inevitable criticism, or that person cannot survive.

It may help to remember that much of criticism is positional, not personal. Even when it comes leaded with personal invective, it may not be personal. Anyone occupying your position would catch it. Leader roles are vulnerable. The higher you climb, the more attractive a target you present.

Joseph Addison once wrote, "There is no defense against reproach, except obscurity."

When we're being criticized we must also learn to listen to the criticism.

Unlike Jesus, we are fallible. Most of us have a tendency to see one-half of the truth at a time. The other half of the truth may need to be supplied by our critics.

The story is told of Abe Lincoln that Edward M. Stanton, his Secretary of War, called him a fool in his absence. The report reached Lincoln, who remarked to one of his associates, "Did Stanton call me a fool?" When he was told that this was the case, Lincoln replied, "Stanton is a wise man. If he said I am a fool then I had better look into the matter."

We must learn to listen to criticism.

Over sixty-two years ago, when I fell in love with my husband, I decided I should learn a little more about architecture since that was my beloved's hopeful career. So, at Ohio State University, one of the elective courses I signed up for was "Art and Architecture." I really struggled the entire semester to get a good grade. I never worked so hard!

And at the end of the semester, my professor called me into his office and said "Marlene, I have some good news and bad news for you. The good news is I am giving you an A. The bad news is I hope this doesn't encourage you."

So, when we're facing criticism, let's listen to it. I never entered the field of art or architecture, because I really have no talent, nor could years of study provide me the ability to have that talent.

Another way of accepting criticism is sometimes we need to ignore it. And this word comes after the admonition to "listen to it." When you have squeezed the lemon and extracted all the juice from it, don't keep the rind. It's a mistake to brood too long over other people's opinions. Ian Keith Falconer, missionary to the Arab world, was strengthened by his family's motto: "They say, what do they say? Let them say." It's a mistake to try to please everybody. If you do, you will never have a policy of your own. You will be a reactor, not an actor. A pacifier, not an initiator.

Joseph Lister, father of antiseptic surgery, was ridiculed by his fellow surgeons, scorned, even ostracized. But he was one hundred percent correct on his germ theory. Every hospital in our country is a tribute to his insight. How grateful we are that he was willing to stick to his business and ignore his critics.

Nehemiah, when he rebuilt the wall of Jerusalem, after the exile, was invited by his critics to come down from the wall and fight with them.

> Now it happened, when Sanballat, Tobiah, Geshem the Arab, and the rest of our enemies heard that I had rebuilt the wall and that there were no breaks left in it(though at that time I had not hung the doors in the gates), that Sanballat and Geshem sent to me, saying, "Come, let us meet together in one of the villages in the plain of Ono." But they thought to do me harm. (Neh 6:1-2)

But Nehemiah replied, "So I sent messengers to them, saying 'I am doing a great work, so that I cannot come down. Why should the work cease while I leave it and go down to you?'" (Nehemiah 6:3). Sometimes we must take our stand and ignore criticism.

However, it is easy to be confused by questions, such as:

> What is expedient?
> What is acceptable to the crowd?
> What will promote the right "image"?
> What will get me ahead?

Beyond these questions are other questions of a higher order:

> What is true?
> What is right?
> Who are we serving, God or ourselves?
> What is consistent with the God we learn to know in Jesus
>   Christ?

We need to settle these basic questions first to help guide us to appropriate answers. In this period of rapid change, in government, businesses, medicine education, as well as in the church, we could choose one of two ways to be guided in making these decisions.

We could try to be everything to everybody. The purpose and goal in doing this would be to insulate ourselves against the winds of change and hope that everything will come out all right. Sometimes called "head-in-sand disease," this policy itself questions nothing, it simply lives out the past, hopes the future will take care of itself, and builds dikes against the pressures of the present. This policy usually leads to lack of growth and character.

The other way is harder but more promising. Be willing to examine everything, not frantically, nor faddishly, or fearfully, but patiently. This way believes that truth cannot be harmed by scrutiny. It believes that God has a purpose for this present time, as well as for past ages. It believes that not all the patterns of the past need to be retained, but that there is a present leading of God's spirit, which can be discovered through openness, through prayer, through discussion and dialogue. This way could lead to a fuller life.

When we have to face the nitty grittyness of life and the critics, we could be a gift to one another. In a community of caring people, we can face our failures and successes and hear the glad news of God's message.

"Through the Lord's mercies we are not consumed, because His compassions fail not. They are new every morning, great is Your faithfulness" (Lamentations 3:22,23).

And from the Gospel, Jesus said: "Come to Me, all you who labor and are heavy laden and I will give you rest. Take My yoke upon you and learn from Me, for I am gentle and lowly in heart, and you will find rest for your souls. For My yoke is easy and My burden is light" (Matthew 11:28-30).

Stained Glass Descending Dove

Good and Evil

I don't know how many times people have asked me if I think the Devil is alive and well.

I certainly do!

Have you ever been tempted? One of my seminary professors said that the biggest failure of Christians is that they don't make friends with the shadowy side of themselves.

Facing this fact, is our hope of advancing good and keeping evil in check. Now that's hard work. My seminary professor was asked by our class where the Garden of Eden was. His answer was his home address. We all laughed, but the good professor didn't. "What do you mean?" we inquired. He went on to tell of the day he stole some money from his mother's purse, bought some candy, came home guilt ridden, and hid in the closet. Why was that the Garden of Eden for him? "Because," he said, "that was the place that I discovered my duplicity."

The Garden story is ours too.

We are capable of great good and great evil at every turn of life. We are inherently and intrinsically imperfect so any relationship we enter into, voluntarily or involuntarily, family or otherwise, will necessarily be flawed. Where is our help? Once again to the biblical Scriptures.

We all are taught to read the Psalms from the Old Testament. Did you know most of those Psalms are assigned to the hand of an Old Testament hero: David? David committed acts of murder and adultery. But David, the Psalmist, asked God for forgiveness in accepting the blame, and shouldered the consequences.

We all need to understand the consequences of wrong acts. And we must accept our blame and pay the consequences as we ask God for forgiveness.

Further looking into the Bible, and understanding these important points, there are two forty-day stories.

Noah is a story about bad things happening to bad people and good things happening to good people. And, most importantly, Noah's response is one of total faith in God. This story is found in Genesis.

> Then the Lord said to Noah, Come into the ark, you and all your household, because I have seen that you are righteous before Me in this generation. "You shall take with you seven each of every clean animal, a male and his females; two each of animals that are unclean, a male and his female; also seven each of birds of the air, male and female, to keep the species alive on the face of all the earth. For after seven more days I will cause it to rain on the earth forty days and forty nights, and I will destroy from the face of the earth all living things that I have made." And Noah did according to all that the Lord commanded him. (Gen 7:1-5)

The second story is about Jesus, whose life is the story of bad things happening to the best of the best people. The Jesus story is likewise one of good people doing the worst of things. The very people that wave branches of honor on Palm Sunday will be the same ones shouting for his crucifixion and death just five days later.

And Pilate said to them again, "What do you want me to do with Him whom you call the King of the Jews?" So they cried out again, "Crucify Him!" Then Pilate said to them, "Why, what evil has He done?" And they cried out more exceedingly, "Crucify Him!" (Mark 15:12-14).

All life stories. And we've all seen evil betrayal in our lives too, haven't we?

I always look at Jesus to see how he handles this painful duplicity of Himself. Jesus is baptized and immediately is lead into the desert to be tempted.

Know this: the place of high spiritual experience and excitement is the exact place of our greatest pain and temptation. Strong light makes strong shadows. The more you are in the limelight, the stronger the shadows become. That is why we must make friends with our shadow side.

In the story of the temptation of Jesus found in Matthew, the devil prepares Jesus for a public ministry by placing before Him every temptation that he will face among the people.

> Then the devil took Him up into the holy city, set Him on the pinnacle of the temple, and said to Him, "If You are the Son of God, throw Yourself down. For it is written: He shall give His angels charge concerning you, and In their hands they shall bear you up, Lest you dash your foot against a stone." Jesus said to him, "It is written again, You shall not tempt the Lord your God." Again, the devil took Him up on an exceedingly high mountain and showed Him all the kingdoms of the world and their glory. And he said to Jesus, "All these things I will give You if You will fall down and worship me." Then Jesus said to him "Away with you, Satan! For it is written, You shall worship the Lord your God and Him only you shall serve." Then the devil left Him and behold, angels came and ministered unto Him. (Mt 4:5-11)

Someone said that two things are painful—getting what you want, and not getting what you want. Jesus being tempted is a bigger word than we might think. It includes the idea of "testing." This kind of temptation, or testing, is not designed to break us down, but to build us up. It's not designed to make us weak, but to make us strong. It's not just a testimony to our human vulnerability, our evil, but also to our good, our glory.

Even being tempted to do wrong is not in itself wrong.

Martin Luther once said, "You can't help the birds flying over your head, but you don't have to let them build nests in your hair."

You know what Mark Twain said about temptation? "It is easier to stay out than to get out."

There are some circumstances of Jesus temptation worth noting.

First it takes place in the wilderness, in the desert, where Jesus is alone for a prolonged period of time. Yet, it is also in the wilderness where almost every movement of spiritual renewal in the Bible begins. Self mastery had to be won first, and then powers of the spirit.

For you and me, the wilderness may be something other than a desert.

It may be a prolonged hospital stay.

It may be a relationship at home that is painful.

It may be helping a family member or friend through rehab.

It could be many things. It is when we feel most alone, that the test comes.

Secondly, note that Jesus has just experienced an emotional peak.

At Jesus's baptism, the spirit has descended upon him, conferring powers that are truly amazing. Jesus is aware of those powers.

The Father's affirming voice has been heard. "You are my Beloved Son" (Matthew 3:17).

It is with us, as it was with Jesus. After a moment of high elation, a moment of great success, an emotional high, the test comes. Remember: the place of high spiritual experience and excitement is the exact place of our greatest pain and temptation.

The shadow is not far from the light. Part of our shadow side is when we lack discernment. That is recognizing the difference between good and evil. We know that discernment means to recognize the difference between one thing and another. Well, discernment has been identified as one of the highest of spiritual gifts.

Here's a fictional story about a Protestant minister anonymously going to the racetrack, that might help our search on the word *discernment*.

The Protestant minister was intrigued by a Catholic priest who would pray over the horses, and he would win. The minister decided to start betting. The priest would pray, the horse would win. It was unbelievable. Then the priest prayed over one horse for the final race. The Protestant minister bet all on that horse. The bell sounded, the horse darted out of the gate and fell dead in his tracks. The Protestant approached the priest and complained about the pattern of praying and winning being broken. The priest looked at the Protestant and said, "The problem with you Protestants is that you don't know the difference between a simple blessings and final rites."

Sometimes we don't discern well. We simply don't perceive something as "simple blessings and final rites." In the very avoidance of tears and pain, we create an evil that is greater than facing our pain would have been in the first place. There is pain in the unexamined life. We are taught and learn well that success and entitlements are more important than anything. However, the spiritual life informs us that we can not know real life until we give up on achieving and give in to God's inexhaustible love.

This is a difficult concept to accept.

Discipline, obedience, and salvation are the high roads to spiritual completeness, not achievement or success, as much of our culture dictates.

Then what is the purpose of life?

Rick Warren, writer of *Purpose-Driven Life*, answers the question "What is the purpose of life?" this way:

> In a nutshell, life is preparation for eternity. We were made by God and for God, and until you figure that out, life isn't going to make sense. I used to think life was hills and valleys, you go through a dark valley, then to the top of a hill. But I don't believe that anymore. I believe that it's like two rails on a railroad track, and at all times you have something good and something evil in your life. You can focus on your purposes or you can focus on your problems. If you focus on your problems, you're going into self centeredness. 'My problems, my pain', but the best way to get rid of pain, is to focus off…yourselves and onto God and helping others.

Grace is standing by each other until God gives what only God can give.

Sometimes, the wait is long.

Walter Wangerin told the story of his son stealing comic books in his early adolescence. They thought the problem was cleared up only to find their son doing the same thing while on summer vacation. The ultimatum came. Quit or get a spanking.

Their son did it again. The showdown came.

The parents believed in paying the consequences if there is a wrongdoing.

So his dad, Walter, went into the room and gave the traditional parent speech that goes, "This is going to hurt me more than it will you." After giving that speech, Walter asked his son to wait a minute because he needed to step out of the room.

In the hallway, the exasperated Walter cried over the fact that his son just would not "get it." After containing himself, Walter went back into the room and delivered The Punishment.

Years later, Mom was driving with their son and she recalled the old days when "your dad had to spank you for stealing."

They both laughed. Then his mother said, "That spanking finally changed you, didn't it?

"Oh no," said their son. "What changed me was when I heard Dad cry in the hallway."

What is the message of Noah's Ark? The drops on the roof of Noah's Ark were not rain, but the tears of God in pain over the evil, rebellious, poor choices humankind made.

But then, the good.

> And God said: "This is the sign of the covenant which I make between Me and you, and every living creature that is with you, for perpetual generations: I set My rainbow in the cloud and it shall be for the sign of the covenant between Me and the earth. It shall be, when I bring a cloud over the earth, that the rainbow shall be seen in the cloud; and I will remember My covenant which is between Me and you and every living creature of all flesh; the waters shall never again become a flood to destroy all flesh." (Gen 9:12-15)

And Noah's Ark-Rainbow came to proclaim, no matter how far we wander, no matter how long we take, God will greet us only with inexhaustible love.

The love finally persuades everyone bent toward evil into something good.

The Ten Commandments: God's Platform

When I was the minister at my church, I recall one Sunday over two thousand ministers across America stood up at their pulpits and did what federal law says they can't do: Tell their congregations how to vote. The reason we were "encouraged" to tell our parishioners to vote was a campaign sponsored by a special interest group challenging the restrictions on "pulpit politicking." The group hoped to provoke a legal battle that would overturn the law's prohibition on candidate endorsements from tax-exempt nonprofits.

All these years of my preaching as a United Methodist minister, we were restricted from endorsing any candidate from the pulpit, because we could lose the Methodist's not-for-profit status. It's really too bad, because I think we ministers have a lot to say about world events, and where God is in the process.

So, we live with good and evil, in the shade of gray.

I heard a fictitious story about a senator whose soul went to heaven and was met by St. Peter at the entrance.

"Welcome to heaven", said St. Peter. "Before you settle in, it seems there is a problem. We seldom see a high official around these parts, you see, so we're not sure what to do with you."

"No problem, just let me in," said the senator.

"Well, I'd like to, but I have orders from higher up. What we'll do is have you spend one day in hell and one in heaven. Then you can choose where to spend eternity."

"Really, I've made up my mind. I want to be in heaven," replied the senator.

"I'm sorry, but we have our rules." And with that, St. Peter escorted him to the elevator, and went down, down, down to hell.

When the doors opened, he found himself in the middle of a green golf course. In the distance was a clubhouse and standing in front of it were all his friends and other politicians who had worked with him. Everyone was happy and in evening dress. They ran to greet him, shook his hand, and reminisced about the good times they had while getting rich at the expense of the people. They played a friendly game of golf, and then dined on lobster, caviar, and champagne. Also present was the Devil, who really was a friendly guy, who had a good time dancing and telling jokes. They were having such a good time that before he realized it, it was time to go. Everyone gave him a hearty farewell and waved while the elevator rose.

The elevator went up, up and up, and the door reopened in heaven where St. Peter was waiting. "Now it's time to visit heaven," St Peter said. So, twenty-four hours passed with the senator joining a group of contented souls moving from cloud to cloud, playing the harp and singing. They had a good time and, before he realized it, the twenty-four hours had gone by and St. Peter returned.

"Well then, you've spent a day in hell and another in heaven. Now, choose your eternity."

The senator reflected for a moment, then he answered, "Well, I would never have said it before, I mean, heaven has been delightful, but I think I would be better off in hell."

So, St. Peter escorted him to the elevator and he went down, down, down to hell. The doors of the elevator opened and he found himself in the middle of a barren land covered with garbage. He saw all his friends dressed in rags picking up the trash, and putting it in black bags as more trash fell from above. The Devil came over to him and put him arm around his shoulder.

"I don't understand," stammered the senator. "Yesterday I was here and there was a golf course, and a clubhouse, and we ate lobster and caviar, drank champagne, danced and had a great time. Now there's just a wasteland full of garbage and my friends look terrible. What happened?"

The Devil looked at him, smiled, and said. "Yesterday we were campaigning, today you voted!"

So it goes with politics and religion, good and evil.

During the last election, an evening television host, David Letterman, produced a skit interpreting of The Old Testament Scripture of The Ten Commandments. A platform committee of a political party is shown racking their brains to come up with a program that would have maximum appeal to all the voters. Every segment of the voting public is represented sitting around a table in some smoke-filled room.

At this point, there bursts into the room a cigar-smoking representative of an old man, evidentially the candidate of the party, holding high a folder containing the candidate's authoritative statement about the kind of platform they ought to come up with. "It has," he says with enthusiasm, "a rather catchy title. It is called The Ten Commandments."

Well, you can imagine how the skit develops. As the candidate runs through The Ten Commandments, each one invokes a louder groan or a protest from around the table. For example, "Honor your father and your mother." Well, there goes the under-thirty vote. "You shall not commit adultery." Well, there goes the yuppie votes, and so on.

The obvious consensus in the group is that the program will doom the party at the polls.

What can they do?

One of them responds, "Maybe we can call them the ten suggestions."

Who should I vote for? I have never endorsed any candidate from the pulpit.

But I can interpret God's word. The Ten Commandments.

Do you know in our country alone there are over fifteen million laws, rules, and regulations, all trying to enforce the original Ten Commandments? These Commandments are the earliest biblical summary of God's program for human community living, found in the book of Exodus chapter 20 verses 1 to 18.

They describe a way of life that God intends to lead His people into a way of life that will be a blessing to them and the succeeding generations. They are God's promises.

The deliverance of the people of Israel from bondage only began with the dramatic events of their escape from the eternal domination of the Pharaoh.

The Ten Commandments are God's plan for leading them out of the eternal bondage of false gods, corrupt thoughts, and perverted relationships, into the glorious inner freedom of Godly authentic people. But here, at this point, the comparison with the Democratic or Republican Party platform stops. These are not "suggestions," but commandments. We can vote against them, to be sure, but they still stand. This is God's program, and unlike many candidates for public office, God keeps His promises.

There are two parts of God's platform.

Part one are the four commandments. They have to do with our relationship to God.

Part two of God's platform are the last six commandments that have to do with our relationship with our neighbors.

Part one: the four commandments. "First, "ye shall have no other Gods before me" (Exodus 20:3).

Our God is whatever we believe in, whatever we value above everything else. Whatever we want to have run our life. That is our God. But God says in his second commandment:

> Thou shall not make for yourself any carved image, or any likeness of anything that is in heaven above, or that is in the earth beneath, or that is in the water under the earth. You shall not bow down to them nor serve them. For I, the Lord your God, am a jealous God, visiting the iniquity of the father son the children to the third and fourth generations of those who hate Me, but showing mercy to thousands, to those who love Me and keep My commandments. (Ex 20:4, 5, 6)

When I look at this, I am convinced that idolatry is far from a dead issue. In fact, idolatry is our number one personal, national, and world problem.

What do we put first? Our career, our happiness. Me, me, me.

These are only a few of the things that we human beings continue to take with that ultimate seriousness, which this commandment says should be reserved for Almighty God alone.

The third commandment in God's platform: "You shall not take the name of the Lord your God in vain, for the Lord will not hold him guiltless who takes His name in vain" (Exodus 20:7).

I was driving by another church in another city and saw a sign outside the church on their billboard that said, "Did you know that God's last name isn't 'dammit'? Find out more about God: come to church this Sunday. Don't take the Lord's name in vain."

How often have we all broken this commandment, especially on the golf course? I'm frequently asked to give an invocation at a golfing event. One of my prayers is: "We know that you're alive and well in our hearts, minds, and souls, as we often hear your name as we're playing our game of golf."

The fourth commandment:

> Remember the Sabbath day, to keep it holy. Six days you shall labor and do all your work: you, nor your son, nor your daughter, nor your manservant, nor your maidservant, nor your cattle, nor your stranger who is within your gates. For in six days the Lord made the heavens and the earth, the sea, and all that is in them, and rested the seventh day. Therefore the Lord blessed the Sabbath day and hallowed it. (Ex 20:8-11)

This commandment about keeping the Sabbath holy is far from being the outdated commandment that I always thought it was. What days of the week, and the way in which we worship, are secondary matters. But the idea, the actual activity, is not secondary, not if we really wish to put God first.

If we really do belong to God, then we must set aside significant time in our schedules to stop everything else and turn to our Creator to refresh our minds on what God's point of view is. To look at our lives and see what God wants us to do for others. Just reflect for a moment on your own weekly schedule. I know I have and try to carve out time to keep holy for God. Whenever I think of this commandment, I try and watch for idolatry and the worship of phony images, and allow time for God to get through. The problem of praying only in times of crisis is that people feel like phonies. In order to overcome feeling like a phony, each morning when you rise, say, "Thank you, God, for another day," even if the day isn't going very well.

God promises to be with us, working with us, if we will let God guide us to use our God-given gifts. If you take me seriously, then you must take your neighbor seriously.

These last six commandments are a place to start thinking about how God calls us to live as women and men with each other.

"Honor your father and mother, that your days may be long upon the land which the Lord your God is giving you" (Exodus 20:12), commandment number five.

The fascinating word in this platform is the word *honor*. I notice it doesn't say, "agree with," or even "like," but "honor." It is respect and caring for our parents as persons.

So many of the ways in which we deal with our elders, from outright rebellion and rejection on one hand, to giving in or paternalism on the other, fail at this important point. Because doing whatever we want, without honoring our parents, are ways that say we have written them off as persons who can understand, can grow, and contribute to our well-being.

Commandment number six: "You shall not murder" (Exodus 20:13).

God loves and values all human beings from the time of conception to the time of death. The sanctity of life in our society has lessened in these past years. You can see it in the moral fabric and ethics we have adopted. Lifestyles are not what they used to be. And the ethical questions of abortion, infanticide, genetic engineering, rationing medicine, and doctor-assisted suicide have completely changed. Now, rather than respecting all forms of life, we have changed our rhetoric and our beliefs. In our society, we are even writing legislation concerning these life and death issues. Should we allow people to die, even hasten their demise, if they are less than perfect?

One legislator has introduced a bill on infanticide that is allowing babies to die. The legislation says, "Mongoloids should be allowed to die, as well as defective infants with malformations, congenital heart disease, and with brain defects." Right now in our country, there are more laws defending the bald eagle and other animals than there are for human beings. In the United States there are over one hundred bills trying to define death. Notice God's commandment does not say, "Thou shalt kill the imperfect, the retarded, the handicapped, the emotionally distressed, or those who want a doctor to assist them in their death."

No. God loves each of us: without exception!

"You shall not murder."

Commandment number seven: "You shall not commit adultery" (Exodus 20:14).

How we Christians have managed to portray God as anti-sex, I am not sure. Because sex, according to the Bible, is God's creation and one of the central ways in which God has made it possible for us to express our love. It is because of this, and not because God is opposed to sex, that God takes adultery so seriously. Adultery is taking what was meant to be used as a sacrament or expression of faithful love and using it for other means, such as selling products, magazines, movies, or for that matter, selling ourselves for pleasure, for profit, for power, for convenience of another person.

God does not approve of this. Maybe someday we will realize that God feels this way, not because Our Lord is against sex, but because God wants us to find meaningful joy and faithfulness with one another.

Commandment number eight: "You shall not steal" (Exodus 20:15). Now there is one that most of us could pass over quickly. For those who think they are exempt from this commandment, there are a few little expressions that we use now and then that could stand some examination. For instance, "Sure everyone else is doing it," "They wont miss this one," "They have deep pockets," "They can afford it," "Business is business," "Pay it back next week." Well, you can supply your own favorite expression or rationalization.

Commandment number nine: "You shall not bear false witness against your neighbor" (Exodus 20:16). Basically, false witness means gossip. You've heard the saying "Gossip; office gossip; party gossip; PTA gossip; Gossip gossip. It makes headlines, and heartaches. Before you repeat a story, ask yourself if it is true; Is it fair? Is it Necessary? If not. forget it!"

Commandment number ten: "You shall not covet your neighbor's house; you shall not covet your neighbor's wife, nor his manservant, nor his maidservant, nor his ox, nor his donkey, nor anything that is your neighbor's" (Exodus 20:17).

Now this one sounds quaint, doesn't it? Manservants, maidservants and ox, and yet, though we have developed slightly more sophisticated forms of coveting, longing to keep up with the Joneses is still a problem that afflicts us far more than we realize. Coveting is an obnoxious insect that gnaws incessantly at the very roots of the joys of our life. Even as we covet the Jones's good fortune, we are strangely unable to appreciate what God has already given us, including the Joneses. I wonder how many marriages are wrecked because husband or wife, or both, keep comparing each other with an illusionary Mr. and Mrs. Jones, instead of working at discovering the unique gifts they have to give to one another.

Well, we have God's platform. Our Creator's ten unshakeable commandments for living and working together as men and women. We can't change them. But we can change the whole attitude and spirit we bring to praying and thinking about them.

John Wesley, the founder of Methodism, said that when he first studied the Ten Commandments, he kept feeling that God was his accuser and his heart was the defender, but then he discovered the good news that God loved him and sought to work with him just as he was. And from that point on, Wesley said he read the Ten Commandments in an entirely new way. After that, he said the whole thing was turned around. "My heart was the accuser and God was my defender, we were working together to find out where I was going wrong and in freeing me to change."

God's platform, the one who brought His people out of bondage, the One who has already come to us in Christ, declaring His love and seeking to deliver us. This platform does not need to be voted on, or elected to office, but becomes our roadmap to not only for four years, but for a lifetime.

Good and Evil.

God's Ten Commandments are the finest values of our Creator's goodness.

Stained Glass Sheaf of Wheat

PATRIOTISM

I am a very fortunate person. I was born in the United States of America. I didn't have to fight for my freedom, but I'm mighty proud others paved the way for all to live in a country where we can be free to create, talk openly, worship our God, and, in general, be free.

And I have many family members who have fought for these freedoms.

Starting with my ancestor, Christopher Strader Sr. He was born in 1745 to Hans Wilhelm Strader, in New Jersey. He died December 21, 1826, at the age of eighty years and nine months.

Patrick Henry, the Governor of the Commonwealth of Virginia, granted a four-hundred-acre tract of land, on November 13, 1786, to Christopher Strader, for service of participating in the American Revolutionary War. The land was on the east side of Buckhannon River, in Harrison County, Virginia. A plate of this survey is on file at Harrison Country Courthouse, Clarksburg, West Virginia. This land, presently, includes the Buchanan Golf Course, and two Strader cemeteries that Tom and I visited on our quest of following the course of our ancestors.

It is recorded that while Christopher and his wife, Elizabeth, lived in Hardy County, Virginia, now West Virginia, he was an outstanding citizen, as is noted by his name appearing in various court records. He took part in subduing the Tory uprising during the Revolution and certificates granted by sundry of the militia of Shenandoah, Fredrick, Berkley, and Hampshire Counties, who were employed in May and June 1781 to suppress an insurrection. The insurrection occurred when John Brake, a wealthy German, located fifteen miles north of Moorefield Virginia, raised a British flag and encouraged local Tories to stand out against taxation and military service.

I am honored to be a Daughter of the American Revolution, because of my ancestor, Christopher Strader Sr. As past Regent of the Philip Perry Chapter in Rockledge, Florida, I have participated in many inspirational patriotic events through the years.

We always honored the Flag of the United States of America, and several times I included this rendition of "The Salute to Our Flag" to remind people of the importance of respecting Old Glory:

The Salute

I stood upon the corner and watched the flag go by,
I gave that flag my best salute,
A tear came to my eye.
The band struck up a stirring march, I drew my shoulders high,
The blood raced through my aged veins,
As the troops went marching by.
Two young men standing next to me, seemed unmoved by what
    I saw,
hats stayed on as the flag passed by,
No cheer, no loud hurrah!
They cannot feel as I do.
Their time may yet arrive, to answer when their country calls
To serve, perhaps to die.
But if they serve their country, and if they might survive, they'll
    remember those they served with, and grieve for those who
    died.
And standing on a corner as they watch the flag go by,
They'll give the flag a proud salute, and tears will fill their eyes."
—Pat Ryan

I'm also privileged to be the wife of a colonel of the United States Army. As a reservist, Tom served thirty years in the intelligence service and the Corps of Engineers. Our eldest grandson, Michael, is serving in ordinance in the United States Navy, now stationed at Norfolk, Virginia, on the USS *Eisenhower*. Our United States Marine grandson, Ben, is serving at Camp Pendleton, California, as a reconnaissance Marine.

Our son-in-law, Bud, is a graduate of the United States Air Force Academy and School of Law at Temple University. He served in the Air Force until his retirement a few years ago. He's still working at the Inspector General's office in Washington, DC.

Proud to be an American, all of us!

The United States of America. Born July 4, 1776.

A birthday is not the end, it's the beginning of a new chapter.

America was born in a revolution. That revolution was led by people who believed that they could govern themselves if they had the chance. People who believed that all people were created equal in worth and should be equal in opportunity; who believed that all were given by the Creator certain rights which governments could not remove. Those statements are familiar now; they were not familiar then.

The poet, Emerson, in his hymn sung at the completion of the Concord Monument, celebrating the battle of Concord the year before, wrote those familiar words.

> By the rude bridge that arched the flood
> Their flag to April's breeze unfurled
> Here once the embattled farmers stood
> and fired the shot heard round the world.

And the shot was heard round the world.

Kings, queens, and courts in Europe trembled at the word *republic*. And old era was dying and a new era was struggling to be born. Two hundred thirty-eight years later, it has proved far more successful in this country than in some other countries which have attempted it. We've been working at this task of freedom and equality, and I'm sure that many of the citizens of other nations would have to grant that we have probably made more progress than ever been expected in a country that is continually absorbing minority groups from around the world.

Our constitution, at the beginning, called a black person three-fifths a human being. That had to change. We fought a war over slavery and it is no more, though lingering effects of it are taking longer to remove than many of us hoped. The republics in history have been both turbulent and short lived. Equality for all is difficult to achieve. After all, when you're in a position of power, prestige, and control, who wants to give that up? Ours is a dream of liberty of common people ordering their own lives. Many minds have struggled with the question of how a "republic" can work. What special conditions must they have to bring a democratic self government?

Scooby Yorkshire, England, was the home of the original "pilgrim" congregation, as they hammered out the shape of the democratic self government for their church life.

As the *Mayflower* lay offshore, they wrote the famous Mayflower pact, pledging to have "just" and "equal" laws. These pilgrims were bold enough to walk out on James I of England, because of the Old Testament example of Moses at the Exodus. This is the first instance of a minority walking out on a ruler who thought he ruled by divine right. The Exodus from Egypt was a decentralizing of the government. And since it was the chief historical event in the Old Testament, which the pilgrims knew backward and forward, its lesson could not have been missed by those early settlers. Later, the little pilgrim colony at Plymouth was swamped by the larger colony of puritans at Massachusetts Bay. The pilgrims were true "congregationalists," practicing democracy in their church life. Ever since these colonial beginnings, churches have been the place where most Americans first experienced being elected by peers to an office and being accountable to a group of people. They learned how to govern themselves in church long before they learned how to govern themselves in the civil state.

In all candor, one must say this is not true of all denominations. But it is certainly true of our United Methodist denomination. That's the main reason I decided to become a United Methodist. Our founder, John Wesley, welcomed women and all minorities to the pulpit, baptizing, serving communion, and preaching the word. We elect our own through a democratic system that was in place long before the Revolutionary War began.

A while ago, I had the honor of giving the invocation for the State of Delaware's Governor Mike Castle upon his election into office. He also proclaimed Delaware Day, commemorating the ratification of our constitution. Just knowing some of the history makes me proud of our State of Delaware.

It was the fall of 1787. Delaware's delegation consisted of John Dickinson, George Read, Richard Bassett, Gunning Bedford Jr., and Jacob Broom, all verbally fought against the Virginia delegation that advocated each state be represented according to its population. Delaware's Dickinson bluntly told James Madison of Virginia, "Delaware would sooner submit to a foreign power than be under the domination of the large states." Meeting in Dover, Delaware, on Monday, December 3, 1787, the delegates elected to Delaware's special convention spent only four days in discussion before unanimously approving the new United States Constitution on December 7, 1787. This speedy response distinguished Delaware as the first state to ratify the Constitution.

The historical scholars report a prediction by all the delegates that "this Constitution would last against all odds." Those who fought in the revolution and those who drafted the Constitution, they overcame all odds.

When some felt overwhelmed, they reached to the Master, our Lord. Listen to what Benjamin Franklin said to the delegates at the Constitution's meeting September 17, 1787:

> I have lived a long time, and the longer I live, the more convincing proofs I see of this truth, that God governs the affairs of men. I also believe that without God's concurring aid, we shall succeed in this political building no better than the builders of Babel; we shall be divided by our little partial local interest, our projects will be confounded; and we ourselves shall become a reproach and by word, down to future ages. I therefore, beg leave to move, that henceforth prayers imploring the assistance of heaven, and its blessings on our deliberations, be held in this assembly every morning before we proceed to business.

Thank you, Benjamin Franklin, for bringing us prayers at the beginning of each session of Congress.

It's been fifty years, July 25, 1962, since the United States Supreme Court first ruled that government-endorsed prayer in public schools is unconstitutional. The landmark decision, which continues to lie at the center of the nation's debate over the separation of church and state, forever changed the way that faith and religion are handled in classrooms.

What a shame that prayers aren't in our schools today.

Watching our leaders, teachers, and friends at prayer is the example our children need to know. We are not alone, even when we feel alone. God is with us always and in all ways.

It was July 2, 1787. Only the abstention of New York marred a unanimous vote for independence from Great Britain. However, it took an all-night ride by Delaware's Caesar Rodney to end the deadlock in the Delaware delegation. An urgent message reached Rodney at his Jones Neck Plantation, southeast of Dover. Rodney was forty-eight years old and suffering from cancer and asthma. He ignored a terrible thunderstorm and traveled through the night, on horseback, to arrive in Philadelphia. Though tired, dusty, and covered with mud, Rodney was in time to break the deadlock in his own delegation, and put Delaware on record as favoring independence.

In 1780, just seven years before Delaware became the first state to ratify the Constitution, John Wesley, the founder of Methodism, requested that the Anglican Bishop of London ordain American-bound Methodist preacher missionaries, but his request was denied. Seeing no other choice, Wesley ordained two of his Methodist preachers, Thomas Veasey and Richard Whatcoat, as Elders. Anglican cleric Thomas Coke, another Methodist preacher, became superintendent with the power to ordain. These three missionaries sailed for New York in the fall of 1784, through storms, high gales, and their ship four times almost sinking. After debarking, the group split up. Coke and Whatcoat stayed together, making their way into the heart of Delaware. On Sunday morning, November 14, 1784, they arrived at Barrett's Chapel, ten miles southeast of Dover.

Delaware historian Dr. William Henry Williams's book, *The First State: A History of Delaware*, states:

> The impact of Methodism on the residents of central and southern Delaware was greater than the American Revolution. On becoming Methodist, most slave holders freed their servants. led by Richard Bassett, a Dover Methodist and a future governor of Delaware, the State Legislature in 1787 made it illegal to sell Delaware slaves beyond the states' boundaries. Through stormy seas, the Methodists began in our country with some of the farthest reaching social reforms for the poor, the imprisoned, the enslaved, than any other religious or secular society.

Following that time period came the War of 1812, a two-and-a-half-year military conflict between the United States of America and the United Kingdom of Great Britain and Ireland, its North American colonies, and its Indian allies. The outcome resolved many issues which remained from the 1776 American War of Independence.

In fact, during the War of 1812, Mt. Lebanon Episcopal Methodist Church was founded. Mt. Lebanon was the church the bishop and cabinet appointed me as pastor from 1983 to 1996. The church had such a historic beginning, we were able to qualify for and approved by the National Historic Register. This bronze plaque says:

> The State of Delaware Historical Society proclaims:" Be it known that Mt. Lebanon United Methodist Church in Brandywine Hundred has been placed on the National Register of Historic Places on the third day of May nineteen-hundred and eighty four.

Now Mt. Lebanon can stand forever as a testament to our country's past and hope for the future. My ordination into the Peninsula-Delaware conference in 1976, two hundred years after our country became the United States of America, was one of the proudest moments of my life. All of our family attended—Mom, Jack, Tom, Debbie, Becky, and Carrie.

A few years ago, on the fourth of July, an enterprising journalist in Wisconsin handed a slip of paper to 122 people on the streets of Madison, Wisconsin. The slip of paper said, "We hold these truths to be self evident; that all men are created equal and that they are endowed by their creator with certain inalienable rights." He asked those people what their opinion was of the words that were written on that slip of paper.

Well, some of the folks said they thought it as very radical. Some said it was silly idealism. Quite a few said it was probably written by some fanatic. There were only 30 out of the 122 people who recognized it as part of the Declaration of Independence.

We are free people.

Let us remember the special conditions that made us too. For the source of freedom. The apostle Paul wrote in his Epistle in 1 Peter 2:15, 16: "For this is the will of God, that by doing good you may put to silence the ignorance of foolish men as free, yet not using your liberty as a cloak for vice, but as servants of God."

We have a great heritage.

So important is our freedom that when an American was arguing with an Iranian about freedom, the American said, "We are free in America to do or say what we please. Why, in America, I can walk straight up to the President of our country and call him stupid, and not a thing would happen to me."

"The same is true in my country," replied the Iranian citizen. "I can walk up to our Iranian leader and say, 'The American president is stupid,' and not a thing would happen to me either."

Presidents George Washington and Abraham Lincoln are two leaders who leaned on the power of Almighty God and brought freedom to the colonies after the Revolutionary War and freedom to the slaves after the Civil War.

When we examine the lives of George Washington and Abraham Lincoln, I think of the words of Paul: "Therefore, my beloved brethren, be steadfast, immovable, always abounding in the work of the Lord, knowing hat you labor is not in vain in the Lord" (1 Corinthians 15:58). Those were the words of our Apostle Paul to all who would hear, and how true that was of our presidents, Washington and Lincoln. They were steadfast, unmovable, always abounding in the work of the Lord.

As George Washington said in his parting address to his comrades-in arms, speaking of morality and religion thusly:

> Of all the habits which lead to political prosperity, religion and morality are indispensable supports, these firmest props of the duties of men and citizens. Let us, with caution, indulge the supposition that morality can be maintained without religion. Whatever may be conceded to influence of refined education on minds of people, reason and experience both forbid us to expect that national morality can prevail in exclusion of religious principle."

And President Abraham Lincoln embraced similar values and a belief in God. A man with a biblical sense of history, in the wake of our country's Civil War, he wrote this at his second inaugural:

> Neither party expected for the war that magnitude or duration which it has already attained. Both parties read the same Bible and pray to the same God and each invoked God's side against the other. The prayers of both cannot be answered. That of neither has been answered fully. The Almighty God has His own purposes.

Both presidents embraced high morals and a deep belief in the guiding hand of God.

When Lincoln was a young lawyer, it is said that he once sized up the case of a prospective client as follows: "You have a pretty good case, technically, but in terms of justice and equity, it's got problems. So you'll have to look for another lawyer to handle the case, because the whole time I was up there talking to the jury, I'd be thinking, 'Lincoln, you're a liar.'" He continued, "And I just might forget myself and say it out loud." A honest lawyer; hence his nickname, "Honest Abe."

These two men—George Washington, the president of our country, who fought through the Revolutionary War, under the declaration that "all men are created equal and endowed with certain inalienable rights;" and the sixteenth president of our country, Abraham Lincoln, who fought the Civil War that finally gave women, men, black, white, inalienable rights of life, liberty, and the pursuit of happiness—were both examples of great leaders and men of God.

What are the sacrifices of being a great leader? In a time our world seems plummeted by one tough decision after another, it is particularly important that we don't trickle down morality.

Paul, the apostle, gives us a foundation for leadership.

As the ongoing influence of his writing dictates some two thousand years after his death, Paul was a leader. More than anyone else, he was responsible for articulating the Gospel. His work is a theological gold mine, which has been pillaged by some of the finest minds in the history of civilization, only to render new insights on a daily basis.

Paul was a man of deep courage, gentle sensitivity, and great vision. From the book of Acts, Paul is sharing a farewell address with the people of Ephesus. This was a large seaport city, well known for its heavy intellectual community. Ironically, it was one of the places where Paul invested a lot of energy only to reap a lot of conflict. It was a place where leading was not easy.

So we discover a sacrifice of being a leader, in the apostle's opening remarks, as he starts his speech by reminding his hearers of his lifestyle.

> From Miletus, he went to Ephesus and called for the elders of the church. And when they had come to him, he said: "You know from the first day I came to Asia, in what manner I always lived among you, serving the Lord with all humility, with many tears and trials which happened to me by the plotting of the Jews; and how I kept back nothing that was helpful, but proclaimed it to you and taught you publicly and from house to house." (Acts 20:17-19)

Like our presidents George Washington and Abraham Lincoln, the apostle Paul understood the ultimate gift of every leader is to be an example.

Isn't it interesting that the most knowledgeable theologian in church history, Paul made no reference to his teaching when he told his friends good-bye. He said nothing about justification by faith, over the power over the flesh, or the role of the church. Rather, Paul said, "Look at the way I lived."

It's a mark of a great leader to understand the significance of the whole over the part. As my husband Tom says, "Don't tell me how you started, tell me how you finished." Although it is a natural human tendency to think the issue at hand is penultimate, history tells us that very few isolated incidences dominate the legacy of a real leader. And even when they do, as time passes, episode gives way to epicenter, and the character of the leader becomes the dominant issue.

Washington and Lincoln are prime examples. To be sure, the signing of the Emancipation Proclamation and the Declaration of Independence were crowning events, but when the "cherry-tree-truth-teller" and Illinois's "Honest Abe" are remembered today, it is more for their character, courage, and consistency.

Real leadership is more a matter of lifestyle than any isolated incident.

One of the most difficult aspects of being a leader is the tendency to be judged superhuman, therefore without feeling. Consequently, some leaders find themselves trapped with their emotions. Expected to always be in control, and methodically brilliant, it seems one of the worst things a leader can do is display an emotion about any given problem. Isn't it refreshing that twice in the Epistle from Acts, the Apostle Paul confesses to having wept over the challenge of the Ephesians? "Therefore watch, and remember that for three years I did not cease to warn everyone night and day with tears" (Acts 20:31). "And when he had said these things, he knelt down and prayed with them all. Then they all wept freely and fell on Paul's neck and kissed him" (Acts 20:37).

The best leader in politics, business, education, or in the home is the one who can laugh, cry, and able to show caring emotions. Still part of the price of leading is the necessity of making tough decisions, choosing directions, and staying with your values and faith, even when it means scuffing a few egos in the process. It is hard to pick one's friends, even harder to pick one's enemies.

It would have been easy for the Apostle Paul to keep all the Ephesians happy. All that was necessary was for Paul to agree with the other religious groups of Gnostics who believed knowledge was the way to salvation. Or Paul could've agreed with the docent's religious notion that Jesus wasn't really human, or he could go along with the Sadducees's conviction, who believed death is the end of every living thing.

Then they would have been one big happy family.

But Paul's ministry would have been totally compromised.

Sometimes, leaders must place popularity on the line, for the sake of principle. Paul didn't lend credence to his detractors by constantly engaging them in dialogue. He simply set out the faith as he knew it, and refused to compromise for the sake of popularity. Paul knew his enemies were constantly plotting to destroy him. He knew they followed him everywhere. Still he boldly proclaimed the truth, recognizing the basic truth that those who are worthy of trust are most often those who are most capable of growth.

He decided it was worth the risk to lead a few to Christ, even if it hastened his own demise.

Likewise, Lincoln and Washington did the same for their country. George Washington led his troops from the front, while shots from British sharpshooters flew across the battlefields around him. This action inspired the American forces to hold together following their courageous leader.

Lincoln stood against his enemies during the Civil War with courage and strength. Irving Stone, the historical biographical writer, described Lincoln as a man who prayed daily and trusted in the Lord for guidance. Lincoln was once told, "Mr. Lincoln, you are sacrificing your political strength by hanging onto this fool idea of equality for blacks. Why don't you stop for awhile so you can consolidate your southern vote. Why you're even losing the northern constituency." But Lincoln had courage as he trusted in God for his leadership.

This inner strength, ideals, and values, and freedom for all people, anchors all of these leaders to their faith.

As Paul writes to the Ephesians:

> And, see, now I go bound in the spirit to Jerusalem, not knowing the things that will happen to me there, except that none of these things move me; nor do I count my life dear to myself, so that I may finish my race with joy, and the ministry which I received from the Lord Jesus, to testify to the gospel of the grace of God. (Acts 20:22-24)

And, as George Washington said, "No people can be bound to acknowledge and adore the invisible hand which conducts the affairs of men, more than the people of the United States. Every step by which they have advanced to the character of an independent nation seems to have been distinguished by some token of a providential Hand."

As Abe Lincoln concluded: "With malice toward none, and charity for all with firmness in the right as God gives us to see the right; let us strive on to finish the work we are in; to bind up the nation's wounds; to care for those who have borne the battle; and for his widow and orphan, to do all which may achieve and cherish a just and lasting peace among ourselves and all nations."

George Washington, Abraham Lincoln, and the Apostle Paul. Great leaders one and all, who embraced these inner qualities of high moral standards, risking themselves with a deep belief in a hand of divine guidance, knowing the consequences of their courage and endurance could bring lonesomeness in their lives.

We have to learn to embrace the sacrifices of knowing we may be lonely on our earthly walk, but we have a friend who walks with us, as did George, Abraham, and Paul.

> Fear not, for I am with you; Be not dismayed for I am your God.
> I will strengthen you, Yes, I will help you, I will uphold you with
> My righteous right hand. (Is 41:10)

And what is a fitting memorial to all the Patriots?

No one has ever identified a more fitting memorial than the one suggested by Abraham Lincoln at Gettysburg. He agonized over our nation's Civil War. On November 19, 1863, he was at the dedication of the National Cemetery where he gave his famous address. His simple words linking the deeds of the present to the thoughts of the future, caused this speech to rank as a masterpiece.

Hear those few paragraphs again:

> Fourscore and several years ago, our fathers brought forth, on this continent, a new nation, conceived in liberty, and dedicated to the proposition that all men are created equal. Now we are engaged in a great Civil War, testing whether that nation or any nation so conceived and so dedicated, can long endure. We are meeting on a great battlefield of that war. We have come to dedicate a portion of that field as a final resting place for those who here have given their lives so that our nation might live. It is altogether fitting and proper that we should do this. But, in a larger sense, we cannot dedicate…we cannot consecrate, we cannot hallow this ground. The brave men living and dead, who struggled here, have consecrated it far above our poor power to add or detract. The world will little note nor long remember what we say here, but it can never forget what they did here. It is for us, the living, rather, to be dedicated to the unfinished work which they who fought here, have thus far so nobly advanced. It is rather for us to be here dedicated to the great task remaining before us, that from these honored dead we take increased devotion to that cause for which they gave the last full measure of devotion. That we here highly resolved that these dead shall not have died in vain; that this nation, under God, shall have a new birth of freedom; and that government of the people, by the people, for the people, shall not perish from the earth.

Abraham Lincoln was the architect; we are the builders. It will be finished when all persons are free.

How do we go about the building of this kind of memorial to freedom? How will freedom be achieved? One area in which the search for freedom has been pursued is the realm of truth.

"Then Jesus said to those who believed Him, 'If you abide in My word, you are My disciples indeed. And you shall know the truth, and the truth shall make you free'" (John 8:31, 32).

Our nation for over 220 years has diligently pursued truth and it has meant a great deal to our progress and growth. We have inscribed the words "Know the truth and it shall set you free" in iron over the gates of our many outstanding universities. We have used them in stone over the doors of libraries. We have used them, with a zeal approaching piety, in the dedication of our laboratories. These words are carved in stone over the entrance of many sanctuaries.

The search for freedom through truth has brought some amazing achievements as byproducts in communication and transportation. One hundred thirty-eight years ago, the telephone was invented, then came the radio, television, VCRs, cell phone, and computers. And what about transportation? There was the tin-lizzy. And out of it evolved the Memorial Day Indianapolis 500, an event to stagger our imagination. I wonder what a spectator from another planet would think if they were sitting today in the grandstands of Indianapolis as the cars go zooming by. Besides telephones and cars, we have a thousand and one things to make life easier. Let us not forget what the pursuit has done in the whole realm of sports. Many years ago, a shepherd in the field took his hook and hit a stone. The stone went a certain distance and when he had time, he walked up to it and hit it again. That has evolved into one of the most amazing sports: golf.

For all these successes, we must admit that finding freedom and peace through the channels of truth have been disillusioning. There are college diplomas found in prison cells and many brilliant minds that created the bombs that killed millions. Even psychology, which has taught us to understand each other better, also enabled us to fool one another more cleverly. Altogether, our search for freedom through truth has not changed the balance of good and evil very much.

Jesus was not wrong when He gave us a well-marked road map. He simply did not say what we have thought He said. We have only part of the map. Jesus did not say, "Know the truth and the truth shall make you free." He said something more. And it is in the more that the answer lies. Recall, Our Lord said, "If you abide in My word, you are My disciples indeed. And you shall know the truth, and the truth shall make you free" (John 8:31, 32).

"If you abide in My word." There is a condition which must be achieved before we have freedom, before we have a lasting memorial. With our typical inclination for brevity, we have left out the most important part. Perhaps the cost is too great for us. Freedom is not in truth, unconditional. But in truth, as it is found in the living spirit of Jesus Christ, permeating all the relations of people with people.

"Abide in My word." If we abide in Jesus's teachings, we will be set free.

We believe every human being is free because every person is a child of God. This is the ideal, but the truth in Lincoln's address was not given to a nation where all people were free.

He knew its achievement would require sweat, blood, tears, and dedication. We will fail our honored dead if we are not diligent in this pursuit. Every day freedom is at stake somewhere. In our home, in our work, everywhere. The pursuit is not out there somewhere. It is right here and now in the way we treat each other every day. If we are to establish a fitting memorial, we must start with motives which are in harmony with Jesus's teaching.

Jesus said, "If you abide in my word, you shall know the truth and the truth shall set you free."

We must begin with a faith that we are all free and we are all children of one God, men, women, black, yellow, white, red, rich, poor, high IQs, low IQs; we are all children of God.

Does it sound too simple? The answer seems too easy, but Jesus said, "Peace I leave with you; not as the world gives do I give to you. Let not your heart be troubled, neither let it be afraid" (John 14:27).

In Honor

For those who have fought
a loud call of thanks
for heeding the call
for filling the ranks
for those who have bled
a wish to be healed
and hope that the pain
will soon be concealed
for those who have died
may your souls find rest
and never again
be put to the test
we call as one voice
yet many are heard
since freedom of speech
breeds conflicting words
but one common theme
that always shall be
is God bless this land
of true Liberty.

—WHS

Stained Glass: Open Bible and Lamp

LIFE CHANGES

Spirituality

A seminary professor of church polity was forewarning us seminary students about the pitfalls of the local church.

He gave us some basic council: "Never alienate the woman's groups; learn to drink all kinds of coffee and never ask what's in the punch?"

And finally: "The best way to split a church is over questions of spirituality. Nothing generates more dissension than the need to pass judgment on the health of one another's souls."

Ah, our souls.

In his book, *The Kingdom Within*, John Sanford uses an illustration that provides a starting point for our examination of our inner pilgrimage. Sanford explains his childhood experience of living in an antiquated New Hampshire farmhouse without the benefit of electricity or plumbing. The family's water supply was drawn from an old well, just outside the door.

And what a well it was. Always providing cool, clear, and perfect water. But then the day came when Sanford's father, a Methodist minister, scraped up enough money to modernize the house. Electric lamps replaced smelly oil burners, the kerosene stove gave way to an electric model, and a new deep artesian well was drilled a few hundred feet from the house. No longer needed, the old well was sealed over to be kept in reserve in case of emergency. And so it was for several years, until one day John decided to check out the old well.

Certain he would find it fruitful as ever, filled with the sparkling water of yesteryear.

Oh, no.

When he pulled back the cover, he discovered the old well was bone dry.

He writes: "It took many inquiries to find out why the well ran dry. A well of this kind is fed by hundreds of tiny underground rivulets, bringing water into the well. When a well is not used, and the water is not regularly drawing the tiny rivulet, it will close up. Our well was dry, not because there was no water, but because it had not been used."

Isn't that true with our own spirituality?

We must keep the rivulets open to the living water of God.

When it comes to communicating with God, we are talking about the closest and most personal experience any human being can muster.

What is right for you may be wrong for me. What appears to be white might be black or gray to someone else.

Jesus speaks to this point in the Gospel of Matthew, concerning prayer. Cautioning his helpers against making public displays of their faith, Jesus not only tells them how to pray, but virtually explains the meaning of spirituality in the process. Jesus says, "But you, when you pray, go into your room and when you have shut the door, pray to your father who is in your secret place, and your Father who sees what you do in secret; will reward you" (Matthew 6:6).

Private prayer, in a private place.

Nothing better illustrates the totally personal aspect of human spirituality.

Yes, we gather in large groups to sing God's praise. We gather in churches to pray, and invocations at many events. But Jesus tells us it's also important we pray up close and personal at a quiet time.

The late Francis Schaefer, who founded the wonderful L'Abri Fellowship, defined true spirituality in his book by the same name. Said Schaefer, "To believe in God, not just when I accept Christ as Savior, but every moment, one moment at a time, this is the Christian life and this is true spirituality."

What is the essence of believing in God every moment? The essence is in the Lord's Prayer. "Thy kingdom come, Thy will be done, on earth as it is in heaven" (Matthew 6:8).

When we accept the fact that a higher power presides over all life, here and beyond, we enter the realm of true spirituality. The fact is, whether we study our Bible, or helping one other human being, we are practicing true spirituality.

There are several characteristics to true spirituality.

There is a sense of humility.

Then there's a sense of forgiveness. The Lord's Prayer teaches us to "forgive us our trespasses, as we forgive others who trespass against us." So the truly spiritual person is the one who lives the faith, ever aware of his or her own weaknesses and more than willing to forgive others.

Also, true spirituality is constantly growing, always adjusting to change. Like the Minister John Sanford's well, the human soul must be constantly receiving new material to stay healthy. However, often life changes and we must search for our Creator in the midst of these areas of gray.

As Paul said in his writings to the Romans:

> Who shall separate us from the love of Christ? Shall tribulation or distress or persecution, or famine or sword? No, in all these things, we are more than conquerors through him who loved us. For I am persuaded that neither death nor life, nor principalities, nor power, nor things present, nor things to come, nor height nor depth, nor anything in Creation shall be able to separate us from the love of God, which is in Christ Jesus Our Lord. (Rom 8:34-39)

We will never be left alone, all through the changes in our lives because life does change.

Zacchaeus

You've been reading about how my life changed throughout the years. Some changes good, some not, some in the realm of gray.

As Benjamin Franklin said, "When you're finished changing, you're finished!"

Life changes.

I just heard about a retiring minister who was saying farewell to his congregation at the church doors for the last time. He shook the hand of an elderly lady as she walked out of the vestibule.

She said, "Your successor won't be as good as you."

"Nonsense," said the minister, in a flattered tone.

"No, really," said the old lady. "I've been here under five different ministers and each one has been worse than the last."

Yes, life changes.

And we find people frequently seeking change throughout the Holy Bible.

From our Gospel of Luke:

> Then Jesus entered and passed through Jericho. Now behold, there was a man named Zacchaeus who was a chief tax collector, and he was rich. And he sought to see who Jesus was, but could not because of the crowd, for he was of short stature. So he ran ahead and climbed up in a sycamore tree to see Him, for He was going to pass that way. And when Jesus came to the place, He looked up and saw him, and said to him, "Zacchaeus, make haste and come down, for today I must stay at your house." So he made haste and came down, and received Him joyfully. But when they saw it, they all murmured, saying, "He has gone to be a guest with a man who is a sinner." Then Zacchaeus stood and said to the Lord, "Look, Lord I give half of my goods to the poor and if I have taken anything from anyone by false accusation, I restore fourfold." And Jesus said to him, "Today salvation has come to this house, because he also is a son of Abraham; for the Son of Man has come to seek and to save that which was lost." (Lk 19:1-10)

As our Gospel lesson tells us, Jesus entered through the town of Jericho and came across a man by the name of Zacchaeus, a rich man, a chief tax collector in the town of Jericho.

The Gospel reading tells us that Zacchaeus is far removed from the peace of himself or the world around him. He collected unjust taxes from the people of Jericho. He was as respected in Jericho as a bootlegger at a temperance convention.

Outcast, reprobate, traitor, bloodsucker. Who would ever think of writing a character reference for Zacchaeus? But where, may we ask, could he have gone wrong? At what point on the pilgrimage of his life had he begun to stray? What forces or events ostracized him from his community and caused him to live in an open collaboration with the enemy of his people, to collect unjust taxes?

What makes a person turn away from God?

There can be many reasons. Was there a tragic break in his marriage, or had he become disenchanted with religion because there were so many hypocrites in the local synagogue? Or was it that he found himself in a dog-eat-dog world and decided that the bigger they come, the better they survive? Could there have been some secret sin for which he could not forgive himself, much less think of asking for forgiveness? What about his apparent preoccupation with money? Did he have a lust for the luxuries which money could provide? Or was it simply a case of neglect. A neglect of public worship and private prayers that gradually led Zacchaeus further and further from God?

We do not know.

These, together with hundreds of other reasons, can warp our view of the world, turn us sour on God, and lead us into a life of meaninglessness.

What we do know, from our Scripture, is "there was a man and his name was Zacchaeus."

Or was that name…yours…or mine?

To put that question turns the page for us and brings us to where we are today. For there are days in the experience of us all when we have gone wrong and have known defeat and felt utterly depressed and outcast. There are times when all of us feel trapped by despair, overwhelmed with problems, paralyzed with fear and wonder whether there can ever be a chance for a spiritual change. For you see, we all know what it means to face strong, masterful temptations. We know what it means, God help us, to settle down after a while in dull apathy, fettered by shackles of despair, and resigned to defeat.

And we know what it means, thank God, to grow dissatisfied with all that, angry at our own inability to change, and to cry, oh God, to find unity and peace within ourselves and a chance for a spiritual change.

Well, says our Scripture, you can change and Zacchaeus points the way.

After years of preaching, teaching, healing, and counseling, Jesus's fame had spread. Some of the citizens of Jericho came to satisfy their curiosity about what this popular figure looked like. Others were bored and welcomed the break in monotony that Jesus and his followers brought to the village, but the unjust tax collector, Zacchaeus's burdened conscience and empty life, drove him to try to see Jesus. Perhaps a glimpse of Jesus would be enough to give him hope for which he hungered.

The Scripture says the crowds closed in, obstructing the sight of the Savior from Zacchaeus, who is reported to be "of short stature" (Luke 19:3).

As the entourage proceeded out of town, Zacchaeus began to feel desperate. He spotted a sycamore tree ahead whose limbs offered his only chance for a view. In total disregard for his own dignity, Zacchaeus dashed ahead of the crowd. To do so, he must take the front edge of his robes in his hand, exposing his legs. All of this is frightfully shameful in the Middle East in those days. No man over thirty dare do this. But, no matter, Zacchaeus had far more to worry about than his size or his dignity. His dissatisfaction with his life drove him to the extremes of doing the unusual and even climbing a tree, if that's the only way he could see Jesus.

This Jesus who heals the lame and blind, raises the dead and forgives sins, and all the while radiating power and love and total acceptance.

At last Zacchaeus made it! Breathlessly, he scrambled up the tree, selecting in advance the branch that would afford him his best view. Perched in position, Zacchaeus strained to see the approaching figure, as the crowd moved toward Jesus. You can almost hear some children giggling and the village women scathing at his disgraceful behavior, sitting there with his legs exposed. Little bother was this to Zacchaeus. He was already isolated from them, had been for years. He knew he needed help desperately, and this one, this Jesus approaching, had changed the lives of many.

Perhaps He held for Zacchaeus a chance for a spiritual change.

With a burning, hopeful gaze, he looked at Jesus passing by, asking himself if he might hold the power that will release him from the captivity of his life.

Then it happened. The first in a series of surprises that Zacchaeus would experience that day.

Calling him by his first name, Jesus addressed him in the familiar language of a friend. "Zacchaeus" (Luke 19:5).

Jesus urges the man to come out of the shadow and to come into the sun.

"I must abide at your house today."

And that was the first surprise.

Jesus knew him. He knew his name, He knew his needs and He sought him out to save him. We don't know all that happened at Zacchaeus's home that day, but we do know what was most important. Jesus offered him a chance of a spiritual change, and Zacchaeus took it.

Zacchaeus said, "If I have defrauded anyone, I will restore the amount four times over" (Luke 19:8).

A strange release accompanied these new themes in his speech. Repentance and restitution had not been a part of Zacchaeus's life for a long time.

As the evening wore on, the crowd in the courtyard became increasingly critical of Jesus's association with Zacchaeus. Their muttering and complaining grew louder. Jesus rose and announced for all to hear. "Today salvation happened in this house. Inasmuch as this man is a son of Abraham; "for the Son of Man has come to seek and to save that which was lost" (Luke 19:10).

An instant silence swept over the group. They retreated. "Son of Abraham!"

It had been a long time, but Zacchaeus remembered from his early youth what this meant. Abraham's faith was the model for every devout Jew. It was not some abstract quality. Abraham's faith was a sure, unshaken confidence in God that comes after a difficult human struggle over recurring doubt and unfaith. A victory gained through God's forgiving grace. And to be son of Abraham meant to participate in that faith and be in a right relationship with God. We hear this from the Epistle lesson from Galatians: "Just as Abraham believed God, in faith and was blessed by God, for his faith" (Galatians 3:56).

What a total change for Zacchaeus!

And what a chance for a total change for us.

Does that sound difficult? Not if we hear our Lord's declaration at the conclusion of the Scripture. "The Son of man is come to seek and to save that which was lost" (Luke 19:10). In no other passage of the Scriptures does Jesus state more clearly the purpose of his birth, his Holy life, His atoning death, and His glorious resurrection and ascension. So, as to say, "I have come so that everyone can have a chance for a spiritual change."

Does it trouble you that Jesus offers to everyone a chance for a spiritual change? Even to the downtrodden, to the sinners, to the unbelievers, to everyone? Be assured that the risk is not with Jesus, but with us. Although Jesus offers us Himself, He never deprives us of our freedom to refuse to accept. He freely gives to every person the right to say no and He deeply grieves when he hears the refusal.

Why?

Remember, it was exactly one week after Jesus passed through Jericho, after helping Zacchaeus, when Jesus was betrayed and arrested in Jerusalem.

On the next day, they raised three crosses on a lonely hill called Calvary outside Jerusalem's walls. On the center cross, between two thieves, hung our Lord, agonizing and in excruciating pain pouring out his blood so that you and I could have a chance for a spiritual change. There we see most clearly what Jesus meant when he said, "The Son of man is come to seek and save that which was lost" (Luke 19:10).

So, when Christ speaks to you saying, "Repent, change your life, follow me," Jesus is standing right beside you offering you and me the power to do the impossible.

The power that changed the incorrigible Zacchaeus.

The power that changed a dying thief and the power that turned thousands of hopeless people into confident believers.

And the power of the Psalm from the Old Testament that says, "I will lift up my eyes to the hills, from whence comes my help? My help comes from the Lord, who will preserve your soul from this time forth and forevermore" (Psalm 121:1).

It is the power of His presence that is as real in our day, as it was in the day of David, the Psalmist, and in the day of Zacchaeus.

We can trust that Jesus knows us completely, calls us by our names, and seeks to find us.

You might be tempted to say, "But I can't change. I can't have hope when my loved ones are dying, and I am sick with nothing to look forward to. How can I live like this? How can I believe?"

Well, Jesus invites you to throw away those doubts and hesitations and join Him in seeking peace by knowing He is always beside you, as He always offers each of us a chance for a spiritual change.

Time and Change

Tom and I have lived in Wilmington, Delaware, longer than we lived anywhere in our life. Occasionally, we go back to our birthplace in another state. Often we made it a point to show our kids where we grew up. My first house has chipped paint and shutters down.

Tom's first home is now a parking lot for university students. But we would tell the kids how lovely that house used to be and I would tell how I put Christmas tree lights around that old evergreen tree my daddy planted for us one Christmas many years ago. And now, the tree is dying and the house has been abused by its new owners.

Life changes!

Every week we lose someone, it seems. And, my mom, who lived to be 105-1/2, lost someone daily. In fact, she was the last remaining person from her high school, business school, and all old friends.

Life changes!

As I reflect on these thoughts, I am convinced, more than ever, that the only way to achieve happiness is to accept change, because it is simply unavoidable in this pilgrimage called life. As Jerome Kagan of Harvard University observed, "Change is far more common experience in human development than continuity. We prepare for continuity, but it is change we must always expect."

Perhaps no biblical writer had a better grip on both the inevitability and the indifference of change than Koheleth, the writer of the book of Ecclesiastes from the Old Testament. Sometimes he's known as the master of reality and the master of despair. He certainly understands the hard edges of life. He observes: "I again saw under the sun that the race is not to the swift, and the battle is not to the warriors, and neither is bread to the wise, nor wealth to the discerning, nor favor to men of ability; for time and change overtake them all" (Ecclesiastes 9:11).

With these words, Koheleth puts his finger on the two dimensions around which the fortunes of change forever revolve.

Time and change overtake us all. It is "time and change" that gives us a faith-centered hope. There's no better mark of God's ongoing concern for humanity than the continuing impact of change in the world around us. We were made to bring glory to God, and nothing accomplishes that more than the human pursuit of improvement and growth.

Time and change deny all of us the absurdity of sitting still. Like it or not, we are destined to change and so is the world around us.

As I reflect on a few scientific changes in my life, they are amazing.

It was in 1940 that Sir Howard Florey, an Australian pathologist, discovered penicillin and its curative effects on various infectious diseases. Thanks to Flordy, thousands of lives were saved during WWII, as penicillin was used to fight infections related to wounds sustained in battle

Today, the influence of antibiotics is largely credited for saving millions of lives.

Life changes!

It was over sixty years ago the people at Vought Sikorsky unveiled a weird-looking airplane without any wings. It had just a shell for the pilot and a giant propeller mounted right on top of it. Better yet, the thing could take off going straight up, and land the same way.

They called it a helicopter. Today, those contraptions are used for traffic control and emergency ambulance service that saves hundred of lives everyday.

Life changes!

Change is the only predictable dimension of human existence. It is a gift from God to keep our eyes on the future and our attention glued to our ever-renewing world.

"Time and change," said Ecclesiastes Koheleth, "affect us all." But it's the way we respond to change that actually shapes our lives. The more we treat life changes as preludes to new blessings from God, the sooner we will be free to give up our death grip on today and freely approach tomorrow. We also know that if we could keep things the same yesterday, today, and forever, it wouldn't be very long until we were bored stiff.

As shapers of our own lives, ours is the privilege to weave our tomorrows. As life changes every day, it is our choice to either look away and live in the fantasy of yesterday, or embrace those changes and shape tomorrow. As believers in God, we need to perceive change as a gift from God. Then we need to respond to these changes in a positive, God-loving way.

This means, however old we are when change happens, no matter how much it costs or who it affects, no matter how simple or complex a change might be, we approach it with the expectant attitude that it holds promise and prosperity for our future.

If we look closely, we can recall numerous examples of artists and musicians who lived long, effective, constantly evolving lives. Think of Monet, Picasso, and Chagall, all of whom defied the restrictions of age to make major contributions long after others would have thrown in the towel. Or what about Stravinsky, Casuals, and Frank Lloyd Wright?

Same story.

Why? Because all of these people made it a point to perpetually embark on new projects.

They didn't wait for life to change them, they changed life. They didn't struggle under the weight of their years, they used the years to reach for the future. They transformed the inevitable, unavoidable changes of life into pedestals for creativity. They trusted what they did not know, while blending it with what they did know.

When he was eight years old, his mom and dad told little Walter they were moving. He couldn't believe it. He didn't want to go. Why would they leave the excitement of a big city like Chicago for a hick town like Marceline, Missouri?

He cried, but it didn't matter. They moved anyway, and little Walter's eyes filled with tears as he said good-bye to his friends and climbed into the family car to head for a farm in Missouri. But, as so often is the case, when life changes, here was something waiting for Walter in Missouri. A part of a bigger plan that the boy could not see.

When it happened, it didn't seem like much, but it was to ultimately establish an empire that would impact the lives of children for generations to come. Once at the farm in Missouri, Walter began to adapt. He learned to love the quiet of the countryside and the melodic sounds of the birds. And then he made his first slingshot. The kids at school told him how to make it, but they didn't tell him what it could do. So when Walter saw a owl sleeping on the branch of an elm tree, he didn't think twice before firing a stone at the slumbering bird.

He hit him.

Square and hard. With a screech, the mortally wounded owl came crashing out of the tree and little Walter watched in horror as it died. Ashamed, he scrambled into the barn and fetched a shovel with which he buried his unfortunate prey. But the owl wasn't gone. It lived on in Walter's thoughts. In Walter's memory. In Walter's dreams. At last, the only way the boy could make peace with what he had done was to draw pictures of that owl.

And soon he found himself drawing pictures of other animals as well.

His shame faded, but his love of animals never stopped growing.

It took years for Walter to tell the truth about what happened in the farmyard in Marceline, Missouri.

And when he did, the world quickly forgot.

Why? Because Walter had long since proved how deeply he cared for the innocent animals of God's creation.

Today, Walter is dead.

But his memory lives on in the scores of unforgettable characters he has indelibly inserted into the consciousness of the world.

And we can all celebrate the fact that Walter Elias Disney was once forced to move from Chicago, Illinois, to Marceline, Missouri.

It is not the changes that shape our lives, but what we choose to do with the changes when they occur.

Annoyances, Worries, and Sins

When we started the Supporting KIDDS (Kids Involved in Death, Divorce, and Separation) groups, there was a great need for kids and their families to share their feelings with other people going through similar crisis. It was my responsibility to facilitate the adults, and we had many other trained volunteers to lead the children's groups. One children's group was for three- to five-year-olds, another six to nine, ten to twelve, and teenagers. There were many challenges over the years with the different groups and their families. And there were many similarities. All of them are areas so small we don't pay attention to them, and that's where they can ruin our lives.

I want to highlight three areas we need to watch carefully, because these "little" things can deprecate our very existence.

First, we need to watch the little annoyances, next, the little worries and, thirdly, the little sins that creep into our daily life.

First, the little annoyances that plague us. It is the little annoyances in life that disarm us from becoming true peacemakers. Strange as it may seem, it is not so much the great problems and tragedies and sins that drive our families and friends away from us and generally mar or destroy our lives. Rather, it is the little annoyances, the little problems, the little sins. Singly, they in themselves are seemingly unimportant, but in their cumulative effect, they can be terrifying and ruinous. It is their seeming insignificance that enables them to create such havoc. We think we can take each annoyance as it comes, but we forget their devastating affect when they pile up over a period of time. So we allow them to nibble at our lives, unconcerned because we don't realize their danger.

It is quite different with tragic situations. We have no trouble recognizing them for what they are. Their very awfulness nerves us to high courage and endurance. Simply because the storm is so great, we are able to summon up resources to weather it. Tragedy often elicits an "I'll show the world" attitude. But one cannot register the same response to petty annoyances. They do not make one rise to great heights, or courage, or resourcefulness, and that is their danger. Rather unnoticed or regarded as unimportant, they nibble away at our life until it is tragically marred and sometimes even ruined.

We all know that in our family life, it is the little annoyances and hurts that grate on our nerves and make us do or say things we are sorry for afterward.

It is the little annoyances that lead to family wrangles, and are behind a great many of those divorces granted on so-called mental cruelty. Oftentimes in our Supporting KIDDS support group, I would ask the divorcing adults what it was that made them finally ask for a separation or divorce.

The reply often is: "Oh, I don't know, it's hard to say. A lot of little things, I guess. Things that have piled up over the years." No clear-cut specific reason, but the cumulative effect of years of petty annoyances, unexpressed affection, and small wounds have amounted to an unbearable situation. And then there was finally added the proverbial last straw which broke the back of the marriage.

The second area that we need to watch is the little problems that beset us.

These, like little annoyances, are not dangerous or devastating in themselves, but taken together, they can ruin all that is fruitful and good in our lives. It is the little problems that drive a person wild. The big problems, like tragic situations, are sometimes foreseeable, and almost always nerve one to much sanity and clear-headedness that they can be met and solved satisfactorily. We often find, to our own surprise, that we have a solution and can face the consequences unafraid.

Major problems, then, are not the real difficulty. It is the little problems, innocent looking, supposedly easily solved, that ruins one's life, or one's usefulness. Virtually disregarded, they bore into one's system, there to plague and fester, eating away at one's mental, physical, and spiritual well-being. None of them important in themselves, perhaps, but together almost overwhelming.

Small problems are like tiny strings with which the Lilliputians bound Gulliver. Each string by itself is easily broken, but bound by so many, Gulliver was helpless. This is the way little problems can affect us, paralyzing us by their very number and ruining our lives.

It is to our advantage, then, to overcome this.

In our support groups, we try to deal with each problem, solving it or isolating it, thus rendering it harmless. And we need to do this as quickly as we can.

There's an interesting quirk to problems. Someone once wrote: "Some of your griefs you have cured and the worst you have survived, but what agonies you have endured from the troubles that never arrived." Jesus, our Lord, made a helpful point about this: "Sufficient unto the day, is the evil thereof" (Matthew 6:34).

Yet, as much as these little annoyances and the little problems are important to watch, this third area needs to be carefully monitored, because it is the little sins that can destroy us.

Small annoyances and small problems can damage and detract our lives from their worth. But of all the distractions, the most insidious and most disastrous are the petty, seemingly inconsequential sins.

It is by all odds these small sins are the most malicious. For, you see, we have the ultimately tragic idea that there is nothing really harmful about a little sin. It is only the big sins that are bad. We have separated lies, for example, into big lies and little lies, and feel that a little lie is harmless. But it is often the little lies that can do the most harm, if only because the big lies are easier to detect. We fail to see that it is the little harmless sin that can become the large and destructive ones in time. You hear a bit of gossip that is too juicy or seems to have too much truth not to pass on. It is a small tidbit, and a relatively harmless one, so it is passed on. But, as gossip will, it snowballs, and in a short time an innocent person's reputation is hurt or irreparably ruined. Or we criticize other people who are doing their best. Do you ever thank someone rather then criticize them?

Gossip and overly criticizing people are only two examples of the insidious, little sins that wreak their havoc on us and other people. But another facet of the insidiousness or little sins is that they can creep into your life while you are unaware of them.

By their very lack of size, as it were, they are able to slip into our life unnoticed, and there they wreak their havoc. We are on the lookout for the large sins. We guard against them constantly, and are not even tempted to embezzle, murder, or kidnap.

We keep the Ten Commandments fairly faithfully, but the little sins slip through.

A little malice. A desire for some revenge. The moments of self-congratulations on the one hand, or envy on the other. Breaking confidentialities, judging others by putting them down in order to build ourselves up. It is sins like these, however small, that prevent us from being our best selves, keeping us from spiritual fruitfulness that damages and destroys much of the good part of our lives.

What, then, should we do to follow our Creator?

Our Old Testament says it well. "Gather my saints together to Me. Those who have made a covenant with Me by sacrifice. Let the heavens declare His righteousness for God himself is Judge" (Psalm 50:5, 6).

We try to do our best and let go and let God do the rest.

The Epistle Scripture says: "God has delivered us from the power of darkness and translated us into the Kingdom of the Son of His love, in whom we have redemption through his blood, the forgiveness of sins" (Colossians 1: 12-14).

Jesus will forgive our sins if we repent and ask for forgiveness.

What was important to Jesus was not what position you hold, or how important you are, but the attitude of your heart. Embracing the attitude of following Jesus will help us.

So we don't allow those little annoyances to eat away and destroy our lives.

So we don't allow the little problems to gnaw away at our better selves.

And we don't allow those little sins to slip through and wreak their havoc.

It's the Lamb Chops

A few years ago, my husband and I were on a cruise, and we encountered force 11 winds, which would be equivalent to a hurricane category 5 winds on land.

The winds blew dinner plates and glassware off their shelves. It was quite frightening over a period of fifty-four hours.

As Tom and I sat there, we had no idea what would happen to us and the other passengers in harm's way.

Life changes!

I asked myself, what Scripture would I choose in this unusual situation?

As we were sitting on this perilous ship, in order to ease the tension, a passenger told a story about a married couple in their early seventies, celebrating their forty-fifth anniversary in a romantic restaurant. Suddenly, a tiny yet beautiful fairy appeared on their table and said, "For being such an exemplary married couple, and for being faithful to each other for all this time, I will grant you each a wish."

"Oh," said the wife. "I want to travel around the world with my darling husband."

The fairy moved her magic stick and two tickets for a lovely luxury liner appeared in the wife's hands.

Now, it was her husband's turn. He thought for a moment and said, "Well, this is all very romantic, but an opportunity like this only occurs once in a lifetime, So, I'm sorry, my love, but my wish is to have a wife thirty years younger than me."

The wife and the fairy were very deeply disappointed, but a wish is a wish, so the fairy made a circle with her magic stick, and the husband became…one hundred years old!

Well then, what Scripture would I choose if I had only one sermon left to preach?

If I had but one last chance to speak to a group of people about whom I cared deeply, such as my family, for whom I would wish only the best, what would be the Scripture I would share? As soon as I entertained that thought, a specific text flashed in my mind.

You've heard it hundreds of times throughout your life. It's from the prophet Micah when he looks at the corruption of Judah and asks theoretical questions. "What does the Lord require of you but to do justice, to love kindness; and to walk humbly with your God" (Micah 6:8). There are some vital values in those words: "Do justice, love, mercy, and to walk humbly with God.

What does "doing justice" mean? Well, it's a lot more than sticking up for the an underdog or even insisting on moral stringency. In the fullest sense of the Holy Bible, doing justice means practicing what is right, establishing character, developing values. The call to "do justice" is a call to look at life through the lens of God's written word with a commitment to sanctify the equality of all human existence in the process.

This doesn't mean we'll follow the letter of the law, for sometimes we simply can't do that. Remember the Supreme Court in 1875 enacted the infamous Dred Scott Law, ruling blacks were not persons, and that erroneous law didn't change for years.

Sometimes our courts write erroneous laws.

The second mandate that Micah sets out for us, is to "love kindness."

You see, I believe the Christian faith is an affirmation of the sanctity of every human being and all of life.

"For God so loved the world that He gave His only begotten Son that whosoever believeth in Him shall not perish but have everlasting life" (John 3:16).

These words tell us, in an unmistakable fashion, that God's first priority is people.

Not pomp, not purity, not pride, not power, but people.

And suddenly, another beautiful principle takes shape before us.

As we give, so we gain.

Isn't that the real message of the incarnation? God became human, so humans could come to God. God gave, so we could gain. So often we want to make this faith thing a lot more complicated than it needs to be.

Recently, I read about a British preacher by the name of Arthur Lax who labored in the East End of London for thirty-eight years.

He was an eloquent speaker, a fine teacher, and a very influential man in the community. One day, he was informed that Henry Bloom, an eccentric old cobbler, had taken ill. As Dr. Lax was passing Bloom's home, he decided to pay him a visit. He managed to get in the door of the tiny little house, but as soon as old Henry spotted the minister's collar, he froze up. He wouldn't speak a sentence of more than six words and replied to most of the minister's inquiries with grunts and groans.

Dr. Lax noted the ragged furniture, the worn-out rug, and the pitiful refrigerator. When he left, he stopped at the local butcher and ordered three pounds of lamb chops, and sent them to Mr. Bloom.

Ten days later, he called on the old fellow again. This time, the octogenarian was a bit less hostile, but certainly not friendly. Again, upon leaving, Dr. Lax stopped at the butcher's shop and sent the lamb chops. On the next visit, old Henry warmed up quite a bit. The two of them talked about childhood memories, even laughed a little about experiences in the church choir. And, again, Dr Lax sent the lamb chops. Then the preacher was called out of town for awhile, and when he was away, Mr. Bloom's health took a turn for the worse, and he died. But on his death bed, he left a message for the preacher.

"Tell Dr. Lax that everything is okay. I'm going to be with the Lord. I've given my life to Him, but be sure to make one thing clear. It wasn't his preaching that did the trick. It was the lamb chops."

If doing justice means working at life on the basis of biblical principles, then loving kindness means putting a premium on lifestyle, as opposed to lip service.

It is not what we say that affirms our faith.

It is what we do.

It is not the sermons, it is the lamb chops.

The prophet Micah said it well. "Do justice, love kindness and walk humbly with God" (Micah 6:8). We need to apply biblical values to our current life in order to reach holistic decisions. Do justice. Then we gain as we give of ourselves.

As Bob Hope once said, "If you haven't any charity in your heart, you have the worst kind of heart trouble."

And finally "walk humbly with God."

I don't think walking humbly means to sag one's shoulders and look at the ground all the time. I think God authored our pride as well as our piety. I think walking humbly with our God is a simple matter of realizing God's plans are more important than our own.

It means taking everything that happens in life and trusting God's purpose for it, even if it feels difficult and painful. We give ourselves over to the will of the loving God who is with us always and in all ways.

Trust our Creator.

Follow our Lord. Deep in the majestic plans of God, there is an ultimate destiny.

A glimpse of the lives of two Frenchmen may underline this truism.

Augusta and Ferdinand were into "big," and Egypt tickled their fancy—the Pyramids, the Nile, the Sphinx, all these colossal realities got their hopes flowing. And sure enough, as they toured this big vista land, Ferdinand got a big visa idea. He wanted to join the Mediterranean and the Red Sea by a water thread: a passageway for ships, linking east to west across the great isthmus of Suez. Such an accomplishment would reduce a journey of thousands of miles around the African continent to a paltry 105 miles.

Most people laughed.

But not his friend Auguste. "If you pull it off," he challenged, "I will design a lighthouse to stand at the entrance of the canal that the world will never forget. It will be big and beautiful and filled with the promise of hope. Twice the size of the Sphinx, it will be more than a mere structure, it will express the idea of east meeting west, to uniting the world!"

By 1859, Ferdinand had secured the blessings of the proper authorities and the financial backing he needed.

And so began the ten-year construction of the Suez Canal.

In the meantime, Auguste was designing a high lighthouse. He made sketches, built models, adjusted and readjusted until he had exactly what he wanted. He took the design to the Egyptian government and they liked it. But not enough to pay for it.

He sought private investors, but found none. So, for the lack of funds, Auguste's design was set aside. Obviously, it was the right time for Ferdinand's dream. The wrong time for his friend Auguste.

But not for long.

Within just a few years, another country way across the continent sought a monument for their special harbor and they found it in that design of Auguste Bartholdt.

Today, the giant lighthouse, bigger than the Sphinx, shaped like a lovely lady, holding a torch to the sky, stands in the harbor of New York City.

We know her as the Statue of Liberty.

Walking humbly with God means trusting the fact that the Creator has purposes often beyond our understanding. That for every dream, there is a destiny; and a loving God shares every step of our journey.

Stained Glass: Cross and Crown.

Blessed Are You and Your Neighbor

The Beatitudes

My mom, Dorothy Durham, lived longer than anyone I've ever known. She lived through two World Wars, the Big Depression, two loving husbands, her caring mom and dad, my Mamaw and Papaw, and all of her friends.

She seldom complained about the difficulties of her 105 years, 5 months, and 5 days of living. Instead, she lived life to the fullest.

The Beatitudes was her favorite Scripture, because she always felt "blessed," as she put it. We shared reading that Scripture many times over our lifetime together.

It's found in Matthew. They are called the Beatitudes because originally each one of them began, "Blessed are you," but the Greek word that is translated as "blessed" may be translated as "happy" (Matthew 5:1).

So, the Beatitudes describe a special kind of happiness. They describe God's kind of happiness. These are really clues to our own personal discovery of happiness. These signs will be like dropping bread crumbs along the path. When you don't know where you came from, the bread crumbs will lead you back.

Discipline, self-control, good judgment, wise choices, good habits are all mentioned. And remember that blessedness buffeted by ill fortune is saved by hope.

The First Beatitude from the mouth of our Savior Jesus: "Blessed are the poor in spirit for theirs is the kingdom of heaven" (Matthew 5:3). Jesus says blessed are those who know they need all the love, understanding, and forgiveness from God. According to Jesus, we start by emptying out all pretense, all self sufficiency, and open our lives wide to the God who made us.

The second Beatitude: "Blessed are those who mourn; For they shall be comforted" (Matthew 5:4). Jesus says blessed are those who admit, and regret, their moral failures, and who feel deeply the suffering and pain of other people. This kind of mourning shows a person who knows how to care. A person who can feel the human situation, whether it's your own or others.

Third: "Blessed are the meek, for they shall inherit the earth" (Matthew 5:5). *Meek* does not mean "weak." Moses was called the meekest of men, but he took on the whole Egyptian government and led the children of Israel out of Egypt into the Sinai as a free people. Quite the opposite of weak. The "meek" person has a quiet inner strength based on an accurate knowledge of himself or herself. You can't intimidate such a person, or make them do what they don't really believe they should. You know what is right and have within you the tender-tough courage to see it through. One anonymous writer puts it this way: "Blessed is the person who is angry at the right time and never angry at the wrong time."

Here is the fourth blessing: "Blessed are those who hunger and thirst for righteousness for they shall be filled" (Matthew 5:6). And what does God require? We heard it in the inauguration speech from Micah: "Mercy, fairness, justice" (Micah 6:8). Did you ever know a truly happy person who didn't want the world to be like that? Did you ever know a truly blessed person who wasn't willing to commit themselves to helping the world be like that?

Number five is lovely. "Blessed are the merciful for they shall obtain mercy." The Epistle of 1 Peter says: "Finally, all of you be of one mind, having compassion for one another; love as brothers, be tenderhearted, be courteous; not returning evil or reviling for reviling, but on the contrary blessing, knowing that you were called to this, that you may inherit a blessing" (1 Peter 3:8, 9).

Number six: "Blessed are the pure in heart, for they shall see God" (Matthew 5:8). This one isn't so easy because all of a sudden I want to turn it around and say, "Then will those who are not pure in heart not see God?" But this clue to blessedness or happiness really has to do with our motives. Why we do what we do. The truly happy person has pure motives and doesn't mind people knowing what they are. They have nothing to hide. They are the same outside as inside. The truly blessed person doesn't connive behind people's backs or paint wrong lies with less wrong lies.

Number seven is important too. "Blessed are the peacemakers for they shall be called sons of God" (Matthew 5:9). Like parent, like child. God himself is the great peacemaker. That's what Christmas was all about. That's what Good Friday and Easter are all about. God's real sons and daughters are chips off the old block. Does peacemaking make people happy? Of course it does. Nothing is sweeter than patching up a quarrel, coming to a fresh and deeper understanding, getting the tenderness in place and making up. It feels so good not to have to carry the burden of resentment.

Finally, the last clue to blessedness: "Blessed are those who are persecuted for righteousness' sake, for theirs is the kingdom of heaven" (Matthew 5:10). Sometimes being blessed means standing up for something you believe is right. When circumstances are at their worst, you can still be happy, fifty fathoms down in your soul, if you believe you are doing what God requires.

An old Chinese proverb says: "If there is righteousness in the heart, there is beauty in the character, if there is harmony in the home, there will be order in the nation. When there is order in the nation, there will be peace in the world."

The One who followed those Beatitudes the best was the One who gave them to us. When we study the four Gospels—Matthew, Mark, Luke and John—the life and career of Jesus of Nazareth, we will know the One who shared them with us, as we endure the vicissitudes in our lives.

God's Plan

We have seven fun-loving grandchildren. They all enjoy where we live in Florida. Close to Disney, Universal Studios, and Sea World! Oh, the glorious rides! At Magic Kingdom, Space Mountain, It's a Small World, the Haunted Mansion, Pirates of the Caribbean, then over to Epcot and Spaceship Earth, Soarin', visiting all the countries; then on to the Tower of Terror at Disney Hollywood Studios and the Safari ride at Animal Kingdom. And of course, going to Universal having a blast watching the Wizarding World of Harry Potter, then on to Sea World and Shamu Express, Manta, and the Empire of the Penguin.

For us grandparents, we enjoy watching.

Watching our grandchildren at play, savoring life. Watching all the people around us with happy faces, hugging one another, smiling at strangers, and even when babies cry, we collectively smile at the unhappy child, wanting to bring back the high spirits we're feeling.

We all seek filling our days with a touch of bringing pleasure, happiness, and joy into our lives.

What is God's Plan for us?

The Old Testament sheds light on what God's plan is for His creation. Most of us find ourselves in the position of the Hebrews in this Exodus story:

> Then the whole congregation of the children of Israel murmured against Moses and Aaron in the wilderness. And the children of Israel said to them, "Oh, that we had died by the hand of the Lord in the land of Egypt, when we sat by the pots of meat and when we ate bread to the full! For you have brought us out into this wilderness to kill this whole assembly with hunger." (Ex 16:2, 3)

Trapped, enslaved, unable to change direction. Sometimes our Egypt is a personal experience of stagnation or paralysis or being up against a problem. Sometimes we find ourselves in this spot, surrounded, overwhelmed by forces which seem to be too much for our energy and wisdom. Well, God has a plan. And from the time of the Exodus until now, it has worked, for those who are willing to try it.

The first step in the plan is to trust. The people of Israel had to trust that God knew and cared about them and what they were going through. In any contest for the most insignificant people on earth, those Old Testament Israelites would have been real contenders for first prize. Their ancestors, at best, had been nomadic shepherds without a home. Now, they were but one among a multitude of such small tribes, enslaved by the Pharaohs, to provide the labor for their architecturally beautiful projects, such as the pyramids. Before they would even consider trying to escape, they wondered if there even was a God. "Oh, that we had died by the hand of the lord in the land of Egypt. For you have brought us out into this wilderness to kill this whole assembly with hunger" (Exodus 16:3).

We do the same thing.

We question God's existence. We question our own existence. Our culture, with all its obvious excesses in other areas, has failed miserably in one all-important aspect—that is, helping people believe that they are irreplaceable and important. We need to help others believe that they are unique and special.

Our scientific, medical, and architectural achievements make the pyramids, remarkable as they are, pale in comparison. Yet, in the process of building our modern civilization, we, too, like Egypt, have lonely enslaved people. I'm thinking about people who feel left out, alone, no support groups, no church families. People who feel nobody really understands their frustrations and emptiness. I'm thinking of countless widows and widowers, divorced, separated, singles, trying to make their way to find fulfillment in a world still geared largely to couples and families. I'm thinking of the elderly who have to sell our possessions and enter into another horizon, and the feelings of diminishment.

Whatever our situation, we are unlikely to do anything about it, to take seriously any promise of freedom, until we can feel that the offer of love and understanding comes from someone who will demonstrate that they understand us.

The people of Israel had Moses. Moses was one of them. Remember, Moses had been exiled because of his concern for what was happening to his people. Moses stopped an Egyptian from beating a slave. He defended a man who was treated unjustly. Moses didn't have to abandon a pretty good life and business as a shepherd, to come back among the people and risk his neck. He could have stayed away. When Moses spoke about the concern of God for them, his words were backed by his life and his deeds.

He walked the talk.

They had Moses. We have our Lord, Jesus the Christ.

Among all the characteristics of Christ, one thing comes through loud and clear: He poured himself out to get across to every person that God knew them and cared about what they were going through. The message Christ lived and died to communicate is the message every one of us has to trust before God can do anything else with us. The Almighty and All Righteous Ruler of the Earth is not a God above the battle, far off and unconcerned about our problems.

No, God is with us through our problems. Don't we talk all the time about God's love? Isn't this the constant theme of our hymns and sermons? Of course it is. However, for all too many of us, God's love remains a lonely abstraction. We never let the good news sink in that this love applies to you and me personally.

The founder of Methodism, John Wesley, said that the turning point in his life occurred when he went beyond believing that Jesus not only died for the world, but realized that Christ had died for him personally. Until we let ourselves and each other take this final step, we will never find the courage to take any other step in getting delivered.

Deliverance for us, as for the Hebrews, begins with trusting that God knows and cares. I believe something similar must happen to us, if we want to be delivered. The gods of the American way of life have been more alluring and productive than those of Egypt. Money, success, pleasure, power, comfort, security, these gods sway over a lot more of our hearts than we might like to admit. We must squarely face the fact that these false gods—power, pleasure, control—cannot deliver us in the face of the worst storms of life. God has set us in the midst of a risky world, a world which continually puts what we value and depend upon, to the test. But, unfortunately, many of us simply do not get the point until we ourselves are let down by our idols—money, power, success—right when we need them the most.

Maybe God did not specifically arrange our current blows and tragedies that beguile our lives, but they are providing us with the chance to learn about the false gods in whom we have placed our trust. However, let us assume that we, like the Hebrews, have begun to question the gods which dominate our culture, and we are ready to take a risk with our real God, our Lord and Savior. At this point, we must take a crucial step in getting delivered.

Step number two: We must move out with God, in a new way.

The people of Israel, if they wanted to be free, had to clear out of the land of Egypt. They had to leave their old surroundings and belongings behind and enter into a new existence out of the wilderness. It is important to recognize that this was not an easy move. Bad as slavery was, at least they knew what it was like. They really didn't know what life would be like after they escaped. Then, too, there was a kind of security in slavery. At least the evils are familiar ones.

When I think about these things, it becomes something of a miracle that Moses could persuade them to finally make the break, to venture into the unknown.

> Then Moses and Aaron said to all the children of Israel, "At evening you shall know that the Lord has brought you out of the land of Egypt. And in the morning you shall see the glory of the Lord; for He hears your murmurings against the Lord. But what are we, that you murmur against us?" (Ex 16:6, 7)

I wonder how many of us, individually, stand at this point. We want to be delivered, but we are hesitant to take this step, to pay the price of Exodus, to risk finding our freedom. We would like to be free, but it is hard to turn ourselves over completely to God, difficult to say right now, "Here I am, Lord, no matter what my troubles, my problems, my personal tragedies, I need your love, I need your deliverance."

Step number three: We need to say, "Here I am, Lord, deliver me."

We want to find deep meaning in life, to discover and experience a living God. But somehow we never can take the time to undertake a serious search, to study, to worship, to pray. Other things are always more pressing and more important at the moment, all of which brings us to the fourth climatic point in God's plan for deliverance.

Hear again the first three steps in getting delivered.

First step is trusting that God knows and cares about what you're going through, and believing that Christ died for you.

Next step, we must squarely face the fact that the false gods— money, success, comfort—cannot deliver us through the worst storms in our lives.

Thirdly, move out with God into a new way of living. Break free and say, "Here I am, Lord, I need your deliverance."

And, finally, it's a climatic point in God's plan for deliverance.

The people of Israel, having made their escape, are pursued by Egyptian border guards. Behind are the chariots of their pursuers. Their resources are exhausted. No way seems open to them. They want to turn back and give in.

> Then they said to Moses, "Because there were no graves in Egypt, have you taken us away to die in the wilderness? Why have you so dealt with us, to bring us up out of Egypt? Is this not the word that we told you in Egypt, saying 'Let us alone that we may serve the Egyptians? For it would have been better for us to serve the Egyptians than that we should die in the wilderness.'" (Ex 14:10, 11)

Moses said to the people, "Do not be afraid. Stand still, and see the salvation of the Lord, which He will accomplish for you today. For the Egyptians whom you see today, you shall see again no more forever. The Lord will fight for you, and you shall hold your peace" (Exodus 14:13).

At this point, the Lord interrupts his servant, Moses, and makes this all important correction:

> Why do you cry to me? Tell the children of Israel to go forward. But lift up your rod, and stretch out your hand over the sea and divide it. And the children of Israel shall go on dry ground through the midst of the sea. (Ex 14:14)

The sea opened up, only when the people pressed on. Literally, they had to be willing to get their feet wet. To risk.

Time and time again, we face situations exactly like this in our own lives. Situations in which our own resources are exhausted, and there seems to be no way out. At this time, we are tempted to do one of two things: return to Egypt and the old life, more bitter than before, or cry to God for a miracle.

And then we come smack up against disillusionment within ourselves. And right behind us is a whole army of thoughts and feelings, urging us to forget about taking Christ seriously, to stop trying to be some sort of hero, to get back to normal. Of course, we think a miracle might change our minds, but we know deep down that sort of thing just doesn't happen, at least not to us.

We say, "Hey, the Lord's not going to provide you with a miracle." That's when we come face to face with disappointment. The chariot wheels of fear and despair are rolling ever nearer, tempting us to turn away from hope and love, and giving into self-pity. Well, at such a time, the word of God to Moses is his word to us as well: "Why do you cry to me? Go forward" (Exodus 14:13). In other words, keep on keeping on. Keep praying, keep trusting in God. Whether you are talking about overwhelming tragedies or personal crises, they are won by people who persevere, who hang in there, just when you thought they might give up. So it is with the critical experiences of life. God's power to deliver us is known in the last analysis only by those who are willing to press on, trusting that what they cannot do, God can!

But, you say, the sea doesn't open up for anyone today.

No?

I have seen a way opened up for people who choose to live in faith rather than to give in to bitterness. I have seen a way opened up to reconciliation for people who choose to keep on forgiving and loving instead of turning back to apathy or indifference or cynicism. I have seen the way opened up for creative service for those who are willing to care and not give in to discouragement. I have seen a way opened up to meaning and joy with God for those who choose to keep praying and worshiping.

The Lord is as powerful to redeem as ever. The sea still opens up, but only for those who press on in faith. The Lord still works miracles, but before God can, you and I have to trust enough to take the plunge. When you are at your lowest, you must remember God is with you.

This beautiful poem that many have shared with me, says it all.

Footprints in the Sand

One night I dreamed I was walking along the beach with the Lord.
Many scenes from my life flashed across the sky.
In each scene I noticed footprints in the sand.
Sometimes there were two sets of footprints, other times, there
    were one set of footprints.
This bothered me because I noticed that during the low periods
    of my life, when I was suffering from anguish, sorrow or defeat,
I could see only one set of footprints.
So, I said to the Lord,
"You promised me, Lord
That if I followed You,
You would walk with me always.
But I have noticed that during
The most trying periods of my life,
There have only been one
Set of footprints in the sand.
I don't understand
Why, when I needed You most
You would leave me."
The Lord replied,

"My precious child, I love you and would never leave you. During your times of trial and suffering, when you see only one set of footprints, it was then that I carried you."

—Mary Stevenson

Love Your Neighbor as Yourself

How do we believe, in our hearts, that we are indeed loved, especially when we're not too sure we love ourselves? Listen to the two great commandments (Mark 12:28-31).

> Then one of the scribes came, and having heard them reasoning together, perceiving that He had answered them well, asked Jesus, "Which is the first commandment of all?" Jesus answered him, "The first of all the commandments is: 'Hear, O Israel, the Lord our God, the Lord is one. And you shall love the Lord your God with all your heart, with all your soul, with all your mind, and with all your strength.' This is the first commandment. And the second, like it, is this: 'You shall love your neighbor as yourself.' There is no other commandment greater than these."

"Love your neighbor as yourself."

What does that mean, "as yourself"? Does it indicate how much love or, for that matter, any amount of love may be withheld from our neighbor? First, though, you must love yourself. If we love ourselves, we should regard our minds as an instrument of God too precious to be prostituted to unworthy ends. We should look upon our body as the temple of the Holy Spirit, and not be debased by smoking, drinking, drugging, and other addictions. To love ourselves is to see ourselves as immortal souls freighted with immeasurable possibilities because, as Ethel Waters once wrote, "I am somebody, God don't make no junk."

Ethel was born in Chester, Pennsylvania, on October 31, 1896, as a result of the rape of her teenage mother. She had a difficult childhood, living in poverty, and never lived in the same place for more than fifteen months. She married at age thirteen but left her abusive husband and became a maid in a Philadelphia hotel working for $4.75 per week. On her seventeenth birthday, she sang two songs at a nightclub and began her illustrious spiritual journey.

In 1950, she wrote her autobiography, with Charles Samuels, naming it *His Eye Is on the Sparrow*, a Gospel hymn she eloquently sang touching the lives of everyone who heard her inspirational presentation.

The theme of the song is inspired by the words of Jesus in the Gospel of Matthew in the Bible: "Look at the birds of the air; they neither sow nor reap nor gather into barns, and yet your heavenly Father feeds them. Are you not of more value than they?" (Matthew 6:26).

Why Should I Feel Discouraged

Why should I feel discouraged,
Why should the shadows come
Why should my heart feel lonely
And long for heaven and home.
When Jesus is my portion
A constant friend is he
His eye is on the sparrow
And I know He watches over me
His eye is on the sparrow, and I know He watches me
I sing because I'm happy
I sing because I'm free
His eye is on the sparrow
And I know he watches me.

This appreciation for ourselves, then, is a yardstick by which to measure our appraisal of our neighbor. As we have regard for the sanctity of our own person, we will have regard for our neighbor's person. As we value our convictions, we will recognize the value of our neighbor's viewpoint. As we prize our freedom, we will help safeguard the freedom of others. For humanity is really one and the person who finds themselves at their deepest level has found something which makes them kin with all other persons. At the deepest level of our beings, we are not separate selves. Your life and my life flow into each other as wave flows into wave. Unless there is peace and joy and freedom for you, there can be no real peace, joy, or freedom for me. You can bring a healing touch of compassion and love to other people only if you have love for yourself. "You shall love your neighbor as yourself" (Mark 12:31).

At this point, it might be wise to look at the differences between *selfishness* and *self-love*.

The selfish person is interested only in themselves. Selfish people want everything just for themselves. That person feels little pleasure in giving, but only in taking. They look at the world in terms of what they can get out of it. The selfish person lacks interest in the needs of others. They judge everything in terms of its usefulness to themselves. Actually, selfishness and self-love are opposites. The truth is, the selfish person does not love themselves enough. In fact, they may dislike themselves.

Some might ask the question of whether doing good things for yourself is not simply self-indulgence. However, doing what you feel good about yourself is really the opposite of self-indulgence. It means satisfying your whole self. This includes the feelings and ties and responsibilities you have to others too. It does mean being self-centered enough to care for yourself and to take care of yourself. If you don't learn how to do that, you can never care properly for others.

Our Scripture says, "Love your neighbor as yourself."

Not "better than" or "instead of," but "as yourself." If we cannot love ourselves, where will we draw our love for anyone else? People who do not love themselves can adore others because adoration is making someone else big and ourselves small. They can desire others because desire comes out of a sense of inner incompleteness which demands to be filled. But they cannot love others because love is an affirmation of the living being in all of us. The clue to all our relationships is the ability to love ourselves. To enjoy being alone with ourselves. To be our own best friend. Some people might worry about falling into the trap of pride and self-righteousness and becoming an obnoxious little Pharisee. But we do not need to worry about that if we remember we are loved by God.

We know that God sees us exactly as we are—our faults, failures, our defensive pride. God sees every piece of us, and accepts us, as we are. Not because we have done lots of dandy deeds to deserve it. And that is the wonder of it.

A while back, there was a popular song called "The Greatest Love of All." Some of the words are, "I believe the children are the future, teach them well, show them all the beauty they possess inside, give them a sense of pride, learning to love yourself is the greatest love of all."

The story of the Cross is the story of God bending down to accept and forgive us, despite our defects and failures, because our Lord wants to affirm our value and worth as persons. If God affirms our worth as persons, what right have we to deny it?

I am to accept myself, with all my faults, silly pretensions, my limitations, my handicaps, my power struggles. I am I. You are you. We are persons in our own right. Infinitely valuable in God's sight, because "God don't make no junk."

Only when we have discovered the power of being who we are will we live the life God gave us. If we can learn to love and nurture ourselves, we will find ourselves happier than we ever imagined.

Oh, we will still be beset by real problems and suffer defeats, because life is not a rose garden. The world is not run for our benefit. There is no escaping the human condition which involves pain and difficulty and loss. But we can bring everything we have to bear upon the challenges life presents and make the most of what it offers us. We can all help ourselves to change, to grow, to be content with the person it is in us to be, that God wants us to become. We can learn to love ourselves to be our own best friend. For if we do, we have a friend for life, because "God don't make no junk."

Now that we are attempting to love and accept ourselves, what does Jesus mean, "to love your neighbor"? "You shall love your neighbor as yourself" (Mark 12:31).

Who Is My Neighbor?

And who is my neighbor?

In the Scriptures found in the book of Luke, Jesus told a story about eternal life The setting is in Palestine. The lawyer asked Jesus, "What shall I do to inherit eternal life?" (Luke 10:25). Our Lord does not reply to his question but asks him another in return. "What is written in the law?" (Luke 10:26).

I believe the lawyer must have been somewhat startled. After all, anybody who has grown up among the people of God knows the answer to this fundamental question of life. So the lawyer proceeds to answer, "It is written, you shall love the Lord your God with all your heart and with all your mind and your neighbor as yourself" (Luke 10:27).

Oh, how easy it was before to say "love your God." How easily we speak such a sentence. It even sounds a bit trite. But just let Jesus stand in front of us and look at us when we say the words, "You shall love the Lord your God with all your heart, mind, and soul and your neighbor as yourself," and all at once this pious little saying penetrates our souls. Then all of a sudden, we hear it spoken by a person who called this week and we spoke harshly, or we did not hear the cries of a person who was treated unfairly, or we spread a juicy piece of gossip. Suddenly we hear them all speaking, because this saying has something to do with all people, for through each person, the eyes of the Lord Himself are gazing at us.

And so it was with the lawyer when he had recited his piece about this religion of love. Jesus said to him, "You have answered rightly; do this and you will live" (Luke 10:28), thereby indicating that this was the answer to all his questions. What the lawyer wanted was to engage in a philosophical discussion of love and eternal life. But Jesus said don't start by thinking about love, but practice it. Many things can be known only by doing and practicing them. I can assure you, this is not easy. It is easier to discuss a thing, or write about it, than to practice it. Reading the Scriptures daily, going to church on Sunday, listening to and delivering sermons about love. This is much easier than to sacrifice oneself for one in need.

But this Jesus begins to pose challenges and raise questions in our mind. Then the lawyer, who wants to justify himself, said to Jesus, "And who is my neighbor?" (Luke 10:29).

The lawyer looked at Jesus with eager expectation. Now, certainly, this Nazarene must begin to philosophize. Now he will have to discuss the meaning and nature of the word *neighbor*, that is if He is to be considered an intelligent person and taken seriously.

And, again, this Jesus once more responds completely differently from what had been expected. Jesus tells a story.

> "A man", said Jesus, "went down from Jerusalem to Jericho and fell among thieves who stripped him of his clothing, wounded him and departed, leaving him half dead. Now, by chance, a certain priest came down that road. And when he saw him, he passed by on the other side. Likewise a Levite passed by on the other side. But a certain Samaritan, came where he was. And, when he saw him he had compassion on him and went to him and bandaged his wounds and set him on his own animal, brought him to an inn and took care of him." (Lk 10:30-35_

And Jesus continued, "So which of these three do you think was neighbor to him who fell among the thieves?" (Luke 10:36).

As I read this beautiful parable, I wonder how I would feel as the wounded man, or the priest, Levite, or the Samaritan. If I was the wounded man being left by thieves who stripped me of my clothing, wounded me, and left me half dead, what would I think when I saw a priest coming down Jericho Road? I would probably think, "Ah, here is a priest who just came from the temple. He must have preached a sermon on loving God and one's neighbor. Thank God that it is someone who is still under the impression of the temple who should happen to come by. Surely he will help me."

In the same moment, the priest saw the wounded person. Why didn't the priest stop? The priest had a different opinion about the concept of the neighbor from that of the wounded man. This is always the case. The person who is appealed to for help and the person who needs help sometimes have different ideas about the meaning of the word *neighbor*.

The priest might have thought, "The poor fellow, lucky it didn't happen to me." Perhaps he even thought of helping, but checked himself thinking, "The same robbers may still by lying in wait a hundred yards away, just waiting to knock me in the head too." Who is my neighbor? This fellow who I don't know at all? This fellow who may be an embezzler, or another criminal, or heavens knows what? My family comes first. If it were only myself, I would sacrifice for him, but I have other obligations. My family, my vocation, and they are my real neighbors.

The Levite, too, passed by on the other side. He may have indulged in similar reflections. "If I get held up with this poor man, I'll miss my lecture." None of us really want to see who our neighbor really is, for to look at our neighbor's misery is the first step in God's love.

Love always seizes the heart first, and then the hand.

On this Jericho Road that runs right through our home road where we live, there are three attitudes we can learn from this parable.

The first attitude can be put this way: "What's yours is mine, if I can take it." That is the attitude of the robbers who lurked in the caves nearby. Armed robbery is a common felony reported on the news. Most of us are not likely to be tempted to become armed robbers. But before we feel too good too soon, are there not ways of robbing helpless people that are not violent ways or even illegal ways? We can vote money out of our neighbor's pockets. The poor can do this to the affluent, the affluent can do it to the poor.

The second attitude is: "What's mine is my own, if I can keep it." This is the attitude of the priest and the Levite. They notice the wounded man lying in the pool of blood. They do not stop. They hurry by. I can even justify their conduct. They weren't bad men. They were clergy! That's what bothers me about this story. They are religious men. They don't lack morality, they don't lack honesty, but a willingness to risk.

Love is a willingness to risk. A willingness to give yourself totally to another person in need. A willingness to stand beside a person who has been treated unfairly. A willingness to stop, listen, and act.

The third attitude on our Jericho Road is: "What's mine is yours if I can share it."

It's the attitude of a person you would not expect to act that way.

To review a little history, in Latin, all Gaul was divided in three parts. So was all of Palestine in Jesus's day. There was the solid conservative, orthodox south, Judea; the northern third was Galilee, mostly gentile, but with Samaritans, a kind of combination of religion and other things. There was bad blood between the Jews and the Samaritans.

No love lost, either way. In Jesus's neighborhood, when you wanted to go from the north down south to the temple at feast time, you didn't go south, you went all the way around the Sea of Galilee and down the east bank of the Jordan through the Rock Desert. Then you crossed the fjord of the Jordan near Jericho and wound up on that long twisty, tortuous, dangerous Jericho Road to get to Jerusalem. You went 50 percent out of your way to avoid meeting Samaritans.

So, when Jesus asked the lawyer, "So, which of these three do you think was neighbor to him who fell among the thieves?" (Luke 10:36), Jesus knew how much the Samaritans were disliked by their neighbors.

The question is: "How does the Samaritan feel this kind of love for people who don't even like him? How does it get started?"

Love is always somebody's initiative. It always has to start somewhere. It starts in a God-touched heart. It comes from people who support you through difficult, trying days. When we are in touch with that love, we witness it and begin to pass it on to others.

We will learn who Jesus is from our distressed people all around us, for it is in them that Jesus meets us. But we cannot go and do and love, if we stop and ask first: "Who is my neighbor?"

We can only love if we have the mind of Jesus and turn the lawyer's question around. Then we shall ask not "Who is my neighbor?" but "To whom am I a neighbor?" Who is laid at my door? Who is expecting help from me?

We have to choose which road to travel on, and which attitude will be ours. Shall we keep our love to ourselves, which becomes like the priest and the Levite, a self love? Or shall we choose the road of the Good Samaritan, who passed Jesus's love on to others? And Jesus asks us all: "So which of these three do you think was neighbor to him who fell among the thieves?" (Luke 10:36).

And, the lawyer said to Jesus, "He who showed mercy on him" (Luke 10:37).

Then Jesus said to him, "Go and do likewise" (Luke 10:37).

Channels

make us true channels
of Your endless love
as we live our lives
and reach for above we struggle with sin
yet strive to be good
we confess past sin
and wish that we could
always make choices
correct in Your eyes
always love neighbors
even when disguised
help us to see that
in all that we do
we can, when humbled,
grow closer to You
help us to know that
You're here ev'ry day
ready to nurture
and guide when we stray.

—WHS

Churches Door

GRATITUDE
AND THANKSGIVING

I heard about a traveler on foot, walking through desolate country, but at nightfall he came upon a monastery. He was welcomed there and given food and shelter. The next morning, as he was about to leave, one of the brothers offered to loan him one of the horses for his journey. Well, as you can imagine, the traveler was overjoyed. This would certainly make his traveling easier. He readily accepted the use of the horse.

The monk then said, "You'll have to understand that this horse has to be ridden with special instructions because he has been raised in this religious environment. The normal commands which you would use to ride the horse will not work."

The traveler asked, "What are the commands that you have taught this horse to follow?"

The monk replied, "When you want to go forward, you must say, 'Thank God!' That's because the religious life starts with thankfulness. If you want the horse to go faster, you will have to say, 'Praise the Lord,' because our lives without praise of God are empty. When you say, 'Praise the Lord,' the horse will jump into a trot. If you want the horse to go even faster, you'll have to say, 'Praise the Lord, praise the Lord!' and the horse will start to gallop. And when you need to stop, say 'Amen,' which is the way we end our prayers."

The traveler said, "Well, I think I can remember those easy commands." He climbed aboard this large steed and he said, "Thank God," and the horse did, indeed, jump ahead. He got comfortable in the saddle and decided he was ready for more speed, so he said, "Praise the Lord," and the horse started to trot. The traveler tired of that quickly and thought now we'll really make some time, so he said "Praise the Lord, praise the Lord!" and the horse started to gallop across the field. Then all of a sudden, the traveler saw a cliff ahead of him. "Whoa!" he said to the horse, but the horse charged ahead, and he was really a powerful animal.

"Stop," the traveler shouted as the horse charged ahead and as he got closer and closer to the edge of the cliff.

Finally, the traveler remembered the commands the monk had given him.

He shouted, "Amen!" The horse stopped, just on the edge of the cliff. He looked down on the long drop where a canyon had been developed by a river sweeping through the valley and then, with a shaky hand wiping his brow, he said, "Thank God!"

Do you remember the command from the monk?

The Case of Ingratitude

When our children are learning to talk, one of the first things we teach our children to say is "thank you." One time, when we took a daughter trick and treating at Halloween, we asked her to say thank you at each home. When we didn't hear her say thank you, we asked if she had something she wanted to say. Instead of saying thank you, she turned back to the lady at the door and said, "More."

There are so many Scriptures in the Holy Bible that speak of "giving thanks." I believe the most amazing Scripture on this topic is from the Gospel of Luke:

> Now it happened as He went to Jerusalem that He passed through the midst of Samaria and Galilee. Then as He entered a certain village, there met Him ten men who were lepers, who stood afar off. And they lifted up their voices and said, "Jesus, Master, have mercy on us!" So when He saw them, He said to them, "Go, show yourselves to the priests." And so it was that as they went, they were cleansed. Now one of them, when he

saw that he was healed, returned, and with a loud voice glorified God, and fell down on his face at His feet, giving Him thanks. And he was a Samaritan. So Jesus answered and said, "Where there not ten cleansed? But where are the nine? Were there not any found who returned to give glory to God except this foreigner?" And He said to him, "Arise, go your way. Your faith has made you well." (Lk 17:11-19)

This powerful Scripture concerns Jesus's healing of the ten lepers, but only one who was healed came back to Jesus giving Him thanks. To understand what it would mean to have the dreaded disease of leprosy, let's look back to Jesus's time when He walked the earth.

In the near east, when someone came down with leprosy, they were immediately separated from the rest of their society. They were given a separate colony of people with whom to live. We tend to think that the primary reason for this is the contagious nature of leprosy, and that is partially true. There is also a further explanation as to why lepers were separated from the rest of society. The people of that time believed that every physical illness was from God. If life was not going well for you, including physical illnesses, then obviously God was punishing you. You had done something wrong.

Therefore, the person with leprosy was not only physically ill, but spiritually ill as well.

What a picture.

These ten men came to Jesus, living apart from their families, outside the community. They can't play with their children nor embrace their wives. Everyone sees them as a threat. They have to wear torn cloths. They have to cover their mouths and wear their hair disheveled, and worst of all, the disease is linked with sin, so the leper is morally judged, and self judged, as a sinner. And what is Jesus's response?

He saw them and healed them. All ten of them. And one of them, when he saw that he was healed, turned back praising God and fell at Jesus's feet, giving him thanks (Luke 17:16.)

And Jesus answered, "Were there not ten cleansed? But where are the other nine? Was no one found to return and give praise to God except one?" (Luke 17:17).

To be sure, ten of them were cured of leprosy, but for nine, the cleansing was only skin deep.

Only in one leper did the healing reach the heart as well.

Only one person was saved from the worst disease of all, the disease of ingratitude.

All of us know what ingratitude is. It is not being grateful for what has been given to us. Few of us, I imagine, are aware that it is a disease. A disease that can do more damage than almost anything else in our lives.

Because of this damage, I want to describe some of the effects of this disease of ingratitude so that you can recognize it and then give you a prescription for a cure. Now, ingratitude usually sneaks up on you. However, there are some symptoms, or signs, that are pretty easy to spot.

Just imagine you are looking into a full-length mirror, and if you're showing any of these signs, beware. An almost imperceptible lengthening of the face. A weakening in the muscles you use in smiling, in laughing, and most of all, singing. Occasional signs in hardness of hearing when you are asked to do something for someone else. A decreasing ability to give compliments. A glowing capacity to find things to complain about. A feeling that there's no hope. An inability to see God's small, wonderful miracles happening around you every day.

These are some genuine signs that the disease of ingratitude is creeping up on you.

And if you think these things are bad, when the disease of ingratitude really takes hold, the results, frankly, are horrible.

For instance, it can make a person almost blind. I don't mean physically blind. There are worse kinds of blindness. The ungrateful person still sees things and people, but they become blind in a more important way. They cease to see what life and people mean to them. They stop truly enjoying. A person with a bad case of ingratitude can be a member of a loving family and be surrounded with friends and neighbors. They can be a part of God's family, and, yet, all they see from day to day are their own expectations. They miss out completely on enjoying what is around them and rejoicing in all that people bring to their lives.

Ingratitude does another thing too.

It paralyzes.

Sure, you can move your arms and legs and you can think, but you can only do it for yourself. Somehow the kind or generous or sacrificial deed or word just never gets done. Never gets spoken. Whatever muscles are used in writing notes, in giving of self, these muscles just wither up, and finally, the most terrible result of all, is loneliness. The person whose heart is infected with ingratitude finds it almost impossible to trust and share with anyone very deeply. Worst of all, they find it very hard to feel that God cares about them. The insidious thing about this disease is that it can infect the heart of someone who outwardly is very healthy and surrounded by every advantage.

In fact, the disease of ingratitude seems far more prevalent among people who are privileged, because they have been given much for which to be grateful.

Finally, I should mention in this diagnosis that the disease is a catching one. I've seen one person who has a bad case of ingratitude give it to a whole group in the space of a few minutes. At a meeting, I have come down with a case of ingratitude myself, because of as small a thing as a harsh comment or a nasty glance.

Well, then, how do we get cured of this disease of ingratitude?

There is only one prescription that I know that can really help. You can't buy this prescription at the drug store. In fact, it isn't something you buy or take at all. Instead, this prescription is something you give.

The only sure cure of the deadly disease of ingratitude is gratitude. Gratitude to God and gratitude to each other.

Let's look at each part.

To begin with, gratitude to God.

We all know that we are supposed to give thanks to God for special nice things that come our way. But what I'm talking about is giving thanks for the tremendous gifts that come to us each day without our asking for them, which we are likely to take entirely for granted and never see how really wonderful they are. The sheer gift of each day of life. The chance to breathe. Food to eat. The gift of citizenship in this country of ours. The presence in our lives of all kinds of people to love and be loved by. And, above all, the miraculous news that Jesus and His special family keep telling us about, reminding us, that God cares about us, believes in us, and loves us. No matter what.

John Newton was the author of the lyrics of a well-known hymn, "Amazing Grace." John lacked religious moral, self control, and discipline, as well as having a career in slave trading. He didn't know about God's love until a violent storm occurred one night while he was at sea. Throughout the tumult, John realized his helplessness and concluded that only the grace of God could save him.

After his boat was saved, John wrote "Amazing Grace," thanking God for a new beginning. "Amazing Grace, that saved a wretch like me, once I was lost and now am found, was blind, but now I see." He wrote these lyrics in 1773, and then became a changed man, openly challenging the trafficking of slaves, thanking God for a new beginning.

What I'm suggesting is that we all need to thank God, not for just one day, but every day. I'm not suggesting this because it's a good idea to be nice or polite or do our duty. I'm prescribing gratitude to God as the basic way in which to avoid the blindness, the paralysis, the terrible loneliness which the disease of ingratitude unfailingly produces.

The second part of the prescription is gratitude to each other.

One of the big points of an education is learning to appreciate things. How to appreciate architecture, art, music, and much more. Something, however, which is much tougher to learn, is people appreciation. People who pass through our lives everyday. Appreciating and enjoying the endless fascinating procession of people who pass through our lives every day. People appreciation takes work. It's an effort that is worth every minute we can give it because it can help us see all sorts of ways in which people can enrich our lives. That's just half of the prescription. The other half is to let people know that we appreciate them. Giving them thanks. There are all sorts of ways in which we can do this. A word, a note, a pat on the back. How we do it isn't as important as really giving our thanks to other people. That sounds like a very small thing, doesn't it? So small and insignificant that we usually don't even think about it. Or we simply never get around to it. I can guarantee that if you make a habit of giving gratitude to people you know, what happens will inoculate you against the deadly disease of ingratitude as almost nothing else can do.

Why? Because we know that every person wants, more than anything else, some sign, however small, that somebody notices and appreciates and is grateful for what they do. There are lots of people in this world of ours who have not been given any signs that even God actually cares about them.

There you have it. A prescription for getting over the worst disease you can get.

But, you know, it's a funny thing. Unlike most prescriptions which you stop taking after the disease is cured, the prescription of gratitude is one you will want to take the rest of your life. In fact, you might discover that gratitude is what our lives are all about.

Now, I mentioned earlier that the disease of ingratitude was very catching. What you need to know is that the truly grateful heart is even more catching. The person who sincerely practices gratitude can brighten up a home and meeting in no time at all.

Jesus said, "Were not ten cleansed? Where are the other nine? Was no one found to return and give thanks to God except this one man?" (Luke 17:17). Then Jesus said, "Arise, go your way. Your faith has made you well" (Luke 17:19).

Now, that's Amazing Grace.

Is the Pain Worth the Gain?

There are so many challenges as we stretch to our Lord through faith and thanksgiving.

Have you ever watched a blind person trying to use their cane? I was watching a blind man in an airport as he encountered a walking ramp. It was quite an achievement for this blind man to even reach the appliance. He walked at a pretty good pace, cane ever in front of him, tapping, probing the unknown. He was probably translating signals, painting a picture in his mind to match the hubbub in his ears. Then he reached the moving rubber track. He tapped once and stopped. Very deliberately, he pushed the tip of the cane firm against the rubber and felt it move.

With that, he stepped aboard and handled it like everybody else, except he kept the cane in contact with the surface and extended as far as he could push it in front of him. When it clicked against the metal track at the other end, he picked up his foot and walked away. It was awesome. I sat there watching him walk the "sidewalk" and thinking about how we grow in our faith.

If we are serious about constantly growing in our faith and giving thanks, then we must develop a cane to keep us from stumbling over the roadblocks dotting our pathways.

So, what are these barriers which keep the Holy Spirit from shaping our lives?

One barrier is busyness. We have to be the "busiest" generation ever. How many of us could make a meeting this very night? Our calendars are so cluttered with activity, it's a wonder we can sit in church for sixty minutes.

The Psalmist gave us a tremendous piece of counsel when he said, "Be still and know that I am God" (Psalm 46:10).

His advice was to stop the rat race, shut down the conveyor belt, and center in God. After all my surgical operations at Mayo Clinic, the downtime helped me to learn how to nourish my relationship to God.

I'm talking about personal time totally devoted to giving thanks and being in prayer. I'm talking about using our cane and tapping it in the right direction, toward God. Most of us are consumed by the need to achieve, the quest for number one. The challenge of excellence, and all of those motives, have their positive dimension, but they fade when they destroy the ability to love and be loved, to care and be cared for, to serve and to be served.

I guess Walker Percy said it best: "It is possible to get all A's and flunk life."

What can we do to eliminate these roadblocks? We must recognize that the future remains in the hands of God, so we need a tapping cane which invests in our Creator.

Yes, we are exceptionally busy—of our own decision. Yes, we are consumed with the pursuit of profit—of our own decision. All are a matter of selected decisions. And so is the decision to choose our Creator.

For even as we choose to be busy, choose to pursue profit, so we can also choose prayer and thanksgiving. Prayer and giving thanks are the two practices which frees us for the future. If we really want to claim the future, we must entrust it to God with daily prayer and thanksgiving.

How do we live our lives with faith, thanksgiving, and trust in God?

I believe the book of James is a practical guide for daily behavior. Now, you need to know that James was addressing his remarks to people who were more than familiar with hassles. James was writing to the Jews of the dispersion.

"James, a servant of God and of the Lord Jesus Christ, to the twelve tribes which are scattered abroad, 'Greetings'" (James 1:1).

Now, the twelve tribes of the dispersion were the poor souls who had been intentionally transplanted from Israel to foreign lands. The tribes were Reuben, Simeon, Judah, Issachar, Zebulun, Benjamin, Dan, Naphtali, Gad, Asher, Ephraim, and Manasseh. They were the scattered people, the descendants of those exiled in Old Testament times. These were the folk who had heard a lot about the promised land but had never been there. Always in the minority, they were accustomed to the subtleties of oppression and indignity of being second-class citizens. For them, life had not been easy. That being the case, what difference should it make for them to believe in Jesus?

James goes right to the heart of the matter: "My brethren, count it all joy when you fall into various trails, knowing that the testing of your faith produces patience. But, let patience have its perfect work, that you may be perfect and complete, lacking nothing" (James 1:2-4).

Now, there is a single word in this little passage that provides a wealth of insight about how faith makes a difference in the way we live. Translated "testing," it is the Greek term *dokimion*, and it means "probed to a purpose." By using the word *dokimion*, the book of James is making it clear that the Lord is not someone who delights in watching people suffer, but rather a loving friend who is intent on strengthening those who bear his name.

Of course, we know that testing is important to all progress. Chemists test new materials through test tubes. Engineers test input/output. Athletics is similar to this. If you've ever played a sport, you know how tiring, how exhausting, and how frustrating it is to your body, mind, and spirit. For me, it is especially so in the game of golf.

Every time an athlete reaches for a new level of strength, it is done toward a purpose. The theory being that the more practice, the better he or she will perform. "The pain is worth the gain," so the saying goes.

Well, in like manner, James says, "Count it all joy when trials come; because you're being tested for a purpose"(James 1:2). Like single strands of cord, twisted together to make a rope.

So the difficult moments of life blend together to produce the backbone and fortitude required to make us victors in the midst of strife. Let's face it, life is filled with some difficult experiences. One of the differences faith makes in the believer's life is the capacity to accept difficulty as a stepping stone toward strength. Another difference that faith makes is a commitment to excellence.

We all have blemishes. We ain't perfect yet. I do believe that following Christ means we are always trying to improve.

"The Whole Gospel for The Whole World through Whole Persons" is the motto of my Palmer Theological Seminary. We do our best, not for ourselves, but for the Master.

If we carry His name, we owe Him our best. This is the heart of what James is telling the scattered Jews and tells us even today.

Yes, life is full of difficult moments. But if we trust the promises of God, we will accept every difficulty as a test for a purpose, an opportunity to improve our endurances and a stepping stone toward excellence in the Master's name.

Worshiping God

One of the most obvious effects of faith and gratitude is the ability to worship God and get something out of it. That's what James is talking about in this passage from the book of James.

Therefore lay aside all filthiness and overflow of wickedness, and receive with meekness the implanted word, which is able to save your souls. But be doers of the word, and not hearers only, deceiving yourselves. For if anyone is a hearer of the word, and not a doer, he is like a man observing his natural face in a mirror; for he observes himself, goes away and immediately forgets what kind of man he was. But he who looks into the perfect law of liberty and continues in it, and is not a forgetful hearer but a doer of the work, this one will be blessed in what he does. (Jas 1:21-25)

All of us bring our baggage to meetings, groups, even church worship services. We have knowledge about ourselves to which no one else has access. We know our shortcomings, our weaknesses. Yes, even our filthiness and wickedness. In order to have a meaningful worship experience, we need to dump that stuff at the door. That's right. James says put it aside and leave it at the door. Don't sit there all bogged down with how terrible you or other people are. Rather, make yourself a deal and agree for the time you're there not to get hung up on your hang-ups. I'd like to post a sign at the entrance to our sanctuary that says, "Check your poor opinion of yourself and others before you enter."

Let's look at James's formula for growth through worship. And it all begins, like everything good, with a receptive attitude. The person of faith and thanksgiving tries to be perpetually open to the word of God. To absorb as much as possible. Let's face it, it's hard to concentrate on God's guidance when our minds are filled with images of children struggling at school, business foul-ups, and the state of the stock market. Even as I've aged, I might not be thinking about the kids, as much as my next doctor's appointment, an upcoming operation, and the procedures inevitably involved.

In fact, every time we enter the sanctuary more concerned about where we are than where God is, we have a problem.

I'm sure that is what the writer of Ecclesiastes was alluding to when he wrote:

Walk prudently when you go to the house of God; and draw
near to hear rather than to give the sacrifice of fools, for they
do not know that they do evil. Do not be rash with your mouth,
And let not your heart utter anything hastily before God, For
God is in heaven, and you on earth; Therefore, let your words be
few. (Eccl 5:1, 2).

The whole idea is to be receptive, open, ready to accept whatever
God has to offer.

Many years ago, I took my eldest grandson, Michael, to New York
to see the Radio City Music Hall show and ice skate at Rockefeller
Center. It is a wonderful experience being together, sharing in the
magic of the city, but amazingly noisy. The cab driver had on the radio,
jabbering to us, the rustle and bustle of the people, horns honking,
ambulance sirens blaring. I'm always overwhelmed by the din of
information swirling around me. All well and good, but it's hard to
think with the constant noise. Once again, I realized what an awesome
challenge it is to find a corner for God's communication.

When Tom and I lived in Wilmington, our property had a large
rock on the side of our home. It was there I took our grandsons, Mike
and Ben, for talks with God. We called it "our God Rock." Quiet time
together, talking with our Creator.

So, the pivotal dimension for preparing for worship is silence. Clear
the tape, shut down in conversation, and listen to the organ music, as
we prepare for the open space the word to be implanted. Our Scripture
from James draws a great analogy as he made reference to the person
who looks in the mirror but refuses to change. "For if anyone is a hearer
of the word and not a doer, he is like a man observing his natural face
in a mirror, for he observes himself, goes away, and immediately forgets
what kind of man he was" (James 1:23).

Encountering the word of God means allowing the light of
unconditional love to illumine our lives and help us cope with our
inconsistencies. None of us should find it possible to worship and
communicate with God and come away without homework.

If nothing else demands that we stretch to the Lord, the awareness that we are loved, without reservation, should send us out into the world every week with a new attitude about the people around us. It centers not in what we know, but what we don't know. Not in what we are, but what we are not. Not in smug achievement, but humble acknowledgment. Thomas Jefferson said it: "He who knows most, knows only how little he knows."

When we worship God, whether by attendance in the sanctuary, or in a corner of our private space, we need to let the light of God illuminate the intricacies of our lives, taking us to new heights of opportunity and reminding us of old anchors of understanding.

Even as it would be foolish to look in a mirror without the will to change things we don't like in our lives, so it is foolish to listen to God's word without the will to adjust our lives in accordance to it.

The person of faith and thanksgiving sees every worship experience as an opportunity to examine the soul, to affirm strengths and address weakness. Not only to hear the word of God, but to do something about it.

The late J. Wallace Hamilton loved to illustrate this point by telling the story of the bedraggled young student who slipped into the back row of a New York church. It happened over forty years ago. The kid was a mess. He had spent the previous night partying and he looked like it: hair askew, shirttail hanging out, trousers wrinkled, eyes bloodshot. He was surprised by waking up during the worship, hearing the preacher say, "Let us pray." The young kid didn't bow his head, instead he started gawking around the sanctuary studying the people who were there. "Why are they here?" he wondered. "What difference does all this mumbo jumbo make to these seemingly intelligent people?"

And then his eyes locked on the man across the aisle from him. It was one of his teachers. A professor of science, a man with many degrees and academic honors. There the professor sat, head down, deep in prayer, obviously humbled before God. And the young student thought, "Now I understand why this professor is so understanding and listens to his students. Now I understand how it is that he is so forgiving with those who taunt him with cynical remarks and even make fun of his clothes. I always thought he acted like a martyr when others hurt him because he didn't stand up to them." The young lad said to himself, "If he can believe in God, surely I can."

A burden lifted from his mind. He went out of the church with a feeling of hope and purpose. The professor never knew the boy was there. That is, he didn't know until twenty years later, long after he retired from teaching. It was then that he received a knock at his door and was met by a middle-aged man and his wife. They were home on furlough from missionary work in Africa and he had looked up his old professor.

Sitting in his teacher's study, he said, "I don't know what it was, sir. I think it was the look on your face. The fact that you were there, the fact that suddenly I realized the way you lived matched the faith you confessed. Whatever it was, it sat right in my heart, and I came to thank you."

You see, we never know when someone is setting a mirror in front of us. We never know when the manner of our living casts a direct reflection on the substance of our faith. We never know when someone might be glancing across an aisle, or sitting in a meeting, taking measure of the gap between what we say and what we do.

But we do know this.

If we are to effectively carry the name of Jesus Christ, we are obligated to not only be hearers of the word, but doers as well.

God's Affirmation: In His Time

When I was a younger woman, I really enjoyed going to the state fair. It rolled around every August, and even though I could care less about cows, pigs, and produce contests, our family always made it to the fairground. Most of the fair was fun. I always liked the horse show, the cotton candy, and, of course, the midway. There, the "carny" people set up their booths and bilked the public, including me. There was only one booth I ever succeeded in winning a teddy bear, and that was the basketball shoot. But there was one part of the state fair that bothered me back in those days. It was the spectacle displays. Each was complete with garish signs and recorded sounds effects. "Come see the three-hundred-pound woman." "See the three-handed boy."

It bothered me then. Today, it seems unconscionable.

Yet, as I look at Scripture, I discover a bit of making spectacles of human beings that didn't start with our state fair. It's been going on for a long time before that. Go with me to the dusty streets of Philippi from the book of Acts.

> Now it happened, as we went to prayer, that a certain slave girl possessed with a spirit of divination met us, who brought her masters much profit by fortune-telling. This girl followed Paul and us, and cried out, saying, "These men are the servants of the Most High God, who proclaim to us the way of salvation." And this she did for many days. But Paul, greatly annoyed, turned and said to the spirit, "I command you in the name of Jesus Christ to come out of her." But when her masters saw that their hope of profit was gone, they seized Paul an Silas and dragged them into the marketplace to the authorities. And they brought them to the magistrates, and said, "these men, being Jews, exceedingly trouble our city; and they teach customs which are not lawful for us, being Romans, to receive or observe." Then the multitude rose up together against them; and the magistrates tore off their clothes and commanded them to be beaten with rods. And when they had laid many stripes on them, they threw them into prison, commanding the jailer to keep them securely. Having received such a charge, he put them into the inner prison and fastened their feet in the stocks. But at midnight Paul and Silas were praying and singing hymns to God, and the prisoners were listening to them. Suddenly there was a great earthquake, so that the foundations of the prison were shaken; and immediately all the doors were opened and everyone's chains were loosed. And the keeper of the prison awaking from sleep and seeing the prison doors open, supposing the prisoners had fled, drew his sword and was about to kill himself. But Paul called with a loud voice, saying, "Do yourself no harm, for we are all here." Then he called for a light, ran in, and fell down trembling before Paul and Silas. And he brought them out and said," Sires, what must I

do to be saved?" So they said, "Believe on the Lord Jesus Christ, and you will be saved, you and your household." (Acts 16:16-31)

Paul and Silas have just returned to the city, when they were confronted by an amoral group of hustlers exploiting a demented slave girl. As the evangelists entered the Macedonian city, they were surprised to see this rag-tag girl lingering in the fringe of their group.

Then, every once in a while, they were startled to hear a voice, seemingly coming from nowhere, crying out to Paul, "These men are the servants of the Most High God, who proclaim to us the way of salvation."

As our Scripture tells us, she was "possessed with a spirit of divination" (Acts 16:16), bringing her masters much profit by fortune-telling. Such attributes made her a likely candidate for exploitation. With Paul and Silas, she had her own midway. The preachers drew a crowd and the con men couldn't resist. Better yet, they discovered whenever the girl got anywhere near Paul, she would begin to scream with immense intensity.

The Bible says the apostle put up with this for several days. But finally his patience wore thin, and realizing her performance was prompted by the subliminal clash between the power of the demon within her and the power of the Holy Spirit within him, he turned to the girl and destroyed her demon (Acts 16:18).

Suddenly, she was free. Suddenly, the scam was over. The hustlers were broke. They were mad and needed to point their finger at the men who brought them this trouble. "And, they brought them to the magistrates and said, 'These men, being Jews, exceedingly trouble our city and they teach customs which are not lawful for us, being Romans, to receive or observe'" (Acts 16:20).

After beating Paul and Silas, they put them in jail. And then they were miraculously freed from prison via a violent earthquake. Their captor, who had questioned their sanity when they were singing while in stocks, suddenly sensed the profound power at their fingertips and posed the big question, "Sirs, what must I do to be saved?" (Acts 16:28).

Paul and Silas went to his home and there the jailer treated the wounds of the preachers, and the preachers treated the soul of the jailer. Then the Bible plays a "gap" game. One verse finds Paul and Silas partying with the family, the next has the police coming to release them from jail.

> Now when he had brought them into his house, he set food before them; and he rejoiced having believed in God with all his household. And when it was day, the magistrates sent the officers, saying, "Let those men go." So the keeper of the prison reported these words to Paul, saying, "The magistrates have sent to let you go. Now therefore depart, and go in peace." (Acts 16:34-36)

We don't know what happened in between.

For some reason, they didn't claim the freedom they had gained. For some reason, they chose to go back to that putrid jail. In the meantime, the magistrates were having second thoughts about locking them up in the first place. So it was no surprise when the local constable said, "Let those men go" (Acts 16:35). But what happened next was a total surprise. When the police sought to lead them out a side door, Paul stopped and said, "They have beaten us openly, uncondemned Romans, and have thrown us into prison. And now do they put us out secretly? No indeed! Let them come themselves and get us out" (Acts 16:37).

At first blush we might get the idea that Paul had a Philippians death wish.

First, he deliberately exposes the scam of the local mafia.

Then he makes a spectacle of himself while in jail. Then he befriends his assailant, he voluntarily goes back to the slammer. And lastly, when the authorities try to give him a break by slipping him out the side door, he refuses to leave until they escort him out the same way he came in. It's an unusual story and it is loaded with information about the dimensions of mature faith.

Mature is one of those tricky words which defies definition. Webster's Dictionary says it means "fully developed." It is derived from the Latin *matures*, meaning "ripe" and "morning." Hence, to be mature is to be "ready at dawn." They knew their place and trusted God to work in it.

Dr. Paul Brand, the noted plastic surgeon, understood this principle. When his mother was seventy-five years old working as a missionary in the mountains of South India, she fell and broke her hip. After an excruciating 150-mile journey to the hospital on a makeshift cot in the back of a rickety old jeep, she received treatment only to discover the only way she could walk was with the assistance of two bamboo canes that were taller than she was. Still, she went back to the mountains to care for her people. Shortly thereafter, Dr. Brand journeyed to her remote village to persuade his mother it was time to retire. He praised her long years of service, pointed out all that she had done, and invited her to come and live with him.

Dr. Brand writes in his book, *In His Image*:

> Granny threw off my arguments like so much nonsense and shot back a reprimand. Who would continue the work? There was no one else in the entire mountain range to preach, to bind up wounds, and to pull teeth. "In any case," she concluded, "what is the use of preserving my old body if it is not going to be used where God needs me?"

So Granny stayed. Eighteen years later, at the age of ninety-three, she reluctantly gave up sitting on her pony because she was falling off too frequently. Devoted Indian villagers began bearing her on a hammock from town to town. After two more years of mission work, she died at the age of ninety-five.

A mature faith has the inner security to endure insecurity. It goes where others fear to tread. I thought of that story when I remembered watching the people at our Supporting KIDDS group. They were willing to continue on, even when life looked most difficult, even when the next step was totally unknown.

Another mark of mature faith is that it recognizes conflict as a means to express values.

Paul had an ulterior motive when the magistrates wanted to sweep him under the rug. He knew the scorn with which Christians had been treated in Philippi and he recognized a tremendous opportunity to stand proud in the face of persecution. It would have been easier to simply slip away into the night, but it would have done nothing for those who would remain behind. Thus, for the sake of principle and the people, the apostle willingly confronted his tormentor. But Paul, seeking to set an example, chose conflict to make his point.

Sure, he risked total failure. But in doing so, he clearly illustrated that Christians have rights as well as pagans. He gave his people something for which to strive. Throughout his ordeal in Philippi, Paul and Silas were never anxious. Confronted with a demented girl, Paul calmly called the demons from within her. Seized by the authorities for disturbing the peace, the preachers offered no defense. Shackled in a rat-infested cell, they sang songs of faith.

And now, freed to flee into the night, Paul says, "Let them come themselves and get us out" (Acts 16:37). And I get the feeling he would have waited a long time before doing anything else.

We might ask, "How could he be in this much control?"

It's simple. He wasn't. But he knew who was. He knew ultimately God always affirmed His people. It happened with Abraham when he willingly entered the wilderness (Genesis 12:1-3). It happened with Moses when he crossed into the Sinai (Exodus 4:29, 30). It happened with David as he approached Goliath (Samuel 17:1-58). It happened with our Lord when it appeared evil had triumphed (1 John 3:8). And it happened in this Philippian jail where Paul was tossed in as a clown and brought out as a conqueror.

God always affirms…in time.

Yes, this is the promise of eternity that we, through the grace of God, can never be ultimately defeated. That one day, "every knee shall bow in heaven and on earth and under the earth, and every tongue shall confess that Jesus Christ is Lord" (Philippians 2:10).

Knowing this, we can be as bold and benevolent as the Apostle Paul. We can expose injustice. Do battle with poverty, Take stands that protect the sanctity of life, because we trust in time as God's tool of triumph.

For All That Has Been, Thanks; for All That Will Be, "Yes, God"

On June 25, 1995, I preached my last sermon at Mt. Lebanon United Methodist Church in Wilmington, Delaware. It was the most difficult sermon I've ever delivered, because I loved that "church in the dogwoods," as it was known in the community.

The title of my sermon was "For All That Has Been, Thanks, For all That Will Be, Yes." That quote came from Dag Hammarskjold, and it was my personal statement to my congregation. And, I add "God" to Dag Hammarskjold's quote.

How do I even begin to lift my thanks to all of you? First, to my supportive family, who were all sitting with us today. My mom, who brought me into this world, along with my dad, who died at the young age of forty-six, but was with me during my formative years, encouraging me to be whatever I wanted to be. Thanks, dearest mom, as you also came to my seminary graduation, my ordination, and the weddings of all our children, and today, my special day of thanksgiving. Our children, Debbie, Becky, and Carrie, who were sixteen, thirteen, and eight years of age when I took my first course at Palmer Theological Seminary in 1972. Your helping fix breakfasts, dinners, housework, along with doing our homework together helped me immensely. My attending seminary twenty years after college left me with a lot of intellectual "catching up" to do. Thanks to you for helping me endure the pilgrimage with your caring encouragements.

And thanks for giving us more family members, with our loving sons-in-law, Joe, Bud, Bill, and beautiful grandchildren, Michael (Boogie), Ben (BJ), Megan (Megablue), and Patty (boom-a-laddie). I am so grateful you've given me the honor of officiating at your weddings and baptizing our precious grandchildren.

And my dearly beloved husband of forty-two plus years, Tom. How did I know forty-two years ago you would be the greatest person in my life year after year? Especially when I changed course in the middle of our marriage. After being housewife and mother for almost twenty years, I blazingly announced: "I'm going to seminary."

But as the great country song says, "You never gave up on me." And what's more, you even participated in making this church everything the saints up above meant this church to be. Thank you, my beloved prince!

"For all that has been, thanks." Thanks to the Master for his calling each of us to be ministers to one another and the entire community.

From our Gospel lesson: "Now, when Jesus got into one of the boats, which was Simon's and asked him to put out a little from the land. And He sat down and taught the multitudes from the boat. Now when He had stopped speaking, He said to Simon, "launch out into the deep and let down your nets for a catch" (Luke 5:3).

Our Lord is strolling along the shore of the Sea of Galilee. The "sea" is not a sea at all. At best, it could be called a moderately sized lake. Thirteen miles long and eight miles wide, it nestles along the gently sloping hills between the Golan heights on one side and a lush, fertile valley on the other. About this time, Jesus spotted some fishermen cleaning their nets. Beside them were their small fishing boats. The Master stepped into one of the boats directing the fishermen, a rather surly character, known as Peter Simon, to "let down your nets for a catch." At this point, Simon let down the nets and caught so many fish that he had to call to his friends for help. And when he realized what miracle had taken place, Simon fell on his knees before Jesus, exclaiming, "Depart from me Lord, for I am a sinful man" (Luke 5:8.) As much as to say, "I don't deserve this miracle, Lord!"

Immediately, our Lord reached forth his hand and lifted the contrite fisherman to his feet. "Do not be afraid. From now on you will catch men" (Luke 5:10).

For all of us, the passage bristles with council. And it begins with Jesus's response to Peter. We might have expected the average person not to choose a sinner. Perhaps to even judge Simon Peter, by making him an outcast, but certainly not giving him all those fish.

Why give him a miracle to encourage this sinner, Peter? But this Jesus comes to us with unconditional love, calling all of us, even if we are snared by circumstance.

My question was, "How can I follow you, Jesus, if I don't have the skills or the finances? Why, I have a family. How can I answer your call?"

More often than not, if we just step back and study the terrain, the Lord provides the answers. But all of this takes a shift in perspective. As the scientist Albert Szent Gyorgyi observed, "Creative thinking consists of looking at the same time as everyone else, and thinking something different."

It happens all around us, in all kinds of ways. While the rest of us were looking at sawdust as the carpenter's necessary nuisance, some genius figured out how to press it altogether and make self-starting fireplace logs. While the rest of us relegated baking soda to a moderate role in the cooking process, some thinker figured out how to use it as an odor eater in the common refrigerator. While the rest of us were grousing over the aggravation of summer burrs snagged in the pelts of our pets, someone whipped out a magnifying glass, studied the clinging power of the pesky plants, and invented Velcro.

The message is simple. When baffled by barriers, fresh insights are as close as a change in perspective. The water in the Sea of Galilee is so clear that as long as one remains close to the shore, it is easy to see the bottom. But out near the center of the lake, the depth is too great for the light and from the surface, it is impossible to see what is below.

It is my deepest conviction that the Master often asks us, all of us, to go into unknown territory.

And, I say to you, twelve years later, "For all that has been, thanks."

Thanks for your wonderful response.

Thanks for your courage to test unknown waters. And most especially, Lord, thanks for the people you've sent our way. The Lord answers every prayer, according to His will. Through the years, just when I thought our time was over, because I couldn't do everything, the Lord sent someone.

I wish the church had a Hall of Fame, the way every other group does.

Certainly the "backbones," a group of women, led by good friend, Eunice Ayres, who encouraged, enabled, and supported our efforts here, would lead the list. Also at the top of Mt. Lebanon's Hall of Fame would be the newsletter Lantern writers, A. Mouse, secretaries, director of music and the choir that have staying powers beyond reproach. To all that helped place Mt. Lebanon in the Historic National Registry. And the sanctuary's bare lightbulbs were all replaced with ten lanterns in each window, six chandeliers, and ten aisle candles. All of these were crafted with pewter, and designed by artesian John Ramsey of Chestertown, Maryland, and modified by Tom Walters, AIA.

To all of you who have joined our church inspiring me to continue facilitating the many support groups we started over the years. And for all of you who've had the courage to join our support groups. The YSPP Youth Suicide Prevention Support Group; the MOVING ON adult suicide prevention support group; FOSTER, Families of Suicide to Enable Recovery; HOPING, Helping Other People in Normal Grieving; and Supporting KIDDS, Kids Involved in Death, Divorce, and Separation.

For your many hours of volunteering to serve in any capacity needed.

And another special outreach of our church was the "Best Foot Forward" program. Our church "in the dogwoods" served the women's prisons in our State of Delaware. "Best Foot Forward" is a joint program of the YWCA, the Delaware Council on Crime and Justice, the Women's Correctional Institute, and our Mt. Lebanon United Methodist Church. This program helps develop self-esteem, basic life skills, physical fitness, job readiness, and has a special emphasis on helping the children of incarcerated women at Woodshaven-Kruse and Smyrna prisons. You've been bringing lunches to the incarcerated women and their children every Saturday, as I led the vespers service, with many of you reading Scripture, singing hymns, and greeting each incarcerated woman and their children with a smile and a feeling of God's love. You've been assisting in this vital outreach since 1987.

"For all that has been, thank you God." Thank you for allowing us to witness more about You.

Although I always knew God was with us, learning more about the nature of God has been a revelation on our journey together.

In order for me to learn unconditional love and grace in this journey we call life, I need to recognize that God is at work in every situation. As the prayer specialist. Hannah Smith said, "Until we can learn to see God in everything, we shall never know contentment." It was the prolific theologian Karl Barth who wrote volumes concerning the divine human relationship. Still, when asked to summarize his ideas about God, what did he say? "Jesus loves me, this I know, for the Bible tells me so."

What it all boils down to is the ability to trust in the Lord as the Author of our lives. He is the potter, we are the clay.

"For all that has been, thanks."

Thanks to my family, Thanks to God for calling each of us. Thanks to you for your enduring helpful responses. Thanks to my Savior for revealing his unconditional love.

"For all that has been, thanks. For all that will be, yes, God."

For all that will be, we must trust in our future. It is easy to see God in the good, happy, pleasant times of our lives, but finding our Creator in the midst of turmoil and trouble is more difficult. Yet God is always with us.

I remember the Sea of Galilee, where Jesus spends a lot of his pilgrimage on earth. It has been several years since I boarded a ferry at Capernaum, along with other United Methodist people in the conference, as we made our way across that beautiful body of water.

It was a cool February day, even though the sun was shining brightly. Most of us assembled on the rear observation deck where we could watch the hills where Jesus delivered the Sermon on the Mount fade into the background. Then when we were square in the center of the lake when we were directly over the deep water, the captain of the vessel shut down the engines and let us drift.

There were prayers and Scripture readings and total silence as all 158 of us basked in the beauty of the moment.

Then, very softly, some of the people began to sing this song:

> When peace, like a river, attendeth my way,
> When sorrow like sea billows roll,
> Whatever my lot, thou hast taught me to say,
> It is well. It is well with my soul.

One by one, the rest of us began singing, until our entire boat sang that phenomenal statement of faith that echoed off the Galilean hills. It was then a strange phenomenon took place. Directly above us, ominous clouds seemed to come, from out of nowhere, looking as though it would rain any minute. But just as suddenly, the sunlight appeared through the clouds, forming the most beautiful spry of glory ever resembling a cross. The combined reaction all of us was a chorus of "oohs" and "yes, God."

When we finished singing, and the clouds dissipated, most of us had tears running down our faces.

"For all that will be, Thanks God."

1871 was not a good year for Horatio Spafford. Early in the year, he lost a teenage son to meningitis. Then, just as he was beginning to recover from that tragedy, the great Chicago fire took place, virtually wiping out his financial base. Then, in the fall, Spafford decided to book passage to Great Britain with his wife and four daughters to visit his wife's family. But a sudden flurry of business made it imprudent for Horatio to make the journey. He sent his wife and children with the promise he would join them in a week. On November 22, 1873, in a heavy Atlantic fog, their steamship, *Ville du Havre*, collided with another boat and sank in twelve minutes.

It took several days for the survivors to be transported to London. It was then that Horatio Spafford received a two-word telegraph from his wife. It said, "Saved alone."

Once again, his world had been unmercifully smashed. By the time he arrived in London, he had written this beautiful hymn. Just imagine penning these words:

> When sorrows, like sea bellows roll, whatever my lot, Thou has taught me to say, 'it is well, it is well, with my soul.

But, even more importantly, imagine how this broken man felt, whose life had been ripped apart by tragedy in eighteen short months. If he was anything like most of us, he was probably blaming himself, scouring his history for the unforgivable trespasses that would result in such a horrible development.

Well, think again, and take a look at the third verse.

If anyone understood the matchless Grace of God, Horatio certainly did, when he wrote "It Is Well With My Soul"

My sin, Oh, the bliss of this glorious thought, My sin, not in part but the whole, is nailed to the cross, and I bear it no more, praise the Lord, praise the Lord, O my soul.

Jesus said, "Whoever would be great among you, must be your servant, and whoever would be first among you must be your slave" (Matthew 20:27).

"For all that has been, thanks."

I will take your teaching and pass on your Lord's unconditional love when I leave here. For I do not leave, I take you with me.

"For all that has been, thanks, for all that will be, yes, God."

We will trust in the future, for we know Jesus said, "Lo, I am with you always, even to the end of the age" (Matthew 28:20). Amen!

God in Focus

God tries in so many ways to reach us. How often we miss seeing Him in our lives.

Do we know where God is? Many of us think our Creator is way out there somewhere, unreachable.

There's a story about a good man who was caught in his home at the time of a terrible flood. Water was pouring down and the dam had been broken. Rescue squads were trying to save the people in that city. A canoeist was paddling up many streets when he came upon this good man, who was now standing at his doorway knee-high in water.

"Come on in, I'll save you," the canoeist yelled.

But the good man said, "No, thank you, God will come and save me."

About an hour later, a rowboat rowed by and the rowers shouted, "We will save you."

And the good man, who was in the water waist deep now, said, "No, thank you, God will come and save me."

Another hour passed and a helicopter with the chair at the end of a long rope whirled by and the pilot yelled, "Get in the chair and you'll be saved!"

But the good man, now standing on the chimney of his water-logged home and with water everywhere, said, "No, thank you, God will come and save me."

Well, a little time elapsed and the good man drowned. When he entered the pearly gates, he asked God why in the world He didn't come and save him. After all, he had been a good Christian, faithfully waiting for God to rescue him. God said to the good man, "My son, I sent a canoe, I sent a rowboat, and I sent a helicopter, but you refused to be saved."

God does come to us, through others, and through many different modes. A God who confronts us simply as exalted, distant, and strange would be a God we would have to avoid, because our Creator would not reach us on the human level of understanding.

God is in our heart, yet we search for Him in the wilderness, or up there somewhere. Sometimes we have such difficulty bringing God into focus.

God wants to know us. When I use the word "to know," I can mean two very different things. I might say, "I know arithmetic, or I know the Star-Spangled Banner," or "I know how to golf or swim." That's one kind of knowing. But if I say, "I know my husband or my children or grandchildren," I mean something quite different.

The first kind of knowing is one way. I know golf, but golf doesn't know me. I am the subject: golf is the object. The second kind of knowing is two way. I know my husband Tom, and I am known by Tom. Each of us knows the other in the same act of knowing. I am the subject and so is he a subject. Not only that, but golf is not changed by my knowing it. That's for sure. But my husband and I are changed by knowing each other.

Some Gospel light might help bring God into focus more clearly.

"For God so loved the world that He gave His only begotten Son, that whoever believes in Him should not perish but have everlasting life" (John 3:16), and verse 17: "For God did not send His Son into the world to condemn the world, but that the world through Him might be saved." This is the second kind of knowing, where both God and us are subjects. Knowing each other, interacting with each other, living with each other. Both of us are changed by knowing each other in this ongoing relationship.

By the way, God is not the only one who was unhappy when we turn Him into an object. Something to talk about, rather than someone to talk to. Other people are unhappy with that treatment too. Sometimes spouses become frustrated when their loved ones treat them like objects. "My wife, my husband, you know, they always talk at me, but never listen to me."

Suppose I tried to treat my husband like an object. Suppose I tacked up on the refrigerator door these instructions: "Tom, please rise at 7:00 a.m. and fix my breakfast. Eggs on Monday, bacon and pancakes on Tuesday...something really special on Sunday." Well, I can tell you, I'd be laughed at from here to breakfast! Whenever we make another person into an object, whether a status object or housekeeper object or money machine object, there's bound to be trouble. Even when an employer thinks of the workers as so many "hired hands" or "units of labor" instead of human beings, that employer is asking for labor problems. Everyone wants to feel his or her value as a person, and hungers for real relationships.

God wants us to know Him.

How does God make that happen? How does God approach us?

I really enjoy taking pictures. It's a fun vocation for me to take a picture and send it off to the person who would enjoy seeing it. We used to take slides and had a slide projector for years. We couldn't get our slide project fixed, it's so outdated. The digital camera has taken its place. Now my digital camera has those thumbnail memory cards. You can slip into a format on your computer and you can instantly print pictures, even e-mail them somewhere in the world where our Marine and Navy grandsons are based. It is truly amazing.

First, you pop in the memory card, and all you see is a blob of color, then you twist the lens and slowly shapes appear. Then you twist the lens some more. Suddenly everything is in focus. There you are at the beach, your mouth stuffed with hot dogs and mustard.

In a sense, God turned on His projector, His memory card at creation and said, "Let there be light," and in the creation, God comes to us in many ways. What are some of the ways God approaches us?

Stand by me in Chestertown, Maryland, with my camera and telescopic lens some years ago, when I watched the lunar eclipse. Let us watch the great starry constellation wheel slowly and majestically through the silent heavens. The light reaching us has been traveling for thousands, even millions of years. One star up there is 250,000,000 miles in diameter and so rarefied you could pass right through it and not know it, except for the temperature. I don't know how you feel, as we look together at the night sky, but to me, God seems vast, far away, majestic, wrapped in mystery.

Or stand with me at the beach after a big storm and let's watch and listen as the surf comes crashing in toward shore. Spindrift sliced off by the wind: power, sheer, irresistible power. And movement spanning millions of years while waves sculpture the edge of the continent and polish each tiny grain of sand.

That's what comes across to me, as I think of the God who made the seas, and the land, and the wind. Or let's take a walk at low tide along a river and look at the tidal pools. We peer down into tiny fascinating worlds, each a perfectly balanced ecological system with plants and animals meant to live together until the next tide.

Or put your snorkel mask off the coast, and open your eyes underneath to see the colorful universe of coral reefs. It's God's genius and artistry that comes across now.

So far so good. But if we leave God as a powerful Creator, or an artist, He still seems awesome and far away. We wonder, does He know about the kid who had leukemia? Does God care? How about someone in pain with cancer, arthritis, dementia, emotional pain, grief? Does He really want to know little old me? How can I be sure?

Well, twist the lens a turn and let's look into the Old Testament.

Now we see God more clearly. We see not God up there in the starry heavens, far off, but God working and involved with people. Throughout the Old Testament, we find God appearing as a patient teacher, working with people where He finds them. God teaches them how to live, how to act justly, how to get along with each other, how to walk before Him and with Him.

God cares about His people. He loves them, and hopes for their love in return.

God brings them out of slavery in Egypt. He guides them through their wilderness wanderings. He gives them the Ten Commandments through Moses. He tells them how to worship in a kind of family reunion. But God's people sometimes turn this personal friendship with our Creator into an outward formal system of religion, with rules, customs, and laws.

People, unfortunately, turned God into an object, a thing, and the life of loving and knowing one another in divine relationships almost disappears. So God decided to come to us in a way that He could best be known, at our human level. To become one of us. To meet us within a human relationship. As the Epistle tells us: "The first man was of the earth, made of dust; the second Man is the Lord from heaven" (1 Corinthians 15:47). The Old Testament Isaiah predicted it: "For unto us a Child is born, Unto us a Son is given; And the government will be upon His shoulder. And His name will be called Wonderful, Counselor, Mighty God, Everlasting Father, Prince of Peace" (Isaiah 9: 6,7).

So, the word that hurled the galaxies of stars out into the millions of light years and space, the word that designed the majestic and beautiful palm trees in Florida, the word that guided the writings of Holy Bible, that word was made flesh in a tiny baby, so that we could meet and know our Creator.

This Jesus grew up as a normal boy. Don't strip him of His humanity, the things God tried so hard to give Him. Jesus ran around the house, went to synagogue, studied the Torah, learned responsibility and knew the call of His heavenly Creator, gave His life to ministry, died under the hostility of those who rejected Him, and rose again in triumph.

Now, with Jesus having lived in our midst, the second kind of knowing, living, and personal fellowship with God becomes possible. The lens is now in the right place.

God comes into focus, and at the human level, God is Jesus incarnate.

The event is at Bethlehem. Those who took the pictures were the shepherds, the disciples, and the Gospel writers. The film, the slide, the memory card is the biblical record, the Holy Bible. Now, we are at the computer/projector. The whole world is the screen and all of its people are the intended audience. And that's the gospel of today, as we are called to present Jesus to the world. How do we do this? By our word of witness, our deeds of caring love, justice, and friendship. We do this through deeds of mission, as we reach out to others.

I pray our light is bright and the lens is clear, and as the picture appears in focus, the miracle happens, the event is now the present.

So we can hear Jesus speak again, as He did when He said "that whoever believes in Him should not perish but have eternal life. For God so loved the world that He gave His only begotten Son, that whoever believes in Him should not perish but have everlasting life" (John 3:15, 16).

Evening Collage

Saturn peeks between the clouds
a darkened bank of vapor shrouds
Spica's calm and gentle rays
Polaris hides behind the haze
but as the evening hastens on
I notice to my right-a swan!
the North Cross shines and Deneb, too
and Vega with its crystal blue
the starry host comes out this night
ablaze with reds and blues and white
a spectacle that few enjoy
and one that we may soon destroy.

—WHS

Stained Glass Spiritus

Starting Over

Tom and I have suffered a lot of health problems over the years. Tom's prostate cancer came when he was just sixty years old. His PSA was high, at a measurement of eight, and the biopsy showed it was cancerous. At that time, I was the pastor at Mt. Lebanon United Methodist Church and teaching medical ethics at the medical center. In my ethics class were all male interns. When I told them my husband's situation, I asked them what surgical urologist they would recommend, and to the man they said Dr. Wein at the University of Pennsylvania. Dr. Wein was well known for his treatment of prostate cancer, and after four weeks of donating his own blood for the upcoming operation, Tom had his radical prostatectomy. After the operation, Dr. Wein came to the waiting room and greeted us with the bad news. Tom's cancer was outside the margins, which meant radiation for six weeks. Surviving the operation was difficult, and six weeks of radiation took a toll on his architectural practice. After forty years of giving his talent, his integrity,, and his diligent service to the State of Delaware, he had to close his practice. Did he whine, or give up on life? No. He started over.

We had a grandson who loved golf. One time, when he was four years old, we took him to a putt-putt green where you line up, putt your ball, try to miss the slowly moving windmill, and drop it in the hole. On the very first hole, he putted the ball, missed the hole, went up to the ball, retrieved it and brought it back to the tee again. Then, as his big brown eyes twinkled, but with a small frown over his brow, he would say, "Starting over." Then he proceeded to putt again, missing the hole. He'd assume the same position, saying, "Starting over."

Starting over is what you do over and over again, throughout life.

The Chinese philosopher, Confucius, outlined seven stages of life.

First, the newborn infant. Wail loudly, drooling, needing round-the-clock care.

Second, school child. Morning face shine, drags foot forward to schoolhouse.

Third, lover. Sighing, composing poetry, marriage, love.

Fourth, parent. Tell children right ways of life, teach others, work at career.

Then, fifth stage, well-fed stomach grows fleshy, expression of eyes severe, mouth spout out wise, sometimes not so wise sayings.

Sixth stage, declining years. Spectacles above nose, stockings oversize, skin shrinks, big, strong voice returned to child's voice, then whistle sounds.

Last stage, end this strange eventful history, second childhood, teeth go, sight go, taste go, ears go, everything goes.

As I reflect on Tom's cancer surgery changing his lifestyle, and my own four cancer surgeries changing my lifestyle, I began to reflect on what our needs are, as we "start over."

First, we all need a sense of belonging. We all want to belong to something or someone. For me, it's God. I know God was present even when I was feeling miserable. That presence came as people called and offered to help. That presence came as get-well cards came to the door. That presence came as I realized how many nurses, doctors, hospital staffs were trying to unveil the mystery of the disease called cancer.

Feeling God's presence through others makes me feel as though I can "start over."

The second value I found I needed as I started over was to have something worthwhile to do. Most of us are concerned about losing a sense of purpose, which leads to questions like, "Why am I here?" If I died tomorrow, would it matter to anyone? After all, the older we get, the more misery, the more suffering and grief we experience. The more we see sadness and bitterness, callousness can set in.

But it doesn't need to be this way.

Dr. Martin Luther King Sr., after he lost not only his son to an assassin's bullet, but also his wife while sitting playing the organ in his church, said, "There is no hate in my heart. I will continue to use what I have left and not cry over what I have lost."

My mom lost two wonderful husbands and all of her friends. We would talk daily and when she mentions someone I have met, she adds sadly, "She just died." To start over at her age is overwhelming. Yet Mom was never bitter, always trying to make her life work as well as she can, and always a welcoming voice when she answered the phone.

Yes, we lose as we age. But we can adapt to our changing circumstances and use the strength we have left, which could be a constant source of inspiration to others. "My soul, waits silently for God alone, For my expectation is from Him. He only is my rock and my salvation; He is my defense; I shall not be moved. In God is my salvation and my glory; the rock of my strength And my refuge, is in God" (Psalm 62:5-7).

God is always with me.

The third common value we need as we "start" over is to feel we are truly loved by someone significant to us. If you have been in a situation where you're feeling alone, abandoned, or in fear of the unknown, you understand what the simple act of someone holding your hand means. My Tom was with me every second before and after surgery.

The hunger for needing to feel loved never subsides. We can be God's messenger to others, to make someone else's life feel worthwhile.

As the Gospel from John says: "This is My commandment that you love one another as I have loved you. Greater love has no one than this, than to lay down one's life for his friends" (John 15:12, 13).

As we start over in our different stages in life, these three common values are vital.

A sense of belonging.

A desire to be useful.

A sense of being loved by someone.

And, a fourth value, the wisdom to live each day as a gift.

Remember the Psalmist said, "Teach us to number our days that we may get a heart of wisdom" (Psalm 90:12).

Each moment is sacred.

I like William Blake's poetic wisdom, as he wrote:

> He who bends to himself a joy
> Doth the winged life destroy.
> But, he who kisses the joy as it flies
> Lives in eternity's sunrise.

Seven stages of life, and our needs as we journey through it, frequently "starting over."

The Ritual

Did you know that the posture of the mind determines the peace of the person? In his latest bestseller, *Peace, Love, and Healing*, Dr. Bernie Siegel tells the story of a physician whose mother was dying of cancer. Doctors had informed her loved ones that it was a matter of three to six months. At this, her daughter decided that even if she couldn't beat the disease, she could at least be the prettiest patient in the hospital, so she headed for the nearest department store and purchased the most expensive matching robe and nightgown ensemble she could find. As she carried the gift into the hospital room, she did have a bit of reservation, remembering that her mother had been raised during the depression and didn't appreciate waste or extravagance. Opening the gift, the older woman paused as her fingers traced the lace on the collar of the nightgown. "Would you mind if I asked you to take this back?," she questioned. "This is what I really want," and she picked up the newspaper and turned to the back page where she put her finger on a designer purse.

Her daughter was shocked. Not only was this the epitome of extravagance, it was also a summer purse and it was now the middle of January. There was no way her mother could use that purse in the summer six months away. And suddenly she realized that her mother was pointing her mind toward tomorrow, locking her sights on the future, reaching for a forbidden horizon. Not only did she intend to live, but to do so triumphantly.

Every three months, when we fly to Ohio to be with my mom, my husband and I always took her to the "mall." She delighted in riding the wheel chair, with us pushing her around to see the window sights and, of course, the sales. Mom loved a good sale, and she knew her fabrics. Even when I was a senior in high school, she made all my clothes. Adept in designing her own patterns, she would ask me, "Which collar do you like?" or "What style skirt?" And I was always able to choose the fabric, even velvet for my high school prom. I've never been a good shopper, but Mom taught me a lot as she touched a shirt or dress and proclaimed, "This is good material."

Mom was able to travel to the mall until she was 105 years young. We had a lovely party for her on her birthday, but she became too fragile to travel to the stores. However, she did tell me what to purchase for her. A summer blouse, and it was February in Ohio. I dutifully found a summer blouse in her small size, and she lived to wear it, before she died.

My mom too lived triumphantly.

All over the world, scores of researchers are discovering there is nothing more significant that the mind in determining the spiritual, mental, and physical condition of human beings.

Of course, this doesn't mean we won't die a physical death, but we need to learn how to be positive thinkers, as minister Norman Vincent Peale said in his book, *The Power of Positive Thinking*.

This shouldn't be news to anyone who has ever read the book of Philippians from the Holy Bible. If anyone ever understood the phenomenal influence of mind over matter, it was the Apostle St. Paul. Locked in a Roman jail, surrounded by rats and roaches, subjected to daily interrogation and perpetual aggravation, Paul may have been the first person to prove the power of confidence over cruelty. His followers marveled at the vigor of his faith. They couldn't believe how he rose above the trauma and terror of imprisonment. How he subdued his captors with kindness. How he diligently displayed the ability to overcome all things, just through faith.

From the Epistle Scripture, Paul writes:

> Finally, brethren, whatever things are true, whatever things are just, whatever things are pure, whatever things are lovely, whatever things are of good report, if there is any virtue and if there is anything praiseworthy-meditate on these things. The things which you learned and received and heard and saw in me, these do, and the God of peace will be with you. (Phil 4:8, 9)

With these words, the apostle makes it clear that he understands the human tendency to think in the negative. In fact, he is underscoring the importance of attitude in shaping the human spirit. What it comes down to is a matter of choosing where to focus our thoughts. What is our best offense?

Do we concentrate on what is right, or do we concentrate on what is wrong? Peace dwells with the difference.

One of the most embarrassing moments in my life occurred during my sophomore year in high school. I attempted to play the French horn. I was also line squad leader of the band, playing at football games and other places when called upon. I think they chose me for my booming voice to get everyone in line. Certainly it was not for my sense of rhythm.

One time we had to play for a group of so-called dignitaries who were lined up in the gymnasium, along with the entire high school. My job was to march my line in rhythm with the rest of the band, and my particular line was pivotal in the procession.

I gave the command, "To the right...march" two beats late. As a consequence, the entire band ended up marching between the first and second rows of dignitaries, laughing all the way. I share that story only to emphasize the value of direction. Not unlike a band, the mind moves according to our instructions.

If we want to focus on the misery, mayhem, and mistakes of ourselves and others, I'll guarantee you depression isn't far behind. Or, as the apostle Paul suggests, we can train our eyes on the good things, "whatever things are true, whatever things are just, whatever things are pure, whatever things are of good report" (Philippians 4:8). That is what Paul was saying to the Philippians and says to us today.

You can practice positive thinking when you're in the waiting room, waiting for surgery of yourself or your loved one. You choose to be a positive thinker. If you want joy in your life, you better concentrate on joyful things. If you want success, think success. If you want harmony, think harmony.

When you start over with newness and change, groove your thoughts in a positive direction. When sometimes joy is the furthest noun we could ever think about. When life is tough. When things don't go just right, think positive.

Sometime ago, the preacher Dexter Wise talked about the Israelites who did not get to enter the Promised Land. After wandering around in the desert for forty years, only a select group crossed over Jordan into Israel. Dexter explained the rationale behind this phenomenon when he made reference to what he called "the Canaan Committee." These were the representatives of the twelve tribes who were called upon to establish a plan to enter the Promised Land. But when they looked at the power of the Canaanites, they considered their bedraggled associates, then they started to tremble. At this point, Dexter turned a phrase that I think is wonderful. He said, "Their eyesight destroyed their hindsight and denied their foresight."

What does that mean? It's very simple. They forgot what God can do. When they looked at the task before them, it seemed so big and they seemed so little that they forgot what God had done for them in the past and they chose to forfeit their future. They gave up. By concentrating on what was wrong, they lost sight of what was right.

Oh, how important it is for any person or any people interested in pressing the cutting edge to remember that fact.

If we want to wallow in the mud, then we have to think muddy. But if we want to be happy, we have to think happy, even when life is giving us a bad turn. That's what a community of caring, supporting people are about. That's what support groups and church families can do for others. Not what are the latest rumors or what are people grumbling about, but what are we celebrating this week. What piece of ministry do we want to affirm.

What are we here for? Our calling is to minister to people. To find their needs and meet them. And to do it all in the name of Jesus Christ who told us in the Gospel of Luke:

> And do not seek what you should eat, or what you should drink, nor have an anxious mind. For all these things the nations of the world seek after, and your Father knows that you need these things. But seek the kingdom of God, and all these things shall be added to you. (Lk 12: 29, 30)

"We must direct our eyesight so that it affirms our hindsight and enables our foresight," as we start over.

Let us travel together on the passenger compartment of the train streaking up the East Coast. As we walk down the aisle, we notice a lady sitting beside an empty seat with a package on it. Taking a second look, we recognize this is the same lady who brought the robe and nightgown ensemble for her mother. We pause and listen as another passenger asks her a question.

"What's in the package?"

"A ritual." she responded, smiling.

"What kind of ritual?"

"Well, five years ago, I tried to give my mother a robe and nightgown ensemble after she had been given just six months to live, and she wouldn't take it. Instead she sent me back to the store to get her a designer purse. Since then, every year for her birthday, I buy her another designer purse.

And here it is. Tomorrow, she celebrates birthday number eighty-nine.

"Finally, brethren, whatever things are true, whatever things are noble, whatever things are just, whatever things are pure, whatever things are of good report, if there is any virtue and if there is anything praiseworthy-meditate on these things" (Philippians 4:8).

Stained Glass Descending Dove

FORGIVENESS

One common hope from all the support groups I facilitated was the hope of being forgiven and learning how to forgive. How do we forgive someone of hurting us so deeply it causes scars that last as long as we let them? How do we forgive ourselves if we've hurt someone else so deeply they don't want to forgive us? What does God say about forgiveness?

The parable of the lost son describes the forgiveness of our loving Father, God.

Jesus tells us this parable in the Gospel of Luke:

> Jesus says, "A certain man had two sons. And the younger of them said to his father, 'Father give me the portion of goods that falls to me'. So he divided to them his livelihood. And not many days after, the younger son gathered all together, journeyed to a far country, and there wasted his possessions with prodigal living. But when he had spent all, there arose a severe famine in that land, and he began to be in want. Then he went and joined himself to a citizen of that country, and he sent him into his fields to feed swine. And he would gladly have filled his stomach with the pods that the swine ate, and no one gave him anything. But when he came to himself, he said, 'How many of my father's hired servants have bread enough and to spare, and I perish with hunger? I will arise and go to my father, and will say to him, "Father, I have sinned against heaven before you, and I am no longer worthy to be called your son. Make me like one of your hired servants." And he arose and came to his father. But

when he was still a great way off, his father saw him and had compassion and ran and fell on his neck and kissed him. "And the son said to him, "Father, I have sinned against heaven and in your sight, and I am no longer worthy to be called your son.' But the father said to his servants, "bring out the best robe and put it on him, and put a ring on his hand and sandals on his feet. And bring the fatted calf here and kill it, and let us eat and be merry; for this my son was dead and is alive again; he was lost and is found.' And they began to be merry." (Lk 15:11-32)

This is the first part of the parable. The perspective of the Father and the younger son. I think I can understand why that younger son wanted to leave his father. According to patriarchal custom of that day, his older brother was going to inherit the major portion of the estate and become head of the family. There was no way the younger boy would get to the top of that scene. He wanted to strike out on his own. Like every young person of independent spirit, he wanted to break free of the apron and money strings. Home was dull, predictable, fenced in with the constraints of custom and the confinements of convention. And there was so much that was fascinating out there that beckoned him. The exciting life of travel and adventure, the future of new experiences, new friends, maybe exciting new investments and, in addition, an anonymity of a kind he could never enjoy in his hometown. So the younger son asked for his money and left home.

For all of us, somewhere in our life, there is a tiny seed from time to time of a yearning to take off, to leave home. Literally thousands of young people run away from home every year. The inner pressure to break loose from the deadness, the constraints of the ordinary routines, throbs in every chest, acknowledged or unacknowledged. A part of this yearning is healthy. It may include a refusal to knuckle to the dead hand of conventions, settle for existing, instead of living. There is a valid and boundless curiosity of being, a longing to discover the full range of your humanity, to taste new meanings, to expand to new potential, the call of self-actualization. But there is a danger in that yearning as well. Self-actualization can be modern language for a very familiar phenomenon with which you and I are familiar, a savage ruthlessness, an egocentric self-centeredness, a determination to do what I want to do, regardless of other feelings. There is the danger of living so willfully by what we want, and what we need, that we brush by or roll over the legitimate wants and needs of those nearby, destroying more than we create.

You know, self-pleasing is expensive. Any person bent on pleasing her or himself is doomed to pay a terrible price. If self-pleasing is my God, it will hurt me, and it will also hurt others. No person ever sinned without wounding someone else. That is true regardless of how secret that sin may be. I may sin and no one knows but God and myself. Yet, even then, I involve others. I rob my own home, my soul, lower the moral temperature of my companions, of my city, and even my world.

Sin was costly to this prodigal son. He set out upon a quest that seemed to him altogether reasonable and legitimate. He was out for that which vast multitudes are seeking today. He was doing the very thing many of our modern psychologists look upon with hearty approval. He was spitting in the face of all inhibitions and claiming the privilege of the freest self expression.

So, was it worth it?

Let's examine the cost of his adventure and see if we are willing to pay the price. What did his self-pleasing cost this son in the Scripture reading? It cost him the fellowship of his father. The moment that self-will becomes the goal of any soul, that moment the soul breaks with God and becomes a homeless wanderer. To go from God is always to go from the heart's true home. It cost him his freedom. What a tragic irony, for it was his freedom he went out to seek.

"Give me," he said to his father, in the hour of his self-will (Luke 15:12). And, when his heart was broken, he said, "Father, I am no longer worthy to be called your son" (Luke 15:19). There is all the difference between those two requests. By "give me," he meant "I'll do what I want, and I'll do as I please." But the road by which he sought to find freedom led into slavery. As Scripture reports, "He went and joined himself to a citizen of that country and he sent him into his fields to feed swine" (Luke 15:15).

Every person who sets out in search of freedom apart from obedience only ends by dressing their soul in chains. This is not mere theory, it is experience. And it cost this prodigal son his very all. The story says that he spent all that he had. He became morally and spiritually bankrupt. The person who persists on the road of serving of self does end by losing all. And, what was the outcome? What did he get for this stupendous investment? He got an empty heart and a gnawing agony that wrung from him this bitter cry, "I perish with hunger!" (Luke 15:17).

The theologian Robert Lifton, in his book, *Thought Reform and the Psychology of Totalism*, calls this hunger that pursuit of immortality. He points out that many people today no longer look for fulfillment after death, so they crave it here and now in this life. And the peculiarly American mode of pursuing happiness, immortality, transcendence, whatever word you want to use, is to hit the road, to leave home, to find a quick fix.

The younger son left home and lost it all in that far country. Whatever may have been his good intentions on making wise investments and faithful friends, he got taken. He wasted his money, energy, his options, living it up until there was no place to go, but down. Events closed in on him, famine hit the country, and he hit the bottom. No food, no friends, nothing. Events close in on us too, don't they? Leaning us up against the wall, shaking, trembling, and asking, "How could this happen to me? What am I doing here? Who am I?"

What would it mean for you to begin to deal with your problem that seems hopeless? What would it mean for you to come back to the abiding continuities in your life which nourish you? For the younger son, it meant that he was ready to face his failure.

He was ready to admit he was wrong.

How often does anyone admit they're wrong? And yet that is the first step to being forgiven, admitting you are wrong.

So the younger son prepared a confession and went back home ready to accept the consequences, ready to accept a much lower status in his father's household. Then, when he left, he expected, he hoped, to be taken in, if not to be welcomed.

Now, for the reaction of the older son in this parable of Jesus:

> Now his older son was in the field. And as he came and drew
> near to the house, he heard music and dancing. So he called one
> of the servants and asked what these things meant. And he said
> to him, "Your brother has come, and because he has received him
> safe and sound, your father has killed the fatted calf." But he was
> angry and would not go in. Therefore his father came out and
> pleaded with him. "So he answered and said to his father, 'Lo,
> these many years I have been serving you. I never transgressed
> your commandment at any time; and yet you never gave me a
> young goat, that I might make merry with my friends. But as
> soon as this son of yours came, who has devoured your livelihood
> with harlots, you killed that fatted calf for him; And he said to
> him, "Son, you are always with me, and all that I have is yours.
> It was right that we should make merry and be glad, for your
> brother was dead and is alive again, and was lost and is found."
> (Luke 15:25-32)

The older son was angry. You bet he was angry. Perhaps he was
thinking about that good-for-nothing kid brother, wasting the family
money, like some eternal playboy, and he was back home without a
dime. Of course he came home: he ran out of money. Where else was
he going to go? Doubtless he had some phony confession to wheedle
sympathy out of his sentimental father. That kid always was his parent's
favorite. The young one, you know, curly hair, cute smile. He had
everybody fooled, everyone but him, the elder brother. The kid's back,
a complete flop. He made his choices. He ought to pay every penny
now and get what was coming to him. He told his father he was too
permissive in those early years, and now was no time to coddle him.
So what does his father do? He puts on a big bash for this good-for-
nothing kid. And everybody's going bananas because he's back home
again. There's no way he's going to that party his father is throwing.

Now, you and I can identify with that kind of feeling, can't we?
Some of us have stayed home for years. We've saved, instead of spent.
We've done our duty. We've taken on our shoulders that family mantle

of responsibility and we have been responsible and dependable, and loyal and trustworthy. And we've worked. Oh my, how we've worked. And we've produced too, and if we've been a little bit successful, well, that's only fair.

Some people may believe that virtue is its own reward. But we never bought that. We call it a work ethic. And the deal was plain. We work hard, do what we ought to do, and then we are rewarded with success. We were taught to achieve, to strive, to win, to climb to the top. And if we should get there, to stay there. And in the process, to achieve.

Well, okay, maybe some of us got so tough, you know, we forgot how to be tender. Maybe we were so living from the outside, measuring our progress by external marks, that we got out of touch, or never got in touch with our feelings.

Wasn't the elder son competing for the top place when he was totaling up accounts, stashing a little more money away in the back, and sighing at the end of another ten-, twelve-, fourteen-hour workday? Tough at times, as with all of us. He must have wondered about that young kid brother. What was that rascal doing? Might have even envied him at times, because he had yearnings too. He'd like to have gone away and explored and met new people and tasted the range of life and discover all there is to know and be and do. But the time never seemed to come and now it was too late.

We can understand, a little bit, the resentment of that older brother. He heard the sounds of this big party for his younger brother who'd done everything he wanted to do. But the kid completely fouled up, and now he was back. And instead of being justly punished, they were making him some kind of hero. It's quite natural that the elder brother simply cannot get it into his head why the father should be so terribly happy and why all heaven should begin to exult. Nobody ever got excited over him, who never found it necessary to come back home because he had always stayed at home. Nobody ever killed even so much as a goat to celebrate over him. It strikes him, this faithful, model citizen, this guardian of tradition, that he is being pushed over to the shady side of life.

We've all felt like that elder brother. We can understand how he desires to punish his younger brother. However, it is the punitive spirit in us that creates enemy lists, justifies the invasion of privacy, overrides personal rights for some abstract purpose. It is the punitive spirit in us that seduces us to regard with scorn those in our own family or in society who make serious, obvious mistakes. We secretly feel morally superior to them, washing our hands of their shame. We even think to ourselves, "They had it coming to them. I'm glad they're getting it." The punitive unforgiving spirit in us is born out of fear. Fear that the very evil and ugliness we ferret out and condemn in others might overwhelm and pollute our lives.

What is this unhappy older brother, if not myself, but some other person? Perhaps my friend? What kind of attitude would this be? Don't we see that this just takes us farther away from God?

Let me ask you something. To whom would you go, if you wanted to be forgiven? Someone whose love for you is deep and unconditional, to be able to receive you, regardless of your self- centered behavior?

Now, listen to what the Father, in our Gospel lesson does:

> And He said to him, "Son, you are always with me, and all that I have is yours. It was right we should make merry and be glad, for your brother was dead and is alive again, and was lost and is found." (Lk 15:31, 32).

The Father, the symbol of God, didn't turn away from the younger, or older son. The Father assures the elder brother of His love of him too. "Son, you are always with me, all that I have is yours." The Father does not say, "Hey, shape up and forgive your kid brother, you're too holy acting." No, the Father honors the elder son who has served him faithfully. And by telling the story this way, Jesus helps us understand that the figure of the elder brother is the type of Pharisee who takes his ethical and religious duties in bitter earnest. After all, the elder brother, the symbol of the Pharisee, faithfully reads his Scriptures, prays, faithfully follows the commandments of God. Some might think the elder brother rather judgmental. But this is not how the Father thinks.

He sees the life of the elder brother also from the inside. The Father says to him, "Son, you are always with me, and all that I have is yours." And, to the younger son, his Father saw him and had compassion. "'For this my son was dead and is alive again; he was lost and is found.' And they began to be merry" (Luke 15:24). The father does not say, "Now where in the world have you been? Do you realize what you've put your mother and me through?"

Likewise, the son does not blame others for his own failure. No, the younger son had his confession prepared. He admitted his failure. He was ready to see what he did was wrong. So he started his confession, "Father, I have sinned against heaven and in your sight, and am no longer worthy to be called your son. Make me like one of your hired servants" (Luke 15:19). And then comes the next part of this parable, that is as beautiful a portion of writing in the Holy Bible that I know. "And he arose and came to his Father; But when he was still a great way off, his Father saw him and had compassion, and ran and fell on his neck and kissed him" (Luke 15:20).

When I read this, I get the feeling that every morning that Father was up looking down the road and every evening before he went to bed, he was looking, waiting, hoping.

Can you see the Father running down that road to his boy? That's what a community of loving people are supposed to do. A Hospitality Inn for you and me, whatever our sins, failures, or struggles.

A minister friend of mine told me about a long-time member of his church who said he was leaving the church. My minister friend asked him why, and the man said, "every Sunday morning when I look into the congregation I see too many weirdos with tattoos, strange piercing, and wild hair."

What a tragic misunderstanding of what a church is meant to be. It's not a club for the righteous. It's not a place for the perfect. The place of worship is a home, where you and I can come just as we are. People who wound each other and are wounded. Who betray and are betrayed. A place where we can bring our awful problems, our dilemmas, our blood, sweat, tears, whatever we've got to bring. A place where we can give up our cover and deal with our problems and receive our true worth as God's children.

There are two ultimate themes of this parable. The first theme of this parable is not the son, but God the Father, who finds us. The second theme is not the faithlessness of people, but the faithfulness of God our Father.

This is also the reason why the joyful sound of festivity rings out from this story. Wherever forgiveness is proclaimed, there is joy and gladness. It's the good news that God always is there for us, waiting for our return.

Now, we must learn how to open our hearts and welcome our prodigal sons and daughters as God our Father taught us.

Stained Glass Sheaf of Wheat

Overcoming Discouragements

Snakes.

I really dislike them almost as much as any God-given creature. That's why I'll never forget being invited to preach at an outdoor church service in Elkton National Park, Maryland. I was the first woman they invited to the self-built wood pulpit. Everyone in the campground was invited to attend, and the Sunday services had been well-received for many years. On this particular occasion, I was responsible for playing the pump organ, leading the singing, reading the Scriptures, and, of course, preaching the sermon. I was really pleased to be asked, especially as a clergywoman.

After I pumped-played the prelude on the organ, I moved ten steps to the pulpit. As I began reading from the Old Testament, I felt some "nibbles" on my right ankle. When I looked down, lo and behold, a bed of infant snakes all curled up in a circle, but one rebel "snakelet" was popping his head up to find some sweet creamy human ankle.

I nearly screamed my head off! But I sure didn't want to be the first woman preacher doing what I'm sure they thought a woman would do, under the circumstances. Scream!

So, throughout the hour of Scriptures, singing, and preaching, I was also kicking under the pulpit. In those days they didn't have clip-on microphones, so I had to stay at the pulpit's mike so the congregation of over two hundred people could hear.

My husband and grandson, who attended that day, still can't believe I made it through that long hour with a hatching of snakes moving on both of my bare ankles. I even had red marks to prove it. That moment made me feel really proud for myself and other females that would eventually follow.

I said to the male deacons and ushers following the service, "Before you invite the next preacher in the pulpit, you'd better clean out the nest of snakes under the pulpit." Immediately, they ran down to the pulpit, found the snakes, and made me proud when they said, almost collectively, "Wow, she didn't even say anything during the service!" And, another gentleman nodded, saying, "Yeah, and she's a woman!"

Often, life is not rosy. God didn't promise us a rose garden. The world is not fashioned to our taste, nor does it conveniently adjust itself according to our moods. There are disappointments, but sometimes disappointments are changed into opportunities.

I heard about a certain woman who received a phone call from the babysitter saying her daughter was sick with a fever, so she picked up some medication at the pharmacy. When she returned to the parking lot, alas, her keys were locked in the car. She didn't know what to do. She couldn't find another key and her husband was out of town, so she saw an old rusty coat hanger that was lying on the ground. She looked at the hanger and said to God, "God, I don't know how to use this hanger, please send me some help!"

Within five minutes, an old rusty car pulled up with a dirty, greasy, bearded man who was wearing an old bike skull rag on his head. The woman thought, "This is what you sent to help me?"

The man got out of his car and asked if she needed any help. The woman said, "Yes, my daughter is very sick, I stopped to get her some medication and I've locked my keys in the car. I must get home to her, please, can you use this hanger to unlock my car?"

The man said sure. He walked over to the car, and in less than one minute the car was opened. She hugged the man and through her tears she said, "Thank you so much, you're a very nice man."

The man replied, "Lady, I'm not a very nice man. I just got out of prison today. I was in prison for car theft and have only been out a few hours."

The woman hugged the man again and with sobbing tears cried out loud, "Oh, thank you, God! You even sent me a professional!"

God does send people our way, but there are setbacks and failures from time to time. Take Jesus in the Gospel of John.

> Now it was the Feast of Dedication in Jerusalem, and it was winter. And Jesus walked in the temple, in Solomon's porch. Then the Jews surrounded Him and said to Him, "how long do You keep us in doubt? If You are the Christ, tell us plainly." Jesus answered them, "I told you and you do not believe. The works that I do in My Father's name, they bear witness of Me. But you do not believe, because you are not of My sheep, as I said to you. My sheep hear My voice, and I know them, and they follow Me. "And I give them eternal life, and they shall never perish; neither shall anyone snatch them out of My hand. My Father, who has given them to Me, is greater than all; and no one is able to snatch them out of My Father's hand. "I and My Father are one." Then the Jews took up stones again to stone Him. Jesus answered them, "Many good works I have shown you from My Father. For which of those works do you stone me?" The Jews answered Him, saying, "For a good work we do not stone You but for blasphemy and because You, being a Man, make Yourself God." (Jn 10:22-38)

It was the Feast of Dedication at Jerusalem. This feast kept in remembrance of the restoration of the services in the temple by the Maccabees after three years' desecration under the Syrian kingdom. Jesus, a rabbi, was walking in the temple in the Portico of Solomon. The people gathered around him and said to him, mockingly, "How long do You keep us in doubt? If You are the Christ, tell us plainly" (John 10:24).

And Jesus answered them, "I told you, and you do not believe. The works that I do in My Father's name, they bear witness of Me. But you do not believe because you are not of My sheep, as I said to you. My sheep hear my voice and I know them, and they follow me" (John 10:25, 26).

"Then the Jews took up stones again to stone Him" (John 10:31).

Note the word "again." Jesus had been threatened before. How do you suppose Jesus felt? Time and time again people just would not listen to him. He must have felt discouraged. We, too, have our moments of feeling discouraged. In fact, like the elevator, we have our ups and downs. Sometimes we are very much up and sometimes we are very much down.

The up phase we like. But the down phase is often hard to take, particularly when it continues over a long period of time and discouragement sets in. I suppose that anyone who is unprepared for discouragement and failure is really not conditioned for life.

As I facilitated the suicide prevention support groups for both teens and adults, I realized that we have trained people to succeed, when we should be teaching folks how to successfully fail. When you think about it, you realize that very few of us have a chance to live on the basis of our choice. The vast majority of us have to settle for something less than we want.

A broken marriage, a painful onslaught of cancer, frustrations at home, a sudden change of health, a bitter disappointment, the death of a loved one. Any of these or a dozen other situations which are part of our lives can get us discouraged, and it's mighty hard to make something redemptive out of discouragement.

The Apostle Paul tried to make something good out of his discouraging times. In the Epistle of Paul the Apostle to the Romans, Paul wrote:

> But now no longer having a place in these parts, and having a great desire these many years to come to you, whenever I journey to Spain, I shall come to you. For I hope to see you on my journey and to be helped on my way there by you, if first I may enjoy your company for a while. (Rom 15:23, 24)

Paul told the people he would see them in passing "as I go to Spain." Paul wanted to go to Spain. He had his heart set on it. In his dream of preaching the good news that the Messiah has come and fulfilled the Scriptures, Paul had plans for reaching the outermost rim of the world. That was his goal. But he never got there. Instead, he got a prison cell in Rome.

Somewhere along the way, we all have to deal with disappointment, disrupted plans, deferred hopes, unrealized dreams.

In his book, *Ride the Wild Horses*, Wallace Hamilton has this line: "Every person's life is a diary in which they mean to write one story but end up writing another."

St. Paul never took his journey, but sat in prison, scribbling on a piece of parchment. Much of the New Testament was written in jail and some of the very best of it would not have been in our hands today if Paul had gone to Spain. Would you dare say that God was in that disappointment helping Paul use the prison cell? After twenty years of missionary wanderings, Paul was quiet enough to permeate the mystery of Jesus the Christ. Paul made, out of that discouraging circumstance, some of the greatest contributions of his life.

It has been suggested, more than once, that life makes progress in a resisting medium. The bird needs the resistance of the air to fly. The fish needs the resistance of water to get traction for its fins. We would not be able to stand up without the resisting action of the law of gravity.

And yet, life's discouragements are so disagreeable. The weight of them so heavy that we dislike giving them credibility for our problems in helping us grow. Still, most of us would probably agree that there are many facets of our character which were achieved through conflict. Perhaps through a crisis which involved initially a good deal of discouragement. Chances are good that the achievement came through powers that were deep within us. So deep we really didn't know we had them, but were called into action by the challenge of opposition and frustration. I know through my own hospitalizations I couldn't get through them without knowing God is present with me through my conundrums.

Sometimes the weight of life keeps us going.

We see it all through the New Testament. Look again at the discouraging interruptions of Jesus's life.

"They took up stones again to stone Him" (John 10: 31).

What does Jesus do? Does He become discouraged? Does He say, "What's the use? You can't talk to these people. Why me?" No, Jesus answered those ready to stone Him, "Many good works I have shown you from My Father. For which of those works do you stone me?" (John 10:32).

And, they answered him, saying, "For a good work we do not stone You, but for blasphemy, and because You being a Man, make Yourself God" (John 10:33).

Jesus answered them, "If I do not do the works of My Father, do not believe Me; but if I do, though you do not believe Me, believe the works, that you may know and believe that the Father is in Me, and I in Him" (John 10:37, 38).

Jesus didn't merely endure the discouragements and frustrations of life, he employed them and used every one of them to promote the purposes of God. Jesus did not merely endure the blows thrown at Him, He made them weapons against evil. Jesus did not merely endure the cross, He used it. The frustration of the cross became the salvation of the world. We might go as far to say that Christianity says we should get something out of everything, even out of discouragement and failure. We should get something out of defeat: learning how to be a good loser. Learning how to go through sickness. Learning how to make every severed relationship, every broke hope, pay a profit. The creative question for us is to ask not "How can I stand this thing?" but "How can I use it for a greater good?"

So, how do we overcome the difficult problems that overwhelm us?

There are no easy answers. If anyone could say, with confidence, "Take steps one, two, three, and all will be well," that person would be a millionaire, or we'd all be robots.

One thing we have learned, there is little value in saying to a discouraged person, "Cheer up, smile, it's National Smile Week." That is exactly what a person cannot do. And it really annoys and irritates us to think that kind of platitude, "Cheer up, all is well," might help.

Insofar as moods of discouragement are under our control, there might be a least a few things we can do. First, tell you troubles to someone that you can trust and who you have reason to believe will understand. A burden shared is a burden lightened. One of the great values of friendships is the support we give each other. Remember, discouragement is a feeling, an emotion, and the first thing to do is to honestly share it with someone who cares enough to give you the healing touch of attention.

Secondly, try to get a realistic view of what causes your discouragement. Perhaps you are a perfectionist with standards set too high. Perhaps you are going in a vicious kind of circle. Sometimes we have to learn to live with the thing that causes our discouragement and realize it is our own attitude that needs changing. Basic attitudes are vital and touch all the lives around us.

How often have you said of a person, " He or she is negative in their outlook." Or conversely when you said, "That person is such a pleasure to be with, always so positive about life." As a matter of fact, religion is basically an attitude toward God, toward people, and toward each other.

Next, we might need to shift our energy focus to other-centeredness. Subordinate ourselves, commit ourselves to something else. It includes reviving our sense of humor, which, at its best, means not taking ourselves too seriously. Self-centeredness and self-pity are great enemies to our happiness. There's a lot of "me first" in our lives. We will find new perspectives in our discouragements when we become a volunteer in projects which benefit the lives of others.

Finally, maybe we need to take a fresh look at our faith in God. Does it need strengthening, some new growth? What we believe in God does matter in how we handle discouragement and our emotions.

The kind of God that we believe in is a creative God who has given us the gift of life. A God who has given us these adventurous years to ride this spaceship earth, with a fantastic variety of other passengers. A

God who forgives and loves us with our pretensions, blunders, failures, and, yes, sins.

The beautiful anonymous soldier's prayer, reported to have been found on a soldier killed in the line of duty during the Civil War, sums up how we should overcome our disappointments and discouragements. It reads thusly:

> I asked God for strength, that I might achieve:
> I was made weak that I might learn humbly to obey.
> I asked God for help that I might do greater things,
> I was given infirmity, that I might do better things.
> I asked for riches, that I might be happy.
> I was given poverty, that I might be wise.
> I asked for power, that I might have the praise of people,
> I was given weakness, that I might feel the need of God.
> I asked for all things that I might enjoy all things.
> I got nothing that I asked for,
> But everything I hoped for.
> Almost despite myself, my unspoken prayers were answered.

If we can practice our faith, we might discover, as the soldier's prayer says, "I got nothing I asked for, but everything I prayed and hoped for." As the Psalmist says, "O Lord, how excellent is Thy name in all the earth" (Psalm 8:9). We, too, can overcome life's discouragements by remembering Jesus didn't just endure his discouragements, He used every one to promote the love of God.

We have to realize we may be discouraged in our earthly life, but we have a friend who walks with us, as He does with all who seek.

> The Lord is my shepherd; I shall not want. He makes me to lie down in green pastures; He leads me beside the still waters. He restores my soul; He leads me in the paths of righteousness For His names sake. Yea, though I walk through the valley of the shadow of death, I will fear no evil; For You are with me; Your rod and Your staff, they comfort me. You prepare a table before me in the presence of my enemies; You anoint my head with oil;

My cup runs over. Surely goodness and mercy shall follow me All the days of my life; And I will dwell in the house of the Lord Forever. (Psalm 23)

May you, too, be encouraged.

Stained Glass Anchor

LOVE

I've had the special honor of officiating at our three daughters' weddings, Debbie, Becky, and Carrie, and, so far, three of our grandchildren, Megan, Ben, and Michael. A special Scripture passage I frequently use for many weddings is the passage from Paul found in the Epistle of first Corinthians. It describes what love is, and it is as true today as it was in Apostle Paul's day when he wrote it.

> Though I speak with the tongues of men and of angels, but have not love, I have become as sounding brass or a clanging cymbal. And though I have the gift of prophecy, and understand all mysteries and all knowledge, and though I have all faith, so that I could remove mountains, but have not love, I am nothing. And though I bestow all my goods to feed the poor, and though I give my body to be burned, but have not love, it profits me nothing. Love suffers long and is kind; love does not envy; love does not parade itself, is not puffed up; does not behave rudely, does not seek its own, is not provoked, thinks no evil; does not rejoice in iniquity but rejoices in the truth; bears all things, believes all things, hopes all things, endures all things. Love never fails, But whether there are prophecies, they will fail; whether there are tongues, they will cease; whether there is knowledge, it will vanish away. For we know in part and we prophesy in part. But when that which is perfect has come, then that which is part will be done away. When I was a child, I spoke as a child, I understood as a child, I thought as a child; but when I became a man, I put away childish things. For now we see in the mirror,

dimly, but then face to face. Now I know in part, but then I shall know just as I also am known. And now abide faith, hope, love, these three; but the greatest of these is love. (1 Cor 13:1-13)

How wonderfully said. Love is patient, kind, does not envy, does not parade itself, is not puffed up, does not behave rudely, rejoices in the truth, greatest of these is love.

Pets Allowed

I love animals, except snakes. We've had three dogs, Buffer, a cocker spaniel, lived for twelve years; Snoopy, a basset hound, only made four years; and Salty, a West Highland terrier, living a full seventeen years. Eighteen gerbils, many fish, turtles, a bird, a large rabbit, and, as a young girl, eight kittens. There is a bond between most pets that seems to rise above all circumstance. No matter where you might have been or what you might have been doing, when you come through the door, your old friend is glad to see you.

When I was a hospital chaplain, it was known that "no pets" were allowed in the patients' rooms, or anywhere else. Then, one day, one of the oncology patients' daughter had a new baby.

Our hospital was called the Alpha and Omega hospital. Alpha, the Greek word for the beginning, and Omega, the Greek word for the end. Almost all babies were born in our hospital and it was rare that a patient on the oncology floor would be a new grandmother, as her daughter, just two floors away, had delivered her a new grandson.

The new grandmother asked me if she could see and hold her new grandbaby, and I found a way to bring her grandson around to her room, through the help of a bunch of good-hearted maternity nurses. She held him and was so thrilled that in the midst of her stage four cancer, she lived long enough to hold this precious child.

All was well, until her roommate said, "As long as she could hold her new grandson, can I hold my new puppies? My precious Labrador just had them two days ago. Please, oh please!"

I didn't know what to say because I knew the rules. No pets. So I cowardly said to her, "You remember the rules? No pets allowed."

But she really wanted to see the new puppy and, in those days, patients usually died in their hospital bed. Going home wasn't much of an option then. So I pranced down to the administration and brought them another challenge. "Could we just have one puppy? Just for a moment. I'll oversee it. I'll diaper it…etc."

Finally, administration okayed the idea, but, "Just this once! And just one puppy!"

So, I happily, hurriedly hustled up to the patient with the newborn puppy's room and joyfully gave her the exciting news. She didn't look as excited as I was.

"What's wrong?" I asked. She leaned over to reach the only drawer in the room, right next to her bed, and pulled out a picture. She opened it up and there was a photograph of four precious Labrador's puppy faces, all looking at me with sad, lonesome brown eyes. The patient, and "surrogate mom" of these cute dogs, pointed to the picture and said lovingly, "You choose which one I can bring in."

Just one. How could I choose which one of those cute puppy heads, with wistful begging eyes? I couldn't choose just one, so I thought it might be an idea if her husband would bring one puppy to her room at a time. I could help him go to his car, pick up a puppy, bring it up for her to see and hug, then return to the car and repeat the process, until she had seen all four of her new puppies. I was actually congratulating myself for such creativity. But, as things go, I should've known self-congratulations are much too sanctimonious.

Once a puppy got on her bed, and the other patients heard the nurses say, "Oh, did you see the cute puppy?" the game was on. Not only did all the patients on the entire oncology unit see all four of the puppies, but the cancer patients looked as though a new life had begun for them.

The experience of watching patients, families, nurses, doctors, unit clerks, housekeepers, and anyone who was walking down the corridors was breathtaking, as all of us joined together in a common love. The unconditional love that animals invariably openly pass onto us.

Faithfulness, loyalty, playfulness, protection, companionship, forgiveness, all are found in the pet-human connection.

Mothers

There's a story about a woman who died and arrived at the gates of heaven. While she was waiting for St. Peter to greet her, she peeked through the gates. She saw a beautiful banquet table.

Sitting all around were her parents and all the other people she had loved and who had died before her. They saw her and began calling greetings to her.

"Hello, we've been waiting for you."

When St. Peter came by, the woman said to him, "This is such a wonderful place! How do I get in?"

"You have to spell a word." St Peter told her.

"Which word?" the woman asked.

"Love."

The woman correctly spelled "love" and St. Peter welcomed her into heaven.

About six months later, St. Peter came to the woman and asked her to watch the gates of heaven for Him that day. While the woman was guarding the gates, her husband arrived.

"I'm surprised to see you," the woman, his wife, said. "How have you been doing since I died?"

Her husband told her, "I married the beautiful young nurse who took care of you while you were ill. And then I won the lottery. I sold the little house you and I lived in and bought a big mansion. My wife and I traveled all over the world. We were on vacation and I went water skiing today, I fell, the ski hit my head, and here I am. How do I get in?"

"Hmmm," said the wife. "You have to spell a word."

"What word?" the husband asked.

And the woman answered: "Czechoslovakia."

Where does love begin?

"Jesus Loves Me" is the song my mom sang to me. She remembered that hymn for her entire 105 years. I'll never forget her teachings, guidance, resilience, determination, and most of all, her love. If you ask me what I consider to be the greatest sin in the world, I would have to answer: it's not worry, it's not pride, nor envy, nor any of the things officially listed in such theological catalogues, as the seven deadly sins.

No, in my opinion, the greatest sin is the sin of taking things for granted, and I mean that in two ways: positively and negatively. Think of all the callousness and insensitivity that has descended upon us because we take the evil things in life for granted.

A hundred years from now, people will be astonished that we, in the twenty-first century, accepted such anomalies as racism, and such barbarities as germ warfare and the Holocaust. They will look back on us in horror, as we now look back on such uncivilized customs as public executions, slavery, and child labor. Little more than a hundred years ago, decent people took these things for granted as part of the natural order. That's how life was until some intrepid spirit saw the disgusting horror of it and helped change these evils.

We also make a habit of taking for granted the good things of life. It is this that sours friendships, breaks up and weakens family life. I really have come to believe that "taking things for granted" is not the eighth deadly sin, but it lies at the root of all the other seven. Pride, for example, is the arrogant assumption that we are self-made people, indebted to no one for anything. We take for granted the unseen hands of parents, grandparents, aunts, uncles, teachers, ministers, and friends that hold us. We take for granted their friendly persuasion, their love and loyalty that have given us a footing on this slippery earth.

Envy springs from the same root as pride. Envy is the suspicion that we are taken for granted, that we are not being given our due. Nobody appreciates us.

Sloth, the drabbest of all the seven deadly sins, is taking for granted and trading on the drive and initiative of other people, while we do very little to make life better for others.

Lust is taking for granted that other people exist for our pleasure.

The list goes on, but in no sphere of life does the sin of taking things for granted wreak more havoc than in the sphere of the home.

I believe the most taken-for-granted persons I know are mothers.

Some ministers are uncomfortable about preaching on mothers' and fathers' days. Some don't like its sentimentality and rank commercialism associated with it. They see it as a folk festival, that unlike Christmas, Easter, the Ascension, have nothing to do with religion. "No theological content," they say. Yet what in heaven's name is theology but reflecting on the meaning of human experience? Theology isn't endlessly discussing God, but discussing everything else, in the light of God, as He has made Himself known in Jesus Christ our Savior.

The Apostle Paul, in his letter to the church at Ephesus, gives us some solid counsel about the essence of life itself:

> Children, obey your parents in the Lord, for this is right. Honor your "father and mother," which is the first commandment with promise; that it may be well with you and you may live long on the earth. And you, fathers, do not provoke your children to wrath, but bring them up in the training and admonition of the Lord. (Eph 6:1-4)

Here we find Paul underscoring discipline, obedience, and the importance of parental examples. I would like to paraphrase an old question to all parents, grandparents, and surrogate family members. "On this day, should you be called into accountability, is there enough evidence in your home for your family to call you a Christian? How does your family know you serve the Master?" I believe there are several observances every Christian parent/grandparent need to give their family, and not take it for granted they will learn it elsewhere. I believe we owe it to our family to witness us in the practice of prayer. I believe we owe it to our family to witness us as faithful stewards as we set aside a portion of our allowance for our Lord. I believe we owe it to our family to witness us as pilgrims of faith. We need to do this in our families and not take for granted they know the Lord.

I recently read a book written by Henry Drummond, a Scottish scientist, theologian, and preacher. He wrote his book because he was provoked by Charles Darwin. He disagreed with Darwin's book entitled *Descent of Man*. He felt Darwin had it topsy turvy.

So Drummond entitled his book *The Ascent of People*.

And in that ascent he saw the mother as a key figure. I remember the illuminating distinction he made between maternity and motherhood. We take it for granted that they are the same. "Not at all," said Drummond. "Maternity is as old as nature. Any woman can get pregnant, if she's not barren."

Motherhood is as new as humanity. Indeed, motherhood is the point at which humanity begins. Maternity is a biological fact, motherhood is a spiritual fact. We take it for granted that mothers care for their children.

It was not always so. There was a time in the history of the human race when there were no mothers and no children. Only offspring, "springers off," as they were called then. The unwanted children were discarded almost as soon as they were born, receiving no care or attention. They were left to fend for themselves. Imagine, even as late as the third century, motherhood was by no means firmly established. It was a widespread custom to expose unwanted children to the elements. Children, especially girls, were abandoned and disposed of without ceremony.

We find that incredible today. What we take for granted is not cruelty, but kindness; not neglect, but nurture.

We are shocked when the headlines report child beatings and abuse, even driving the children in strapped car seats into the water to drown.

We accept care and love as the norm, forgetting the decisive part that Christianity has played with its insistence on the reverence and sanctity of all life.

All through the Old and New Testament, you will read, "Honor thy father and mother." "Honor your father and your mother, as the Lord your God has commanded you, that your days may be long, and that it may be well with you in the land which the Lord your

God is giving you" (Deuteronomy 5:16). Have you noticed this is the only Commandment of the Ten that has a promise attached to it? When parents are dishonored, that is when family life is imperiled. It has struck me again, with force, that men who have insisted most on honoring their mothers were statesmen of the highest values.

The great Semite statesman, Moses, author of Exodus, Leviticus, Numbers, and Deuteronomy.

The great English statesman, Prime Minister Winston Churchill.

The great American president, Abe Lincoln.

Besides desiring, with passion, the unity of their countries, they also had this in common, a checkered, difficult, dysfunctional home life.

Moses was a foundling with several adopted mothers, who were not available to him. His mother, Jochebed, had to give him up, due to the customs of his day.

Churchill had a mother who was incapable of loving her children. There are no more poignant letters in English literature than Churchill's schoolboy letters home, almost beseeching his mother to show some interest in him. Taken from his autobiography, *My Early Life*.

And Lincoln's mother was hardly a paragon of any virtue, known to move from man to man. Lincoln's mother died when he was nine, and he was raised by a stepmother.

Yet it was these statesmen, these reconcilers, these builders of their countries, who most earnestly pled for honoring the fifth commandment, "Honor your Mother and Father," and who honored their mothers themselves. When the ties of their mothers were not strong, they took the initiative and honored them, regardless of their mothers' faults. And because they began there, they carried over into history the same uplifting, reconciling spirit.

There is a beautiful tribute to moms written by Erma Bombeck, entitled *When God Created Mom*.

When the good Lord was creating mothers, God was into His sixth day of overtime when the angel appeared and said, "You're having a lot of problems with this one."

And the Lord said, "Can you imagine this? She has to be completely washable, but not plastic. Have 180 moveable parts, all replaceable.

Run on black coffee and leftovers, have a lap that disappears when she stands up, and a kiss that can cure anything from a broken leg to a disappointed love affair. And six pairs of hands. But it's not the hands that are causing me problems," said the Lord. "It's the three pairs of eyes that mothers have to have."

"That's the standard model?" asked the angel.

The Lord nodded, "One pair that sees through closed doors when she asks, "What are you kids doing there?" when she already knows. Another pair in the back of her head that sees what she shouldn't but has to know; and the ones here in front that can look at a child when the child does wrong and still say, "I understand and love you" without so much as uttering a word."

"Lord," said the angel, touching the Lord's sleeve gently. "Let's relax and work on this tomorrow."

"I can't," said the Lord. "I'm so close to creating something so close to myself. Already I have one who frequently heals herself when she is sick, can feed a family of six on one pound of hamburger, and can get a nine-year-old to stand under a shower."

The angel circled the model of a mother very slowly. "It's too soft," she sighed.

"But tough," said the Lord excitedly. "You cannot imagine what this mother can do or endure."

"Can it think?"

"Not only think, but it can reason and compromise," said the Creator.

Finally, the angel bent over and ran her finger across the cheek. "There's a leak," she pronounced. "I told You, You were trying to put too much into this model."

"It's not a leak" said the Lord. "It's a tear."

"What's it for?"

"It's for joy, sadness, disappointment, pain, loneliness, and compassion."

"You are a genius," said the angel.

The Lord looked caringly, "I created her, but she created the tear."

Fathers

On February 20, 1942, Butch O'Hare was flying a routine night reconnaissance flight over the South Pacific when he spotted nine speckles two thousand feet below him. Within moments he had slipped close enough to detect the twin-engine Japanese bombers on a direct flight path to his home carrier, the USS *Lexington*. Now it was decision time. He could break radio silence and warn the carriers, or he could initiate his own attack. Already the enemy aircrafts were too close for his fellow pilots to launch before the first strike. Hence, for Butch O'Hare, the decision was simple. He flipped on his radio switch so as to transmit the sounds of battle and mounted his assault.

Before it was over, five of the nine Japanese bombers had been dumped into the Pacific Ocean. For his efforts, Lieutenant Commander Henry Butch O'Hare became the first Naval aviator ever to win the Congressional Medal of Honor.

Today, every air passenger who passes through Chicago reconnects with his name via the world's busiest international airport. However, the courage of Butch O'Hare didn't develop in a vacuum. It was shaped by a Chicago gangster, who was Al Capone's number-one lawyer. "Artful Eddie O'Hare," as he was also known, single-handedly kept America's biggest crook, Al Capone, out of jail for nearly ten years.

In return, the shady barrister was given control of the windy city's dog tracks. He became a very wealthy man, of course. However, the price for all this was a severely tainted name. Thus, when Artful Eddy's boy, Butch, decided he wanted to attend the United States Naval Academy, he ran smack into the FBI's road block. That's when the courage of a father, Artful Eddie O'Hare, appeared. Rather than see his son suffer the consequences of his own rancid life, the old man turned state's evidence.

He talked, he diagrammed, he cooperated against the mob, for the State of Illinois. All the while, he knew what fate awaited him. Still, he pressed on, convinced the most significant gift he could give his son was the right to establish his own reputation.

Two shotgun blasts killed Artful Eddie. But that didn't keep his son from entering Annapolis en route to that fateful day when he would prove a hero in the skies of the South Pacific.

Fathers.

Fathers are so significant, even when they make mistakes. Few fathers will experience such dramatic circumstances as did the O'Hares. Nonetheless, I'm firmly convinced that the deeds of the father continue to have a life-shaping influence on their children. I know the remembrance of my beloved own father, my father-in-law, my grandfather, Papaw, and my husband Tom, have all positively influenced me over the years.

Being a father is challenging. I don't think we celebrate Fathers' Day as we should. It's hard to find good greeting cards. Here's one with a picture of a pipe or a golf club or a fishing pole. I couldn't find one card that associated father with the Christian faith or the church or God.

Oh, I finally found one. It was a full page advertisement that appeared with a scripture passage: "Honor thy father on Father's day, give Old Granddad." I also heard about three boys who were in the schoolyard bragging about their fathers.

The first boy says, "My dad scribbles a few words on a piece of paper, he calls it a poem, and they give him fifty dollars."

The second boy says, "That's nothing. My dad scribbles a few words on a piece of paper, he calls it a song, and it gets one hundred dollars."

The third boy says, "I got you both beat. My dad scribbles a few words on a piece of paper, he calls it a sermon, and it takes eight people to collect all the money."

I think it's time to get back to the basics. Let's remember our fathers and their vocations and talents they've been given. As we invest in our future, our ambitions and our lives change. We might call the stages of this journey dependence, independence, interdependence with the accompanying emotions of admiration, aggravation, and appreciation. But the greatest of these is appreciation. That's why I always welcome Mothers' and Fathers' Day. It is alleged by some that they have nothing to do with religion. If that is so, I don't know what religion is, because I've been reading the wrong Bible.

My Bible has a great deal to say about fathers, mothers, and children. My Bible has theology that is bound up with those personal relationships, and what personal relationship is more crucial and more vital than those at the heart of the family? This is where God reveals himself.

From the Epistle in first Corinthians, St. Paul is mapping a lifestyle to the believers at the church of Corinth. In these verses, the Apostle sets forth several ingredients which can be applied to the art of being a father. For starters, the wise old teacher makes a great case for being supple, flexible. St Paul says:

> For though I am free from all men, I have made myself a servant to all, that I might win the more; and to the Jews I became as a Jew, that I might win Jews; to those who are under the law, as under the law, that I might win those who are under the law; to those who are without law, as without law (not being without law toward God, but under law toward Christ), that I might win those who are without law; to the weak I became as weak, that I might win the weak. I have become all things to all men, that I might by all means save some. (1 Cor 9:19-22)

When I first read those words, I didn't care for them. I'm just not too pleased with people, who, like chameleons, shift personalities to adjust to the terrain. They seem hard to trust. But then, I studied the passage a little closer and noted that the real issue is not one of wishy-washy values, but of honoring others.

Paul didn't suggest it would be wise to constantly change allegiances. He did suggest it is very prudent to meet people where they are rather than expecting people to adjust to us.

That's a very important message for families. I'm concerned that with our capacity to constantly meet the desires and needs of our children, we may be leading them to believe the world will always accommodate them and there are no failures, no problems. But we will experience a lot of failures and problems. The world is not anybody's oyster.

William Arthur Ward, a Christian writer of Fountains of Faith, observed: "If you would be interesting; be interested. If you would be pleased; be pleasing. If you would be loved; be lovable. And if you would be helped; be helpful."

The bottom line for all of us is the ability to make the most of every situation. We are called to adjust to the terrain and witness to the love of Christ with the ability to bend with the wind. Years ago, when I was an adolescent during World War II, my parents taught me to plant vegetables in the Victory gardens. If we expected to help in the war effort, if we expected to survive the winds of war, we had to do something to make it work.

So our Scripture says we are called to be flexible. When we do this, we must live with a purpose. I'm sure St. Paul was imagining the skeptical squint of the Corinthians when he wrote these words: "I have become all things to all men" (1 Corinthians 9:22). Shortly after, Paul announced his purpose: "Now this I do for the gospel's sake, that I may be partaker of it with you" (1 Corinthians 9:23).

And that message he knew from hearing the disciples repeat Jesus's words, as we find them in the Gospel.

> No one can come to Me unless the Father who sent Me draws him; and I will raise him up at the last day. It is written in the prophets, And they shall all be taught by God. Therefore everyone who has heard and learned from the Father comes to Me. Most assuredly, I say to you, he who believes in me has everlasting life. (Jn 6:44, 45)

We, too, must pass this message onto our children and grandchildren. We must have a sense of purpose. Purpose that's centered and not confusing. I've known a lot of people who are confused about their purpose of life, especially as we get older. Saint Paul explained his focus in the first chapter of Philippians: "For to me, to live is Christ, and to die is gain" (Philippians 1:21). He was fully centered in the Master.

From Apostle Paul's 1 Corinthians, we see he underscores being flexible, then he lifts up a sense of purpose, and finally he puts the spotlight on perseverance. "Do you not know that those who run the race, all run, but one receives the prize? Run in such a way that you may obtain it" (1 Corinthians 9:24). In other words, hang in there, don't give up, always be optimistic.

It was Bishop Fulton J. Sheen who recounted the story of walking up to a ten-year-old at a little league baseball game in Rochester, New York.

"What's the score?" asked the noted preacher and teacher.

"We're down eighteen to nothin'," said the lad.

"Oh, that's a shame," said the Bishop.

"No, it ain't so bad," responded the boy. "We ain't come up to bat yet."

There's something to be said for planting that kind of spirit in all our youngsters. It is the very attitude by which twelve nondescript characters launched a ministry for their Master, Jesus, which now encompasses the world. So for all of us, let us listen to the words of St. Paul as he spoke to the Corinthian church. Be flexible, have a purpose, and persevere!

This special poem by our special son-in-law, Bill Sharp, was written on my husband's seventy-fifth birthday.

For Pop

What stripe of man is this I see
marching through life confidently
with agile mind and steady hand
creating a business that would stand
what stripe of man is this I hear
wandering through love's blissful year
who found a wife to share his all
one with whom to stand or fall.

what strip of man is this I sense
embracing more togetherness
as three children rush to his side,
a spoonful of wisdom he shares with pride
what stripe of man is this I know
soon struck by cancer's merciless blow
who chose to fight and not succumb
whose years are lengthened, this battle won
as promising as the Florida sun
your twilight years have thus begun
so at this moment I'd like to say,
God bless you, Pop, and Happy Birthday!

—WHS

Love, Sweet Love

There are many good jokes about love in marriage. It was expressed by a thank-you note I received back in the day. "Dear Rev. Walters, I want to thank you for performing our marriage ceremony. It was beautiful the way you brought my happiness to a conclusion."

Of course, sometimes no matter what you try to do to make your marriage work, it doesn't turn out well. I remember hearing about a husband surprising his wife by bringing some magic back into their marriage by doing some little unexpected act of love for his spouse for absolutely no reason at all. So this husband decided it would be fun to surprise his wife with a box of candy, a bouquet of flowers, and a little formality. So, instead of going through the back door unannounced, he went to the front door and rang the doorbell. When the husband's harried wife yanked open the front door and saw him standing there smiling beneficially, extending the bouquet of flowers and box of candy, she blurted, "Oh, this is great. After a day like this! I got a call from school because our son talked back to the teacher. Susie fell down the basement steps and knocked one of her front teeth loose, the baby is sick, the washing machine broke down, and now, to top it off, you come home drunk!"

Love, sweet love.

Jesus says:

> You have heard that it was said, "An eye for an eye and a tooth
> for a tooth." But I tell you not to resist an evil person. But
> whoever slaps you on your right cheek, turn the other to him
> also. If anyone wants to sue you and take away your tunic, let
> him have your cloak also. And whoever compels you to go one
> mile, go with him two. Give to him who asks you and from
> him who wants to borrow from you do not turn away. You have
> heard that it was said, "You shall love your neighbor and hate
> your enemy." But I say to you, love your enemies bless those who
> curse you, do good to those who hate you and pray for those
> who spitefully use you and persecute you, that you may be sons
> of your Father in heaven; for He makes His sun rise on the evil
> and on the good, and sends rain on the just and on the unjust
> (Matthew 5:38-46).

We are to love one another as God loves us, it's that simple. It
means caring about the true interest and welfare of everyone, even
those who are our enemies. For this is the way God, as we see Him
in Christ, deals with you and me. Well, that sounds easy enough,
doesn't it?

Too easy.

The story is told of a hiker who was nearing the top of a modest
mountain when suddenly the ground under his feet began to give way.
He started to slip and then to slip uncontrollably down the steep face of
the hill. As he fell, he had the good sense to grab a tree branch, but the
further cascades of stones left him hanging in thin air. In desperation,
the man prayed, he pleaded, and bargained. Finally out of the heavens
came a voice saying. "Let go of the branch."

To which the man replied, "Is there anyone else up there I could
speak to?"

Love your enemies? I would like to ask God, "Is there anyone else
up there I could talk to?" That's a difficult admonition.

The Greeks have six different meanings to the word *love*. *Eros*, a sexual love. *Philia*, a friendship. *Ludus*, a playful love. *Philantia*, a love of self. *Parma*, a longstanding love. Agape is the one Jesus speaks about.

Agape love is unconditional.

Christian love is a continual responsibility It does not end when we have tried one course of action. It only begins. Neither failure nor success lets us off the hook. We have a continual responsibility to look at and deal with the consequences of what we have done, good or bad, or as usually is the case, a tangled mixture of the two. In fact, what we do may be nowhere near as important as the way in which we deal with the consequences of our actions. And this is particularly true of the way we deal with failure.

Here, we need each other. We need to confess to one another our discouragement and despair, not in order to get some kind of sympathetic permission to drop the whole matter because we have done the best we can, but to get the kind of creative forgiveness that says, "Yes, you did fail, this time. Now let's see why you did and figure out what to do next." What is it we humans need more than anything else? Is it money, health, prestige, affection, security, or a million other things? The deepest need by far is for a love that seeks to discover and meet that need, that will not give up, that keeps on trying in spite of everything.

I love the country western song that Crystal Gayle made popular that says, "You never gave up on me, when I was given love up on you."

Love acts, and love listens. As Sam Levinson said, "Love at first sight is easy to understand. It's when two people have been looking at each other for years that it becomes a miracle." Love is tenderness, not toughness. We hear nice guys finish last. But toughness is not real strength. Real strength is a flow of inner energy through the whole person that brings a dimension of caring, instead of aggressive toughness.

Tenderness is obeying the inner law of your nature, but without the negative part of what God made when God said, "I will make you in my image" (Genesis 1:26).

The Psalmist says, "The Lord is merciful and gracious, slow to anger, and abounding in mercy. He will not always strive with us, Nor will He keep His anger forever, He has not dealt with us according to our sins, Nor punished us according to our iniquities" (Psalm 103:8, 9, 10). Gentleness is real strength St. Francis de Sales said, "Nothing is so strong as gentleness; nothing is so gentle as real strength."

In Hal Lyon's book, *Tenderness is Strength*, he lists four ingredients that belong to tenderness.

First, tenderness is genuine, it is real, no pretending. In a relationship, one has to be real. That means we are in touch with our feelings. Tenderness cannot be put on, like cosmetics. It comes from the deep center of the real you.

Secondly, gentleness, tenderness in a relationship cherishes the other person. I can not find a better word. To cherish is to want someone's best, to prize and value someone dearly and deeply.

Thirdly, tenderness is marked by emphatic understanding. In a tender relationship, you really feel what the other person experiences. God's prophet, Ezekiel, in the days of the Babylonian exile, was supposed to speak to the exiles, and he knew they were in exile because of their idolatry and disobedience. He says, "So the Spirit lifted me up and took me away, and I went in bitterness, in the heat of my spirit; but the hand of the Lord was strong upon me" (Ezekiel 3:14). He was really going to tell them off, but then, "he sat where they sat" (Ezekiel 3:15).

And lastly, tenderness implies a sense of trust. I can trust you with my failures, with my weakness, with my dreams, because our trusting relationship is strong and alive. This implies that I can afford to admit imperfection and that I can both forgive freely and expect to be forgiven freely. Our Lord Jesus is a superb role model of tenderness. Jesus attracted children because of His tenderness. He was gentle and observant to nature itself. Hence the parables, "Are not two sparrows sold for a copper coin? And not one of them falls to the ground apart from your Father's will" (Matthew 10:29).

"So why do you worry about clothing? Consider the lilies of the field, how they grow; they neither toil nor spin; and yet I say to you that even Solomon in all his glory was not arrayed like one of these" (Matthew 6:28).

Jesus was especially tender to women, including women who were outcasts (John 8:2-11). He could cry tears at his friend Lazarus's tomb (John 11:33-36). He could tell stories of the prodigal son (Luke 15:11ff), and the good Samaritan (Luke 10:30). But, for me, nowhere does Jesus's tenderness seem so visible as in the Upper Room (Luke 22: 10).

The Cross is just hours away. He has wanted an intimate meal with His disciples and what do these disciples do? They have an argument over which of them was the greatest (Luke 22:24). Jesus could be angry, or frustrated, or exasperated, and we would certainly understand. How many times do we feel exasperation when things don't get done the way we wanted them to? And we get frustrated. I do, all the time, and I must daily remind myself of Jesus's response. It was not in anger. Jesus didn't harshly say, "Will these disciples ever learn? You can't teach them anything."

No.

Jesus, in great tenderness, explains the difference between His kingdom and the power structures of this world.

> And He said to them, "The kings of the Gentiles exercise lordship over them, and those who exercise authority over them are called 'benefactors.' But not so among you; on the contrary, he who is greatest among you, let him be as the younger, and he who governs as he who serves. For who is greater, he who sits at the table, or he who serves? Is it not he who sits at the table. Yet I am among you as the One who serves." And then Jesus says, "And I bestow upon you a kingdom, just as My Father bestowed one upon Me." (Lk 22:24)

And the Apostle Paul could write to his friends in Ephesus from his prison in Rome: "I, therefore, the prisoner of the Lord, beseech you to have a walk worthy of the calling with which you were called, with longsuffering, bearing with one another in love, endeavoring to keep the unity of the Spirit in the bond of peace" (Ephesus 4:1, 2). And then he says, "And be kind to one another, tenderhearted, forgiving one another, just as God in Christ also forgave you" (Ephesians 4:32).

So much more can be said about love. Love is enduring. Love builds community. Love is unselfish, knows how to suffer, and lays its life down for a friend. But Jesus's words about love can never be separated from His giving of Himself in love. It was not fanaticism, or a search for martyrdom that led him to accept the crucifixion. It was a need to be where we are, to help us, to give us life for death, because loving is always leaving oneself to go toward others.

When you've experienced you are loved like that, and accept a love like that, then you have experienced unconditional, agape love.

Through a Mustard Seed

Jesus gave many of his answers through parables. In fact, the disciples asked Jesus in the Gospel of Matthew, "Why do you speak to them in parables?" And Jesus answered them, "I speak to them in parables because seeing they do not see and hearing they do not hear, nor do they understand" (Matthew 13:10).

And then Jesus tells them a parable, saying, "The kingdom of heaven is like a mustard seed, which a man took and put in his garden; and it grew and became a large tree, and the birds of the air nested in its branches"(Luke 13:18, 19).

Now, if we are to understand this parable properly, we must first understand the mood of the people who have gathered around Jesus. They are partly discouraged and partly expectant and excited. It makes quite a difference whether a person looks at this Nazarene with the reserve of a sympathetic spectator. This costs nothing. Or whether that person has given up their job and staked everything on just this one person, Jesus. This is actually what the disciples around Jesus had done. And, now, quite understandably, they are asking, "What's going to come of it? What will be the outcome?"

The answer seems to be...nothing. Almost nothing is happening.

Sure, a few poor people have been helped, a few sick people have been healed, but this is a small thing really, and the Jesus movement had, so to speak, fizzled out.

The intellectuals and political establishments rejected Him, or worse, simply ignored Jesus. The capital city acted as if He did not exist. The Greek and Roman centers of culture paid no attention to this Galilean. And now Jesus has asserted that the Kingdom of God had begun. But, when a man asked, quite realistically, "Where?" the results looked pretty small. The few dirty children who ran after Him, the beggars and the few hangers-on from the outskirts of society. These certainly cannot be the Kingdom of God. Are these the kind of things we're asked to put our faith and trust in? The Kingdom of God seems to be represented by so few people and from the outposts of society. But how many people do we need? We would like a large quantity, wouldn't we? We would like to look out upon the congregations and count the numbers.

I'll never forget a lesson in numbers I learned on my first speaking engagement thirty-eight years ago. I laboriously prepared my notes and went over my topic repeatedly, only to find one person attending that evening seminar on "death and dying." I went ahead with all gusto and, after the talk, the one person in attendance, called me over and said, "I suppose you're disappointed that I was the only one here."

And she looked at me as I tried not to show disappointment. Then she said, "Just remember, God called you to be faithful to Him, and not to worry about how many people come to listen." God certainly sent the right person to me that evening.

My disappointed attitude was similar to the mood of the disciples as it is reflected in the parable. They, too, were disappointed. They thought the Kingdom of God might move out, perhaps starting a new regime.

Then Jesus paints a picture of the Kingdom of God.

> And He said, "The kingdom of God is as if a man should scatter seed on the ground, and should sleep by night and rise by day, and the seed should sprout and grow, he himself does not know how. For the earth yields crops by itself; first the blade, then the head, after that the full grain in the head. But when the grain ripens, immediately he puts in the sickle, because the harvest has come. "To what shall we liken the kingdom of God? It is like a mustard seed which, when it is sown on the ground, is smaller than all the seeds on earth; but when it is sown, it grows

up and becomes greater than all herbs and shoots out large branches,so that the birds of the air may nest under its shade." (Mark 4:26-31)

Here the question arises. Did Jesus mean by this statement that everything starts from a seed? That Christianity would conquer the world?

No, He did not.

When Jesus speaks of the mysteries of growth, He is not thinking so much of the quantitative process by which His church grows ever larger, and finally a mighty Christian invasion conquers the world. Rather, the fact that in His church there is an indwelling love which must try and touch everything around it. Jesus is indicating to us that this quantitative way of counting is false. It is just numbers. Jesus tells us just the opposite. He tells us every small way we treat each other, every seemingly insignificant way we listen and care for and love one another, is vital.

The great theologian, Peter Marshall, tells the true story about a trip many years ago an English family took. One day their son found a swimming hole and jumped in, seized with cramps, and shouted for help. It happened that in a nearby field a farm boy was working. Hearing the cries for help, he came running and dove in, dragging the young English boy out of the water. The boy's parents, of course, were very grateful and visited the farmer's broken-down cottage to thank the youth who had saved their sons life.

"What do you plan to do with your life?" they asked the boy.

"Oh I suppose I'll be a farmer like my father", the boy answered. "But I always wanted to be a doctor."

Observing the people were poor, the English gentleman said, "You shall have your heart's desire and study medicine. Make your plans and I will take care of the costs."

So, the boy became a doctor.

It was December 1945. Sir Winston Churchill was dangerously ill with pneumonia in North Africa. His doctor asked Sir Alexander

Fleming, the discoverer of the new wonder drug, penicillin, to fly over to Africa to attend to the sick statesmen.

Taking off in a fast bomber, Sir Alexander Fleming arrived within a few hours, administered the new drug, and for the second time in Churchill's career, saved his life. It was the young Winston Churchill whom young Alexander Fleming had pulled out of the swimming hole so many years before.

And this is what the parable of the mustard seed means. The emphasis is not upon external growth and bigness. Not the total Christianization of our planet. No, this parable has nothing to do with increasing denominational memberships statistics. This is rather a matter of the growth of the person. If we do not scatter and spread our seeds about, helping others, teaching, loving, and caring, then we will be infected by moral and mental decay.

Sometimes only a single seed of God's word falls into a human heart. "Follow me," and Matthew, the tax collector, became a messenger for the whole world (Matthew 9:9). "Behold, the lamb of God," and John the Fisherman became a witness who feeds our faith to this day (John 1:29). And to Martha, Jesus said, "If there is one of you who has not sinned, let him be the first to throw a stone at her;" and none condemned (John 8:7). And Saul on his road to Damascus met Jesus and became the writer of our Epistles in the Holy Bible (Acts 26:14-18). Paul and Silas found that out too. They were in prison and an earthquake split the foundations; doors opened; prisoners' chains loosened; and the keeper of the prison saw all prisoners leaving; and by Roman law in those days, drew his sword and was about to kill himself. But Paul told the keeper the prisoners were staying and not to kill himself. And the keeper, on his knees in thanksgiving, said, "What must I do to be saved?" Paul said, "Believe on the Lord Jesus Christ and you will be saved" (Acts 16:30).

Seeds of love saved them all. How do we gather up God's seeds of love? We must be in commune with the roots of our souls through prayer. Theologians Martin Luther and John Wesley prayed each day, not despite their busy lives, but because only could they accomplish their gigantic labors, if they prayed to God. The word of God falls like a mustard seed onto our hearts and contains within itself tremendous power.

It takes years to become a tree and bear fruit. If the kingdom of God is to grow like a mustard seed, we must let the word of the Lord germinate, grow, and flourish within us. But if Jesus is to grow in hearts, we must grow smaller and ever less important.

In my wedding prayers to the bride and groom, I ask this: "Lord may they not expect that perfection of each other, that alone belongs to thee."

Jesus says, "If you have faith as a mustard seed, nothing will be impossible for you" (Matthew 17:20).

Seek first the kingdom of God. Seek to receive and keep this smallest seed in your heart, then pass on God's seed of love to others.

Stained Glass the Mustard Seed

Morality and Love

Sometimes it's difficult to know what's right. How do we choose to make faithful moral decisions in this world of ours?

Apostle Paul sheds light on this when he says:

> And He Himself gave some to be apostles, some prophets, some evangelists, and some pastors and teachers, for the equipping of the saints for the work of ministry, for the edifying of the body of Christ. (Ephesians 4:11, 12)

Paul is trying to teach the people at Ephesians moral standards. "I, therefore, the prisoner of the Lord beseech you to have a walk worthy of the calling with which you were called" (Ephesians 4:1).

Show your love by being tolerant with one another. Don't listen to cunning craftiness and trickery of men, but climb to the height the Lord God has given each of us the capability to achieve. We achieve this by growing in every way to Christ who is the head.

In today's world, these words are as fresh and new as they were centuries ago. Today is a time when there's widespread outburst of drugs and crime, few moral standards and reports that continue of bribery in high places, along with copycat crimes, needles in cereal boxes, and poisoning in some over-the-counter pills.

We're not quite sure what's happening, whether the moral fabric of society is pulling loose and we're somehow contributing to this and how we avoid falling into the same moral corruption. This concern has been with us as long as the human race has been on the planet. It's with us every time we say a moral yes, or a moral no. It's with us all during the year as we try to inculcate the capacity to make moral judgments with our friends, our neighbors, our families, and every human being we touch along life's journey.

What motivates our moral choices?

Lawrence Kohlberg in his book, *The Story of Psychology*, found six stages of moral development for humankind. I'm paraphrasing by adding my own observations of choosing motivational levels.

The lowest motivational level is the fear of punishment. We can all remember old tapes from childhood, "If you don't put that hammer down this instant, I'm going to tell your father when he gets home." We put it down. Fear of punishment.

But the fear of punishment is the motivational level of many adults too. When they put out their tax forms or testify in court, or perhaps even go to church or the synagogue. The government or God will zap you if you don't shape up. Our whole criminal justice system operates largely at the level of fear of punishment. We call it deference. Even the action of nations who spend billions of dollars to scare one another into decent behavior. This is part of human nature, I suppose, but it's a pity that so much attention and so much money is spent at the lowest level of moral motivation that we never get around to asking whether we might do something constructive at some of the higher levels.

The second level of motivating us is the promise of reward. From the stick, we advance to the carrot. The children will get dessert if they eat their vegetables. Contributors to the campaign will get juicy appointments if we win. Good Egyptians, Good Russians will get economic aid. Good Christians will go to heaven when they die. A great deal of moral decisions are made at this level. Early parole for good conduct. If you describe rewards in terms of expectable goals, this level is really not bad, but it's not very high either.

The third level of moral motivation is a conformity to an expected norm. The norm is outside you, even as the punisher is outside you, and the rewarded is outside you. We are still on external forms of motivations, only this time, it's the group of your peers, or a society that puts expectations on you, and to win their approval, you conform.

We all do this.

Sometimes, it's pretty innocent, sometimes it isn't so innocent. If you are a student, you may get drunk after a football game, not because you really want to, but to win the laugh and the "in" feelings of your group. Or we can contribute to the office for a fundraiser, or support a birthday party of a colleague. Perhaps you don't want to, but because you're afraid to be one conspicuous holdout. Or you may vote Republican or Democrat because your family or social group has this perspective and you want their approval. We can do bad and good, under peer group pressure. We might commit perjury, or defame an opponent, if we want group approval badly enough. We could even rise to heroism in battle and win a medal of honor from the same level of motivation.

Level four is a bit higher. The motivator this time is God, or the state or government. We make a moral decision in response to what we think is a divine command. God says, "Do it," and you obey. The state says, "Do it," and you do. We can call this level "obedience to a command." This level may actually free us from lower levels at points. From fear of punishment, for example, or a concern for reward. It might even free you from pressure from your peer group. Yet even this motivation is external. God who speaks through the Ten Commandments through a moral code through Bible verses and traditions can be an external motivation coming from outside you. Yours not to reason why; but to do or die.

So you might believe that God is anti-homosexual, and anything you do against the gay community pleases Him.

People hear God's voice telling them to do or not to do all kinds of things. We may burn a heretic to the glory of God, as the Protestants and Catholics have done in the past. Or we may build a hospital to the glory of the same God. The motivator is still out there. A system of ethics, standard of conduct, something that you perceive has a divine voice. And you obey.

Now, we've gone through four levels of motivation.

However, we need to remember the lessons from our great leaders.

Neither the Old Testament prophets nor Jesus or St. Paul were satisfied with external motivations. They talked about a coming era when the law of love would be written on people's hearts. When people would love others, and not do it because they felt forced, coerced or pressured.

Recall these words from our Jesus:

> Then He called the multitude and said to them, "Hear and understand. Not what goes into the mouth defiles a man; but what comes out of the mouth, this defiles a man." (Mt 15:10)

It isn't what comes into a person from the outside that defiles them, they are defiled from the inside. It's what is inside that counts. It's not just the outward act, like stealing, but it's the inward thought, hate. The kingdom of love is not a kingdom of horses and chariots and race cars and cheerleaders, but a kingdom of truth which is rooted inside us.

Where are we on this motivational scale? Are we still at the first four levels of external motivation? If so, something inside us needs to grow. We need to have our life internalized. Our inner springs of motivation need to grow. This is the difference between the first four levels of motivation and that which follows. So we cross a very real boundary when we go from four to five on this scale of moral motivation.

For now the motivator becomes inside of us. It's an inward consent to a perceived truth. We say, "This is the way I see it." We take a stand. We speak out of our own conviction. And this is where the real struggle to find the truth begins. Now we aren't just reacting to an external source. We are really trying to sift through our own convictions, insights, understandings, and commitments.

My boss says it's all right. The Supreme Court says it's all right. The government says it's all right.

But "I don't think it's all right!" Every human being made in the image of God has not only the right, but the responsibility, to say that. This is part of the glory of our humanness, to be a moral decision maker. Inward consent to a perceived truth. The question is no longer, "Is it legal?" But "is it right?" "Is it just?"

It's a totally different question than those at the lower levels of moral decisions. The kingdom of truth requires that something inside of us is born and starts to assert itself, starts to grow, mature, stand up for what we believe is right. One truly wonders about the brilliant people who are implicated in a variety of scandals. Whether there was a suspension of this personal inward monitoring in order to please the goal of a team. I covet this strength for all of us. When we see the world in a new perspective, then we will have the courage to make moral decisions on our own at this higher level. So, as a student, you refuse to cheat on a test when others in the room are cheating because you're unwilling to conform when you know it isn't right.

When we sit in a board room and some policies are being discussed for a corporation or organization, you will take responsibility and your judgment will lead you to ask, "Is this just?" "Is it right?" When we hear a racial slur, we immediately rectify it.

Level six only deepens level five. Total commitment to a supreme relationship other than one's self. A person's life becomes focused in a supreme commitment beyond one's self. This is Saul on the road to Damascus meeting Jesus (Acts 13:9). This is Albert Schweitzer heading for Lambarene in Africa. This is Dag Hammarskjold in his quest for peace. This is Martin Luther King in his walk for freedom.

And then, we learn how to find peace and enjoyment of our lives. Jesus said to His disciples:

> At that time the disciples came to Jesus, saying, "Who then is greatest in the kingdom of heaven?" And Jesus called a little child to Him,, set him in the midst of them, and said, "Assuredly, I say to you, unless you are converted and become as little children, you will by no means enter the kingdom of heaven. Therefore whoever humbles himself as this little child is the greatest in the kingdom of heaven. And whoever receives one little child like this in My name receives me." (Mt 18:1-5)

Have you ever watched little children enjoy life? What is there about childhood that we adults would like to recapture? It may be the level of trust, or openness which sometimes the scars of cynicism obscure with experience. It could be the sense of playfulness of being at home in the world. It could be the sense of creativity, or spontaneity, or all of these taken together, which belongs to the kingdom of the child. The kingdom of play, in the deepest sense, is the kingdom of trust.

Now, where are we on this scale? How do you grade yourself?

Are you at the lowest level of moral motivations? A fear of punishment, promise of reward, or obedience to a command?

I think most of us would like the motivation to be inside of us. Where the law of love is written in our hearts. Where there is an inward consent to a perceived truth, and then a total commitment to someone other than yourself. When that happens, we'll dislike nothing in the world except falsehood and evil, we'll fear nothing except cowardice. We'll be governed by our admirations rather than by our disgust. We'll covet nothing that is our neighbors' except their kindness of heart.

We will think seldom of our enemies, often of our friends, and everyday of God, because motive and caring are the most important guideposts on the footpath to peace and the level of choosing moral answers in this life of ours.

Agape Love Remembered

When I started this chapter on Love, I mentioned our children/ grandchildren's weddings. They were glorious, memorable days, forever commemorated. Those moments were truly times of shared love with our family.

Also remembered is the most loving experience I have ever witnessed. It was also a day of great sadness. Isn't that often the paradox of life?

Sometimes when we're most gratified with overwhelming love, there can be enormous sorrow.

A remarkable day forever remembered.

It was July 11th, 2013, and my 105-1/2-year-young precious mom died. Tom and I were just returning from overseas, and our daughters called our cell phone to grievously tell us that their Nana died the night before we arrived home from Europe.

Our daughter Becky drove all night from Fairfax Station, Virginia, and daughter Debbie, who detests flying, particularly alone, flew from Philadelphia to Ohio.

Our other daughter, Carrie and family were out-of-pocket, with missionaries from their church, helping build homes for others in need.

Becky and Debbie stayed with Nana for over three days, holding her hand, stroking her fingers, rubbing her back, talking to her, never leaving her side. They were with her comforting, loving, caring, wiping her lips, whispering, "We all love you, Nana."

This is truly agape, unconditional love, the love Jesus tells us about, asks us to do. "A new commandment I give to you, that you love one another, as I have loved you, that you also love another" (John 13:34). A love that they witnessed as they held onto their Nana and each other, and now will pass that love onto others. Their lives have been completely spiritually changed as they felt the Lord with them as their Nana took her last breath, and God took her home.

Jesus said, "Greater love has no one than this, than to lay down one's life for his friends" (John 15:13).

A loving poem from the heart and soul of our son-in-law, Bill Sharp, summarizes our collective unconditional love for my Mom, and their Nana.

Mom in imitation *Time* magazine created by friends,
Rose and Bill Caufield

For Nana

Long weekends spent
in the Ohio shade
good times remembered
new memories made
sound advice given
yet a gentle ear
that heard of changes
one hundred five years
and yet while the world
seemingly passed by
a beacon of strength
unchanged would just sigh

and remind us all
to smile and not frown
and not let hard times
get us too far down
and now that your days
on this earth are through
we want you to know
that we will miss you
always our Nana
in thought you will be
smiling and teaching
the way it should be
may warm summer sun
shine now and not cease
while you walk with God
in eternal peace.

—WHS

100th birthday, family and Mom

FINDING PEACE

There was a fictional story written about an atheist who hired an attorney to bring a discrimination case against Christians and Jews, and their observances of Holy days. The argument was that "it was unfair that atheists had no such recognized holidays."

The case was brought before a judge. After listening to the passionate presentation by the lawyer, the judge banged his gavel declaring, "Case dismissed!"

The lawyer immediately stood, objecting to the ruling. "Your Honor, how can you possibly dismiss this case? The Christians have Christmas, Palm Sunday, and Easter. The Jews have Passover, Yom Kipper, and Hanukkah, yet my client and all other atheists have no such holidays."

The judge leaned forward in his chair, saying, "But you do. Your client and you, counsel, are woefully ignorant."

The lawyer said, "Your Honor, we are unaware of any special observance or holidays for atheists."

The judge said, "The calendar says April 1 is April Fool's Day, found in the Old Testament, Psalm 14:1, where it states, 'The fool has said in his heart, "There is no God. They are corrupt. They have done abominable works, There is none who does good."'"

Thus, the judge continued, "It is the opinion of this court that if your client says there is 'no God', then he is a fool. Therefore, April 1 is his holiday. Court is adjourned!"

Even though it might be a fictional event, nevertheless, it's cleverly and appreciably written, as it brings a new dimension to peace of mind, body, and soul.

Oh, it was such a great birthday party! People laughing, glasses clinking, music playing. She had a twinkle in her eye. She was having a good time, greeting friends, telling stories, catching the spirit of the day. She even felt better about herself than she had for a long time. Then she was walking into the family room and all that was up, suddenly came tumbling down.

She didn't know...he...was going to be there. It had been two years since the divorce. Still, whenever she saw him, her world did a flip-flop—stomach tensed, heart raced, palms sweaty, and blotches would jump all over her face.

How long will this last? Would she, could she, ever find "peace"? How do we live life here on this place called earth with a modicum of peace? What does this word, *peace*, mean? Webster's dictionary says it is "a state of tranquility or quiet, freedom from disturbance."

The etymological notion behind the word *peace* is the concept of "fastening to something in order to find stability." So, in our pursuit of "peace," we need to pay attention to those things with which we have developed attachments.

Inevitably, the level of our tranquility will be paralleled by the nature of our allegiance. Tunnel vision of any sort, excess concern, in any way, leads to an overload of anxiety and worry. If we want peace, we can't find it while questioning the motives of others, or grumbling over perceived wrongs and blaming others. If we want a sense of personal serenity, we should get rid of all our grudges. Few of the biblical heroes had a better grip on this principle than the rumble tumble boy who became a handsome king, David, from the Old Testament. Adored by many, despised by some, he knew the difficulty of life with a high profile. From the time when he first played the harp for Saul, to his epic encounter with Goliath, during his liaison with Bethesda, his triumphs over the Philistines, and even as he mourned the murder of his beloved son, Absolom, David was the subject of pointed criticism from one end of Israel to the other.

If anyone had the right to bear a grudge against treacherous enemies, it was David, and yet he wrote this:

> Rest in the Lord, and wait patiently for Him; do not fret because of him who prospers in his way, because of the man who brings wicked schemes to pass. Cease from anger, and forsake wrath; do not fret-it only causes harm. For evildoers shall be cut off; but those who wait on the Lord, they shall inherit the earth. (Psalm 37:7-9)

First of all, as we seek peace, we must release our resentments, and get rid of our grudges. In short, we need to close accounts with our old adversaries. It's ironic how grudges and resentments have such an ugly way of showing up at special occasions. You can count on Christmas, Easter, weddings, and funerals to sometimes bring out the worst in people. Perhaps it's because of the forced proximity prompted by these events that cause all the agitation.

Whenever I counseled couples for their upcoming weddings, I asked about second marriages, involving either sets of parents, or children who should sit on one side of the aisle. What might cause some "upsets" by either family? Problems more likely arrive if you haven't addressed them before the actual day. Sometimes, latent hostilities have prevailed for many years. It's truly surprising sometimes. I've seen it in my church, when mothers, fathers, stepmothers, and stepfathers refuse to sit on the same side of the aisle, let alone the same pew. It's also not unusual to find family members sitting ten rows back, lost in the crowd, cut out of the loop, because something as festive as a marriage is being celebrated.

It doesn't have to be that way.

Not too long ago, I officiated at a wedding where the bride appeared at the narthex holding the arm of her father. Halfway down to the altar, they paused and her stepfather took her other arm. Together, the three of them approached the altar, pride aside, beaming at "their" daughter and new son-in-law. When I asked the question, "Who gives this woman to be married to this man?" They answered, in unison, "With her mother, we do."

Obviously this was a family who knew how to move on and celebrate their new life. Bearing grudges, resentments, anything that denies free and open communication, is a foil to inner tranquility. We can't measure ourselves by the accomplishments of others. Self-esteem is not centered in how we compare ourselves to others, but how we feel about ourselves. We can't always be numero uno.

That might be what David meant when he said, "Rest in the Lord, and wait patiently for Him" (Psalm 37:7).

So we look at another point in finding peace.

We refuse to measure ourselves on the basis of the accomplishments of others. We need to accept ourselves as we are, and as God accepts us. We take a giant step toward peace when we cultivate the habit of dealing with others by realizing that we're only here a little while. Let go and let God.

As the Psalmist David wrote: "Cease from anger, and forsake wrath; do not fret-it only causes harm" (Psalm 37:8).

The dictionary defines *wrath* as "retributory anger." We know what that is. It is the "I'll get you back" kind of animosity that inevitably does more harm to the bearer than the recipient. Sometimes we just get so incensed over the behavior of others that we can't let go of it. Still, if peace is honestly a concern, we can go a long way by simply learning to focus on the positive while abiding the negative.

When we learn to appreciate what God gives us and leave the rest to our Lord, our peace is in our heart. In the final analysis, there is no greater denial of the love of God than finding the negative, therefore worrying about everything in life.

If paganism can be defined as "a rejection of a loving God," then worry and negativity may be the most pagan of all practices. It suggests there is no loving Creator who will ultimately care for all living things. It suggests there are no options other than those we can detect or project. It suggests the ultimate victory of evil over good. It laughs in the face of Resurrection.

And here is the real ploy. Worry, bearing grudges, resentments are more concerned with loss than gain. They simply do not take into account the fact that God has been with us, is now with us, and will always be with us.

How do you know God is with you this very moment?

We need to feel God's presence in our lives. If we believe ours is a God of love, and if we really believe God is always with us, we should fear nothing. Then we are free to throw our arms around life and live it to the fullest, but we can't do that while clinging to the past or longing for the future. We can only do it now. We can't always choose what happens to us, but we always can choose how we are going to respond. We don't know if we'll have arthritis, or if we'll lose our spouse, have an accident, or a divorce, but we can choose how to respond. As the Psalmist David says, "Rest in the Lord, and wait patiently for Him, cease from anger; and forsake wrath; do not fret-it only causes harm. For evildoers shall be cut off; But those who wait on the Lord, shall inherit the earth" (Psalm 37:8,9).

And that should be our response too.

I've known a very fine gentleman for many years now. His faith was strong, even though he knew he was dying. Cancer had moved through his entire body. It started in the prostate, and moved into his bones. It started almost three years ago now. When I visited him, he knew the end was not far off. "You know," he said, "I really wanted to see my daughter Peggy graduate, but I'm not gonna make it. I can't go to work anymore, can't even read more than a few minutes. But, I'll tell you what I can do. I can watch the birds outside my window. Every day my wife puts bird seed in the feeder, and I watch God's creatures living, yet for another day. Gosh, they're precious, aren't they? All sizes, all makes, so unassuming. And I love it when my wife comes in and I stare at her more than ever before. She is soft, gentle, caring, and loving. Let me tell you something really special. It's the 'little' bump on her nose. Just check it out. She hates it but I love it. I've loved it for years."

A few minutes later, his wife came in carrying a tray with a morphine milkshake and small fruit salad for herself. Her smile was touching. I stood to leave and noted her eyes filled with tenderness. Upon reaching the door, I looked back. She had placed the tray on the table and was bending over to kiss his head. My eye went to her nose. It actually looked like my nose, a little bump in the middle, that happened to me from a car accident in my youth. And now, looking at her, I realized my bump was beautiful too, just as my Tom would tell me many times. I walked out to my car and just sat there wondering why life has to come to an end before we learn to live it one beautiful moment at a time.

Peace.

As I look over Scripture, Jesus is talking with His disciples and he says,

> Therefore I say to you, do not worry about your life, what you will eat or what you will drink; nor about your body, what you will put on. Is not life more than food and the body more than clothing? Look at the birds of the air, for they neither sow nor reap nor gather into barns; yet your heavenly Father feeds them. Are you not of more value than they? Which of you by worrying can add one cubit to his stature? So why do you worry about clothing? Consider the lilies of the field, how they grow; they neither toil nor spin; and yet I say to you that even Solomon in all his glory was not arrayed like one of these. Now if God so clothes the grass of the field, which today is, and tomorrow is thrown into the oven, will He not much more clothe you, O you of little faith? Therefore do not worry, saying 'what shall we eat" or 'what shall we drink?' or 'what shall we wear?' For after all these things the Gentiles seek. For your heavenly Father knows that you need all these things. But seek first the kingdom of God and His righteousness, and all these things shall be added to you. Therefore do not worry about tomorrow, for tomorrow will worry about its own things. Sufficient for the day is its own trouble. (Mt 6:25-29)

Peace.

The truth is, people who have peace make it a practice to live in the present. They don't spend a lot of time sweating over past mistakes. And they sure don't wear themselves out worrying about tomorrow. Peace is in the present. It is choosing not to wallow around in yesterday's memories, regretting what is no longer possible or grieving over unrequited sins. Rather, it is a matter of taking exactly what you have and using it to enrich the moment. It is enjoying a morphine milkshake with someone you love. It is refusing to dull the luster of what we have with fragments from the past or fears about the future. It is exactly what I think the Psalmist was helping us understand when he observed: "This is the day which the Lord has made; We will rejoice and be glad in it" (Psalm 118: 24).

There's another point from Scripture that Jesus makes to that crowd on the shores of the Sea of Galilee. First, He reminded them that peace is in the present. "Sufficient for the day is its own trouble" (Matthew 6:34). Then, we add to our inner tranquility by truly realizing how short our sojourn is on this earth. "Therefore do not worry, for your heavenly Father knows that you need all these things" (Matthew 6:33).

If we really want to make the most of every moment, we would begin to treat other people as if it were their last day on earth. It doesn't mean we never disagree or that conflict never arises or difficult decisions should always be coated with sugar-coated niceties. No, it just means life is a lot more meaningful when we remind ourselves that it doesn't last forever and its quality content is largely in our hands.

Peace is in the present. Then we realize the shortness of our journey. And, finally, in simple trust, we find an anecdote to anxiety. This is really the essence of this entire passage. Jesus, in essence, said, "Look at the birds, they have no pension plans, cost of living clauses, and they do alright. And, look at the flowers, they have no clothing allowance, yet they are arrayed more beautifully than any human who ever lives."

So, we should worry? I like the final verse and find it so easy to write and preach about, but living it is difficult. "Therefore do not worry about tomorrow, for tomorrow will worry about its own things. Sufficient for the day is its own trouble" (Matthew 6:34).

Many groups have understood this truth. People attending our support groups I facilitated through the years tried to live one day at a time. There's no better way to engage life's challenges than to release the past, embrace the present, and trust the future to God. And that really is the bottom line. Trust. If we really trust God, we take life in stride and keep on growing.

On the other hand, if we feel we have to control everything in order to make it right, worry is an unavoidable reality.

In the final analysis, there is no greater denial of the love of God, than worry. If paganism can be defined as a rejection of a loving God, then worry may be the most pagan of all practices. It suggests there's no loving Creator who ultimately cares for all life. It suggests there are no options other than those we can detect or project. It suggests the ultimate victory of evil over good. It laughs in the face of the resurrection. And, here is the real surprise. Worry is predominately attached to maintaining the status quo. It is more concerned with loss than gain. It simply does not take into account the fact that God has been with us, is now with us, and will always be with us.

Here's a marvelous piece written by a young lad by the name of Jason Lehman. He calls it "Present Tense."

> It was spring. But it was summer I wanted, the warm days and great outdoors.
> It was summer, but it was fall I wanted, the colorful leaves and cool air.
> It was fall, but it was winter I wanted, the beautiful snow and the joy of the holiday season.
> It was winter, but it was spring I wanted, the warm and the blossoming of nature.
> I was a child, but it was adulthood I wanted, the freedom and the respect.
> I was twenty, but it was thirty I wanted, the youth and the free spirit.
> I was retired, but it was middle age I wanted, the presence of mind without limitations. My life was over, but I never got what I wanted.

If we want peace, we have to learn how to stop worrying and trust in God.

Grow with the Flow

I really like my hair dresser, Sal, at the Imperial Salon. I've been with him now over eight years. What I like the most is his ability to make my hair "obey," with good perms, color, and cuts. I've always had the feeling that he knows how to "grow with the flow." If something doesn't go right, he grows in changing it to make it better for all his patrons.

That's what people who have peace of body, mind, and soul do. They grow with the flow. Instead of retreating within the self, they grow.

St. Paul was concise with his counsel to his young companion Timothy.

> But in a great house there are not only vessels of gold and silver, but also of wood and clay, some for honor and some for dishonor. Therefore if anyone cleanses himself from the later, he will be a vessel for honor, sanctified and useful for the Master, prepared for every good work. Flee also youthful lusts; but pursue righteousness, faith, love, peace with those who call on the Lord out of a pure heart. But avoid foolish and ignorant disputes, knowing that they generate strife. And a servant of the Lord must not quarrel but be gentle to all, able to teach, patient, in humility correcting those who are in opposition, if God perhaps, will grant them repentance, so that they may know the truth, and that they may come to their senses and escape the snare of the devil, having been taken captive by him to do his will. (2 Tim 2:20-26)

With these words, the wise old teacher Paul reminds his young follower, Timothy, that the kingdom of God is an interdependent network of believers. It's a team of people, all with different attributes, yet working together to achieve harmony and peace. By this, he tells young Timothy we can't be whole unless we are together.

None of us are totally self-sufficient. We were made to live in community. So when a crisis strikes, we don't turn inward, which only brings depression, and isolation. That is why support groups are so successful. People share their problems with others who understand. No matter how massive the problem might be, difficult situations tend to shrink when we share it with others.

Nothing puts life in perspective faster than an open-caring encounter with other people. That was the concept the Master had in mind when He told us: "Then Jesus said to His disciples, If anyone desires to come after Me, let him deny himself, and take up his cross, and follow Me. For whoever desires to save his life will lose it, and whoever loses his life for My sake will find it" (Matthew 16:24-27).

If Apostle Paul's words to Timothy do anything, they confirm the fact that we human beings find wholeness and peace in healthy interdependence. I personally don't know what I would do without my best friend, my husband, and some of our family members. The Scripture from 2 Timothy says, "In a great house there are not only vessels of gold and silver, but also of wood and clay" (2 Timothy 2:20).

Everyone is important.

Peace is heavily dependent upon the capacity to contain our bent to see ourselves as self-sufficient and to reach out to others for understanding and acceptance. Even under stress, we must try and share ourselves in some kind of community. During our weekly suicide prevention support group, one of the members shared with us this composition that he found from *The Compassionate Friends Newsletter*, October 1986. It is entitled "Just Walk with Me."

> I have a problem. I want to tell you about it. No, I really don't. I'd rather keep it to myself, handle it alone. I do think it would be good for me to share it with you though. I don't want to because I am afraid of what you'll say and how you'll act. I am afraid you might feel sorry for me in a way that makes me feel pathetic. like I am some 'poor thing.' I am afraid you'll try to cheer me up.
>
> Please just walk with me. All those other things seem so much brighter and sharper, smarter and expert. But what really takes love is to "Just walk with me."

Being There

Of all the treasures we human beings can share with each other, there are few more helpful than our simple tender caring Presence.

It is called "being there."

It is a key ingredient to peace of our heart, mind, and soul. During my years at seminary, I remember over and over the professors stressing that the most important attribute wasn't necessarily what you were saying at a funeral or memorial service, it was the fact that you were there. I've thought about that many times over my years, and somehow, what we say is never quite as important as what we do.

Several years ago, Sidney Harris, the *Chicago Tribune* columnist, was asked, "If you knew you had only one column left to write, what would you say?"

Harris pondered the question for a while before responding, "I'm not sure exactly how I would flesh it out, but the last column would include three points.

1. You gain your life, by giving it away.

2. Being and becoming are the proper ends of human life; and having is only a means.

3. We are all part of the great chain of life and we must make a lifestyle of forging stronger links with others and not breaking them."

And, from our Scripture, "But in a great house there not only vessels of gold and silver, but also of wood and clay, some for honor and some for dishonor" (2 Timothy 2:20).

Ours is the calling to purposefully hold together all the vessels of the household. Whether they are gold, silver, wood, or clay is not the point, valuing each one as important to the household, that's the point. Reaching for peace of mind means coming to understand that our lives are enriched and enhanced in contact with one another. Indeed, peace comes when we share honestly and openly with one another.

When someone has peace, they refuse to seek self-justification in easy alibis that make them appear noble to themselves and others. They are up front, honest, with no false pretenses. If we desire inner tranquility, then we must learn to admit we are wrong, absorb bad breaks, and move on.

The Scripture that may direct us is one of the more revealing images in the New Testament. Jesus spoke this parable to some who trusted in themselves that they were righteous, and despised others.

> Two men went up to the temple to pray, one a Pharisee and the other a tax collector. The Pharisee stood and prayed thus with himself, "God, I thank You that I am not like other men-extortionists, unjust adulterers, or even as this tax collector: I fast twice a week; I give tithes of all that I possess, And the tax collector, standing afar off, would not so much as raise his eyes to heaven, but beat his breast saying; 'God be merciful to me a sinner!' I tell you, this man went down to his house justified rather than the other; for everyone who exalts himself will be abased, and he who humbles himself will be exalted." (Lk 18:10-14)

Jesus had run headlong into the society of judgmental law-making prudes. In that day, as in ours, there were plenty of people who perceived themselves as flawed procurators for the cause of purity. These were people with ironed wigs and icy eyes, who always enjoyed pointing out the errors of others. They didn't get much sympathy from Jesus, who already broke the laws of healing on the Sabbath, talking with women in public, and touching unclean lepers. Having been challenged one too many times by their self-righteous arrogance, the Master told this parable. It seems as though Jesus was the first person to relate to some of the principles we need when we have an inner peace. What are some of the principles we need for inner peace? We need to realize that we can't get to this "peace" until we own up to our mistakes. In the sense of human wholeness, there is very little space for either "pitiful Pearl" or "alibi Bob."

Peace comes when we learn how to roll with life's punches and admit our errors.

The only time we can truly stand up straight is when we have done just that. A person who can effectively be all things to all people simply does not exist. Carl Sandburg had a cute story of the "classy chameleon." According to Sandburg, this was the chameleon of chameleons. Capable of split-second color changes, the chameleon was the envy of all his friends. And then came the day when he happened upon a Macgregor plaid, blew all his circuits, and had a nervous breakdown.

People who pride themselves on error-free lifestyles are destined to a familiar fate. Like that Pharisee rattling off his list of accomplishments, these people simply have their priorities misappropriated. Flawlessness is not a life requirement for those who know the unconditional love of God. Honest acceptance of human inconsistencies is.

I think of a story related about Frederick the Great's visit to a Berlin prison. The King of Prussia, renowned for his eccentric tastes, was immediately accosted by inmate after inmate vigorously protesting innocence. One man alone remained silent and aloof. Frederick called to him, "You there, why are you here, in this prison?"

"Armed robbery, your Majesty."

"And are you guilty?"

"Yes, indeed, your Majesty. I entirely deserve my punishment."

Frederick instantly summoned the warden.

"Guard, release this guilty wretch at once. I will not have him kept in this prison where he will corrupt all the fine innocent people around him."

There is something refreshingly disarming about admitting our mistakes. As a sign in a therapist's office advises: "It is important to be who you is, because if you is who you ain't, then you ain't who you is."

Apostle Paul informed the people of Rome none of them were perfect, all have sinned, and had come short of the glory of God.

> Therefore, as the elect of God, holy and beloved, put on tender mercies, kindness, humbleness of mind, meekness, long suffering; bearing with one another, and forgiving one another, if anyone

has a complaint against another; even as Christ forgave you, so you also must do. But, above all these things put on love, which is the bond of perfection. And let the peace of God rule in your hearts, to which also you were called in one body; and be thankful. Let the word of Christ dwell in you richly in all wisdom, teaching and admonishing one another in psalms and hymns and spiritual songs, singing with grace in your hearts to the Lord. And whatever you do in word or deed, do all in the name of the Lord Jesus, giving thanks to God the Father through Him. (Col 3:12-17)

People with peace know that truth and have no problem owning up to their inadequacies. They don't make alibis or indulge in self-pity.

It's also important, in order to experience peace, to learn how to handle bad luck. We all know that tragedy has no respect for persons. Whether we deserve it or not doesn't have much to do with what happens to us in this life. Does anyone in their right mind think that those who died in 9/11 deserved to die? Innocents. It's just not fair or acceptable.

I do not accept these things. I have to ingest them. We all know there are times in life when the breaks simply do not go our way. Murphy's Law is in effect. "Anything that can go wrong will go wrong." No matter what happens to us, or around us, or inside us, the sun will come up in the morning and the world will keep on moving. Peace comes when, after we've grieved, we willingly move on to the next day.

The late Bishop James Pike often coached his followers to practice what he called "holy carelessness." What he admonished was to "do your homework and leave the rest to God." Any person who has ever taken an examination or competed in an athletic contest or delivered a speech knows what that means. We do our best to be prepared, but can't touch all the bases and know all the consequences. There is great wisdom in "holy carelessness," placing the whole concern in God's lap with a commitment to live with the consequences.

If we want peace, we must try and master this process. We refuse to make excuses or pity ourselves in the process. We accept the rest, trusting in God's promise that He will walk through the waters with us.

In my husband's Army Reserve magazine, there is a single phrase that captures the essence of turning the page, and moving on. It reads: "If lost, climb, and conserve and confess." It's written by Donald Rumsfeld, as one of the primary rules he learned in pilot training. If you get lost, you need to "Climb, conserve, and confess."

Isn't that great? If your life is upside down, climb. Find a better perspective from a new position. Conserve. Don't waste energy by stewing over spilt milk. Save some energy for challenges yet to come. Give yourselves the opportunity to recover. Confess. Admit you made a mistake.

Develop a new and fresh perspective. That is what happens when we move on and step into the next day.

There is no such person as a perfect human, save Jesus the Christ. "So there really is not a bit of sense in keeping up a false pretense."

> Peace comes when we
> own up to our errors
> take in life's bad luck
> and move on to tomorrow.

One of the most humble observances ever made by the Apostle Paul was written in Romans: "For we know that the law is spiritual, but I am carnal, sold under sin. For what I am doing, I do not understand. For what I will to do, that I do not practice; but what I hate, that I do" (Romans 7:14, 15).

I doubt there is any other passage in the Bible that carries any more liberating potential than this. If only every human being on the face of the earth could come to understand that perfection is beyond reach, we might all manifest not only a deeper affection for one another but for ourselves as well. People who have peace have come to terms with their weakness and struck a balance between what they expect of themselves and what they can actually accomplish.

Several years ago, in the middle of all my ten major operations, a friend of mine gave me a poster that had a straggly cat, face filled with fear, staring right at me, hanging on one paw's claw, grasping tightly to the overhang of a table, with the caption underneath reading: "Hang in there!" There are some things we simply cannot do. I can't climb mountains or swim with sharks. More and more every day, there are "things" I simply cannot do anymore. The sooner we accept ourselves as we are, the sooner we can enjoy what we can do. When we expect too much of ourselves, it does nothing but increase our levels of frustration and multiply our potential for misery. On the other hand, when we set expectations that are challenging, and reachable, it isn't very long until we find ourselves rising to new levels of performance. As any long-distance runner can explain, one doesn't begin training for a marathon by running thirty miles on the first day. Great performances always require patient preparation.

When we succeed at striking a balance between what we expect of ourselves and what we can actually accomplish, we will save ourselves from sustaining false images. People with peace, like the Apostle Paul, know their faults and confess them. We need to share our humanity and stand up together. We need to understand our errors and own up to our weaknesses.

The key is to admit it, try not to expect too much of yourself and make the most of the moment. Not only that, but it's equally important to practice honest self-indulgence.

Apostle Paul said, "What I do, I would not, and what I would, I do not" (Romans 7:19). We all know that feeling. The last thing in the world we need to do in response to such frustration is to quit on ourselves. We've all had our down days: can't find our car keys, the garage door gets jammed, you've waited all day for a maintenance person who never shows up. Sometimes, we have to pamper ourselves. There are days when we need to relax, do yoga, light candles, sit back in a hot bath, and close our eyes.

Nothing can separate us from the love of God. But, like every other gift, the gift of grace can be yours only if you reach out and take it. The catch is in the taking.

Paul couldn't always do what he wanted to do.

Neither can we.

Paul often did what he didn't really want to be doing.

So do we.

We need to understand not only what we're going through but what others go through and share our journey together. That's why all those support groups became so vital. We need others to understand us, share with us, and guide us on our troubled paths.

The Gospel of John says it: "And the Word became flesh and dwelt among us, and we beheld His glory, the glory as of the only begotten of the Father, full of grace and truth" (John 1:14).

As we gain our inner peace, there is no experience, no crisis, no tragedy, no calamity that we can ever encounter, apart from the loving presence of God. "And the Word became flesh and dwelt among us."

A Light in the Darkness

Two thousand years hence
from that Holy Night
the vision seems blurred
and no longer bright
centuries passed since
the story was told
the herald's warm tale
feels suddenly cold
we search for a place
where Christmas lights shine
and find battered streets
where conflicts unwind
how can we find peace
in this war-torn world
where hatred's dark flags
constantly unfurl
the message of love
the birth of a child
visions of angels
to that mother mild
are lost in the dust
of violent crimes
loving one's neighbor

is hard in these times
and yet, through this mire
of conflict and hate
the story is told
and darkness abates
the herald's voice sings
muffled but still heard
the vision exists
still seen although blurred
the darker the night
the brighter the star
we cannot forget
who we truly are
each one a vessel
for God's holy grace
each a reflection
of God's holy face
the choice is now ours
to see or be blind
to passively dream
or open our minds
the message of Christ exists all around
in each humble sight
in each gentle sound
the challenge is here
we must make the choice
to proclaim God's love
we must be the voice.

—WHS

Stained Glass Star of Bethlehem

AND THE WORD BECAME FLESH AND DWELT AMONG US

At my church, Mt. Lebanon United Methodist, we were honored to be given a beautiful piece of sculpture, "The Dream of Isaiah." This mahogany wood piece of sculpture was five feet high by two feet wide with the full figure of Mary holding her Son, Jesus, standing on a carved Isaiah's head underneath, with the inscription: "The Dream of Isaiah."

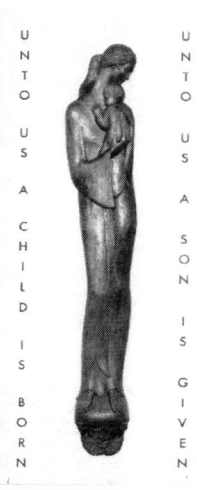

Dream of Isaiah

The incredible piece of inspirational sculpture was created and carved by Wilmington Delaware's outstanding, widely acclaimed, and internationally recognized sculptor, Charles Parks. Charles, his wife

Inga, and his administrative assistant, Joan Anderson, are dear friends of ours. This sculpture was donated by John and Marion Cowan, friends of the Parks. The sculpture was lovingly placed on the side curtain at the left of our altar. It remains there, always a remembrance of the "Dream of Isaiah" from the Old Testament, Isaiah 7:14: "Therefore the Lord Himself will give you a sign; Behold, the virgin shall conceive and bear a Son, and shall call His name Immanuel."

Who was this prophet Isaiah?

About the year 720 BC, there was born, in the city of Jerusalem, a boy to whom was given the name Isaiah, which in Hebrew means "Jehovah saves." This meant that Jehovah would save his people, not only from political disasters, but from national wrongdoing and from evil of every kind.

It is written that Isaiah had a prophetic vision when he was a young lad. Scholars say he entered the temple and that he had a vision that changed his life. In a prophetic trance, he saw Jehovah, God of Israel, tell him that he would send a servant to save his people. Isaiah heard the word of God and relates it in the book of Isaiah. These words refer to the coming of our Lord and are called the Messianic Prophecy.

What is the background of these chapters and the Isaiah prophecy? They belong to the period of the Syto-Ephraimite War, 745 BC. It was a desperate, frightful time for Judah. A mere remnant of a once-proud nation was living in captivity in Babylon, a theme made poignantly contemporary when fifty-two of our own country men and women were taken by the Iranians and finally released after fourteen months, back in 1979 to 1981.

In the sixth century BC, however, all that was left of God's chosen people were in exile. The future didn't look good for them. Many of the people who were captive integrated themselves into Babylonian culture. They figured, why not blend into the environment? Why not idolize the idols of greed, lust, lasciviousness? It was a time of uncertainty. The new power in the area was Persia, and all thought that it was only a matter of time until Cyrus the Great exercised his sovereignty, even over Babylon.

No one was sure what might happen. Nothing about the prospect looked good. And then the prophet Isaiah tells them, those desperate people, those captive countrymen and women, "not to worry, someday a child will be born, with the great name, Emmanuel, meaning, 'God is with us.'" The new king will not be like the poor King Ahaz. The new king is then described throughout the book of Isaiah. The new King Immanuel would arrive as a suffering servant afflicted and despised, a Man of sorrows.

You can imagine how the captives felt when this upstart, this so-called prophet, Isaiah says:

> He is despised and rejected by men, A man of sorrows and acquainted with grief, And we hid, as it were our faces from Him; He was despised, and we did not esteem Him. Surely He has borne our griefs and carried our sorrows, Yet we esteemed Him stricken, Smitten by God and afflicted. but He was wounded for our transgressions, He was bruised for our iniquities; the chastisement for our peace was upon Him. (Is 53:3)

Jesus, our Lord and Savior, was going to come, not as a king, but as a lowly servant, fulfilling the prophet Isaiah's prophecy. Thus says the Lord: "In an acceptable time I have heard You, and in the day of salvation I have helped You; I will preserve you and give You as a covenant to the people, that You may say to the prisoners, Go forth, to those who are in darkness, show yourselves" (Isaiah 49:8, 9).

That was back then, and then, five hundred years later, the prophet Isaiah's predictions came to pass: "The word became flesh and dwelt among us" (John 1:14).

Mary the Mother of Jesus

How could this happen? How would the word become flesh?

> Now in the sixth month the angel Gabriel was sent by God to a city of Galilee named Nazareth, to a virgin betrothed to a man whose name was Joseph, of the house of David. The virgin's name was Mary. And having come in the angel said to her, "Rejoice, highly favored one, the Lord is with you; blessed are you among

women!" But when she saw him, she was troubled at his saying, and considered what manner of greeting this was. Then the angel said to her, "Do not be afraid, Mary, for you have found favor with God. "And behold you will conceive in your womb and bring forth a Son and shall call His name Jesus. He will be great and will be called the Son of the Highest; and the Lord God will give Him the throne of His father David. And He will reign over the house of Jacob forever, and of His kingdom there will be no end. Then Mary said to the angel, "How can this be, since I do not know a man?" And the angel answered the said to he, "The Holy Spirit will come upon you, and the power of the Highest will overshadow you; therefore, also, that Holy One who is to be born will be called the Son of God." (Lk 1:26-35)

After the visit of the spirit of God, the teenage girl went with haste to the city of Judah to visit the elderly wife of Zacharias and Elizabeth, who was also expecting.

She knew who this was, and she acknowledged the same with these wonderful words: "Blessed are you among women, and blessed is the fruit of your womb" (Luke 1:42).

Mary responds with what is come to be known as "the Magnificent," one of the most powerful pieces of literature the world has ever known. Loaded with meaning, it begins with the paradox of blessedness. You see, with every blessing is also a burden. Whether we're talking about the writings of Tom Clancy, the voice of Pavarotti, or the honor of birthing the Son of God; the flipside of every gift is the responsibility to do something with it.

Yes, Mary was chosen, selected, singled out to give birth to the "Wonderful Counselor, the Mighty God Immanuel, the Prince of Peace." But she was also chosen to raise a child with a mission bigger than life. And, perhaps most difficult of all, she was chosen to one day watch that child become a man who loses His life on a hill called Golgotha in the hands of an angry mob, and a government more interested in expediency than justice.

The flipside of every blessings is the burden of doing something noble with it.

Mary knew the honor of being "chosen." And she knew the importance of answering the call when it comes.

Listen to the verses that immediately precede this Scripture. Having been informed of her role by a visit from the Holy Spirit, the courageous young Mary responds:

> My soul magnified the Lord, And my spirit has rejoiced in God my Savior. For He has regarded the lowly state of his maidservant; For behold, henceforth all generations will call me blessed. For He who is mighty has done great things for me, And holy is His name. And His mercy is on those who fear Him From generation to generation. He has shown strength with His arm; He has scattered the proud in the imagination of their hearts. He has put down the mighty from their thrones, and exalted the lowly. He has filled the hungry with good things, And the rich He has sent away empty. He has helped His servant Israel, In remembrance of His mercy, As He spoke to our fathers, To Abraham and to his seed forever. (Lk 1:46-55)

Isn't it interesting that this young girl from Nazareth, suddenly informed she is most blessed among women, would leave the comfort, safety, and familiarity of her hometown to "go with haste to a Judean town in the country" to visit an older woman who waited sixty years to become a mother herself? So why did Mary go to Elizabeth? I think it was to underline, for all of us, our utter dependency upon the grace of God. It doesn't matter if you're fourteen or sixty, your life and everything in it is under the guidance of Almighty God.

The link between the two is rather obvious.

Having been surprised by the mysteries of life, both Mary and Elizabeth accepted their calling as a gift from God. The young sought out the old, and together they took strength from each other while embracing the challenges before them. The message is that the old is never separated from the young.

God is the Author of all life, so all our lives are interconnected.

Even as I am writing this, even as you are reading, somewhere in this world there is a youngster who will someday be President of the

United States of America. Someone will write another book on the reverence and sanctity of life. And, in the fullness of time, it shall come to be.

The bridge between the old and the young is the Spirit of God.

Luke tells us that Mary stayed with Elizabeth for three months. Just imagine the relationship they must have forged. I see them visiting the marketplace and bartering for household goods. And I see them praying together for patience and wisdom and the courage to train up a child in the way he should be, that when he is older he will not depart from it.

If only in our time, we would learn to obliterate the lines between the old and the young and allow the one to learn from the other. If only we could graciously learn that the one does not supersede the other and both are better for the sharing.

What a magnificent passage of Scripture.

The Spirit of God visited Mary, called her out of the crowd, chose her. But think of Mary's response. Just think of her options. She could have cowered in fear and refused the honor of her calling. She could have summoned Joseph and tried to misguide his affection in order to camouflage her own condition. Or she could have run off with some local scalawag to escape embarrassment and provide a father for her child at the same time. But she did none of this.

She didn't deny, she didn't hide, and she didn't flee. Rather, she embraced the situation and sought the glory of God in the midst of it. That's the beauty of this poem. It is full of vision.

She seized the moment to concentrate on all she could come to be. What did Mary say? She said: "And His mercy is on those who fear Him from generation to generation, He has shown strength with His arm; He has scattered the proud in the imagination of their hearts. He has put down the mighty from their thrones and exalted the lowly, He has helped His servant Israel, In remembrance of His mercy" (Luke 1:50-54).

I don't know how you feel about this attitude, but I think it's unbelievably inspirational. Of all the options this young lady had, this is incredible. Imagine yourself, not even fifteen years old, engaged to be married, a child of humble means and virtually no education and this angel appears and announces you're pregnant. And what would you do? The question is, when life thrusts a change upon us, how do we respond? Do we invite the best or anticipate the worst?

When the most horrendous change that could possibly have happened in her life confronted young Mary, she had that choice. She could have become a victim, but she chose to be a servant, and the world has never been the same since.

> And it came to pass in those days that a decree went out from Caesar Augustus that all the world should be registered. This census first took place while Quirinius was governing Syria. So all went to be registered, everyone to his own city. And Joseph also went up from Galilee, out of the city of Nazareth, into Judea, to the city of David, which is called Bethlehem, because he was of the house and lineage of David, to be registered with Mary, his betrothed wife, who was with child. So it was, that while they were there, the days were completed for her to be delivered. And she brought forth her firstborn Son, and wrapped Him in swaddling cloths, and laid Him in a manger; because there was no room for them in the inn. Now there were in the same country shepherds living out in the fields, keeping watch over their flock by night. And, behold, an angel of the Lord stood before them, and the glory of the Lord shone around them, and they were greatly afraid. Then the angel said to them, "Do not be afraid, for behold, I bring you good tidings of great joy which will be to all people. For there is born to you this day in the city of David a Savior, who is Christ the Lord. "And this will be the sign to you: You will find a Babe wrapped in swaddling cloths, lying in a manger.," And suddenly there was with the angel a multitude of the heavenly host praising God and saying: "Glory to God in the highest, And on earth peace, good will toward men!" (Lk 2:1-14)

On that night of nights, what led up to that moment at the inn?

The law of the land in Jerusalem in those days demanded that people return to their hometowns for a census-taking. The Romans wanted to know how many subjects they really had and where they came from. So Joseph, Mary's husband, had to leave Nazareth and went way down the Galilean area of the Holy land to his hometown of Bethlehem, some eighty miles to the south. It didn't matter that his wife was well into her ninth month of pregnancy. The family had to go. It was the law. So for eighty miles, Mary endured the rocky spine of a walking donkey, only to arrive at Bethlehem and discover their reservations were lost, the computer at the Bethlehem Hilton was down. There was "no room for them at the inn." The only place for them to stay was in the stable, with the donkeys, cows, sheep, and goats.

Now, if you were going to pick a time and place for the Son of God, the Mighty Counselor, the Prince of Peace, to be born, this would not be the time, and certainly not the place.

But, life's timetables are in God's hands. Joseph and Mary understood that and trusted God's purpose in every portion of their circumstance. Can you imagine that happening in our country today? Expecting a mother in her ninth month to ride a donkey eighty miles in order to register to vote? We certainly would not vote for the person who enforced that bad law.

But Mary did, and so did Joseph. They trusted a plan that was bigger than their perception. And while they were trying to find a place in the stable, a group of shepherds huddled watching their flock by night were about to have their lives turned totally upside down.

And while Mary, Joseph, and the Baby Jesus were snuggling into the dusty hay of a back street stable, Herod was looking for his would-be successor amidst the marble, gold incense, and myrrh of the upper classes.

God's purposes often elude our perception.

Sometimes life doesn't make sense. Maybe it's an illness or a financial problem or a domestic difficulty, and it just doesn't seem fair, right, or acceptable.

I'm sure Mary felt much the same way when Joseph came home with the news they had to travel eighty miles just to register to vote. When we believe God is the Master of our lives, we learn how to go with the flow, how to trust the moment, how to endure the trials in pursuit of the triumph.

When we realize life's timetables are in the Hands of God and the Hands of God are at work even when we cannot see them, it follows that waiting, plain old simple waiting, is an act of faith.

Paul caught it in his letter to the Galatians when he wrote: "But when the fullness of the time had come, God sent forth His Son, born of a woman, born under the law" (Galatians 4:4).

God really does have a plan for our lives and we are here to do our part in it. Sometimes that means waiting. If your life is out of sync now, cut the pace and wait. Stop the process. Time out.

The Old Testament prophet Habakkuk taught the principle in the second chapter, third verse of his book when he wrote: "For the vision is yet for an appointed time; But at the end it will speak, and it will not lie. Though it tarries, wait for it; Because it will surely come, It will not tarry" (Habakkuk 2:3).

In our ever-fast-mega-bit world, waiting is one of the hardest orders any of us can receive. Waiting for anything. However, in the divine-human relationship, waiting is an important part of the process.

One of my indurate moments of waiting is the night our Lord and Savior was born, how difficult it was, as a youngster, and even now, an oldster, to wait for Christmas morning. Yet learning to wait is one of life's most important lessons. We spend a good portion of our lives waiting. For the doctor, dentist, traffic, babies to be born, someone to call, gates to clear at the airport, waiting for time to pass. Waiting is a pivotal part of life. It's also a pivotal part of faith.

Isaiah told us: "But those who wait on the Lord shall renew their strength; they shall mount up with wings like eagles, they shall run and not be weary, they shall walk and not faint" (Isaiah 40:31).

The question is, how do we wait on the Lord?

The Epistle of James gives us some hints in the seventh and eighth verses of his fifth chapter: "Therefore be patient, brethren, until the coming of the Lord. See how the farmer waits for the precious fruit of the earth, waiting patiently for it until it receives the early and latter rain. You also be patient. Establish your hearts, for the coming of the Lord is at hand" (James 5:7, 8).

If we are to fully comprehend the power of these words, we need to put them in context. The people to whom James was writing were absolutely convinced that the Messiah was on the verge of returning. For them, every day was marked by expectation and every night by the assurance that tomorrow would be the day.

So, as the days melted into months and months into years, they found their faith beginning to waver. Like children (and many of us adults) subjected to an endless Christmas Eve, they were growing weary beneath the weight of the waiting. So our Scripture, the book of James, starts by saying, "Be patient, see the farmer: wait for the fruit" (James 5:7).

No one has a better appreciation for the virtue of patience than the farmer. Although James intended his letter for the staid elders of the temple, he knew they were quite familiar with the farmers who peopled the countryside. Long in partnership with Mother Nature, the farmers made a lifestyle of getting in rhythm with the seasons. For them, waiting was essential to success. So it is for all the people of faith.

It is this knowledge that God is forever at work in our midst that should give us the patience to wait. If we know that God is at work, and realize that God shares our journey, then what are some of the characteristics of waiting? As we wait, we wait for the moment.

We've moved to Florida a few years back, and cleaned out extra baggage, keeping only what is necessary. Letting go of unnecessary "things," I said to myself, "If I haven't worn or used this in the past five years, someone else might use it."

Then, practice being prepared.

If our faith is a daily period of prayer and meditation, we must practice it. If our faith is a personal relationship with Jesus Christ, we learn to cultivate it. If it's a faith in helping others, whether they're grieving or being treated unjustly, we must spare nothing in the struggle. What matters is that you keep your faith alive.

James said, "The Coming of the Lord is at hand" (James 5:8).

Over two thousand years ago.

Yet when we consider the millions of years the world has been in existence, that two-thousand-year segment is a forty-page chapter in the midst of a thousand-page book.

There are many spry octogenarians in our community. One told about having a bad knee. After a thorough examination by the physician, the doctor looked this man with the bad knee straight into his eyes. "Joe," he said, "the problem with your knee is simply a matter of old age."

Joe leaned forward with a twinkle in his eye. "Don't kid me, doc," he said as he laughed. "The other knee is the same age."

Even if knees are not, time is relative.

We live in a time period where we want everything done now, make that stat. A preoccupation with hurry-hurry often leads to unsatisfactory solutions. It's true, what we are about is important, and today does have a wonderful way of shaping tomorrow. But nothing is more important than trusting the Sovereignty of God over a span of time.

And as the farmer must wait for the rains before reaping the crops, so also are all of us destined to wait upon the handiwork of God as the ultimate Author and judge of history.

Every moment is precious, every experience an opportunity. Even in the waiting, there is much to be gained. Let the word go forth that when the Son of God was born, the first announcements didn't go to the king or queen or high political places. No, Jesus came to the common people. Those who were glad to be doing their jobs, helping each other, raising their children, trusting in God. The Lord comes to us where we are. Broken, incomplete, searching, sometimes succeeding, sometimes failing, but always waiting and in need.

Mary, the Chosen Lady
Once upon a midnight clear
a woman lead her partner dear
to southern town where there would be
a birth to change our history
for chosen lady was with child
the unexpected mother mild
in humble corners she did lie
whilst herald star passed slowly by
pangs of labor she did endure
commoners and kings came to her door
to pay homage to this one
rumored as God's chosen Son.

(WHS)

Stained Glass The Lily

Prepare the Way for a Suffering Servant

The Israelites also felt like an abandoned people, their leaders led as slaves to a foreign land. Their hope of survival slim, but still stirring in their hearts was the hope of an ancient covenant, the call of Patriarchs Abraham, Isaac, and Jacob. So when the prophet Isaiah rose to address his people, some hope caught a gust of wind of promise.

Said Isaiah:

> Go through, go through the gates! Prepare the way for the
> people; Build up, Build up the highway! Take out the stones, Lift
> up a banner for the peoples! Indeed the Lord has proclaimed To
> the end of the world; Say to the daughter of Zion, Surely your
> salvation is coming; Behold, His reward is with Him, and His
> work before Him And they shall call them The Holy People,
> The Redeemed of the Lord; And you shall be called Sought
> Out, A City Not Forsaken." (Is 62:10-12)

Imagine the scene. The Persians have ruined Jerusalem. Then, after
pillaging the city, they rounded up all the men under sixty, all those
with any education, and all those with wealth and marched them off
to Babylon. The only people left in Jerusalem were the feeble and
dependent. Oh, there were a few young women with children, but
virtually all the vital people had been exiled. Every corner was marked
by soldiers of the occupation. It was hopeless. But Isaiah was telling
them that just because you can't see what God is doing, don't assume
you are forgotten. God knows where you are and what you need and
God will come to you.

The promise of Christ is not just a little sweet boy born in a manger
or a shepherd spotting a star or wise men bearing gifts. Undoubtedly
all those things happened. But the real promise is that this child was
fulfilling God's Promise. In this nondescript son of a carpenter was the
timeless affirmation that love is greater than hate; peace more powerful
than war. The people who were captive back in the prophet Isaiah's
time couldn't understand this new servant-peaceful image. After all,
they were destitute. They needed immediate help, not someday help,
and even then, certainly not a suffering servant, a Man of sorrows.

The image of the suffering servant has long been misunderstood,
even when Jesus, our Immanuel, was born, lived, and became a part of
our world. Jesus's own disciples believed their Immanuel, the Master,
was one who would display power. Remember two of Jesus's own
disciples, the Zebedeboys, James and John, wanted power they thought
would take political, even military force. But Isaiah had a different

vision. He had a sign from God and God's revelation to Isaiah was a vision of a suffering servant.

In His first sermon, which He appropriately preached at His home synagogue in Nazareth, Jesus took a text from the Old Testament Book of Isaiah. Isaiah 61 describes the Messiah not in triumphal terms, but in terms of lowly service. Hear the prophet of Isaiah from the Old Testament:

> The Spirit of the Lord God is upon me, because the Lord has anointed Me to preach good tidings to the poor; He has sent Me to heal the brokenhearted, to proclaim liberty to the captives and the opening of the prison to those who are bound; to proclaim the acceptable year of the Lord, and the day of vengeance of our God; to comfort all who mourn. (Is 61:1-3)

And Jesus said, from the New Testament:

> The Spirit of the Lord is upon me Because He has anointed Me to preach the gospel to the poor. He has sent Me to heal the brokenhearted, to preach deliverance to the captives and recovery of sight to the blind, To set at liberty those who are oppressed, to preach the acceptable year of the Lord. (Lk 4:18)

And then Jesus closed the Torah, looked directly at the congregation, and said, "Today this Scripture is fulfilled in your hearing" (Luke 4:21).

Isaiah wasn't the only person preparing the way for Jesus.

Christmas was scheduled to happen over five hundred years earlier than it did. At least that was what Isaiah, the unknown prophet of the exile in Babylonia, thought. And with his moving story found in Isaiah 35, the Christmas vision of the chosen people reached its climax. "And the ransomed of the Lord shall return, And come to Zion with singing, with everlasting joy on their heads. They shall obtain joy and gladness, And sorrow and sighing shall flee away" (Isaiah 35:10).

When Persia took over the Babylonian Empire and the new Emperor, Cyrus, allowed the exiles to return to rebuild Jerusalem,

Isaiah expected Christmas to come and a new age in world history to begin.

But it didn't. Five long centuries intervened. To understand the hopes and hatreds of Jesus's day, it is necessary to understand just how long and dark those centuries were. It took the returning exiles almost one hundred years of struggling to make Jerusalem something more than a frontier settlement. For four hundred years, there was no Jewish nation at all.

In view of the circumstances, it's truly a miracle that the Jews returned any sense at all of being a special people with a special destiny. But they survived. They survived by holding on to the past and desperately looking to the future. Utterly deprived of nationhood, they became a people of a building and a book. The building, the temple, rebuilt with infinite blood, sweat, and tears, the center of an elaborate and exalted system of worship and sacrifice. Its rabbis were the acknowledged leaders of the people.

The book, The Torah, viewed chiefly as the summary of God's will, the law, the scribes, second only to the rabbis in authority and influence. The Jews resembled nothing so much as survivors of a disaster at sea, holding on desperately to pieces of the wreckage, praying hopefully that rescue was coming. As their present situation grew, if anything worse, they clung all the more fiercely to the hope that God would not let things go on like this much longer.

God would come to the rescue, and when He did, when God sent the Promised One, all the nations that had oppressed and humiliated his people would suffer a retribution more terrible than anything the world had ever seen. Then, in the middle of the second century BC, it seemed that the time had come. Pushed to the wall by the Syrian Emperor, Antiochus, a man whose cruelty was outstanding even in the long history of oppression, the Jews, under a family called the Maccabees, revolted. After a guerilla war against overwhelming odds, they took Jerusalem and established the first truly Jewish Kingdom since the fall of Judah four centuries before.

The Jewish Feast of Lights, or Hanukah, celebrates this fantastic victory. At last, they were a nation again ruled by a new Maccadeen dynasty. But that didn't last long. Once more their hopes were dashed. In less than one hundred years, a short time as history goes, they were back in bondage, this time to the most powerful empire of all—Rome.

Once again they lived on hope and little else.

Such is the stage on which John the Baptist makes his impressive entrance around 28 AD.

> In those days John the Baptist came preaching in the wilderness of Judea, and saying, "Repent, for the kingdom of heaven is at hand!" For this is He who was spoken of by the prophet Isaiah, saying: "The voice of one crying in the wilderness; Prepare the way of the Lord, Make His paths straight." (Mt 3:1-3)

Making his home in the wilderness, from which the people of Israel had originally emerged to invade the promised land, John the Baptist looked and sounded like those long-ago prophets who spoke directly for God, who announced a new word from the Lord. And that announcement was that Christmas was coming, that God was finally moving in to establish his rule. And then, Jesus came from Galilee to John at the river Jordan to be baptized by him. But John tried to prevent Him, saying, "I have need to be baptized by You, and are You coming to me?" But Jesus answered and said to him, "Permit it to be so now, for thus it is filling for us to fulfill all righteousness. Then he allowed Him" (Matthew 3:14, 15).

But what happened next is amazing for all of us to read and know how God the Father touched His Son.

> Then Jesus, when He had been baptized, came up immediately from the water; and behold, the heavens were opened to Him, and He saw the Spirit of God descending like a dove and alighting upon Him. And suddenly a voice came from heaven, saying, "This is My beloved Son, in whom I am well pleased." (Mt 3:16, 17)

No wonder John the Baptist attracted attention. And no wonder Herod Antipas, Roman puppet ruler in the region, decided to get him out of the way. He clapped John into prison and then, as a favor to his stepdaughter Salome, had him beheaded.

St. Matthew's Gospel report of John's appearance and message is a poignant episode from his last days in prison.

> Now it came to pass when Jesus finished commanding His twelve disciples, that He departed from there to teach and preach in their cities. And when John had heard in prison about the works of Christ, he sent two of his disciples and said to Him, "Are You the Coming One, or do we look for another?" Jesus answered and said to them, "go and tell John the things which you hear and see: The blind receive their sight and the lame walk; the lepers are cleansed and the deaf hear; the dead are raised up and the poor have the gospel preached to them, And blessed is he who is not offended because of Me." (Mt 11:1-5)

Yes, we celebrate the manger scene, the shepherds, angels, Mary, Joseph, but we need to see Jesus grown up. The Man who touched lepers, who befriended tax collectors, who challenged the phoniness of the Pharisees, who demonstrated in the temple, who, wherever he went, broke down the racial, religious, social barriers between people, and who poured himself out in concern for human need.

The baby Jesus fits in with our trees, our colored lights, and the presents and Santa Claus and all the rest. We have room for the baby. The baby doesn't raise serious questions about our priorities. The baby doesn't call us to make any radical changes.

Yet, if we want to get at the real joy and power at the heart of Christ-mas, we need to confront the man this baby grew up to be. Because it is only as we let the whole story of Jesus's life and death speak to us that we can find faith and hope which can stand up to the darkness in the world and in our private lives.

Christmas. The gift of Christmas is God's gift of Himself through Jesus Christ and His transforming presence can be taken with us wherever we go. Jesus comes now, not only as a baby to be cuddled and adored. Jesus comes as a Lord with nail prints in his hands, scars of a love that survived hate. Jesus comes as God with us, questioning us, prodding us, saying as He did of old, "Be of good cheer! It is I. Do not be afraid" (Matthew 14:27).

Quietude
The Lord Jesus stands in God's world now with us,
as a reconciler, healer, challenger, and transformer.
Searching for a quiet place
longing for the slightest trace
of peacefulness in hectic times
of solitude that redefines
a simple note, a simple song
can whisk away the slightest wrong
and for a moment all seems right
and all is well this Holy night.

(WHS)

Stained Glass Window

THE HOLY LAND

Just over three hundred United Methodists visited the Holy Land in March 1994. There we followed the life of our Lord and Savior, Jesus the Christ.

As a United Methodist clergy with twenty-two members of my congregation aboard, it was my responsibility to have morning devotions on my bus. It was quite an exceptional honor to deliver the Scriptures around Jesus's time on earth, and actually now walking his walk with my own legs.

After boarding our buses in Tel-Aviv, we departed for the city of Jerusalem, settling in our hotel. Our first stop was the steps from Hasmonean times that connected the City of David with the Upper City. Jesus came down the steps on Palm Sunday, and each of us descended, feeling the words of that first Palm Sunday.

Palm Sunday

Now when they drew near to Jerusalem, and came to Bethphage, at the Mount of Olives, then Jesus sent two disciples, saying to them," God into the village opposite you, and immediately you will find a donkey tied, and a colt with her. Loose them and bring them to Me. And if anyone says anything to you, you shall say, "The Lord has need of them' and immediately he will send them." All this was done that it might be fulfilled which was spoken by the prophet, saying "Tell the daughter of Zion, 'Behold, your King is coming to you, Lowly and sitting on a donkey, a colt, the foal of a donkey.'" So the disciples went and did as Jesus commanded them. They brought the donkey and the colt, laid their clothes on them, and set Him on them. And a very great multitude spread their garments on the road; others cut down branches from the trees and spread them on the road. Then the multitudes who went before and those who followed cried out, saying: "Hosanna to the Son of David! Blessed is He who comes in the name of the Lord!" Hosanna in the highest." (Mt 21:1-10)

Palm Sunday is recorded by all four of the Gospel writers. Matthew and John tell us that the roots of that day's events lay in the Old Testament book of Zechariah, the prophet who looked for the coming of a King who would save the land of Israel from destruction. "Rejoice greatly, O daughter of Zion! Shout, O daughter of Jerusalem! Behold, your King is coming to you; He is just and having salvation, lowly and riding on a donkey" (Zechariah 9:9).

As Jesus's disciples moved slowly from the suburb of Bethany over the Mt. of Olives, they come in sight of the Holy City. The crowds built up, word got around quickly, from lip to ear. The news began to spread that the Nazarene prophet was here and He is coming toward the temple area. The procession moved slowly and Messianic shouts were heard, "Hosanna, Blessed is He who comes in the name of the Lord!" The very idea of Messiah conjured up, in those days, the idea of a warrior king and possible liberation from Rome.

But Jesus had rejected this model of a powerful warrior king and instead came as the prophet Isaiah predicted. "He was oppressed and He was afflicted, Yet He opened not His mouth; He was led as a lamb to the slaughter, And as a sheep before its shearers is silent, So He opened not His mouth" (Isaiah 53:9).

There was no violence from Jesus. Our Savior was a servant with no show of power. Jesus didn't want to control anyone. His disciples were not armed. God's kingdom cannot be rammed down people's throats. His only defense was His defenselessness.

It was a dangerous visit on the first Palm Sunday. Jesus literally took his life in His hands. Of course, now we have taken that Palm Sunday episode and are able to sing about it. We even had palm branches we waved to make sure that we captured some of the excitement when we walked those steps on our trip in the Holy Land. But in Jerusalem on the first Palm Sunday there was a real possibility of violence.

Then, why did Jesus go into Jerusalem? The reason? Ninety percent of the Jews lived outside the country. They lived all over the Mediterranean Basin, all over Mesopotamia. There was no way that Jesus could reach them except one. His willingness to go to Jerusalem and meet them during the Passover. Jewish Passover is a feast celebrating the escape from Egypt under the leadership of Moses. It was there that each family brought a lamb to the temple to be offered. It was a time when representatives of the whole Jewish dispersion would be in the capital city at the temple.

Jesus came as a servant. Servant-hood should not be thought of as demeaning or cringing behavior, nor should it be thought of as without a price. If you would be an agent of reconciliation, there are times when you have to accept the ministry of personal presence with all its risks and promises.

Jesus, on that Palm Sunday, and throughout His life, demonstrated how He interpreted His role as Savior and Messiah. His victories in the world would not be won by force, but by humility, service, sacrifice, and reconciliation.

I believe that is the way Jesus still comes, not as a conqueror on a white horse, or a gatherer appearing in the sky to only collect the righteous.

Now, on the first Palm Sunday and Monday, the day after, we had two dramatic pictures of our Savior Jesus. On Sunday, Jesus's triumphal entry into Jerusalem and then Monday, Jesus's return to the temple in Jerusalem.

> So the multitudes said, "This is Jesus, the prophet from Nazareth of Galilee." Then Jesus went into the temple of God and drove out all those who bought and sold in the temple, and overturned the tables of the moneychangers and the seats of those who sold doves. And He said to them, "It is written, 'My house shall be called a house of prayer,' but you have made it a 'den of thieves.'" (Mt 21:11, 12, 13)

There were reasons that led Jesus to the temples and his ire with the merchants who were selling their goods at a large marked-up price. As pilgrims came into the Holy City, they had to have their money changed into temple money, and the merchants in God's temple were overcharging, sometimes 20 percent. In addition, each man had to pay to gain entrance to God's house. So that Monday morning, Jesus saw the people being cheated out of the money they had struggled all year to save. Always sensitive to the needs of the poor, Jesus had seen the high priests' own family taking advantage of the poor. Angry at this overpricing, this monopoly, Jesus drives out the herds of animals. He overturns the exchange tables, sending coins of a dozen reams rolling across the paving stones, and to the priests in charge, Jesus cried, "My Father's house shall be called a house of prayer, but you have made it into a den of thieves" (Matthew 21:13).

Jesus has only said what the common people have thought and have been afraid to say. Jesus both comforts and disturbs. We all need to be both comforted and disturbed. Ironically, when we often receive the most effective comfort is precisely when we are being disturbed.

The Apostle Paul writes in the Epistle:

> Therefore if there is any consolation in Christ, if any comfort of love if any fellowship of the Spirit, if any affection and mercy fulfill my joy by being likeminded, having the same love being of one accord, of one mind. Let nothing be done through selfish ambition or conceit, but in lowliness of mind let each esteem others better than himself. Let each of you look out not only for his own interests, but also for the interests of others. Let this mind be in you which was also in Christ Jesus. (Phil 2:1-5)

Jesus comes to us as a teacher and servant. Jesus puts Himself in the middle of the action. If you would be a person willing to help others, there are times when you have to accept the ministry of personal presence with all its risks and promises.

There is absolutely no way for God to bleed off the hostilities of the human race without providing a vulnerable servant in the midst.

Jesus rides into the city, the day of Hosannas, and a day of the Lord's passion.

As you can see, that triumphant entry really wasn't triumphant at all.

To the people, Palm Sunday was no more than a passing fancy. Where was their support when Jesus was being tried for treason just four days from then?

And what will it be for us?

Will it be a talk without the walk?

Will it be the apathy without availability?

Will it be the worship without discipleship?

For this is the way the Savior rides.

The Cenacle: Upper Room

The next day we were in the Holy City, we were taken to Mt. Zion, the Cenacle, ascending some stairs to a cold room. This is the "Upper Room," we were told.

It seemed so gray and cold when we entered, but suddenly I was "strangely warmed," just as John Wesley had been in his Aldersgate experience on May 24, 1738. John wrote:

> While I was hearing the Preface to the Epistle to Romans, and hearing the change which God works in the heart through faith in Christ, I felt my heart strangely warmed. I felt I did trust in Christ. Christ alone for salvation; and an assurance was given me that He had taken away my sins, even mine, and saved me from the law of sin and death.

That was exactly how we felt in that Upper Room, and I'll never forget the sensation and warmth that moved through my body. It was here that Jesus chose to share a meal with His disciples. He wanted this meal to be His last act with them. Knowing what was ahead, He chose to observe the Passover on Thursday, rather than the usual Friday night.

In an account of the Lord's Supper:

> Jesus rose from supper and laid aside his garments, took a towel and girded Himself. After that, He poured water into a basin and began to wash the disciples' feet, and to wipe them with the towel with which He was girded. Then He came to Simon Peter. And Peter said to Him," Lord, are You washing my feet? Jesus answered and said to him, "what I am doing you do not understand now, but you will know after this." Peter said to Him, "you shall never wash my feet!" Jesus answered him, "If I do not wash you; you have no part with me." Simon Peter said to Him, "Lord, not my feet only, but also my hands and my head!" Jesus said to him, "He who is bathed needs only to wash his feet, but is completely clean; and you are clean, but not all of you." (Jn 13:4-10)

The dinner was set for Jesus and His disciples, but there was no servant present to carry out the usual courtesy of washing the dust of travel from the feet of the guests. The basin, however, with the jar of water and the towel were there. Who should be the servant to cleanse the feet of the guests? Caught in the net of their pride, the twelve all held back from volunteering for the job of being the servant.

The table was set. But how should the disciples sit? In what order? Only a few days before, James and John asked to sit next to Jesus. It infuriated the others, for they were the youngest of the disciples. Matthew was the richest, Peter was chosen for the difficult tasks. John was the beloved disciple. Who was to take the lowest place and wash their feet?

Gradually they took their places. Jesus rose, took off His outer robe and knotted a towel around His waist like a servant who washes the guests' feet.

One by one, the Master washed the dust from the feet of His disciples. Our Lord washed the feet of Matthew, who had given up a rich business to leave all and follow Jesus. Then the feet of James, the fiery brother of John. Then John, the youngest of them all. Then Philip, the attractive, timid spirit, and Andrew, who had introduced the others to Jesus, and then Judas, who watched Jesus, eyebrows lifted, body turned aside.

Finally, He came to Peter who was overcome to see His Master take the role of a servant. "Master," he cried, "are you to wash my feet?"

And the Master answered, "If I then, your Lord and Teacher, have washed your feet, you also ought to wash one another's feet. For I have given you an example, that you should do as I have done to you. Most assuredly I say to you, a servant is not greater than his master, nor is he who is sent greater than he who sent him" (John 13:14-16).

Then they ate together the Passover feast.

> Jesus took the cup and gave thanks, and said, "Take this and divide it among yourselves; for I say to you, I will not drink of the fruit of the vine until the kingdom of God comes." And He took bread, gave thanks and broke it, and gave it to them, saying, "This is My body which is given for you; do this in remembrance of Me." (Lk 22:17-20)

> Likewise, He also took the cup after supper, saying, "This cup is the new covenant in My blood which is shed for you" (Luke 22:20). And then He spoke those fateful words: "But behold, the hand of My betrayer is with Me on the table. And truly the Son of Man goes as it has been determined, but woe to that man by whom He is betrayed!" (Luke 22:21).

A few tense moments followed and Judas rushed out of the room. He had risen from his chair, swiftly strapped on his sandals, seized his cloak, swinging it around his shoulders, and made for the door.

As he opened it, Jesus's eyes followed him. There in the oblong of the open doorway was the intense indigo of a star-strewn sky across which the moon sent a pool of radiance, then the door closed on Judas. It wasn't long until he betrayed Jesus for thirty pieces of silver.

> Then, one of the twelve, called Judas Iscariot, went to the chief priests and said, "What are you willing to give me if I deliver Him to you?" And they counted out to him thirty pieces of silver.

So from that time he sought opportunity to betray Him. (Mt 26:14, 15)

And soon after he betrayed His Lord, he hung himself.

Then Judas, His betrayer, seeing that He had been condemned, was remorseful and brought back the thirty pieces of silver to the chief priests and elders, saying, "I have sinned by betraying innocent blood." And they said, "What is that to us? You see it!"

Then he threw down the pieces of silver in the temple and departed, and went and hanged himself. (Mt 27:3-5)

What a night! The jealousy, the struggle to be first, the Master washing their feet, the bread and cup, God's gift to our earthly bodies, the exposing of the unfaithful, the escape to make the betrayal.

While we visited the Upper Room back in 1994, each United Methodist pilgrim partook of the Holy Eucharist, and also heard words from St. Paul's writings from 1 Corinthians:

For I received from the Lord that which I also delivered to you; that the Lord Jesus on the same night in which He was betrayed took bread; and when He had given thanks, He broke it, and said: Take eat; this is My body which is broken for you; do this in remembrance of Me." In the same manner, He also took the cup after supper, saying, "This cup is the new covenant in My blood this do, as often as you drink it, in remembrance of Me." For as often as you eat this bread and drink of this cup, you proclaim the Lords' death till He comes. Therefore whoever eats this bread or drinks this cup of the Lord in an unworthy manner will be guilty of the body and blood of the Lord. But let a man examine himself, and so let him eat of that bread and drink of that cup" (1 Cor 11:23-29).

The apostle Paul says that the crucial thing in communion is our eyesight. It's whether or not we discern the presence of the Lord's body. What does Paul mean "seeing the Lord's body"? It means seeing that Christ died for me and you. No one is left out. Thousands of books have been written about the meaning of communion. But I believe the Holy Eucharist's basic meaning is very simple. Christ intended it to be a personal event, that He was giving His body to be broken and poured out for each of us. In spite of everything Christ did, his healing, teachings, parables, Jesus tried to point to this fact of God's unconditional love.

Did you ever wonder why Christ chose a meal as the central reminder of the meaning of life and death? A meal is something that people share with each other. What does this have to do with seeing the Lord's body? In the very next chapter of his letter, St. Paul describes what he calls the "new body of Christ."

> For as the body is one and has many members, but all the members of that one body, being many, are one body, so also is Christ. For by one Spirit, we were all baptized into one body, whether Jews, or Greeks, whether slaves or free, and have been made to drink into one Spirit. (Cor 12:12, 13)

St. Paul says we are all called together. We are now Christ's arms and legs, making God's love believable and visible for one another and the world. That's why the cliquishness of the Corinthians was so blasphemous to Paul. Their blindness to the Lord's body by their gossip and judgment of others was wrong. He said that when we partake in communion, we should pray for others. Paul is pointing out that they are blind to one all-important principle of the Christian faith. Nobody can receive and enjoy God's love for very long, unless she or he is at the same time willing to pass it along to their neighbor.

We are here to see each other in the light of that love, to be transformed from a crowd of isolated individuals into one body bound together by a power that is bigger than all of us. Seeing the Lord's body means seeing ourselves called to participate in that body. Called to rededicate ourselves to the mission of that body in a broken world.

The word *sacrament, sacramentum* in Latin, originally meant the oath which a Roman soldier took to give his life and obedience to

Caesar. Why then did the early Christians call communion the sacrament, the *sacramentum*? Because in receiving the bread and the wine, they felt they were also offering themselves to serve, not Caesar, but God, as they had come to know Him in Jesus the Christ.

Communion

The bread of heaven and grape from a tree
we come to this table on bended knee
our challenging lives, the fear of swift death
conflicts amidst each and every breath
looking for sanctum and finding it here
sing praises to God whose vision is clear
of unified souls harmoniously
living their lives.

—WHS

Stained Glass The Chalice

The Stations of the Cross

During our magnificent trip to the Holy Land, we saw where the angels appeared telling the good news that a Savior was born, the field of shepherds, the model of Jerusalem in the second temple period, the walls of Jerusalem, the Masada, a shrine for Jews, as a symbol of courage, the many cisterns built to accommodate and hold rainwater, and the Dead Sea, that many in our group tried to swim in. The Dead

Sea is forty-seven miles in length, ten miles in width and specific gravity is 1,166, which stops our bodies from sinking. It is the most salt-saturated water in the world.

We saw Jericho, the sycamore tree Zaccheus climbed so he could see and touch Jesus, and the Jordan River. The river twists in a 160-mile long bed and descends from three thousand feet at Mt. Hermon. Jesus was baptized five miles east of Jericho, and we all took vials of water from the river.

I have used that water, baptizing many children and adults, including our grandchildren. What a special memory for me!

Continuing our journey, we walked the steps of Jesus, the Stations of the Cross, the last days of His life, where He was:

1. Jesus is condemned to death.

2. Jesus carries His cross.

3. Jesus falls the first time.

4. Jesus meets his mother.

5. Simon of Cyrene helps Jesus carry the cross.

6. Veronica wipes the face of Jesus.

7. Jesus falls the second time.

8. Jesus meets the women of Jerusalem.

9. Jesus falls the third time.

10. Jesus is stripped of His garments.

11. Crucifixion: Jesus is nailed to the cross.

12. Jesus died on the cross.

13. Jesus is taken down from the cross (Deposition or Lamentation).

14. Jesus is laid in the tomb.

Witnessing and walking these Stations of the Cross left me speechless. Tears of sadness and humiliation tumbled down my cheeks. How could people do that to anyone, much less a man who shared His love with everyone He met, our Savior, our Lord Jesus the Christ?

Standing there, an immediate thought weaved through my subconscious. A well-known Delaware physician called my home a week before our Holy Land trip and asked if he could bring something to me. He gave me a necklace with a crucifix two inches high and one-and-a-half inches wide, made of gold, with Christ crucified on black enamel.

Engraved on the crucifix are these words: "1827 gage d'amitie."

Sadly, my doctor friend died three days later, but I will treasure the thoughtfulness of this friend, who gave me his cross that was a family heirloom, from 1827. Those words *gage d'amitie*, in French means "token of friendship."

I remembered that cross from antiquity, and the gracious friend, when I walked the eleventh Station of the Cross. The Station where Jesus was crucified. Although not traditionally part of the Stations, the Resurrection of Jesus is sometimes included as a fifteenth station. Even though the Resurrection of Jesus was not a part of the Stations, it is the centerpiece of Christianity.

After his death by crucifixion, Jesus is placed in a tomb which is discovered early Sunday morning, to be empty.

> Now after the Sabbath, as the first day of the week began to dawn, Mary Magdalene and the other Mary came to see the tomb. And behold, there was a great earthquake; for an angel of the Lord descended from heaven, and came and rolled back the stone from the door; and sat on it. His countenance was like lightning, and his clothing as white as snow. And the guards shook for fear of him, and became like dead men. but the angel answered and said to the women," Do not be afraid, for I know that you seek Jesus who was crucified. "He is not here; for He is risen as He said. Come, see the place where the Lord lay. And go quickly and tell His disciples that He is risen from the dead, and indeed He is going before you into Galilee; there you will see Him. Behold, I have told you." So they departed quickly from the tomb with fear and great joy, and ran to bring His disciples word. And as they went to tell His disciples, behold, Jesus met them, saying "Rejoice!" And they came and held Him by the feet and worshiped Him. Then Jesus said to them, "Do not be afraid. Go and tell My brethren to go to Galilee, and there they will see Me." (Mt 28:1-9)

Jesus had been tried, taunted, and terminated. His followers were dejected and depressed. Two of the women, Mary Magdalene and Mary of Bethany, can't stand the vacuum of His absence any longer and went to the tomb, perhaps to just be with Him. Upon arriving, they were met by an angelic messenger, who explained that Jesus had been raised from the dead. They looked in the tomb, found it empty, and were heading back to tell the others the good news when they run headlong into the Master Himself.

"Do not be afraid," Jesus says to them. "Go tell the others I will meet them in Galilee" (Matthew 28:16, 17).

But Some Doubted

Then the eleven disciples went away into Galilee, to the mountain which Jesus had appointed for them. And when they saw Him, they worshipped Him, "but some doubted" (Mathew 28:17).

But some "doubted."

For anyone who had ever questioned the authenticity of the resurrection, this is helpful to hear. It starts with the observation that doubters are in good company. These were friends of Jesus, best friends. They knew His special-ness. They had watched Him give sight to the blind, speech to the dumb, sound to the deaf. They were there when Jesus silenced a slashing storm with the simple command, "Be still." They had watched in awe as Jesus fed five thousand people with five loaves and two fishes. And they marveled when the Master restored peace to the demented mind of men and challenged the stoners to cast the first stone if they had never sinned.

If anybody had cause to believe in the divinity of Jesus, it was these three disciples who had shared His life so closely, so intimately, so personally. And, yet, the Scripture says, "When they saw Jesus, they worshiped Him, but some doubted."

We all doubt. It's unavoidable.

They may have seen Him perform a myriad of miracles, but they also saw Jesus die, and the one experience wasn't sufficient to blot out the other. Of course they wanted to believe Jesus was all right. They loved Him. But the gap between what they wanted and what they had experienced was simply too big, and some doubted.

I remember my favorite game when I was a little girl. We all played it, especially when it was inclement weather. Other times, when the weather was nice, we'd play "kick the can" or "tag." It was a simple game called "I Doubt It." One person would make a statement, the others had to discern whether or not it was true. If you thought it was not true, you had to challenge the speaker by saying just three little words, "I doubt it." That's where the rub came. If you challenged a true statement, it cost you a point. On the other hand, if the speaker succeeded in bluffing the whole group with a false statement, it cost everybody a point. I have thought about that silly but fun children's game at least once a year around Easter, as I've heard people lift their voices to proclaim: "Christ the Lord Is Risen Today!" I have wondered how many of these people are mouthing the words, while silently thinking, "I doubt it."

What is *doubt* anyway? Is it anything other than an absence of certainty, a need for more information, a sense of skeptic intensity? Doubt is a natural response to unnatural events. So it should be no surprise that "some doubted."

It is when we are not absolutely certain about something, but keep going anyway that our faith comes to the fore.

John Wesley, founder of Methodism, once said, "Preach until you believe." Theologians have observed "doubt is not the opposite of faith, it is the essential part of it." But faith should never discourage action.

Remember, it was sixty miles from Jerusalem to Galilee. Not an easy walk, even today with modern roads. It was one thing to benignly smile when the women claimed to have met Jesus in the garden, quite another to hike sixty miles to meet Jesus. After all, Jesus said to the women, "Do not be afraid. Go and tell My brethren to go to Galilee, and there they will see Me" (Matthew 28:10). And that's exactly what the disciples did. Even though they weren't sure, they went to meet the Master anyway. Faith works that way. It pushes us to put ourselves on the line, even when the consequences are uncertain.

It took the apostle Paul to Rome; the apostle John to the Isle of Patmos; Joan of Arc to the Prison at Roen, Normandy; Martin Luther to the door of All Saints Church in Wittenberg, Saxony; John Wesley to Aldersgate Street in London, England; Martin Luther King Jr. to Selma, Alabama; Mother Teresa to the gutters of Calcutta, India.

And faith brings us to where we are today.

Certain?

It doesn't matter. The point is, even when uncertain, we act in faith.

Remember my reference to the late Reverend Dr. Leslie Weatherhead, the man who pastored London's City Church from 1936 to 1963? In his book, *Christian Agnostic*, he describes the World War II war years, when catastrophe was a calculated part of every British day. Dr. Weatherhead found himself dealing with life's most difficult questions.

"Why is my husband missing? Why was my child killed? Why does God allow the evil personified in Adolph Hitler to even exist?" At first, Weatherhead sought to concoct rational answers to all such questions, but it wasn't long before his mind was fatigued and his soul was empty. It was then that he created a label with the initials AFL, then he stuck it into the second drawer on the side of his desk. The meaning of those letters:

A, awaiting
F, further
L, light

And, every time he encountered one of those confusing issues, a question that couldn't be answered, an event that defied explanation, a tragedy in the face of justice, he wrote a description on a piece of paper and put it in that drawer and called it "awaiting further light."

I think we all need a drawer like that, a place where we can put things that outrun our capacity to reason; a place where we can confidently contain concerns for which we are yet to develop responses. Just as crime scenes that are sifted through each drop of blood and saved until finally DNA was discovered to unveil the mysteries.

Here is where faith comes into the picture.

Faith, in the deepest biblical sense, is not something we have, it is something we do. Faith is not a noun, it is a verb. And we use a lot of it every single day.

When I'm driving I-95, I've got faith that the oncoming drivers will not cross the line and enter my lane. When I step aboard an airplane, I've got faith that the pilot wants to live as much as I do. When I step onto an elevator and press a button, I have faith that the cables and hydraulics by which the little box moves are appropriately installed, allowing me to rise ten, twenty, thirty stories, without fear of falling.

Most of those "faithing" moments are anchored in experience. I've been down I-95 thousands of times without ever encountering problem traffic, save twice. I've flown thousand of miles and I've ridden on thousands of elevators, never to have one fall. Does that mean I never doubt these phenomena? Of course I doubt. Every time I use the inside lane, my attention is riveted on the traffic. On airplanes I cover up my runway anguish, but it is always there.

And so it is with the divine human relationship. There, too, experience has taught me to trust the love of God. I believe God loves me more than I can mess up. I believe God has a plan for my life. I believe that Jesus Christ was God who became human in order to lead us to God.

When we pause, when we doubt, God proceeds.

Look again at this marvelous passage.

The women find the Master and He tells them to rally the disciples for a meeting in Galilee. Though shrouded with grief, they trudge sixty miles north, and when they get to the mountain, our Lord is there.

Scripture says, "And when they saw Him, they worshiped Him, but some doubted" (Matthew 28:17).

But don't stop the story there.

> Then Jesus came and spoke to them, saying, "All authority has been given to Me in heaven and on earth. Go therefore and make disciples of all the nations, baptizing them in the name of the Father and of the Son and of the Holy Spirit. teaching

them to observe all things that I have commanded you; and lo, I am with you always, even to the end of the age." Amen! (Mt 28:18-20)

It has always been the task of the Master to achieve His ends through earthen vessels. Tax collectors, street fighters, street walkers, and yes, even those who doubt. Remember, our Lord did not say, "You people who aren't too sure, please step to the side, I have something to say to the others." Jesus didn't disqualify anybody, confident or doubting. It didn't matter to our Lord. He commissioned all of them to make disciples and promised to stay with them forever.

When we pause, God proceeds.

The Road to Emmaus

In another Gospel account of the Resurrection, it was two days after our Lord's death on the Cross. Since Saturday is the Jewish Sabbath, Sunday for the apostles would be like our Monday the day when we go back to work. For the followers of Jesus, it means going back to their fishing nets and boats, their barnyards, the grassy hills, back to whatever they left behind, before they took up with this man called Jesus.

Now behold, two of them were traveling that same day to a village called Emmaus, which was about seven miles from Jerusalem. And they talked together of all these things which had happened. So it was, while they conversed and reasoned, that Jesus Himself drew near and went with them. But their eyes were restrained, so that they did not know Him. And He said to them, "What kind of conversation is this that you have with one another as you walk and are sad?" Then the one whose name was Cleopas answered and said to Him, "Are You the only stranger in Jerusalem, and have You not known the things which happened there in these days?" And He said to them, "What things?" And they said to Him :"The things concerning Jesus of Nazareth, who was a Prophet mighty in deed and word before God and all the people and how our rulers delivered Him to be condemned to death, and crucified Him. But we were hoping that it was He who was going to redeem Israel. Indeed, besides all this, today is the third day since these things happened. "Yes, and certain women of our company, who arrived at the tomb early, astonished us. "When they did not find His body they came saying that they had also seen a vision of angels who said He was alive." And certain of those who were with us went to the tomb and found it just as the women had said; but Him they did not see." Then He said to them, "O foolish ones, and slow of heart to believe in all that the prophets have spoken! "Ought not the Christ to have suffered these things and to enter into His glory? (Lk 24:13-26)

It was here, on the road to Emmaus, that Jesus came to these two men. And it is on our roads to Emmaus that Jesus is most likely to come to us. Wherever we go to escape life is exactly where we should expect to be confronted by our Lord. Whenever we give up and try to call it quits, Jesus comes calling and drawing us back to life. That's the one thing we can expect when we try to leave. Our Lord doesn't want us to give up.

Why? Because Jesus gave up his life that we might not give up on ours.

Our Lord lived and died that our life might be saved, changed, transformed into a resurrected life.

When Jesus comes to give us this new life, he will more than likely come as He came to these two men, on the road to Emmaus.

The disciples were embarking on an exciting adventure with a man called Jesus. He was a nobody from a country village, the son of a carpenter, but when He spoke, it was is if God Himself were present and speaking to His people. They had cheered triumphantly with the crowds as Jesus entered Jerusalem on that first Palm Sunday They had watched admiringly as their leader drove the money changers out of the temple. They were overwhelmed when they heard Judas had betrayed their Master, and Peter had denied Him three times. They were distressed and uneasy when they saw their beloved teacher stand tall before Pilate. They hovered in fear among the angry mob when

He was crucified as a common criminal on Calvary. They had grieved with the other disciples when Jesus lay alone and forsaken in the tomb. They had even been present when the women ran breathless from the garden grave, reporting the amazing fact that the tomb of their Lord was empty. They had hoped that Jesus was the one to redeem Israel, but for them, Easter morning came and no light broke forth from the horizon, no army of angels came to avenge the killing of their Lord.

They saw only dark clouds of doubt, despair, and even personal disaster for themselves. So, fearing for their own safety, they had turned their backs on Jerusalem and were headed toward Emmaus, the little village which was about seven miles from Jerusalem. They wondered why Jesus didn't do something to save Himself as He had saved others.

After all, Jesus was divine, the Son of God. He could have exercised His divine power at any time He could have called forth an army of angels and slain King Pilate and his whole court, on the spot, if He wanted to. He could have thrown thunderbolts of lightning and burned those Scribes, Pharisees, and those who yelled, "Crucify Him," if Jesus wanted to. With a single blow, our Lord could have eliminated the vast armies of Rome and knocked mighty Caesar from his throne, if He wanted to.

But He didn't.

Our Lord was nonviolent. He did not resist, nor did He summon this potential power.

No. Just the opposite.

He struggled under the beatings, the heavy load of the cross, and suffered the pain of the nails, the mockery of spit, blood streaming down His face, the agony of hanging in the sweltering heat of the noonday sun.

And He was crucified.

Our Lord knew that this life is not all that there is. There is more. A greater life than we have ever known. A life not limited from dust to dust, but a divine life.

But we can never gain life, earn it by our own merit, attain it by our own goodness. This new life is a gift. A gift from God.

Even if we could be with these two men on the road to Emmaus and walk and talk with Jesus, even if we could have walked in their shoes and experienced for ourselves the horrific death. Even if we were there and heard with our own ears the witness of those women on that first Easter morning, "He is raised! He is risen!" Still, we could not believe unless we believe God gives us a new life, a resurrected life.

It's not enough that Jesus went to the cross and died for us.

It is not enough that He rose from the grave for us.

Something must happen in us and to us.

A Stranger

Tell me, have you ever met the Risen Christ in another person? Was there something about that other person whose sacrificial, self-giving love was so genuine, so free from any ledger sheet or trade-off? "I'll love you if you love me." Not conditional love, but love that was given unconditionally, and you felt you were the object of it?

I have.

And it was a total stranger. I still don't know his name. In most of the Easter stories, Jesus appears first as a stranger on the beach, a stranger in the garden, the Upper Room, on the road to Emmaus, and then He is finally recognized. He is seen as real.

I met this "stranger" on Easter Sunday sixty-one years ago. Tom and I were on our honeymoon, March 24, 1953. We were in Ft. Lauderdale, Florida, and had just received a phone call from home. The message, from Tom's parents, said that my dad had just become ill and we better get home fast. My dad had never been sick a day in his young life, so it was a shock to hear the news.

We had driven Tom's family car to Florida, so we tried to find an airplane seat for me so I could get home and be with my mom and dad.

Finally, after many phone calls, we found one seat from Jacksonville, Florida, to Atlanta, Georgia, but no seats from Atlanta to Columbus, Ohio. It was Easter break for many college students, which made it impossible to find any airplane seats. I climbed on my first airplane flight ever, leaving my new husband behind driving to meet his dad who arranged to fly down to the only place he could get a flight, Louisville, Kentucky, helping Tom drive home from Florida to Ohio.

I was scared stiff, so I sat with my seat belt on, well into the flight, when you're allowed to remove them. Beside me sat this big ol' cowboy. I knew he was a cowboy from Texas because his huge ten-gallon hat had the word "Texas" engraved with bold thread. This ol' cowboy started making conversation with this scared, young twenty-year-old girl.

He said, "Say, sweetie, you can take your seat belt off now."

I just sat there ready to cry buckets, not knowing how I'd find my wonderful, but now sick, dad. But instead I just stared out the window biting my tongue. The cowboy tried several times to open the conversation, but I didn't respond. I didn't utter a word.

After a half hour in flight, a stewardess came over and said "Mrs. Walters."

I hardly knew my new name, I've only been "Mrs. Walters" for ten days.

"Yes," I murmured.

The stewardess replied, "I'm so sorry, but we have no seats available on the flight from Atlanta to Columbus, Ohio. I know this is an emergency and you need to get home, but there are no seats left."

The ol' cowboy said, "What's the matter, dearie?"

I didn't answer.

We landed in Atlanta, Georgia, and I departed the plane, not knowing what I was to do.

My new husband Tom was going to drive to the Atlanta airport from Jacksonville, Florida, due to arrive much later in the evening.

Suddenly, my name was paged, over and over. "Mrs. Thomas Walters, to the TWA desk, please."

I ran over to the TWA desk and the attendant said, "We have a seat for you to Columbus, Ohio. It leaves in thirty minutes."

"Oh," I said as happily as one can exclaim, under the circumstances. "I thought all the seats were taken on that flight," I recalled.

"Well," said the attendant, "they were, but someone gave up his seat."

"Who?" I asked.

She said, "You can thank the man in the Texas cowboy hat," and pointed in his direction.

I looked over and the cowboy and his hat were heading down the terminal. He gave me a wave and tipped his ten-gallon hat.

I attempted to run after him, but he disappeared in the Easter throng.

A stranger gave up his seat to an ungrateful, young, newly married girl. One he did not know. One who was anything but pleasant and had remained a complete stranger.

And although the news from home was tragic, my forty-six-year-old dad suddenly died from an aneurysm of the brain, something special happened to me at that airport that Easter.

Easter happens to us, despite our losses, our defeats, and disappointments. The little deaths and the big ones.

The Easter event didn't give those early Christians a new lease on life, it gave them a lease on a new life.

And Easter happens to us, as it did to them, without His immediate presence, when we discover in our own experiences that no matter what darkness we are in, a light is shining there, and nothing can put it out. Nothing can separate you or me from the love of God.

> Jesus came singing love,
> He lived, singing love,
> He suffered, singing love.
> If love is to continue,
> we must do the singing.

Questions

> Whence cometh distant ray
> On most this mournful day
> When piercing steel my Lord did slay
> Rending useless the words I pray
> Whence cometh distant light
> When noon turned into night
> Giving false hope to followers
> Quenching the fire that was their plight

My Lord has thou forsaken me?
Why have you turned away?
Where are we to turn to now
On most this mournful day?
We see the distant light
Somehow it seems to grow
We see the holy herald
And somehow seem to know
That midst the blood and anguish
That Midst the flow of tears
For those who hold their faith
The humble Lord appears.

—WHS

"Christos: Everlasting Arms." Sculpture by
Charles Parks, donated by Joan and Burt Anderson.

Is Life a Puzzle?

I started another support group, GOLTA (Grief of Loss through Abortion), aimed at trying to help women who had abortions deal with their grieving. The group lasted about six months, with a so-so attendance, and it fizzled out.

I remember one time being asked to speak on a panel of pro choice versus pro life choice issues. I was asked, by the television reporter, "Do the girls who have abortions have any remorse?" I honestly had to say, "A few do, but I really don't know how many. So few 'talked' about it to others. It could be they felt guilt, or were embarrassed, but some were glad to have the choice." My pro-life friends weren't pleased with my comment, but it was truthful. What should our response be to those millions who've had abortions? Most importantly, we must pass God's love onto the woman who had the abortion as well as the woman who chose life.

That's the most difficult ethical moral dilemma I've had to try and understand. Why would someone decide to take the life of a human being that was developing in your own body? I just wish all people would love their life enough to pass that caring onto another human being, whether the baby is in the womb or born alive. Just as the GOLTA support group was faltering, other support groups were growing with each session.

The two suicide prevention support groups, one for teens, the other for adults, were growing so rapidly, I was deeply concerned I couldn't help their overwhelming situations, especially the adolescents.

As I mentioned in an earlier chapter, the buddy system worked quite well. They really did call one another to talk, getting support with their shared problems. What's more, the teenagers were bringing friends to the group. Friends who weren't necessarily suicidal, but caring and wanting to learn how to help.

I created a brochure on the warning signs of suicidal people, and the young teens helped me prepare it. We named our young suicide group YSPP (Youth Suicide Prevention Program), and we called the brochure "Is Life A Puzzle?"

And, this is what it says:

Is Life A Puzzle? It sure is.

Suicide is now the number two killer of young people between 15-24. Since the 1950s, the rate has tripled. Reported suicides are, however, just the tip of the iceberg. Many deaths that are self inflicted are reported as accidents or homicides by officials.

The tragedy of an adolescent suicide reaches far beyond the untimely death of a teenager. Parents, siblings, friends, teachers, even communities, are often devastated by this ultimate rejection. Many survivors of a teenage suicide suffer severe guilt, depression, unresolved grief and acute family and work performance problems, and they are at high risk for suicide themselves, nine times higher than the general population.

What can we do to help prevent suicide?

First, Recognize the Warning Signs of suicidal people:

More withdrawn, uncommunicative and isolated from others, than usual.

Deep depression and feelings of worthlessness.

Expressing suicidal thoughts, even jokingly.

A change in manner, some air of giving up that you can't quite pin down, but makes you think, "something is wrong.,"

Written material that seems disorganized or has heavy themes or overt references to death.

A quiet settling of affairs, such as the giving away of prized possessions.

An increase in cuts, bruises and accidents.

Persistent boredom and/or difficulty concentrating.

Running away.

Drug and /or alcohol abuse.

Noticeable changes in eating or sleeping habits.

Then, Get Help. Adolescent suicide is preventable. You can help!

1. Listen, Don't dismiss the adolescent's problems as trivial.

2. Trust your suspicions that the person may be self-destructive.

3. Communicate your concerns for the well being of the person.

4. Talk openly and freely and ask direct questions about the person's intentions. Try to determine whether they have a plan for suicide. The more detailed the plan, the greater the risk.

5. Encourage the person to seek help from a clergy, school counselor or teacher. If the person resists, you may have to get the necessary help for them.

6. Call the police if the situation is immediately life-threatening.

7. Do not leave the person alone if you believe the risk of suicide is immediate.

8. Do not swear secrecy to the suicidal person. You may lose a friendship but you may save a life.

9. Do not debate whether suicide is right or wrong. This may make the person feel more guilty and worthless.

Then, along with the Mental Health Association of Delaware, we were able to provide a Suicide Prevention Hot-Line Emergency Service in all three counties of Delaware, New Castle, Kent, and Sussex.

Our Mt. Lebanon United Methodist Church absorbed all the printing costs of the brochures, the use of their facilities, their volunteers who provided coffee, tea, and cookies for the participants, and my facilitating all the groups.

We also initiated a group of concerned citizens, who were involved in children's activities, as teachers, law-makers, counselors, parents, clergy, and friends. Together, we met many times at my church and developed a not-for-profit organization called "Delaware Council for the Prevention Of Suicide in Youth, Inc."

We were able to receive funding from membership dues and grants. This Recognition of Exemption status was granted in 1987, three years after the YSPP group began. Gradually, as I approached retirement in 1995, the Mental Health Association of Delaware assumed the leadership.

Speaking to many schools, churches, and community events about the prevention of suicide became an important outreach for our church to our community.

In 1989, I presented to the International Association for Suicide Prevention XIVth International Congress in Hamburg, Germany, the results of surveys I've given to the YSPP support group.

The title of the presentation was "The Cultural, Social and Behavioral Effects on the Adolescents Attending the Suicide Prevention Support Groups."

The essence of the talk emphasized these points.

Suicide is the number-two killer in adolescents from ages 10 to 22 in the United States. This was in 1983, an average of twelve teenagers each year from 1970 to 1983 committed suicide. In 1983, there were 358 suicide attempts. In the fall of 1983, these alarming statistics prompted some concerned people to organize three groups.

This presentation to the May 1987 IASP Conference is an overview of the support groups and our efforts in reaching the youth who are depressed, suicidal, or both.

In attempting to evaluate our suicide prevention support group, we surveyed the population of these adolescents. The survey was conducted by our Suicide Prevention Council and given to each person who attended the YSPP held during the years of September 5, 1983, to May 10, 1987. These groups were held in two locations: Mt. Lebanon United Methodist Church and Rockford Center, a psychiatric hospital for adolescents. Rockford Center's Support Group was initiated by counselors employed by Rockford Center. I facilitated this support group as well as Mt. Lebanon's. The Rockford Hospital's support group was for their inpatient suicidal population. Mt Lebanon's support group was help for outpatients who are suicidal.

This study, over a four-year period, was intended to guide counselors, facilitators, families and teachers, enabling them to understand some of the reasons why our youth are attempting to take their own lives.

All youth surveyed have participated in the groups four times or more, and both the young people and their guardians signed an informed consent agreement. There were a variety of cultural and social differences in terms of age, family structure, race, environment, and training. In all, 997 participants completed the survey. However, some significant commonalities are unveiled in the study. Our survey to the youth in our suicide prevention groups asked the question, "Does the support group help? If so, how?"

The responses were, yes, 96 percent.

How?

1. People listen, 92 percent.

2. We can express our feelings, 95 percent.

3. It helps to know others have the same problems, 94 percent.

4. We participated in the "buddy system" where we could call one another when we felt we needed help or wanted to "just talk," 96 percent.

The vast majority of the youth (98 percent) thought the support groups helped in all the categories. A small percentage (2 percent) thought about suicide more after attending the support groups. Over 96 percent of the attendees of the support groups were relieved to talk about their suicidal feelings to people who understand and care to help.

Other commonalities of all age groups included: Around 75 percent of the youth surveyed felt they lacked coping skills and wanted to learn coping mechanisms. Over 70 percent wanted someone to listen to their problems. Over 65 percent had real or imagined fears of failure.

IS LIFE A
PUZZLE?

YSPP

A GUIDE TO INFORMATION AND
SERVICES FOR FAMILIES & YOUTHS
IN DELAWARE

A project of the
DELAWARE COUNCIL FOR PREVENTION OF SUICIDE IN YOUTH

YSPP

Why We Started yet Another Support Group

The most alarming statistic was the answer to the question, "Did you have any losses, death, divorce or separation in your family over the past three years?"

Amazingly 82 percent had lost a significant other, either through death, divorce, or separation. Two years later, a group of concerned citizens began to look at the statistics on divorces and what effect it was having on families. Remember one of the questions on the survey suicidal members of our support group answered was "Did you have any losses, death, divorce or separation in your family in the past three years?"

The overwhelming statistic, 82 percent, had a major loss. Then, a companion question that followed in that survey was: "How do you cope with your losses?"

A startling 78 percent said they coped in this order:

1. Alcohol
2. Drugs
3. Suicide

Those were the top three coping mechanisms the young adolescents used.

My hope and prayer is that if we can deal with these vital issues of death, divorce, and separation, then when they happen to our children, we can learn healthy coping methods while the overwhelming grief is still fresh and not yet obliterated by negative defense mechanisms, such as alcohol, drugs, and suicide.

We invited a variety of agencies, nurses, psychologists, counselors, funeral directors, physicians, school teachers, guidance counselors, and corporations to see if they might be interested in investigating the importance of a project to help guide families to learn how cope with their divorces, deaths, and separations.

In February 17, 1989, we met at Mt. Lebanon United Methodist Church, forty-two people in all. And for many months, we developed programs for all age groups.

We called the group Supporting KIDDS (Kids Involved in Death, Divorce, Separation). We refined a training program for facilitators. Four psychologists, six elementary school teachers, four nurses, and three school counselors led the groups. One night, we met for divorced and separated families. We structured the groups in this manner: children four to six were in a group with a trained facilitator. Ages seven to ten were in another group. Ages ten to twelve and thirteen to eighteen completed the children's program.

I facilitated the adult family members who were going through a divorce. On another night, we had the same style groups, but for families who were grieving over a death of a family member or friend.

All the groups met at Mt. Lebanon United Methodist Church in Wilmington, Delaware. We were so fortunate to have the well-known artist, Carolyn Blish, donate fifteen of her children's paintings for the areas, at the church, that housed our support groups. Although Carolyn was a member of another church, she heard about our suicide prevention YSPP and Supporting KIDDS groups and wanted to donate something special. How very blessed we were to receive her lovely paintings. Carolyn specializes in painting children, and her love is the Lord. She says this about her paintings and her Creator: "Faith is seeing the unseen as reality. Hope is the pigment waiting to be used. Love is the brush applying paint to the canvas. Painting is the closest thing to prayer that I know. My faith is the most important substance of my life. I believe every work of fine art bears witness to Him."

Thank you, dear friend Carolyn Blish.

These support groups met until I retired in 1995, and another group used the name Supporting KIDS (Kids Involved in Death). I was always pleased that another group captured the importance of helping our kids, but sorry no one sponsored a group who would help kids whose families divorced or were separated.

A biblical phrase keeps running through my head:

> Then little children were brought to Him that He might put His hands on them and pray, but the disciples rebuked them. But Jesus said, "let the little children come to Me, and do not forbid them; for of such is the kingdom of heaven." And He laid His hands on them and departed from there. (Mt 19:13-15)

We must watch over the children. We must not avoid our task of helping children to deal with their feelings around the sensitive, difficult issues of death, divorce, and separation. If we do not help them, we have placed the primary burden of coping with family change onto the children, who are not yet equipped with that skill. Then we would be allowing our children to bear the psychological, economic, and moral brunt of their losses.

And from what the children are telling us, they recognize the burdens that have been put on their slender little shoulders.

When we started our Supporting KIDDS death component, it was my responsibility to interview the new clients. We had decided to accept children ages four to eighteen, but that was changed when one family with three children, ages three, seven, and nine were speaking to me about the tremendous loss of their husband and father. I was paying little attention to the little three-year-old girl.

Just about the time they were leaving, she came up to me and tugged at my jacket. "Hey you, I hurt too."

I unknowingly said, "Did you fall and hurt yourself?"

The three-year-old pointed to her heart and said. "I hurt too. My daddy died too."

From that moment on, we decided to take three-year-olds in our program.

There is nothing more difficult to evaluate than a "prevention" program. During the years after we started the suicide prevention support group (YSPP), we did not lose any participant in our group to suicide. This fact was printed in the July 4, 1988, *Newsweek* magazine, page 50, as they featured our suicide prevention support group: "Hundreds of teenagers have now joined groups for suicide prevention at Mt. Lebanon United Methodist Church. A few of these kids have seriously contemplated suicide, but called a buddy or a hot line in time."

Supporting KIDDS groups grew to more and more participants with each eight-week session. We had so many who wanted to join our groups, we had waiting lists. However, we were still in the experimental stages of our development of these support groups. We did have hope and faith to believe the groups will have a positive impact and should be considered as a possible prevention of suicide in your community, so we can prevent the taking of God's greatest gift, the gift of life.

We all have a lot to learn all through life, as we open ourselves to our Eternal Father, watching and inquiring and learning.

Children Learn What They Have

If children live with criticism, they learn to condemn

If children live with hostility, they learn to fight.

If children live with ridicule, they learn to be shy.

If children live with shame, they learn to feel guilty.

If children live with tolerance, they learn to be patient.

If children live with encouragement, they learn confidence.

If children live with fairness, they learn justice.

If children live with security, they learn to have faith.

If children live with approval, they learn to like themselves.

If children live with acceptance and friendship, they learn to find love in the world.

—Dorothy Law Nolte

Kids Involved in Death, Divorce and Separation

Supporting KIDDS

WHEN IS A PERSON A PERSON?

When I began my ministry, it was because of the Delaware abortion law that would allow women to have an abortion if the embryo would cause "undue emotional stress" for the pregnant woman. That was Friday, June 13, 1969. Since that time, the United States Supreme Court on January 22, 1973, *Roe v. Wade*, declared "a pregnant woman is entitled to have an Abortion until the end of the first trimester of pregnancy without any interference by the state."

Each state was then allowed to determine "when" they would allow a legal abortion. Some states, such as Delaware, do not have a time period on "when in the nine-month pregnancy there would be a time an abortion could not be surgically done."

Since that time, God only knows how many abortions in the first trimester, second trimester, and last trimester there have been in our country.

I delivered a prayer for the New York Right to Life convention back in 1979, and was asked to repeat my remarks at many Right to Life conventions in other cities and states.

My remarks were:

> At this New York Right To Life Convention, with special remembrance of the International year of the child, I bring news from the State of Delaware.
>
> This summer, at our medical center, two tiny infants were born alive through saline abortion procedures. One weighed two pounds, four ounces, a boy. The other, a girl, three pounds,

four ounces. These were late trimester abortions, which are allowed in our state. These two babies survived insurmountable difficulties. However, two alert nurses, who cared about the whether the babies lived, took the little ones and placed them in the premature nursery.

What is the truth here?

We've heard it said, that saline abortions would result in rapid deaths for the baby, but that isn't true. The babies lived for many hours before they were discovered.

We've heard it said, saline aborted babies would have permanent brain damage, but that isn't true. These babies, after months in our ICU nursery, have tested perfectly normal.

We've heard it said, these would be 'unwanted' babies, but that isn't true, the babies have been easily adopted.

To these two babies and the many millions of unborn children, I dedicate this prayer today:

O God, We Come To You Today In The Midst Of All Kinds Of Death.
There Is…Death In The Air We Call Smog,
Death In The Water, We Call Polution
Death In The Cities, We Call Racism
Death In Infanticide, We Call Alleviating Suffering
Death In Euthanasia, We Call Mercy
Death In Suicide, We Call Ones Own Right.
We Come Asking For Life; New Life For Ourselves; For All People; For Our World. Make Us Aware Of Your Presence And Power, God
Come Like A Breath Of Fresh Air
Come Like A Drink Of Clear Water
Come Like The Embrace Of Another Person
Come Like Protection In The Womb
Come Like Compassion To A Helpless Infant

Come Like Reverence For All Life, As You Make No Distinction Between Quality Or Non Quality; More Precious Or Less Precious.

We Thank You For This Company Of Caring Friends.

We Ask That Whatever Else Is Said About Us, It Will Be Said.

That In The Midst Of Death, We Brought Life To The Unborn

To The Sick And Maimed, And To All Life, We Brought Your Love.

Amen.

—Reverend Marlene Walters, Chaplain
Wilmington Medical Center General Division)

Moral Dilemmas

Her name was Dorothy.

She's been sitting in a wheelchair for the past two years. She's in the nursing home for over three years. Her eyes aren't what they used to be, nor is her hearing. She'll never walk again due to a broken hip and shoulder, when she was 103 years young.

Gone are the years when she could truly enjoy the holidays, birthdays, or the fun of living. She can remember some of those early years, careful preparation for guests, last-minute dashes to the supermarket, the days of shopping in the mall. Then, her voice had a sparkle in it. So she sits and waits and falls asleep.

What quality of life does she have? Is she really a "person?"

His name is Ralph. He's a thirty-two-year-old man who was diagnosed as having Hodgkin's, stage II, two years ago and underwent chemotherapy treatments. After recurrence of the malignancy, radiation was given, apparently unsuccessfully. By this stage in the natural history of the disease, metastases of the cancer to other sites are almost inevitable, and the latest liver function studies are suggesting possible liver metastases. Now he has developed a productive cough, and the x-ray indicates bronchopneumonia.

He says, weary of all the hospital procedures, "Just leave me alone. And please some good doctor or nurse, give me something to hasten my dying."

Shouldn't we follow his wishes?

Should he be allowed to die, with a "little" overdose?

The four-day-old infant was being maintained on a respirator due to severe respiratory deficiency. While there had not been time for chromosomal analysis by karyotype, all evidence pointed to a diagnosis of Trisomy 18, a genetic disorder leading to mental retardation, growth failure, and numerous anatomical abnormalities. While there have been scattered reports of patients with the anomaly living to adulthood, 87 percent die within the first year of life.

The family doesn't know what to do. Wouldn't it be more loving to let their child die a "normal" death?

Is this infant really a "person?"

When I started my "teddy bear" journey in 1969, with the original abortion law in the State of Delaware, and entered the ministry, there have been many new laws and, shockingly, the consequences of *Roe v. Wade* are 56,405,766 total abortions from 1973 to 2011, based on numbers reported by the Guttmacher Institute.

What has been happening in the field of medical ethics since the abortion ruling on January 22, 1973? *Roe vs. Wade* has brought forth forty-one years of controversies.

The most recent arise from congressional attempts to reverse or modify the decision. *Roe vs. Wade* boils down to this: a woman has a constitutionally protected right to seek an abortion. It is an absolute right during the first three months of pregnancy. After that, and up to the point of viability, which the court defined as the capacity of meaningful life, the right may be limited only by the states interests in protecting the health of the mother. After viability, which the court reckoned to occur at the seventh month of pregnancy, the right may be limited and even proscribed by the states interest in "the potentiality of human life, unless abortion is necessary to preserve the life or health of the women."

Note the word *health*. The court, in a companion case to *Roe*, recognized a very broad definition of health, including the pregnant women's emotional well-being. The right to an abortion could easily be exercised in the third trimester of pregnancy, thus abortions were virtually unlimited.

A wide range of scholars holding both pro- and anti-abortion beliefs quickly pointed out the numerous problems with *Roe v. Wade*. These included mistakes in history, science, and law, but the essential difficulty was, as it remains today, that *Roe v. Wade* imposed on the nation a view of the abortion issues lacking constitutional warrant. In other words, "when is a person a person, and protected by the Constitution?"

A right to abortion, obviously, can't be found in the Constitution of our country. The Supreme Court could not find, nor has found a way to describe when a person is a person, and therefore protected. With the fetus's status as a human being in limbo, the most the court would say was that fetuses beyond the thirty-eighth week have "potential life." A curious phrase, inasmuch as some fetuses of even lesser age have survived outside the womb. Miraculously, some have survived despite efforts to abort them.

We had a case in our State of Delaware at the WMC hospital where I was a chaplain. It was reported in The Morning News on June 7, 1979, by reporter Jane Harriman: "Two infants were born alive following a saline abortion. The salt solution injected into the mother's womb usually kills the fetus. However two nurses detected a pulse in the umbilical chord and immediate life-support measures were taken."

In fact, the nurses called me and reported the incident. I'm forever grateful the babies (fetus) were resuscitated and later adopted by caring people. By the way, the mothers' who wanted an abortion tried to sue the hospital because they "wanted a dead fetus, not a live baby."

One of the most serious consequences of the court's decision touches the deepest foundations of our society. Our system of law depends on respect for individual life, a value rooted in the Judeo-Christian ethic. The question is, can the court's decision on *Roe v. Wade* be reconciled with that value?

Since 1973, the essentially legislative character is indicated by the stream of litigants who have gone to the court asking for clarification.

When is a person a person?

Most states do not have a law to protect the baby in utero. The potential mother can have an abortion even in the third trimester, the last three months of pregnancy.

Why would they be born alive? Because the only methods of delivery of a late abortion, means that the baby cannot easily be "lifted out" of the womb. They are too large. As we know from the aforementioned news article, the saline solution often doesn't work. The other second trimester abortion technique, a surgical opening of the womb through a small abdominal incision, to remove the fetus has a much higher incidence of live fetuses.

Another question is posed: At what point does the fetus, the baby, have rights?

There have been hundreds of court cases concerning late month abortions, throughout these years. The most infamous was a Dr. William Waddell case in California. Dr. Waddell was brought to trial by two nurses who testified that he not only ordered them to not help resuscitate a two-pound twelve-ounce girl, born following a saline abortion, but also Dr. Waddell was seen actively strangling the aborted baby. Testimony in both trails indicated that the baby girl had survived the abortion performed on her seventeen-year-old mother, that she was alive in the newborn nursery, and she had a good chance of survival as a normal child. Both juries did not convict the physician. They asked a question for which there is still no answer even though it's been deliberated by many juries all these years.

The jury asked, "How could it be all right for Dr. Waddell to kill the baby on the morning of March 2, while still in the womb of her mother but murder, if he killed the same baby several hours later in the newborn nursery?"

Another case, Dr. Kermit Gosnell, was charged with killing infants who had survived abortions. He even trained his employees to use surgical scissors to sever the newborn's spinal cords just below the base of the skull. Though Gosnell refereed to this practices as 'snipping,' the word doesn't convey the nature of the act. Imagine, if you will, cutting through a chicken neck with kitchen shears. Over half a dozen eyewitness testimonies, and the tiny bodies recovered from the freezer at Gosnell's "house of horrors" abortion clinic. The judge dismissed the murder charges against Gosnell for the deaths of three of those infants.

The news was shocking. How could anybody fail to see the abundance of evidence that these infants had been born, had struggled to live, and had been murdered? These cases point dramatically to the unresolved legal, medical and moral dilemmas in our abortion practices.

This practice is called "infanticide."

Now I am back to the beginning of my journey. Remember when I attended the Wilmington Medical Center's workshop with Dr. Joseph Fletcher? He was advocating infanticide and euthanasia. In fact, Dr. Fletcher wrote a book on infanticide, *Tentative Profile of Man.*

Dr. Fletcher, a theologian and professor of medical ethics, has proposed a set of "positive human criteria specifically designed to serve as indicators of personhood" in decisions regarding abortion and infanticide.

Here is a sampling of his list in his book:

1. Minimal intelligence: below 40 on a Stanford -Binet is questionably a person, below 20, not a person.

2. Self-control: if the condition cannot be rectified medically, a person without control is not a person.

3. Capability to relate to others.

4. Communication, person who cannot communicate, is not a person.

5. Balance of rationality and feeling: a person can be neither coldly rational nor given over completely to feelings.

And, so on, ad nauseam. The following are excerpts of Fletcher's statements from a January 1982 interview:

> There is no doubt that the general trend unethical thought is to terminate the lives of defective newborns. If a child has demonstrated low IQ or had severe physical disabilities, then its life should be mercifully ended. The mere fact that a child is a moron, using the Stanford-Binet IQ classifications, doesn't necessarily suggest that it should not be allowed to live, but clearly, in the case of idiots, those with IQ's of 20 or under, they are simply not human beings. Why not end their lives?

What is infanticide? It is allowing babies to die. The Spartans in 600 BC put many of their babies to die. They didn't need a reason to put their babies on the hillsides to die. Whether they were handicapped, without fingers, arms, female, or whatever reason. Female infanticide has been for centuries a prominent and socially acceptable event in two related areas of the world: India and China. Even today, the extent of the problem is measured in frightening proportions: "at least 60 million females in Asia are missing and feared dead, victims of nothing more than their sex." Worldwide, research suggests, the number of missing females may top 100 million. Should we save our defective infants or allow infanticide? Another important legal question that is being debated in our society today.

> When the killing of unborn children is made legal, is the next step the rationalization of killing unwanted infants?
> When is a Person a Person?

As Dr. Seuss said in his *Horton Hears A Who* book, "A person is a person, no matter how small."

The acceptance of abortion but not infanticide in the United States has been justified on the grounds that a baby is alive while a fetus is not. But when does science say human life begins? Dr. Robert George wrote an excellent book entitled *Embryo*, and describes it thusly:

Human embryos, whether they are formed by fertilization (natural or in vitro) or by successful somatic-cell transfer (cloning), do have the internal resources and active disposition to develop themselves to the mature stage of a human organism, requiring only a suitable environment and nutrition. In fact, scientist distinguish embryos from other cells or clusters of cells precisely by their self-directed, integral functioning. Thus, human embryos are what the embryology textbooks say they are, namely, human organism-living individuals of the human species- at the earliest development stage.

Science has clearly and decidedly proven that a new human life begins at conception. That is fertilization, the moment sperm and ovum meet and form an entirely new self-directing living organism of the human species with its own individual DNA distinct from both mother and father.

The procedure to discover if your "baby" in utero is deformed is called amniocentesis. It's a procedure in which amniotic fluid is removed from the uterus for testing or treatment. Amniotic fluid is the fluid that surrounds and protects a baby during pregnancy. This fluid contains fetal cells and various chemicals produced by the baby. Amniocentesis is performed to look for certain types of birth defects, such as Down syndrome, sickle cell, cystic fibrosis, muscular dystophy, Tay-Sachs, and similar diseases. Because ultrasound is performed at the time of amniocentesis, it may detect birth defects that are not detected by amniocentesis, such a cleft palate, cleft lip, club foot or heart defects. There are some birth defects, however, that will not be detected by either amniocentesis or ultrasound. If you are having an amniocentesis, you may ask to find out the baby's sex; amniocentesis is the most accurate way to determine the baby's gender before birth.

Does amniocentesis mean you'll abort the baby if he/she is found to have an anomaly? What would you do if you had a handicapped infant? If you're a parent, do you remember when you found out you were pregnant? The first question from others, usually was, "What do you want, a boy or a girl?" And the answer usually was: "I don't care as long as it's normal."

So, again I ask, when is a person a person and granted a right to life?

In an article from *Fidelity* magazine written by James Bruen Jr., he states this commentary:

> Abortion may be the silent holocaust, but it is not invisible. Newspapers advertise its availability; feminists tout its necessity; politicians genuflect before this "reproductive right," and prolifers express outrage over its legality. Infanticide, however, is almost invisible.

One case, in particular, brought a lot of attention in the media. Baby Jane Doe was born October 11, 1984 with spina bifida, failure of the spine to close properly and hydrocephalus, excess fluid on the brain. The first neurologist who examined her recommended the usual treatment for babies in her condition, surgery to close the spinal opening, and insert a shunt in her head. The parents consented and the baby was transferred to the hospital for surgery. However, the parents then heeded the advice of another physician who recommended no surgery.

What should our courts do? Should the family accept the child? Or does the handicapped child have rights to life?

When does a person have a right to be protected by the Fourteenth Amendment?

The Fourteenth Amendment to the United States Constitution was adopted on July 9, 1868, as one of the Reconstruction Amendments. The amendment, particularly its first section, is one of the most litigates parts of the Constitution, forming the basis for landmark decisions such as *Roe v. Wade* (1973). The amendment's first section includes several clauses: the Citizenship Clause, Privileges or Immunities Clause, Due Process Clause, and Equal Protection Clause. The Citizenship Clause provides a broad definition of citizenship, overruling the Supreme Court's decision in *Dred Scott v. Sandford* (1857), which held that American descended from African slaves could not be citizens of the United States. The Due Process Clause prohibits state and local government officials from depriving persons of life, liberty, or property without legislative authorization." (From Wikipedia, the free encyclopedia).

When is a person a person with inalienable rights?

There have been two Supreme Court cases in our country that have attempted to identify personhood.

One was written in 1857: the Dred Scott Case; and the other, in 1973, *Roe v. Wade*.

The *Dred Scott v. Sandford* was a landmark decision by the US Supreme Court in which the Court held that African Americans, whether slave or free, could not be American citizens and therefore had no standing to sue in federal territories. In this case, Dred Scott attempted to sue for his freedom. In a 7-2 decision, the Court denied Scott's request.

Roe v. Wade ruled that a right to privacy under the due process clause of the Fourteenth Amendment extended to a woman's decision to have an abortion, but that this right must be balanced against the state's two legitimate interests in regulation abortions: protecting prenatal life and protecting women's health. The Roe decision defined "viable" as being "potentially able to live outside the mother's womb, albeit with artificial aid," adding that "viability" is usually placed at about "seven months (twenty-eight weeks) but may occur earlier, even at twenty-four weeks."

Fortunately in 1868, the Fourteenth Amendment overturned the Dred Scott decision by granting citizenship to all those born in the United States, regardless of color.

Let's hope and pray reversing the *Roe v. Wade* decision will grant citizenship to all persons who are formed at conception.

What does the Holy Bible say about "when is a person a person"?

Genesis 2:7 is the clearest: "And the Lord God formed man of the dust of the ground, and breathed into his nostrils the breath of life; and man became a human being."

When the Holy Bible refers to pregnant women, the term "with child" occurs twenty-six times in the Bible. The term "with fetus" never occurs once. In Luke, we are told that Elisabeth conceived a "son" and that the "babe" leaped in her womb. "Now in the sixth month the angel Gabriel was sent by God to a city of Galilee named Nazareth" (Luke 1:26).

"And it happened, when Elizabeth heard the greeting of Mary, that the babe leaped in her womb; and Elizabeth was filled with the Holy Spirit" (Luke 1:41.)

Note, God does not say that a "fetus" leaped in her womb. He says the "babe leaped." This is the exact same word that God uses to describe Christ in the manger after he was born: "And this will be the sign to you: You will find a Babe wrapped in swaddling cloths, lying in a manger" (Luke 2:12).

"And they came with haste and found Mary and Joseph, and the Babe lying in a manger" (Luke 2:16).

In God's eyes, the unborn babe and a newborn babe are the same. They are both human beings.

Where do you draw your line as to "when is a person a person"?

Help Me

THE CHOICE

We are proud grandparents of an adopted grandson, Michael. He's now thirty-one years old, serving in the United States Navy, married, and having a son this year.

Thank God Mike's birth mother made the choice of having her baby and not aborting him. Now, that's agape unconditional love.

Thank God our daughter Debbie, his adopted mother, raised him with all her love.

And, that too is agape unconditional love.

Michael is the light of our lives and touches everyone around him. What a wonderful gift of life!

I dedicated my book *Virtual Grace* to Mike with this inscription:

> Adoption…is a gift from God.
> Adoption…is a gift from the birth-mother.
> Adoption…is a gift from the adoptive-mother.

Michael Andrew Orga, our precious adopted grandson, I dedicate this book to you who has proven beyond words, the gift of life is God's greatest gift. We are thankful you are a part of our family as you have so beautifully passed on God's love to everyone you meet. That is the greatest gift anyone could return back to God. That is Virtual Grace.

Virtual Grace

In 1976, I wrote a poem I called "Where."

Where, O where are the boys and girls today
Who would've been here from yesterday?
The ones whose mothers decided against
Their birth and their adolescence.
Oh where, oh where are the things in the sea?
On the earth and in the air?
The ones pollution did prevent
Their tender love and care.
Oh where, oh where are the people who dissent?
The ones who're jailed for discontent.
The ones who learn by making mistakes.
Room for all, we should make.
Oh where, oh where are the old, sick and maimed?
Their loves, their lives no longer aimed
On life anymore; they're in their place
Tucked aware in much haste.
Oh, where, oh what's left on Mother Earth today?

The perfect person in every way.
The one who'll obey, learn and respect
A society that's correct...
In the minds of a few
Cause that's all that's left.
Oh where, oh where are the rest today?
They're up there somewhere, the Good Book doth say,
Where all are welcome in any way.
I'd rather be there.
Oh where, I'd rather be there.

Stained Glass Descending Dove

IS LIFE WORTH THE PRICE?

How would you feel taking care of this patient?

The patient is a male who appears his reported age. He neither speaks nor comprehends the spoken word. Sometimes he babbles incoherently for hours on end. He is disoriented about his person place and time. He does, however, seem to recognize his own name. I have worked with him for six months, but he did not recognize me in this time period.

He shows complete disregard for his physical appearance and makes no effort whatsoever to assist in his own care. He must be fed, bathed and clothed by others. Because he is edentulous, his food must be pureed, and because he is incontinent of both urine and stool, he must be changed and bathed often. His shirt is generally soiled from almost incessant drooling. He does not walk. His sleep pattern is erratic. Often he awakens in the middle of the night, and his screaming awakens others.

Most of the time he is friendly and happy. However, several times a day, he gets quite agitated without apparent cause, then he screams loudly until someone comes to comfort him.

How would you feel?

Frustrated, angry, disappointed, upset, wanting to quit trying. Perhaps throw in the towel, saying "What's the use?"

You would feel all of those emotions. I certainly did.

But I got over it because I was taking care of my six-month-old grandson.

Why is it so much more difficult to care for a ninety-year-old than a six-month-old with identical symptoms?

We need to change our perspectives. The aged patient is just as loveable as the child. Those who are ending their lives in the helplessness of old age deserve the same care and attention as those who are beginning their lives in the helplessness of infancy.

Yes, we elders need to be loved just as much as we needed love in our infancy. In fact, because we loose spouses and friends as we age, our needs are magnified, and our losses are great.

For those who believe in God, we are comforted knowing God is with us. The Psalmist said: "I have been young, now am old; Yet I have not seen the righteous forsaken, Nor his descendants begging bread, He is ever merciful, and lends; And his descendants are blessed" (Psalm 37:25).

It is this joy in witnessing that gives the elderly a zest for life. Though active work is finished, there can still be testimony by life and word which is fruitful.

So the Psalmist says:

> O God, You have taught me from my youth; and to this day I declare Your wondrous works. Now also, when I am old and gray-headed, O God, do not forsake me, Until I declare Your strength to this generation, Your power to everyone who is to come. (Psalm 71:17, 18)

The Holy Bible shows a great reverence of life for their aged. Our elders have much love and wisdom to pass onto us. What did the older people I knew pass onto me when I was growing up?

Can you remember the first older person that left and impact on you as a child?

I remember mine. They were my grandparents. I was fortunate enough to have both my maternal grandparents living well into my thirties. My maternal grandfather, Papaw, Henry Strader, died when he was ninety-seven, and I was thirty-two, expecting our third child.

Papaw, during my childhood years, had plenty of time for me. He worked for fifty-five years in Ohio. Papaw never received Social Security or pensions, because both those legislations came about after he was forced to retire. This left both my Papaw and my Mamaw, his wife, my grandma, with a slim income. They lived in a rented double, and rented out rooms upstairs to college students. Papaw and Mamaw taught me all kinds of values, but most of all how to unconditionally love and the enjoyment of life. I didn't realize, until many years later, they were poor, and Mamaw had to prepare three large meals a day for her roomers. It seemed to me they were there for me regardless of the day or night.

And I loved Mamaw's ghost stories. Everyone of her eerie tales I would later retell to my children, and several times I would retell them to their Girl Scouts, during a retreat on a moonless night in front of the campfire. When my grandparents died, I truly mourned.

What should we do about keeping the elderly alive? A great number of medical questions surround the issues of cost and aging. Should the elderly ill, be given something to hasten death? Who decides when that should happen?

How much does it cost to keep someone alive? It depends of the condition of the person in question. Dying is by no means cheap. CBSnews.com said, "It sometimes costs up to $10,000.00 a day to keep someone alive in an ICU unit."

Is Life worth the price?

It is estimated if you're sick more than a six-month period and need round-the-clock care, it would cost you between half a million to a million dollars. All your life you've worked for the last process…dying.

Why not pass those bills and allow doctor-assisted suicide?

Why stick around when you're sick and going to die anyway?

Is life worth the price?

Jesus said, "Love your neighbor," and then Jesus describes the neighbor as everyone. Cancer patients-lepers in Jesus's day. Unwanted children-orphans in Jesus's day. Everyone regardless of how ill or old or their handicaps or infirmities. Does this love stop when we reach a certain age or infirmity?

Not according to Jesus.

The Commandment is to "love your neighbor" (Mark 12:30).

Stained Glass The Scroll

Right to Die

Should we allow a person to choose when they have a "right to die"?

It's difficult to oppose a person's right to self-determination concerning decisions about treatment. If our country decides that it's a person's right to their own body, then we need to see these decisions may fail to take into account that:

1. A significant fraction of patients pronounced terminally ill by their attending physicians survive for a much longer period of time than predicted.

2. With the rapid advance in medical science, today's "extraordinary" measures may become tomorrow's standard procedures.

3. Extraordinary measures may make a "terminal" illness less painful and distressing. There are times that tube feedings, chemotherapies and radiation therapy might prolong life and are sometimes purposeful allowing the patient to die without enduring the pain of bed sores, that is connected with malnutrition.

Do we have a right to die?
Should someone be designated to assist in a suicide?
Who decides who is "terminal"?

The article entitled "Terminal is for Buses, Not Patients," written by Justin Stein, MD, states:

> It is very distressing to hear about reports on the management of cancer patients with terminal disease. The use of the words, "terminal cancer," does great disservice to patients and the medical profession. I am reminded of Dante's Inferno, "Abandon hope all ye who enter here!" The word 'terminal: signifies the abandonment of hope. We should not revert back to the days when there were hospitals for the incurable. The words "terminal" should not be used by oncologists. If a physician who is treating a patient with cancer takes away all vestiges of hope, there is very little left for the patient.

Does the right to refuse treatment mean I have a right to die? It's called euthanasia, and it's a Greek word meaning "good death."

When we look at the medical ethics of euthanasia, it becomes easier to decide who is a person. After all, if we allow abortion, the killing of "normal" human cells, then why not let people die by terminating their already "dead" human cells? After all, when a person is close to death, shouldn't they be allowed to die alleviating a lot of misery, suffering and financial costs.

What is the practice of euthanasia?

The book of Ecclesiastes says:

> And there is nothing new under the sun. Is there anything of which it may be said, "See, this is new?" It has already been in ancient times before us. There is no remembrance of former things, Nor will there be any remembrance of things that are to come By those who will come after. (Eccles 1:9-11)

No, there's nothing new under the sun, just new ways of doing them.

The history of euthanasia goes back to ancient times. The first recorded use of the word euthanasia was by Suetonius, a Roman historian, in his De Vita Caesarum-Divus Augustus, to describe the death of Augustus Caesar. Augustus's death, while termed "a euthanasia," was not hastened by the actions of any other person. Withdrawal or with-holding treatment was practiced in history, the correct term for this is orthothanasia, which means "passive death." In this method, the actions of curing the patient are never applied and his death is made easy in a passive form.

There are four different classifications for euthanasia. They are:

> Voluntary passive, involves a person that dies with his consent.
>
> Involuntary passive, involves a person permitted to die without his consent.
>
> Voluntary active, involves a person's death at his will, possibly with doctor-assisted suicide.
>
> Involuntary active, where a person is killed without knowledge or consent.

The first objection to euthanasia came from the Hippocratic Oath which says, "I will not administer poison to anyone when asked to do so, nor suggest such a course." But according to NOVA, The Hippocratic Oath Today article by Peter Tyson, "Today, most graduating medical-school student swear to some form of the oath, usually a modernized version. Only 14% of modern oaths prohibit euthanasia, 11% hold covenant with a deity, 8% foreswear abortion and a mere 3% forbid sexual contact with patients."

So, with the Hippocratic Oath out of practice, where is the opposition to "not administering poison" to anyone when asked to do so, nor suggest such a course?

What are the criteria for defining when a person is not a person anymore, but a dead person?

In the Lancet article, "Medical diagnosis of death in adults: historical contributions to current controversies, in the 18th century, one way of determining if a person died, was to hold mirror, soap bubbles, feather or candle to the nose to detect respiration."

And, in the nineteenth century, death was determined by the lack of a heartbeat. Fortunately some trepid soul decided to beat on the heart, with what we now call CPR, and brought some "dead" people back to life. And, thanks to modern technology, we can now transplant hearts and other organs.

What is the definition of death today?

1. Total cerebral function, usually assessed by EEG as flat-line brain waves.

2. Spontaneous function of the respiratory system, and 3 spontaneous function of the circulatory system. (What Is the Medical Definition of Death? Dorland's Illustrated Medical Dictionary, 31st Edition).

When you look at how the definition of death has changed, through the centuries, you realize how far medicine and science has evolved changing the definition from "holding a mirror under the nose, to flat EEGs."

It's obvious defining death is impossible to determine. Each generation of scientists, doctors, and willing patients to undergo difficult procedures will bring a new definition of when is a person dead. Even though a flat EEG is the definition of dying today, tomorrow, with new technology, someone will find a way to start the brain moving to a normal EEG, much as Dr. Friedrich Maass performed the first equivocally documented chest compression in humans in 1891, followed by the first American case of closed-chest cardiac massage, performed by Dr. George Crile in 1904.

When is a person not a person? And therefore dead?

Physician aid in dying (PAD), or assisted suicide, is legal in the states of Washington, New Mexico, Oregon, Montana, and Vermont. The key difference between euthanasia and PAD is who administers the lethal dose of medication. Euthanasia entails the physician or another third party administering the medication, whereas PAD requires a ballot initiatives and "legislation bills."

The range of euthanasia bills is immense in our country. It was even suggested that people in custody, condemned of rape, murder, should be offered a highly lethal amount of drugs for self administration or administration by the warden or warden's agent.

Although that legislative action didn't pass, the question remains: "When is a person not a person?"

What does the Holy Bible say about euthanasia? Euthanasia is an effort to hasten death. The point is not how, but why we want to hasten death?

Euthanasia takes life and death decisions out of God's hands.

Deuteronomy 32:39: "Now see that I, even I, am He, And there is no God besides Me; I kill and I make alive; I wound and I heal, Nor is there any who can deliver from My hand."

Exodus 20:13: "You shall not murder."

Genesis 1:26: "Then God said, 'Let Us make man in Our image, according to Our likeness.'"

1 John 2:2: "And He Himself is the propitiation for our sins, and not for ours only but also for the whole world."

Every human being is a redeemed child of God. The Bible teaches that we are made in the image of God, so every human life is sacred.

> For you have formed my inward parts; You have covered me in my mother's womb. I will praise you, for I am fearfully and wonderfully made: Marvelous are Your works, and that my soul knows very well, My frame was not hidden from You, When I was made in secret, and skillfully wrought in the lowest parts of the earth. Your eyes saw my substance, being yet unformed. And in Your book they all were written, the days fashioned for me. When as yet there were none of them. (Psalm 139:13-16)

Stained Glass Open Bible and Lamp

LIVING WILLS

Many proponents for "the right to self-determination concerning their decisions about medical treatment," advise writing a living will. This is a legal document.

Living Will Declaration

This is an important legal document. A living will directs the medical treatment you are to receive in the event you are in a terminal condition and are unable to participate in your own medical decisions. This living will may state what kind of treatment you want or do not want to receive.

Prepare this living will carefully. If you use this form, read it completely You may want to seek professional help to make sure the form does what you intend and is completed without mistakes.

This living will remains valid and in effect until and unless you revoke it. Review this living will periodically to make sure it continues to reflect your wishes. You may amend or revoke this living will at any time by notifying your physician and other health care providers. You should give copies of this living will to your family, your physician and your health care facility. This form is entirely optional. If you choose to use this form, please note that the form provides signature lines for you, the two witnesses whom you have selected, and a notary public.

To my family, health care provider, and all those concerned with my care:

1, _____, direct you to follow my wishes for care if I am in a terminal condition, my death is imminent, and I am unable to communicate my decisions about my medical care.

With respect to any life-sustaining treatment, I direct the following: (fill in.)

_____If my death is imminent or I am permanently unconscious, I choose not to prolong my life. If life sustaining treatment has been started, stop it. but keep me comfortable and control my pain.

Date: and your signature.
Witness.

While I taught medical ethics to the interns at Christiana Care Health Services, I would invite each intern to write his/her own "living will." Even though the above Living Will is the one accepted by the legal system, still the internists did not know entirely how to interpret the document. How would they treat this patient if other medical issues ensued?

So I asked them to write a Living Will they would be able to enact, if they received this from a patient/family under their care.

Not one could write a medically sound Living Will that would cover every medical problem they would encounter. But some tried.

I've chosen one written by Maryna Mannes, author of this *Last Rights: A Case for the Good Death*, that attempts to cover every medical situation a person might encounter.

Read it and the response immediately following, and determine what you might do.

The Living Will

TO: My Doctor, My Lawyer, My Closest Relative, My Dear Friends.

I ask each of you, in concert or individually, to assure that certain measures be taken to end my life should I fall victim to the following circumstances.

Singly or together, they would deprive me of all that I cherish most in living, preferring death to their loss.

This document to be resigned by me every two years to and until the event that loss of consciousness through accident or illness precludes my signature. In this case, the wishes expressed are to be carried out by the person herein addressed.

1. Any disease or accident that would leave me unable to take care of my own bodily functions or deprive me of independent mobility.

2. Progressive deterioration of mind as evidenced by total loss of memory, only partial consciousness, chronically irrational behavior, delirium or any other evidence of advanced senility.

3. Any condition requiring the use, beyond two weeks, of mechanical equipment for breathing, heart action, feeding, dialysis, or brain function without a prognosis of full recovery of my vital organs.

4. Any progressive deterioration of muscle, bone, or tissue requiring an increasing dependence on intravenous substances and without realistic hope for recovery consistent with my definition of such.

5. I do not wish to survive a stroke that impairs my ability to speak or move, nor any accident or disease resulting in vision too impaired to see or read, or in total deafness.

A world without beauty heard or seen, is no world for me.

A life without freedom and movement, is not life for me.

If age and illness deny me these, I choose death. And if a difference of opinion among your results in ignoring or only partially acceding to these requested, then I beg that one of you provide me with the means to take my own life while in a conscious state.

Signed_____

Date_____

Witness_____

In answer to this Living Will, here are the succinct questions doctors, nurses, and family members should address, before they adhere to the wishes of anyone who would sign this Living Will document. This is a response to that Living Will written by Maryna Mannes.

TO: all those caretakers who will take care of anyone who signs this Living Will.

In response to the Living Will, Marya Mannes is a real bundle of joy.

She would "do in" even the well cared for. She wants life to march by her door in brisk formation, stepping high and singing loud...or off with your head!

You bet death is a dirty word.

And, the anti-abortionists are right. Abortion really does lead to mercy killing and the promoters are using exactly the same language and the same tactics. And the same media is flooding us with the same hard soft sell.

All in the name of "mercy, personal rights and freedom."

As a care provider, I have a few thousand questions to address to the signers of the "LIVING WILL," because I may be the one expected to administer it. If I misinterpret what you sign, or just let my fatigue show near the end of a wild eight-hour shift, I may just shove you into the great beyond before you are ready.

Do you present this document to me when you check in?

Do you give it to the gal in admitting so you can be put in a special section? Should we call this section, Hospice, or the End Room?

Do I accept it from trusted relatives or from friends? How do I know who this is? Will the untrusted ones look different?

Do I only follow your doctor's orders? Suppose she/he takes off on a world tour? Can the resident or intern write in final orders?

By bodily functions, I assume you mean bladder and bowel control.

As so few patients following surgery are left with this dignity, does the need for a catheter, or an enema put you in the "worthless" category?

How many soiled beds should I allow you before I put you out of your misery...and mine?

All of us exhibit signs of senility at least once a day, including people who write and publish LIVING WILLS.

Do we put you through a memory and sanity test each hour? What's the passing score?

How about two weeks and one hour, or two weeks and one day, as the limit of dependence on some life saving gimmick?

Who does the countdown? What constitutes "full recovery" of vital organs?

Emphysema is an irreversible condition of the lungs: no way can I make this vital organ whole again.

How do I resolve this?

Do I ask you if you have had enough intravenous feedings? Do we, in committee, decide?

Or will there be a standing House order?

And, if I chicken out, can I leave scalpel or syringe or pills at your bedside?

What if you botch the job?

Do we all get another chance?

Do I tell you when I bring in the final dose?

Do I insist you take it, even if you change your mind?

How do I keep the confidence of my other patients who get nervous with all this insanity swirling around them.

Only a society on the skids, decadent, and economically insecure, gets so preoccupied with 'death with dignity.'

Abortion hasn't spread enough death in the land, now we're being told we must legalize suicide and mercy killing.

Let's outlaw LIVING WILLS and DEATH WITH DIGNITY and bring back SANCTITY OF LIFE!

Right now, federal regulations require every hospital and health program that receives any Medicare or Medicaid funds to inform you, upon admission, of your rights regarding an advance directive. As a result, many facilities are giving patients a Living Will or Durable Power of Attorney to sign at the time of admission. This is usually a difficult time to sign anything when you're under stress and there's so much paperwork.

Many hospitals are instituting "futile care" guidelines which may preclude the wishes of a patient who is unable to communicate.

Is this the way to have our wishes communicated to our health care givers?

In 1978, I wrote this poem on how to heal people.

Healing People

If human hearts failed only from disease,
Science alone
Might heal them.
If all our wounds were in muscle and bone,
Medicine alone
Might seal them.
Not only the 'deaf' are unable to hear,
Not only the 'blind' cannot see.
Some who are 'crippled", are walking about,
and some 'confined', think they are free.
Healing of people cannot be complete
By just making
The body whole.
What does it profit a person to save their life
But suffer the loss
Of their soul?
Medicine and theology are lifeless science
Knowledge
Without feeling.
Hospitals and churches are unable to cure—
People
Do the healing.
Building a community of care and concern
Giving science a human history.
Building a people who cure one another
By caring,
Unveiling God's Mystery.

"Welcome to all."

HOSPICE

When I was a hospital chaplain at the Wilmington General Hospital in Wilmington, Delaware, Dr. Bob Frelick, chief oncologist during the 1970s to 1980s, started weekly health care group meetings, to evaluate all cancer patients in his oncology unit.

I was fortunate enough to be the Hospital Chaplain representing the spiritual dimension,. Social workers, dieticians, floor nurses, physical therapist and occupational/speech therapists all attended these weekly meetings. We reviewed each cancer patient, suggesting different treatment programs for their needs.

The oncology team effort became so important, we made a film of our special partnership. The film is entitled, *When the Blues are Running*, and it was produced in 1978 by Arden Film Inc. It depicts a cancer patient and family member as they go through the process of his radiation, chemotherapies, and different treatments, in concert with the aforementioned hospital team.

The film is eighteen minutes long and was used for teaching purposes to medical students, churches, hospitals, CONTACT, and any group who wanted to learn how to undertake unity in teamwork.

We were the forerunner of a group called Hospice. The big difference was, we made no "final" decisions that a patient had six months or less to live. We treated each patient as though they had forever to live.

Hospice is distinctive in the definition.

> Hospice care is a type of care and philosophy of care that focuses on the palliation of a chronically ill, patient's pain and symptoms, and attending to their emotional and spiritual needs. In the United States the term is largely defined by the practices of the Medicare system and other health insurance providers, which make hospice care available, either in an inpatient facility or at the patient's home, to patients with a terminal prognosis who are medically certified to have less than six months to live. (Wikipedia)

While I appreciate and approve of hospices as they take care of the patient, even allowing pets in the rooms, family beds to rest beside their loved ones, pain control and palliative care, I have questions to ask those who are thinking about choosing hospice.

To the family members and patients, please get at least two opinions. And, ask your physicians these questions:

How do you determine who has six months or less to live?

At what point in an illness does the emphasis switch from treatment to pain control?

Does the physician make that decision alone? Or should there be other doctors, nurses and health care people to make the final decision?

If no diagnostic work is to be done when a patient is in a hospice, how does one know whether the palliative care is simply masking the symptoms of a separate and easily treatable condition?

Might a backwoods physician in another community deem a patient ready for hospice where a more sophisticated physician would find the patient's condition treatable?

Should a physician, hospital or hospice have legal protection against malpractice suits when the patient is in a hospice, or when the patient with a living will has his life support system withdrawn?

Might hospice care be denied or granted based on such variables as what cultural milieu the patient represented or how the physician and others perceived the patient?

After all, the real goal is to allow the patient to die in comfort, and I've watched many hospice patients live much longer than the six months, without "extraordinary" treatment. One wonders what might've happened with "extraordinary" treatment?

Remember, procedures regarded as extraordinary five years ago are viewed as ordinary today. While I am concerned with the no treatment stance of hospice, none can fault the humanistic and supportive goals. To the cancer patient, feelings of loss of control, loneliness and isolation are as big a problem as that of pain. But, why not provide this kind of care to all patients? Those who are taking medical treatment, as well as those who are not taking medical treatment? Let's not limit care to only those with "terminal disease." Let's not set a new system of care that has to be separately justified for financial help. Instead, let us be committed to each other in empathy and care throughout life.

Since it's been decided, when you enter a hospice program, you don't need any treatment, except for palliative care, why live those extra days or months in pain, distress, physically, mentally and emotionally wasting away to nothingness?

One of the concerns I have is the possibility of hastening the death of one who is labeled "terminal."

After all, under hospice care, the decision has already been made that you only have six months or less to live. If the goal is to alleviate suffering, many ask this question: "Wouldn't it be more merciful to hasten the process, rather than let the patient suffer and slowly die?"

Hastening the dying process would be active euthanasia, or the act of commission, when someone gives the patient medicine to die.

Hence, the act of omission, only giving palliative care, could easily become the act of commission, which is called physician-assisted suicide.

PHYSICIAN-ASSISTED SUICIDE

When I taught medical ethics, I always asked each class this question, "Who wants to suffer, raise your hand?" As you can imagine, no one raised their hand. No one wants to suffer.

It's a similar question to the one people would ask any pregnant woman, "What do you want, a girl or boy?" Answer: "I don't care as long as it's 'normal.'"

What is normal anyway? What is suffering?

They are two questions of which there are no answers. For one person, "normal" means one thing and to another person another thing. The same with suffering. I know a Navy man who's had sixty-one major operations and nineteen procedures, and he's still fighting for his life. It's his choice, you might say. Of course it's his choice. It's always been your choice to live or die.

Living Wills, Hospice, Physician-Assisted Suicide only reassures what you already had.

Refusal of treatment.

So, why legislate and enact these moral dilemmas?

Several years ago I read the book, *The Final Exit*, by Derek Humphrey. This book tells people how to commit suicide.

If you're in emotional, psychological, or physical pain, then it is better not to live with all those problems. Better to be relived of all your pain and suffering.

The Concern for Dying Society, also known as Death with Dignity, or the Euthanasia Society of America, have presented workshops on how to commit suicide. How to get the necessary equipment and do it right, so you won't bollix the attempt.

One of the main reasons I started suicide prevention support groups is precisely because I wanted to stop people from killing themselves. Should I encourage the people in the suicide support groups to die because they want to?

This May 2014 at the University of Delaware, a forum explored the question of whether Delaware should adopt "Death with Dignity" laws that allow "an option for patients with six or fewer months to live, to hasten an inevitable death. As *Lifeline* newsletter reported, "During the Q&A afterwards, it became clear that most young people in the audience supported the "right to die."

If we usher in "Death with Dignity," or physician-assisted suicide, what kind of society are we presenting for ourselves and our youth? When people came to the suicide prevention support groups, they were looking to society for guidance and support for life. They want someone to give them encouragement to their cry for help.

Is this the message we want to give our youth? It's okay to kill yourself, or assist in suicide, even if the person is terminally ill and wants to die.

You might say, "What does our youth have to do with refusal of insertion or continued maintenance of a feeding tube when a patient is dying?"

First of all, it sends a clear message to our young people, that there is a life not worth living. The impetus is on the chronically ill. A person who is very sick may experience psychological pressure. Pressure to avail themselves to die.

Secondly, it is not a great logical leap, given human nature, to suggest that availability may lead to encouragement, which may lead, in turn, to irresistible psychological expectation that I should not attempt to live, given any form of diagnosis that is thought to be "terminal." As is so often the case with reforms and their unintended consequences, a mechanism designed to give a patient a choice, may result in the patient being left without a choice.

Coercing patients to "give up on their lives" is as unjust as forcing them to endure unbearable pain. In today's medical world, pain can be controlled.

Thirdly, in the message to our youth, who will be their role model? Usually, a role model is someone who rises beyond the call of duty and performs extraordinarily. A person who we look up to who has, even in the face of huge odds, overcome life's discouragements; pain and suffering.

Who will be the role models for our youth? Will our role model be the person who commits suicide? We can always decide there is a good reason someone commits suicide. "Oh well, they were terminal anyway. The cancer got them."

"I remember they said that they 'didn't want to live 'hooked up on machines."

Doctors and emergency care professionals have difficulty knowing what to do when a person is rushed to the Emergency Room with a Living Will. "Should we treat or under-treat?" they've wondered. Often they under-treat if there is a Living Will, and over-treat if there's no Living Will.

To my knowledge, there's not one physician or hospital that forces you to have treatment, if you say "no treatment." Informed consent was used with all patients, and if comatose, their family members consented to treatment. If the patient or the family did not wish to continue treatment, comfort and pain control became the final objectives.

DNRs (do not resuscitate) is quite common in all legitimate health care facilities.

So, why do we need physician-assisted suicide?

Sometimes if takes too long to die. And it costs a lot of money, even if we're in a Hospice facility.

This opens up the question of judgment of quality of life over against sanctity of life. Uselessness over against worthwhile-ness.

If quality of life is the answer, then we must ask ourselves these questions. Will more laws open the door to active euthanasia? Which means, ending a life.

People in that category could be people with Alzheimer's, dementia, "severe" handicaps, mental retardation, emotionally unbalanced; even murderers on death row. Whomever is in control decides to assist in your demise.

But, you say, that's why we have Living Wills and Hospice. They will protect those who really want to die; to die. However, those decisions will be made, without trying medicine, spiritual or emotional intervention. Because, when you're suffering, you feel as though you need to "get out of the way."

There are always difficulties defining when any illness is in fact, irreversible or hopeless. Does hopelessness connote meaninglessness, thus inhibiting the use of prudentially justifiable therapy for the seriously ill? Will those responsible for not feeding people in persistent vegetative state, always act in the best interest of the patient, thus depriving the patient of some safeguard against human caprice?

"Just let me go with my Lord." Of course, as Christians, we know there's our Savior waiting for us. But to hasten death is to undermine God's will.

However, the apex of our Christian faith is the perception that the suffering that accompanies all society, can be overcome by the divine sharing of it.

The main thrust of the Cross, in Christian faith, agrees with the purpose of scientific techniques, such as IV feedings, organ transplants, and other man/woman-made technologies. Both the cross and scientific mechanizations are against the negativeness of destruction of life.

However, as history has shown, even the best purposes can be twisted, becoming corrupt. Therefore, the moral and religious imperatives of justice, love and compassion need to be continually interfaced with the ongoing debates concerning all of medical ethics.

Love is a covenant.

Justice is a covenant.

For the Christian community, the covenant in Scripture, is to love your neighbor as yourself. The sick is a neighbor, the dying is a neighbor.

Even the comatose person is a neighbor.

I have witnessed so many people who've shown their love to one another, but there's one situation I'll never forget.

I was the chaplain in the hospital when a young woman was admitted in the emergency room due to a car accident. She was placed on every piece of life saving equipment that was invented. They called her Jane Doe because the car had been stolen and the police were attempting to locate her next of kin.

Some of the hospital staff thought she should be allowed to die.

"What's the use? No one is around to love or care for her," some of the nurses said. "What's the point? Why are we tube feeding? Why did the doctors give her a tracheotomy?"

Others weren't too sure.

Nevertheless, Jane Doe caused a lot of talk in staff meetings, as to the worthwhile-ness of Jane's life. And the price of keeping Jane alive, especially when it appeared there was no one to pay or take responsibility for her life.

When our hospital team members met, we decided we needed to care for Jane by not only changing her tubes, but talking to her, telling her we care, even if she couldn't respond.

As each hospital staff person entered Jane's room to change the respirator or turn her, or any of the other perfunctory duties we had to perform, each staff member would talk with Jane Doe.

She could not hear, see, or respond.

She was completely comatose.

When I went into her room, I would read inspirational stories I would find in my "Thought Conditioners" or "Daily Bible Readings" resources.

The nurses and other staff members would tell Jane about their daily activities.

One time I heard several nurses, as they turned Jane, and changed her IVs and diapers.

"Oh Jane, I had the nicest date last night, let me tell you about him."

The nurses became close to one another through Jane. At staff meetings, they enjoyed telling one another about how Jane was doing today. They actually communicated with each other through her.

For six weeks we continued this routine, until one morning, I was paged.

The nurses were crying. "Jane has died! Oh no, Jane died!"

At the hospital chapel memorial service for Jane, amazingly each staff person said words of appreciation to Jane and what she had done for them.

I sat and listened as each caregiver of Jane Doe came to the pulpit, one by one and spoke. "Jane gave me love." "Jane passed on her caring." "I hope Jane knows we did everything we could to save her."

Even though Jane Doe never regained consciousness, she was able to bring love to each person, because we showed each other how we cared for someone who couldn't respond or return our acts of kindness.

I remained there, embraced by the sunlight as it reflected the patterns of the stained glass' window, the praying hands, the doves, the Star of David, the Cross of Jesus, and my heart, once again, 'became strangely warmed'.

Through Stained Glass, we are touched by each person we meet, radiating faith, hope and love, but the greatest of these is love.

Love from someone who had no quality of life, but taught us God's gift of agape unconditional love.

The same gift of agape unconditional love that our daughters gave my mom as they wiped her brow, held her hand, and gave her water.

The same gift of agape unconditional love that our Lord Jesus gives each of us.

"A new commandment I give to you, that you love one another, as I have loved you, that you also love another. By this all will know that you are My disciples, if you have love for one another" (John 13:34).

"This is my commandment, that you love one another as I have loved you. Greater love has no one than this, than to lay down one's life for his friends" (John 15:12, 13).

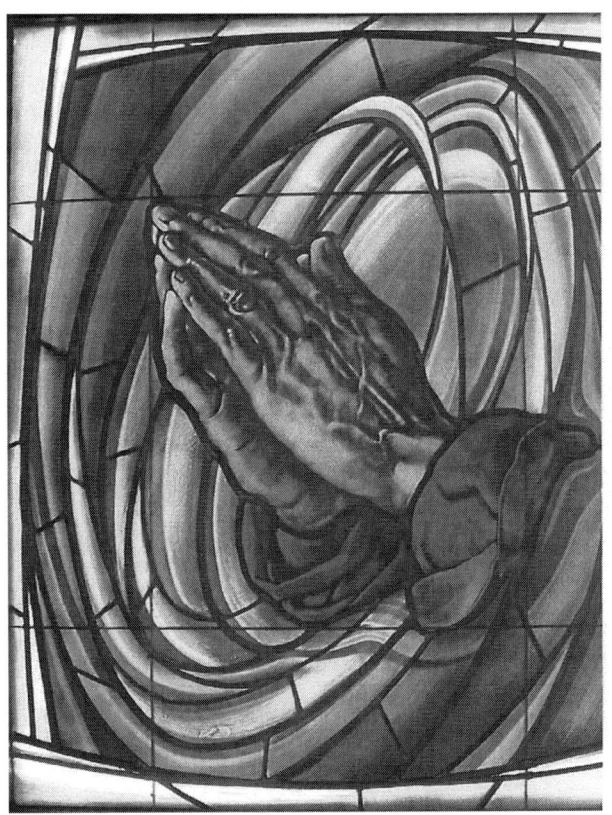

Stained Glass Praying Hands